CHAIN REACTION

CHAIN REACTION

By

Ross E. Goldstein, Ph.D.

This book is a work of fiction. Names, characters, places, and incidents either are products of the author's imagination or are used fictitiously. Any resemblance to actual events or locales or persons, living or dead, is entirely coincidental.

Copyright © 2011 by Ross Goldstein, Ph.D.

All rights reserved. No part of this book may be reproduced, scanned or distributed in any printed or electronic form without permission. Please do not participate or encourage piracy of copyrighted materials in violation of the author's rights. Purchase only authorized editions.

Goldstein, Ross
Chain Reaction: A Novel

ISBN: 978-1452842264

Cover Concept by rb-d.com
Book Design by redbat design
Author photo by Rachel Kawalek
Printed in the United States of America
10 9 8 7 6 5 4 3 2 1

For Nancy, Chase and Graham.
Your support and inspiration are the backbone of this work.

CHAPTER ONE

The smell was an express link to days passed — the lightly acrid, rubber, pungent odor of a bicycle shop, with its low notes of oil and grease. It transported Cal to his teens and his apprentice mechanic years, in this very shop, in fact — The Spinning Wheel. And at its helm was Jason, still there behind the counter with his grease-smudged smile, greeting Cal. His smile was the only clean part of him.

"Well, big dog. Long time no see. Thought you were in the witness protection program, or something, dude."

Cal dipped his head and shrugged. "Yeah. Witness protection program, you bet. Just sorting some shit out. You know." This answer was his stock reply, the bare minimum expressly designed to ward off inquiry into the details of his life. When it came to explaining the last few years, Cal was of the belief that you shouldn't show people a work in progress... as if the motions he went through each day could be called progress.

Jason snapped the magazine shut and tossed it on a box of parts. He lifted his eyes. "If it's work you're looking for, I'm pretty full staffed — if you can call my latest learning project here a staff." He motioned toward Luke, a beanpole kid wrestling a broom across the repair room floor.

Cal planted his hands on the countertop as if to say he was glad to be on this side of it. "No, I think I've found my professional calling pulling espressos for you guys down at Peet's." He braced for the inevitable, the next question that was already forming on Jason's lips, and decided to preempt it with a shift of focus. "Actually, just need to get my bike broken down and boxed. It's out in the car."

Jason wasn't deterred. "Nice. You used to break your own bike down. Now that you're a professional espresso man, you have us doing the work." Jason paused for a response that wasn't coming. "You going back on the circuit?" Jason's eyes lit with the promise of gossip. "Not in this lifetime." Cal smiled. "Those days… well, no, I'm just going over to Italy with my dad. He's doing one of those cycling trips in Italy and invited me along."

"Very nice. But think you can hang with your old man? He doesn't seem to be slowing down any."

Cal chuckled at the reputation that his father had developed in the cycling community. Fierce. Every ride a race. "He's something, all right. But he promised me that it was a recreational ride. Nothing too heavy. Besides, I still have thirty years on him."

"Thirty years and thirty pounds," added Jason. "Well, no matter. Italy, man. It's the mother country for cyclists. You might even run into some of your old…"

Cal cut him off. "The Giro is over and the pro teams have moved north, getting ready for the Tour. This is, like I said, recreation. I'm a tourist. One step above baggage on this trip." He sighed. "A trip to Italy, good food, warm days, beautiful women? Besides, if I don't take a break from latte hell, I'm going to lose my mind."

"You can't go wrong with Italy, man."

"Do you think you can have it ready to go by this afternoon? I'm on a plane tomorrow."

"No problem. We'll give you a call later today when it's done," said Jason. "Hey, when you come back, let's go out for a spin. Some of the guys would be really happy to see you."

"Kick my ass, is what you really mean," Cal responded. "I'm only coming out of retirement for this one trip. Then it's done, and I'll be pulling lattes for you Mill Valley wannabe pros every Saturday again. You couldn't put me back on the circuit with a promise of guaranteed wins, my own masseuse, and all of the fine wine in Europe." Cal grinned and turned to leave. Glancing back, he called out to Jason, "And hey, just don't fuck up my bike. Remember, I taught you all you know about bikes, and I didn't teach you enough."

As Cal opened the door of his beat-up Toyota Forerunner, he glanced back at the shop window and its gleaming bike frames in a rainbow of colors. He hadn't been in a bike shop in over three years. He hadn't even thrown his leg over a bike saddle for anything more than a quick trip to town since that summer, three years ago, in Europe. The shop hadn't changed a bit since his last visit except for the bikes. Technology had advanced at a staggering pace. New materials, new brands, new bits and pieces. But the shop? Still stuffed to the gills with equipment. Parts spilled out of bins with no obvious sense of place or purpose. Jerseys cascaded off of the racks. How many hours had he spent sitting in the shop listening to the local heroes spin their stories of races won and opportunities lost, of gaps closed down, and chases that never quite made it? And the ones that did. Then, he'd become one of those guys—one of the ones the next generation of future racers talked about. Immersed in the bike shop's smells and colors, he'd felt as though time had dissolved — but outside, on the threshold again, he reminded himself that he didn't belong in that world anymore.

* * *

When Cal was out of earshot, Luke dumped a dustpan of used ferrules and cable ends into the trash. His boss was still reading the magazine. "Who's that guy?"

Jason rolled his eyes. "Are you kidding me? That guy? Cal Scott? That guy was only the best racer to ever come out of California. US amateur champion two years running. Made it to the pros. Raced professionally in Europe with T Mobile. Had it made..." He drifted off.

"So what happened?"

"Dunno. Nobody does. Moved back here a couple of years ago and hasn't ridden since." He pushed Cal's bike by its stem into Luke's grip and grinned. "Get it boxed up for him. And whatever you do, don't fuck it up."

CHAPTER TWO

Cal swept through the door of Peet's Coffee and snaked through the mid-morning crush of patrons. He nodded to the regulars, the group of fiftyish guys who showed up each day and argued politics, the young moms with their oversized strollers, the "third-placers" who set up shop and freeloaded on the wi-fi. He always wondered about these people. Didn't they have somewhere they were supposed to be?

He worked his way back to the door that led to the employee side of the counter and donned his apron. He reached across to the shelf to grab his nametag and pinned it on the apron. Cal's merely bore his name; he had resisted the urge to copy the playfully rebellious gesture of many of his fellow Peet's employees and use a goofy, codeword pseudonym. The guys were big on adopting the names of characters from literature. Here was Tashtego and there went Raskolnikov. The girls tended more toward the icons of pop culture, a Paris here and a Lady Gaga there. Management looked the other way at these little ironic gestures. They helped morale, softened the too-sharp distinction between those who worked behind the counter and those who visited on the other side of it. But no pseudonym would work for Cal. He was born and raised in Mill Valley, graduating from Tam High down the street. Those who didn't know him personally knew his parents. And those who didn't know his family had probably heard about him through the cycling buzz. Now, he was just another of the privileged kids who broke out of town, but boomeranged back to its dead-end service jobs.

Cal didn't hate the work, although the rudeness and impatience of some of the regulars could get annoying. In fact, there was something about the rhythm and pacing of drawing the espresso drinks, steaming the milk, and dropping the right amount of foam onto the top of a cappuccino that was almost hypnotic. When he hit his groove, when he was on his game—and he was one of the best—the efficiency of the motion and the repetition of the steps reminded him a lot of one of the best parts of cycling. You did the same thing over and over again. You eliminated any missteps. You developed a stroke, a cadence, even a grace and elegance about it, and you could lose yourself in time.

Claire, the day manager, saw Cal emerge from the back room and smiled her usual, inside-joke smile that she reserved for him. He was pretty sure she had a crush on him, but since she was the manager, and well, there was the whole sticky side of relationships, anyway, it was not happening. He got decent tips from customers, too, when he worked the register. He had his father's looks, handsome in a boyish way: dark blond hair and grey-green eyes, hooded by eyelids that seemed to be permanently at half-mast, and olive skin. His six-one frame had been shaped by years on the professional cycling circuit. Strong, muscle-cut legs supported a lean chest and arms. Cal had entertained the idea of hitting the gym to get a little balance in his body, but never got to it. Besides, all those years of cycling competition, years when he had learned that racing cyclists never lift anything for fear of putting on extra bulk—weight they would have to call on their legs to carry over hills and through sprints—left him with a disdain for buffed chests and big arms. The pro cyclists' credo when it came to extraneous effort went something like this: Never take stairs when you can ride an elevator, never lift anything you can roll, never carry your own luggage, never stand when you can sit, and rest the legs each and every chance you get. Only the sprinters, who relied on the explosions of torque their arms generated from pushing and pulling on the bars in blazing fast finishes, did any upper body work. And the sprinters stood out in a gaggle of competitive cyclists like muscle cars in a parade of electric vehicles.

"Hey, Lance Armstrong. We need you to drop the peloton of the morning rush. Take over for Brad," Claire called out.

Cal appreciated the cycling reference. Claire could get away with teasing him. She had trained him in the art of making the perfect espresso and had given him some great lessons on how to keep the customers smiling, things like remembering their names, making eye contact, always being willing to make a drink over again if it wasn't hot enough, dry enough, wet enough, or just not right in some other, more obscure, way. "Do it with a smile and you'll be rewarded," she always told him. Cal had been at Peet's for a couple of years now and was still wondering what the reward was.

"Got it," Cal replied, and slid behind the machine, tapping Brad on the shoulder, so he could step away. He eyed the computer screen perched above the gleaming Pavoni machine. Orders were backed up fifteen deep. Cal set to work and started the process of knocking the orders off, one by one. His hands moved as fast as a Las Vegas blackjack dealer's. Make the drink, call the name, put the drink on the counter, and watch as the owner turned away with the fruits of his labor. Sometimes, they said thanks, but more often, they were so engrossed in conversation or in such a hurry to move on that they simply grabbed and moved. Cal titrated the amount of contact he had by shifting the angle of his head. He could keep his head down, focused on the machine, use it as a blind, actually, and disappear, or he could lift his eyes over the Pavoni and connect with the recipient. He liked having the choice. Some days, he just wasn't up to small talk, and this was one of them. The trip to the Spinning Wheel, Jason's invitation to join the guys on the ride, and the impending trip with his father were on his mind. He needed some time to think.

It took a good half hour of focused, rapid movement, but Cal finally wiped away the drink backlog. He took a deep breath and glanced back at the latest entry onto the screen. That's when he saw the order flash on the screen. "Triple espresso, extra, extra hot, macchiato cup, panna, FOR HERE." He froze. Only one person ordered that drink. Lisa. It was her signature.

He looked up and saw her standing in front of him. Tall and lean, with high cheekbones circled by an aura of curly, thick, dark hair that complemented her dark eyes, coloring that she had inherited from her Latin parents, Lisa was standing right in front of him. She must have been standing there for a couple of minutes, watching him, Cal realized, not saying anything until the drink order gave her away.

"Yep, that's me. I was wondering when you would catch on."

"Yeah, triple espresso… that's a fierce order. You aren't the only one who can handle a triple. But the 'panna,' in a 'for here' cup? The 'panna' and the cup gave it away."

"Well, you taught me that. Need panna to cut the acid and no way will I drink anything out of a paper cup. 'Go ceramic or go home.' Isn't that what you used to say? How have you been? It's been a long time."

"It has been. Not since I left to go to Europe. It has been a long time."

"I followed you through the web. Saw some of the early posts you put up on Facebook and then…"

"Yeah. Facebook. Well, it got too hard to keep up with when I was traveling with the team. But now? Not a lot to post lately. You're back in town?"

"Just for a visit. Had a break from work."

"You still in New York?"

"After I finished design school. Took an internship and they offered me a job, and then I met… well, there's a lot of ground to cover and…"

Cal studied her face, looking for a clue to guide him. He wanted to extend the conversation. There was certainly a lot of ground to cover. Lisa and he had dated in high school all the way through graduation. When it came time for college, Lisa went across the Bay to Berkeley, and Cal stayed in Mill Valley, took some junior college classes at College of Marin, and focused on his racing career. Time and distance had separated them, but with Lisa, he felt a connection that transcended the discontinuities. He had thought about her often.

"Look, I get a lunch break in an hour. Can you hang around and…"

"I'm showing my friend Peter around Mill Valley right now. He came in with me from New York. But…" Lisa frowned as she considered the logistics. "I'll meet you in the square in an hour. We can catch up then."

Cal looked across the counter and, for the first time, noticed the guy standing a few paces behind her, looking at Lisa and him. Tall, slightly disheveled with long hair and a few days' growth on his face, he had the look of studied indifference that worked so well on the dating scene. It was a mysterious look that Cal could never quite pull off. It seemed like disarray had become a fashion statement. Cal nodded a weak hello to her friend who responded with an equally unenthusiastic wave.

The next hour floated away. When Claire yelled down to him to take his lunch break, Cal didn't need a second notice. He yanked his apron over his head, bolted through the door, and made his way across the street to the square. He saw Lisa seated on the bench and steered over to her.

"I saved a place for you," she said, motioning with her hand to the empty space on the bench next to her. Cal plopped down and looked at her. She was every bit as beautiful as he remembered her. He blushed and shook his head. "You look great."

"Thanks. So do you. I don't have a lot of time, so here's the short story. Yes, Peter, the guy you saw in the shop, is my boyfriend. We met at the commercial design studio in New York where we work, and, I know you probably don't want to hear it, but he's a really great guy and a terrific artist. He's really a great photographer with an amazing eye. I think you'd really like his work."

"You're right. I don't want to hear about him. But you? You're doing good?"

"New York is amazing. The energy there is so exciting. I miss Mill Valley and the laid-back pace here sometimes, but…?" She paused a beat. "New Yorkers wouldn't call this 'laid-back,' though. They'd call it something like 'ambiguous,' or 'lost,' or something like that."

"I get it," Cal responded. He didn't need Lisa to tell him that Mill Valley was a little sleepy. Feeling the urge to make a quick excuse, he continued, "I'm just here in between…"

Lisa cut him off. "I heard that you came back. You could have told me yourself."

"Well, when I came back, I was pretty busy getting settled and then I just…" Cal knew how lame the excuse sounded and let his voice trail off. Lisa picked up on his discomfort and continued.

"The thing with T Mobile didn't work out? I don't get it. They were so hot on you."

"No. T Mobile didn't work out. It's a lot like dating. You start out hot and heavy and then you get to know the other person's quirks. And then, those things that you found really charming in the beginning aren't so charming. And then, you start to get really annoyed by the same shit that attracted you in the first place."

"Is that what happened to us? Did you find my idiosyncrasies annoying?" Lisa jumped in with mock dismay. "What was it? The extra hot thing? With the coffee?"

Cal laughed at the way Lisa personalized his comment. It was one of the things he loved about her. She could work several different tracks at the same time in any conversation.

Cal decided to take her up on her facetious comment. "No. I could take the extra hot. It was the panna." He laughed quietly. "You know what the situation was between us. Different worlds. Different goals. Way different worlds."

"I know. But still…"

Cal ignored her comment. "Way different worlds. Sometimes, I wonder if I made the right decision. But there it is. Like my father says, 'You made your bed. Now sleep in it.'"

"So what did happen?" Lisa asked as she furrowed her brow in focused concentration.

Cal shrugged off the question and gave her what he gave everyone: the management, differences, not cut out for a German team, life on the road, and living out of a suitcase.

"But you were getting results?"

"Yes." Cal looked off in the distance, as if the answer to her implied question could be found somewhere on the horizon. He dredged up more reasons: lots of travel, nowhere to call home, and the long weeks of training. He'd practiced the excuses all so well for his father. They rolled off his tongue like lyrics from a song.

"Cal," Lisa began as she fixed on him with her penetrating stare. "You were the hardest working guy on every team you ever raced for. Remember? How many times were you late to pick me up because you lost track of time on a training ride? I used to drive you to your races, out in the middle of nowhere, leaving in the dark to get you to a seven a.m. start somewhere in the central valley. It must have taken a lot of 'differences,' as you call them to get you to leave." Lisa paused for a second. "Did you get fired?"

Cal froze. "No," he snapped. That's just like Lisa, Cal thought. No subtlety. "I left on my own."

Lisa sensed her way to the next sore subject. "And from what I hear, you're living at home now?"

"At home. You got it. The folks are killing me with kindness. I think I'll stay there for the rest of my life."

"No, really. Is it okay?"

Cal realized that his irritation was getting the better of him—that he hadn't had time to process the experience in The Spinning Wheel and it made him edgy. "Look, Lisa, I can't really say, in all honesty, that it's what I'd like to be doing right now, living at home. I'm twenty-five years old, and I wake up each morning looking at the same wall I saw waking up in high school. My father looks at me like an alien who landed in his living room. I was living the dream, as far as he was concerned. In the pro peloton. He has a way of looking at me that makes me want to crawl into a hole."

Lisa gave him a contrite look. "Your dad could be pretty intense when it came to competition."

"And I'm about to go to Italy and ride with him there for a couple of weeks. Sometimes, you can't get enough of what you really don't want. I think he sees it as some kind of a healing experience for us."

"So what's wrong with that? You love cycling."

"Right. I did love the sport. But sometimes I think it's a little like loving sausage until you go to the sausage factory and see what goes into it."

"Cal, it's your future that you're talking about, not sausage. You should consider it, at least. Tell me that you will."

"You're so damned hard to say no to."

"That's because I was always one of your biggest fans. You know that you can't disappoint your fan base." Lisa's phone buzzed, announcing the arrival of a text. "It's from Peter. I've got to get going. We're going to an art opening in San Francisco this afternoon."

Cal rose from the bench with Lisa and the two stood facing each other. Cal shifted from foot to foot, feeling awkward. He started to say more—thinking she'd hear him out, or at least that he should apologize, but she reached out and put her arms around him and pulled him close.

When she released him, she stood back and looked him in the eye. "Cal, promise me that you'll take it seriously. The whole racing thing, I mean. Let me know how it goes. Get back on Facebook or something."

"Facebook?" He didn't know if she was serious. "Only if you promise me that you'll think seriously about the dweeb that you're dragging around."

Lisa started to rise to Peter's defense and then saw Cal's smile. "Okay, babe. I'll think seriously about the dweeb. It's a small price to pay, if it means that I can get you motivated to do something about your situation."

CHAPTER 3

Cal leaned over the pile of clothes scattered on his bed. He sorted through the mound, paring the pile down to the minimum. Behind him, his room was filled with trophies and ribbons earned from races across America. There was the California Cup championship trophy with his gold medal from the Junior Olympics hanging around the top. Next to it, on top of his dresser, stood the US Amateur championship trophy. If a stranger walked in he might think he was in a trophy room.

Sometimes, when Cal came back from the shop and lay in his bed reading, his eye would land on the hardware, the archeology, the evidence, of his success, and he would stare at it like it was some kind of a religious shrine, one whose particular significance and meaning was lost on him. It seemed that he and someone — who? his mother probably — were engaged in a kabuki play. He would put the trophies away. Then, a few days later, they would magically, it seemed, reappear. He had tried throwing it all out a couple of years before, not too long after he had moved back home. But it was no use. His parents insisted that he would want them some day. If not today, then maybe when he had his own children. His own children? At twenty-five, in limbo, no girlfriend, let alone much of a social life, they might as well be talking to him in a foreign language.

Packing his cycling gear for the trip, Cal fingered a couple of jerseys from his old racing team. He deliberated whether to take them. There was the Mako jersey from his local racing club. Then, there was the bright blue, stars-and-stripes jersey that he had been awarded for winning the US Nationals. He had a drawer filled with jerseys, each one marking the history of his racing career. No, he decided, definitely not the US national jersey, nor the T Mobile jersey, which was the last one that he had worn as a pro. He dropped it down on the bed with a pair of gloves that tumbled out from its folds.

He picked the gloves up and turned them over in his hand. On the inside, roughly scrawled in magic marker was the name, Yves Drummond. They were a parting gift from Yves, one of the few souvenirs from their T Mobile days that he valued. He slipped the left glove on his hand, and held his hand in front of his face. They still fit. He paused for a moment, and then dropped the gloves into his bag.

The final parcel was compact and sparse, just like his hopes. Traveling light was a survival skill he developed on the pro racing circuit.

Cal heard the door close and the sound of his mother ascending the stairs. True to form, she was climbing them two at a time, always in a rush, urgent to get to the next task. She turned the corner and entered Cal's room — a quietly attractive woman, fit in the way that modern women manage in today's era of gym time, spinning class, and long hikes with her lady friends. With a quick disapproving shake of her head, she peeked over his shoulder to see what he was packing.

"Is that it? You have everything? Did you pack sunscreen?"

Cal replied with a chuckle, "You just couldn't hold back, could you? Sunscreen? Check. Change of underwear? Check. Clean socks? Got it. Anything else?"

She walked over and rested a hand on his shoulder. "Yes, one more thing. Attitude. Take a good one, not the dark one that you've been dragging around like an anchor. It's cycling, Cal. Something you used to love."

Cal looked up from his packing and responded in a frustrated tone. "Yeah, I wish it was that easy. Just pack a good attitude, like it's something you put on and take off. If only…"

"If only what? Cal, this is a chance to ride and have a good time with your father. He wants you to enjoy this trip. He wants you to have a good time with him. Your father has accepted…"

"Accepted? Accepted? If I get one more question about why I'm not on the Tour, why I left the team, or what I'm going to do next, I'm going to explode. I've tried to explain it. He doesn't accept it. Here's a typical conversation: I come home from work. He says, 'We need to talk.' I say, 'About what?' He says, 'Cycling.' I say, 'What's there to talk about? I don't race anymore. You don't like it.' End of conversation."

"Cal, don't be a jerk. You don't want to race anymore. We get that. How could we not? At least give your father the benefit of the doubt. He's working on it. He just thinks that you had the world eating out of your hand…"

"The world? You mean bicycle racing, Mom. And bicycle racing is just… It's just a thing. Something that people do. Something that I was good at, but maybe it wasn't right for me. Neither of you gets that? Why is it so fucking hard?"

His mother crossed her arms and gave him a look that was equal to his own anger. "It is so *fucking hard* because we wanted you to win. Why? Because it made you happy. We know how good you were. Are."

In the distance, a car horn sounded. Cal looked at his mother with frustration and turned sharply to zip up his bag.

"There he is now. You need to get a move on. You know how he hates to wait. Now go enjoy."

Cal cut her short. He moved to the door, not giving her a chance to continue. As he passed by, on the way out the door of the room, she reached out to give him a hug, but he was already out of her grasp.

Cal loaded his bike, nestled in a bike box carpeted with stickers, souvenirs from different races and events, into his father's Porsche Cayenne. He slid into the passenger seat and accepted his father's outstretched hand in a shake. It was more formal than friendly. His father backed out of the driveway and guided the car down the street.

The trip was underway.

• • •

Cal glanced across the car and noted that, like his mother, his father dressed with a sense of purpose and fashion. They were about to take a long flight, so his clothes were casual, but not sloppy: loose jeans, a cashmere turtleneck, leather jacket, and a sporty driving cap. It all seemed to fit and match. Cal sometimes wondered if he was adopted.

Paul, Cal's father, didn't look fifty-three. And he was proud to tell people his age, just because he liked their disbelief. He would even pull out his driver's license to prove it. For the same reason, he still spoke proudly in his scrappy, south-side-of-Chicago accent; he wanted people to know how far he'd come. He had learned young that chances for success come around rarely. If you let one go, you never knew when the next one might arrive, if ever. He had used that strategy to succeed in school and on the playing fields, ultimately winning a scholarship to the University of Wisconsin in football, despite being an undersized running back at only 185 pounds. His playing time was mostly scrub time at the end of games, but on those rare occasions when he hit the field, it was as if the very outcome of the game hung in the balance. He often reminded Cal that if it weren't for the opportunity sports brought him to go to college, and his "life or death" approach, he would be bagging groceries in a Safeway, instead of living in the upscale suburbs of San Francisco, driving expensive cars, wearing the latest fashions, and slugging it out in the courtrooms.

Paul rarely lost a case. And if he did, the opposing attorney knew that the next time he faced him, he would be met with a ferocity that made the first encounter seem casual. Paul was cagey as an athlete, even cagier as an attorney. It was a strategy that worked for him, and one that he had tried to infuse into Cal's personality. At times, especially when Cal was a junior on his way up, it looked like it had worked.

"You got everything?" Paul asked. "I mean, did you go through your stuff and make sure you have everything you need?"

"Yeah, bike, shoes, helmet, shorts, jersey… Don't think I'm going to need much of anything else."

"Well, we might take a day and go into Venice and see some museums. You'll need to have some nice clothes to do that. You can always borrow some of mine."

Cal smiled and let it pass. "So Dad, just what is the agenda here?"

Paul brightened. "Well, four-fifty flight to Marco Polo Airport in Venice. We arrive tomorrow afternoon. Drive to the hotel. From there? It's riding, son. You're going to love Bassano del Grappa. Great climbs, lots of rolling hills, and good company on the road. They even have their own velodrome. Lots of the pro teams train there, so there's always a group to join on the road. And Luigi, the hotel owner, will treat us like royalty. Your responsibility is to have a good time. And me? I'm in charge of organizing all this shit."

"Yeah," Cal quipped. "Business as usual."

Ignoring the sarcasm, Paul pressed on. "It's going to be a great trip. I know you rode a lot in France and Belgium with the team, but this is Italy and it will be a totally different experience. Besides, it's a great time to be in Bassano. There's a great local race taking place right where we'll be staying. 'Le Scale di Monte Grappa.' I thought it'd be a good finish to the trip. Some of the best amateur racers in Italy will be competing. Thought you might enjoy watching it." Paul caught the look on Cal's face. "Whoa! Don't get all bent out of shape, Cal. I'm not saying that you should do the race. I'm merely telling you that there's a big race happening while we're there. Stop with the paranoia. I'm not signing you up. Besides, you haven't ridden or trained in, what?"

"Too long."

"No way would you be ready to do something like Le Scale. It's a bitch of a climb. Nearly the whole race is going straight up the side of Monte Grappa. That would be a cruel re-entry into competition. Not in the shape you're in."

Cal eyed his father suspiciously. "Yeah, right," he said. "No way I'm in any kind of shape for something like that."

What he wanted to say was that there was no way he was emotionally ready, or psychologically ready, to turn a pedal in a competition. He wanted to say that he wished they could just relax together, but his father usually had an agenda that was fifteen degrees off of what he said it was. It was a good skill for a lawyer, but not such a good trait for a father trying to resurrect a relationship with his son. Successful attorney, accomplished amateur bicycle racer, marathon runner — there wasn't much his father had attempted that he hadn't completed. Paul had been the driving force in Cal's early years. He not only facilitated the physical aspects of Cal's training, even going so far as hiring coaches and trainers. He also drilled him with his philosophy: "Never give up. No matter how much you hurt, the other guys must be hurting, too. The race goes to the rider who can take the most pain. Use your head. If you can't beat them with your legs, beat them with your mind."

The rest of the ride to the airport passed in near silence. Cal speculated on what wheels might be turning in his father's head. Was he really willing to take Cal on a trip to Italy with no ulterior motive? Would he allow him to go and ride with no other agenda than a nice trip to Italy? Could the leopard really change its spots?

CHAPTER 4

In the darkened cabin of the 747, Cal tossed and turned, relentlessly seeking a comfortable position, while the other passengers slept, tucked into their seats, blankets pulled snugly up to their shoulders. The hum of the engines droned in the background. Inside the cabin, the whole experience of being on a plane, headed to Europe, his bike in the hold beneath him, kicked off a cascade of memories. More vividly than he would have ever expected, his mind snuck back to a bright, sunny day in Belgium.

The spring classics, that's what they call them, the early season torture chambers in Belgium and Northern France. These one-day races were a graveyard for riders who hadn't done their winter training. There were no easy courses in these races, which served as preliminary tests for the bigger tours that come later in the season. Now, in the middle of the Tour of Flanders, one of the most brutal and demanding of all of the masochistic exercises that passed for spring racing in Belgium, Cal knew there was no place to hide. The Belgians regarded the Tour of Flanders as their private national championship. And, if the hostility toward foreigners wasn't daunting enough, the harshness of the conditions made the racers feel like they had been put in a refrigerated box and bounced around for five hours. The wind was blowing sideways across the course, making it almost impossible to hold a straight line. The dark landscape matched his mood. The peloton was in danger of splintering, as riders dove and swerved to stay in the draft of the riders in front of them, avoiding the wind that made even the flat roads seem steep. It was the kind of race where riders felt like they finished a race years older than when they started.

The race had started out predictably enough. An easy rollout, followed by a steady acceleration once the flag was dropped on the outskirts of town. The noise of the crowd was deafening, if you paid attention to it, but Cal, like the rest of the peloton, was more focused on the brotherhood of riders that comprised the peloton. He liked the intimacy in the peloton, borne out of the need for all to survive, despite the reality that only one can win. Riders bumped elbows and slid their knuckles against the hands of other riders, separated by millimeters in the close quarters of the herd. Cal was thrilled to be in the mix. He enjoyed the background soundtrack, music to his ears, of riders speaking in a dozen different languages, some saying hello, others announcing their presence to a closing rider, and some simply reacquainting themselves with teammates from previous teams. His body buzzed with excitement.

Cal's T Mobile team had worked well all afternoon. Keeping their designated leader, Franz, well sheltered from the wind, they had each taken their turns at the front, shredding the wind for a couple of minutes, and then slipping to the side, so that the next rider in line could take up his turn. Efficiency was the name of the game. Each pull at the front was an equation made up of time, distance, and effort. Pull long and hard enough to keep up the pace, but short enough to keep something in reserve, so that you didn't get dropped when your turn ended and the rest of the team cycled through.

The early breaks had all been chased down as the race entered its final kilometers, and the peloton was assembled into clusters of hard-working groups. Each team worked for position, figuring out the best place in the road, the optimal angle against the wind, dosing the right amount of work to maintain the prime position for the final assault. The riders eyed each other nervously, on high alert for the next push, the next acceleration, or the next shift of strategy that would reveal the cards a team was holding.

The churning pedals and spinning wheels of his teammates surrounded Cal. Proud to be in the black and white kit, with the iconic pink T of his T Mobile team, he pedaled fiercely, locked in a battle to the end with himself, the road, the weather, and one rider in particular, a beast dressed in green, riding to his right. A rider's glasses and helmet can sometimes hide his identity. But not today, not in this crowd. The number twenty-one pinned to the bright green Liquigas jersey, identified him as the lead rider of the Liquigas team, but Cal didn't need a number—the rider's form on the bike was enough. The ease with which he managed to stay seated even in the toughest of climbs, the way his powerful legs flattened the steepest pitches, and the intensity of his pace at the front, unassisted by any of his teammates for the last hour, all gave away his identity. It had to be Castillo. Luis Castillo, winner of more professional races than any other Spaniard, was most recently the winner of the Vuelta, Spain's version of the Tour de France. Castillo ate competing riders like a hungry lion. Cal resisted the urge to pinch himself. There he was, neck and neck with Castillo. Did he really belong there, next to this icon of competitive cycling?

Castillo cocked his head to the side, studied Cal, and winked at him. "He fucking winked at me?" thought Cal. "How can he be so comfortable when I'm turning myself inside out? He looks like he's actually enjoying this." Cal remembered his father's counsel—the old line about winning with the mind. Was Castillo messing with him by winking, now, when the course seemed to be getting even more difficult?

Trailing behind Cal and Castillo, waiting like vultures for them to falter, was a large pack of twenty-five riders, churning to the finish line. As they crossed under the banner announcing the final ten kilometers, one of Cal's T Mobile teammates, Franz, the veteran captain, the leader of T Mobile on the road, pulled up to him and pointed to the earpiece in his ear. He leaned in to Cal and said, "Radio. Gerhardt has something he wants to tell you." The radio that connected the *director sportif*, the team director, trailing them in the team car, with the riders on the road, was something new to Cal. Amateurs raced without radios, so the riders were essentially free operators, on their own. But the pro ranks had instituted the use of radios some years back, and the whole team was now in constant communication with the director. The director was like a traffic manager, conducting the team strategy, telling this one to come back and get water, the other one to hold up and wait for the team captain, and negotiating, urging riders, and sometimes issuing commandments to go harder, even offering words of inspiration, or threat, when their legs began to flag. The old guard despised the radios, harkening back to an earlier time when riders were forced to make their own decisions and determine their own strategy. That was an era that celebrated the riders more than the management, they believed. They believed that the radios took the romance, the artistry, out of racing, along with the sense of adventure and the creativity of freelancing on the fly.

In the current day peloton, the riders carried on a love-hate relationship with the radios. The love stemmed from the sense of security that the radio afforded, a tie with the other riders and the team car, a link to convey the request for help, a wheel to replace a flat tire, or a call for information about the shape of the race up ahead. On the other hand, a rider tethered to the team car was robbed of his individuality, which explained why some riders would "accidentally" allow the earpieces to fall out of their ears when too much chatter from the car became a nuisance, or directions contradicted the rider's instincts or intentions.

Cal heard the rough, guttural sound of Gerhardt's voice over the radio. He sometimes had trouble with Gerhardt's German accent, but Gerhardt's voice punched through the earpiece, ringing with authority. "Good going, Cal. You've done good today. Your job is almost done. Now, we come soon to the five-kilometer mark. Castillo and his Liquigas friends are marking you, and we need to break their legs. I want you to jump at the five-kilometer mark. Castillo doesn't know you, but he won't let you get too far up the road this close to the finish. He'll chase and so will the others when they see him go. They'll be marking him closely. Burn them out. Soften them up. Can you do this?"

Cal bent his head toward the microphone clipped to his shoulder. "Yeah. I feel pretty good. I can take it out."

There was a pause from the car and then Gerhardt came back. "Good. Now listen closely. We counter-attack with Franz when we get to the last sprint. Your job is to make them chase you. Don't worry about winning it. Castillo will eat you alive if it comes to a two-up sprint.

When you go out make sure that you don't gap Franz. Got it? Race smart now, don't try to be a hero. Watch out for Castillo. He's smart and he'll let you do the work, breaking the wind for him. Don't pull him all the way to the finish line."

Gerhardt's directions were clear. Take it out and make Castillo work. Soften him up for the final sprint. Cal got that. But still, he wondered, why not just go for the win? He had come this far and was feeling like he had good legs today. No knock on Franz, but why give him the win? He felt strong and knew that the uphill finish to the line meant an advantage to him. He was ten pounds lighter than Castillo, a pure bonus when it came to climbing. Cal saw the finish in his mind. He could imagine himself crossing the line with his hands lifted in the air. Almost. Nothing was guaranteed, but you didn't find yourself in the lead pack at the final kilometers of a race like this by accident. He turned the cranks. He suffered the pain. He pedaled 'til he felt like puking, and now, so close to the end, he was supposed to be a decoy for Franz? The gods were shining on him, he thought, and who knew when he might get another fat chance like this. His father had always impressed on him the virtue of opportunity. It was the ideal situation to prove his worth to the rest of the team, and Gerhardt, to show them that he deserved to be among them.

The group powered underneath the five kilometer banner, waving in the wind overhead. Tension sparked between the riders. Cal wasn't the only one thinking of standing on the podium. The riders were watching each other like cops on a stakeout, waiting for the next move, deciding when the time for a final flight to victory had arrived. Even the most fatigued riders, the ones who were going on fumes alone, could muscle it through to the end at this point. But orders were orders, and Cal was too new on this team to be a rebel.

The time to go had arrived. He slipped his hand down the bars to the shift levers and clicked twice. The chain jumped over to the smaller rear cogs, and he immediately felt the resistance in the pedals, gaining more torque with each pedal stroke. He moved out ahead of the pack, first just a few yards, and then, stroke by stroke, a couple more and a couple more, until there was a measurable gap between him and the pack. The wily veteran, Castillo, saw the move and reacted. He latched onto Cal's wheel and nestled in comfortably behind him, taking advantage of his draft. No surprise jump was going to catch him napping. Gerhardt had called it. Castillo was chasing and now was the time for Franz to position himself for his counter-attack. Cal looked back to locate Franz, but saw only Castillo, who was now locked onto Cal like a caboose. He looked again, craning his neck to see beyond Castillo, and what he saw was even more surprising. The rest of the lead group, including Franz, was slipping backward, losing contact with him and Castillo. The break, initiated by Cal as a decoy, was actually working.

Cal knew the problem he had created. "Uh-oh," he thought, "I could be fucked here. If I keep going, I take Castillo with me. He simply relaxes in my draft, saving his energy for the final jump, when he comes around me. In a sprint, Castillo's a killer. I lose. The team loses. I need to put distance between Castillo and me before the line, and take advantage of the uphill just before the finish."

Cal maintained his blistering pace, turning the pedals, ramping up the power like a turbine. He glanced back again. Castillo was lounging, surfing his draft, and still no Franz in sight. "Where the hell is he," wondered Cal, as his stomach tightened and his legs started to scream. It was decision time. He considered the option of softening his effort on the pedals and waiting for Franz to catch up. Castillo would love that. No way would he sit up and wait. He would move up the road and have his arms up in a victory salute before the rest of the peloton made it into the final sprint.

"Fuck it. I'm going." He thundered down on the pedals, pitching his bike from side to side in a last effort to detach himself from Castillo's grasp. His lungs ballooned with oxygen, and his legs exploded like pistons, hammering down on the cranks. But it was futile. Castillo matched his push and stuck his wheel directly behind Cal's. Only a millimeter or two separated the two riders. They were alone. The reality of his situation hit Cal like a brick. His acceleration had done just what he was told not to do. Castillo was playing him. He was pulling Castillo, who was using him like an engine to power their two-man train to the finish. And Franz? He was stuck in their wake, somewhere down the road, eating dust.

This was exactly what Gerhardt didn't want to see: Cal pulling Castillo to the finish and losing to him at the line.

Cal took a last glance, thinking, hoping that maybe Franz would magically pop into view. But still, nothing but empty road behind them. No Franz. Now Cal had no choice. He had to be committed to the finish line sprint. There was no alternative but to go for the win. Anything less than a win would fry Gerhardt. Cal took another gear with a smooth click of his shifter, imagined that he was leg pressing a thousand pounds with his right leg, and stomped on his pedals. Out of the corner of his eye, he saw the green of Castillo's Liquigas jersey as he pulled even with him, matching him stroke for stroke. The crowd was shrieking with excitement as the spectators lent their voices to the effort of the riders. With a last, exploding, lung-bursting lunge, Castillo launched his bike forward and bore down on the pedals with every ounce of his weight. Cal felt the sweat from his brow stinging his eyes, his neck cramping as he threw himself into the next stroke. The crowd dissolved into a blur, as he focused on the finish line a hundred meters in front of him, begging him to hurry.

In that moment he heard a sickening crack. His right leg plunged down to the ground, and his whole body catapulted skyward off the saddle. He left his bike behind him as his body traced an arc over the road. He was airborne, heading headfirst toward the barrier. Oddly, time slowed as he headed into empty space. He had time to think, "This is going to hurt."

He tucked his head at the last moment and took the impact on his left shoulder, spun forward, and tumbled to a stop against the mesh barrier separating him from the screaming fans. It took a moment, but he knew the pain was coming, sharp at first and then a deep, dull ache like a sledgehammer. He tried to breathe in, but found that his lungs were compressed. He leaned back against the barrier and gathered himself. Slowly, the air filled his lungs, and he rested his head back against the barrier. A quick inventory of his limbs comforted him. Nothing was broken. But his hips, elbow, and knee were seared with road rash, and sent a red light flashing in his brain. He looked up just in time to see the last of the trailing pack swerve to avoid him in their rush to the finish line. Castillo was long gone. He could tell from the crowd noise that his arrival was being celebrated. And he was left to pick up his bike and walk across the line.

Nice, he thought. Time waits for no one.

A couple of the fans behind the barrier leaned over and helped him to his feet. He stood unsteadily and noticed one of the fans holding a piece of his bike. It was the right crank. It had just snapped off clean, and in a flash, he realized what caused his crash. All of his weight was bearing down on the crank when it gave away, projecting his body over the handlebars. It happened, but rarely. Too bad it happened at the exact moment when he was ready to notch his first pro victory.

"Fuck! Fuck! Fuck!"

Cal limped with his bike across the finish line. The collected fans called out their approval. Cycling fans can be sadistic that way; they like to see their heroes suffer. But they also saluted the courage it took to crawl across the finish line. It all seemed so much more authentic that way. A crash in the final sprint — that was the bonus. A real wreck was the highlight of the day. "Fucking ghouls," he thought. Nevertheless, he was going to finish. He avoided making eye contact with the fans. He also knew that he was going to get a ration of shit from Gerhardt. His final pull towed Castillo to the line. The acceleration dropped Franz from contention. All that, and all he had to show for the effort was a broken bike and a healthy portion of skin on the pavement.

The bike was no problem; there was no shortage of spare parts. This was pro cycling, after all. They traveled with a bicycle shop-worth of equipment, all free from their sponsors, just for the honor of saying that a pro team is using their equipment. But fucking up the final sprint to the finish? Putting in an accleration that had dropped the team leader? There were no parts to replace this.

Cal wound his way through the crowd at the finish

line. A couple of the more generous competitors patted him on the back.

He saw the crimson red of road rash on three points for the perfect three-point landing: his elbow, knee, and hip. His legs, already scarred from many crashes, looked like a patchwork of different pigmentations. Same with his elbow. His shorts were shredded. If he weren't stinging so much from the crash, he might have felt a little embarrassed by his ass hanging out the back of the torn shorts. But, what the hell, he thought, the fans liked the up-close-and-personal exposure of cycling. And if it was up-close-and-personal they wanted, what could be more up-close-and-personal than his ass?

Cal continued his limp march toward the team bus. Other riders, those still making their way across the finish, many of whom had seen his fall, called as they passed by, "Tough break, kid. You had it made."

"Yeah, thanks. Fucking crank."

"Blame it on the team mechanic. That's what they're there for. They take the shit when the equipment fails."

"Thanks, I'll keep it in mind."

Castillo circled back to Cal and clapped him on the back and said, "*Bueno*. That was one hell of a sprint. You really pushed me. Thanks for the lead out. Next time, you might want to get your team to work for you a little bit, instead of leaving you out there on your own."

Cal looked up, surprised and flattered to get Castillo's attention. "Yeah, thought I had you there. Nice push at the end. I'm still learning some of the ropes here."

Castillo chuckled, "Yes. Learning the ropes. Here's the way to see it. Three years learning curve. First year, you learn how to just hang in with the pack without getting dropped. It's survival. Second year, you learn how to compete for the win. You see what needs to be done, even if you can't do it yet. You're learning when to work, what work to do, who to work with, and some of the politics of cruelty. Third year, you actually start winning. People start working for you, instead of using you for the cannon fodder. Based on what I saw on the road today, you have good legs. Maybe for you it's not three years. Maybe less. But *tranquillo*. Calm yourself. Take your time. Mind your team. You're strong, but nobody wins on this circuit alone. Your team makes you. And it can break you. Don't forget that."

"Thanks for the advice," Cal replied. But before he could say more, Gerhardt, the manager of his team, pulled up next to him in the team car, slammed on the brakes, and jumped out, almost tripping as he bolted out the door, crossing the road to get to Cal. He was fuming, spitting out words. "What the hell was that?" Gerhardt asked angrily. "Didn't I tell you to not to drop Franz? Do you know what that means? It doesn't mean to go for the win. Team strategy. You're a decoy. Your job is to take the legs out of them, not to try for the win, even if you feel like you have the legs. Today was Franz's day, not yours."

Cal tried to explain that he thought he had a chance for the line.

Gerhardt held up his hand. "I don't care how goddamned strong or lucky you are. And you went pulling that asshole" — pointing at Castillo, who was eavesdropping with a satisfied smirk — "all the way to the finish line with you. Your effort dropped Franz. Left him out in the wind by himself? After you were told what to do? What are you? Some kind of American cowboy?"

"But I…"

"No excuses. I know you think you're good enough to win right now. But you aren't. And even if you are, you aren't winning until I decide you are. Right now, you're a rookie. Act like it."

"But I looked for Franz, and I didn't see him. I had the line in sight. If it weren't for the crank breaking, I'd have taken the line. I thought I could take Castillo."

"You didn't see Franz because you dropped him by accelerating too fast. Castillo baited you into taking the pull. If you weren't so willing to work with Castillo, like a *domestique* for that bastard, Franz would have been there. Next time you ignore the team strategy, don't bother to stop after the finish line. Ride all the way back to the hotel and pack your bags." He yanked the car door back open, but he turned around again, purple-faced. "Oh, and as for the crank breaking? If you're stupid enough to think the reason you lost was because of the crank, you're asking for more disappointment. The crank broke, but even if it didn't, Castillo was playing you like a fiddle. He had you lined up and was just waiting for the last sprint to pass you."

The last comment hurt more than anything Gerhardt had said before. Was Castillo simply setting him up? Well, he thought, we'll never know. And after all that work, not a word about how he was feeling, patching up his road rash? Nothing? Welcome to the pros, indeed.

Franz wheeled his bike up to Cal and placed an arm around his shoulder. Cal winced when his hand brushed his left shoulder. Franz' face was covered with the grit and grime of a full day on the road and his brow was furrowed with exhaustion. "Look. What you did is a rookie mistake. Today, you showed strong. But who knows, tomorrow maybe you have no legs. But don't get sideways with Gerhardt. He's the master at this chess game called pro cycling, and he makes and breaks champions."

Cal limped over to the team bus and climbed the stairs, taking them one at a time. The rest of the team was already gathered inside the bus, engaged in various stages of post-race ritual. Some were slamming down fluids, while others were being attended to by team support staff, fetching dry clothes and energy bars, stretching or massaging their legs. In quiet exhaustion, they recapped the day's events, revisiting critical moments of the race, commiserating, and talking with enthusiasm about how good the showers at the hotel were going to feel. As Cal emerged from the stairs, several of the riders looked up and followed his progress silently. He made his way to the back of the bus and sat down alone.

Behind him, Franz entered the bus. His eyes flashed around the bus as he took in the scene. He saw Cal, and in a loud voice, he addressed the team, "Well, today? Tour of Flanders? Fuck Belgium and fuck the wind out here. Fuck the Flemish and fuck their beer. Okay, maybe not the beer. Let's take a moment guys, and thank our newest rider, Cal. He put his body on the line, literally, today. He worked like a dog out there in the wind. And if it weren't for the sorry crank set that our sponsors gave us, he'd be up on the podium right now, instead of sitting in the back of the bus." Franz raised the water bottle he had been sipping. "So a toast to Cal. You learned something today about the peloton. Today, you learned how quickly a colleague in the peloton turns into a competitor. Thanks to that asshole Castillo for teaching you that."

There was a smattering of applause and murmurs from the other riders. Franz continued. "Second, you learned that nothing is given in the race. A win isn't a win until you actually cross the line first. It doesn't matter how good your sprint looks." Again, there were nods of agreement. "But we learned something about you today. You got up and walked across the line with your bike after a beautiful crash. I saw you pop off your bike like a piece of toast popping out of the toaster. I watched, of course, from the safety of the trailing group. But it still was a sight to see. That takes heart. We won't forget that."

A murmur spread through the rest of the riders in the bus. The teammates, one by one, made their way to the back of the bus and offered a friendly pat or a word of encouragement. Cal sank back into the seat. At least, he thought, if the management of this team didn't respect him, the riders did. For now, that was all the consolation he was going to find.

* * *

"Are you okay?"

Cal's eyes sprung open and he found himself looking into the face of the flight attendant.

"Huh?"

"You were having a dream. I thought you might be more comfortable if…"

"Oh, thanks. Yeah, I guess I'm okay. Thanks."

Cal slowly rose from his seat and made his way back through the sleeping passengers to the bathroom. He envied the sleeping passengers, lined up like eggs in a carton. How do they sleep so soundly when he couldn't even find a comfortable position? he wondered.

Emerging from the bathroom, Cal encountered his father, holding court in the galley with a couple of the flight attendants. With an open bottle of wine in one hand and a glass of wine in the other, he filled the flight attendants' glasses.

"And then, when we finally got to the Champs Elysées to see Armstrong finish, we were so drunk we thought the riders were riding backward, so I yelled out…"

Seeing Cal, Paul offered to fill a glass for him. Cal waved it off with his hand.

"This is my son, Cal," Paul said to the flight attendants. "He's coming with me to Italy to ride. Of course, he's the real rider. Professional. Me? I'm just in it for the fun. Isn't that right, son?

"Dad, nothing you do is 'just for the fun.'"

Paul's face took on a look of inquiry. "I don't think we need to get into that now." The flight attendants, sensing the tension between Paul and Cal took the opportunity to busy themselves with preparation for the morning meal. "Look, son. This is going to be fun. That was then, and this is a different time. Different set of circumstances."

"Yeah. I suppose." Cal started to make his way out of the galley, but his father rose, too, and followed him back to their place in the egg carton of seats. They were still the only two awake. He'd brought an extra glass, and although Cal once again refused, Paul poured him a glass anyway. He settled a hand on Cal's shoulder and forced him to toast.

"To possibilities," he said.

Cal buried his face in the glass, but let the wine touch his upper lip without drinking. He had nothing against drinking. He just resented the way his father had steamrolled his refusal no more than a couple of minutes before.

Paul downed a draught. "Look, I have you cornered, son, so hear me out and then I promise I'll leave it alone." Cal bristled, but his father was on a roll. Cal was held captive, just like a jury that was damned well going to accept his defense, like it or not. "You were a rookie. You were in with the best riders in the world. What did you expect? Nobody breaks into professional cycling and starts winning from day one."

"Yep," Cal said. "Maybe, Dad."

"You could have hung in there. It would have worked out different. I know it."

Cal began turning the glass on the plastic tray, as if trying to screw the lid on his anger. "Yep, I bet you do."

"Look, I watched you from the first race you ever entered. You expected to win every time, every competition. When it doesn't happen, well, it can get discouraging. But that's life. Sometimes, it gets discouraging. That's when you need to dig a little deeper. When you're in the pros…"

"Shut *up*, Dad." Cal's fury rattled loose. He banged the tray with his fist. He hit it harder than he intended and wine sloshed onto his knee, but he didn't care. "You don't know what happened. You weren't there. Don't assume you know everything."

"Hold on, son. I know you. I always believed in you. You just let it all get to you. You just let your mental guard down."

The conversation felt like *déjà vu* to Cal. He looked at his father with perplexed fury.

"I think you talked yourself out of the sport. You had a great future and you let it slip away. Pissed it away… after all the work you did. If you decide that you want it again, it's there for you."

His dad was like a dog with a bone. He chewed and chewed. Cal paused. How many times had they gone over this? What was it going to take to get his father to stop asking why? The truth? Was his father ready for that? Was *he* ready for that? The couple sitting in the next row stirred in their sleep, and Cal realized they were playing this out for an audience. "Fine," he told Paul, "I quit. I just quit. I'm a quitter. Your son is a quitter. I couldn't do it—the picky eating, the ridiculous rituals, the crushing training. I wanted it all my own way because I'm a quitter. Now that that's settled, can we just let it be?"

Sensing that Cal's self-flagellation was going nowhere, Paul switched directions.

"Look," he said emphatically. "You had a false start, maybe. No denying that. Maybe you were thrown in too young. Maybe you got fucked over. T Mobile has a reputation for chewing up riders. I don't know. But I do know that all those ribbons and trophies that you won, that your mother still has on the wall, didn't come from nowhere. They weren't 'gifts.' You had it going on. And you could have it again, if you put your heart into it."

"End of sermon?" snapped Cal, with a dismissive tone.

"Yeah, sure," Paul replied. "I know you stopped listening to me years ago."

Cal closed his eyes and fell back against the seat. "Stopped listening to you," he thought. "Really? Who wasn't doing the listening?"

Cal's mind churned. He turned the conversation with his father over in his head, trying to make sense out of the disconnection between them. They spoke the same language, but the words had different meanings. "When did that start?" he wondered. "What was it going to take to make it end?" Finding no answer to the question, he looked at the door of the cabin. If he could have walked out of the airplane, he would be on his feet and leaving by now. He stared ahead, lost in an exasperated silence.

For all their arguing, Paul seemed indifferent to conflict, calloused by years in the courtroom. He sighed and patted Cal on the shoulder again. "And now that the sermon is over, we can get on to the important stuff. Like figuring out where another bottle of this Barolo is hiding in the galley."

CHAPTER 5

The trip from Marco Polo airport in Venice to the Hotel Villa Palma in Bassano passed quickly. Paul had made the trip many times before and navigated the roads confidently. It was like a jigsaw puzzle, and it wasn't unusual to approach an intersection and see multiple arrows pointing the way to Bassano del Grappa, each indicating a different direction and kilometer reading. Cal dozed. He awoke from time to time to see his father making confident decisions on the most direct route. The chaos of signs struck him as particularly Italian; style was more important than efficiency, a philosophy that would never be tolerated in ever-practical America.

The one hundred kilometers that separated the airport in Venice and the small city of Bassano del Grappa took them through some of the most scenic parts of the Veneto region of Italy. As they approached the town, they saw the soaring, jagged mountains of the Dolomites brushing against the high, full clouds. At this time of year, the mountains were still capped in snow, while the temperature through the foothills was a comfortable low seventies, perfect riding weather. Cal continued to nod off as his father wheeled the rental car through the small towns and villages that punctuated their route. The tinny radio in their rental car churned out a steady diet of American hip-hop music, an irony that only reinforced just how small the world had actually become. At the end of each song, an Italian DJ came on the air and, with machine gun pacing, spat out the local news and information. Cal had picked up a little Italian language from a couple of his Italian teammates, enough to get by in a restaurant or hotel, but the speed of the phrasing perplexed him. On most teams, English was the common denominator, so communication was possible, albeit somewhat reduced in complexity to the bare minimum of cycling related phrasing: "go," "attack," "wait," "work together," "eat," "pass through," and so on. Cal envied, in particular, the central European riders, the ones who were able to converse in English, German, Italian, and French. He didn't think of himself as stupid, but he was humbled when he compared himself to someone like Franz who could handle sequential questions in an interview in three different languages.

Bassano, as the locals called it, was a picturesque little Italian village known for its cycling environment. Many of the professional teams trained in the hills surrounding the town. As the rental car approached the city center, Paul and Cal passed gaggles of riders as well as solo cyclists out for a warm day's training ride. The sight of so many riders brought a smile to Cal's face. It was good to be back again in an environment where "share the road" signs were unnecessary — and riders were an accepted part of the landscape. Italian drivers were the most courteous to cyclists. How could they be otherwise, Cal thought? Their grandmothers still rode bicycles to and from the marketplace, baskets loaded with vegetables, meats, and pastas.

The route to their hotel took them through the town center. Its plaza was crowded with middle-aged men arguing, Cal imagined, over espresso drinks and housewives, engaged in animated discussion while their children savored *gelati* and *biscotti*.

In the near distance, Monte Grappa loomed over the town, six thousand feet of gray granite summit that sparkled in the sunlight. Cyclists traveled from far and wide to climb the seventeen twisting miles to the summit. But for those with racing in their blood, Monte Grappa was best known for its signature event, the climb from Bassano to Monte Grappa's stormy summit, an annual race that drew the best of Italian cycling nobility. Le Scale, literally the stairs, was a regional rite of passage for riders with pro dreams.

As Paul piloted the rental through the gates of their hotel, La Villa Palma, Cal felt like he was falling backward in time. The Villa, which had been in Luigi Palma's family for over a hundred years, was an Italian testimony to luxury from another era. A circular driveway led to a grand set of stairs. Behind the ornate front door stood a reception area with soaring ceilings, classical paintings on the wall, and tapestries suspended from the vaulted heights. Although The Villa had seen its better days, Luigi had managed to retain vestiges of its earlier grandeur. The dining room still served its elaborate meals on linen and was set with sterling silver cutlery. No two of The Villa's thirty rooms were alike. Each had its own idiosyncratic layout: a bathroom in the shape of an L, a sitting room that dwarfed the adjacent bedroom, and doors that led to nowhere. If short on modernity, The Villa Palma was long on personality.

Pulling into the driveway, Cal's eyes scanned the architecture. This was going to be different from the typical tourist hotel that the team frequented when he was traveling with T Mobile. Hotels for traveling cycling teams are chosen for efficiency and logistics, not comfort. Nice, he thought. At least there was this consolation prize for traveling with his father.

As Paul and Cal unloaded their bike bags and suitcases from their car, Luigi scampered out the front door to help with their bags.

"Signor Paul. *Come stai?*"

"*Bene, e tu?*"

"*Non c'e male.* Not too bad. Welcome. How was your trip?

"Long, Luigi. Very long."

"So we must make sure that it's worth the effort then. You're here and you're my guest, so everything will be taken care of."

The two men embraced with a warmth that generated a feeling of a genuine fondness. Remembering that Cal was standing with the bike bag in his hand, Paul stood back and motioned toward his son.

"Luigi, this is my son, Cal. Cal, say hello to my old friend, Luigi."

Cal dropped the bag and extended his hand, which Luigi gripped and shook with the enthusiasm of a man priming a pump. "Nice to meet you, Signor Cal. Your father and I are old *amici*, old friends. I have heard a lot about you over the years."

"Yes, my dad has told me about you, too. Says that you're one of the most rabid *tifosi* in all of Italy."

"Me? *Si, si*, but in Italy, we're all serious cycling nuts. And here in Bassano, we are even more so. The Giro d'Italia, the greatest of all cycling races, wouldn't be complete if there weren't at least two stages in this region. We grow up as cyclists, we live for the races, and we die thinking that life would have been fuller if we had only seen more stages. The Giro is how I first met your father. He was a regular watching the Giro here for many years. That, and he knows that my kitchen makes the best *papardelle* in the whole region. Is that not correct, Signor Paul?"

"Too true, Luigi. In fact, I consider a visit a waste if I don't put on at least a couple of pounds each visit. All the climbing, all the hours spent turning the pedals on the road that we do here, can't offset the calories in even one helping of your *papardelle*."

Luigi turned to Cal and said with a deferential tone and a nod of his head, "I'm truly honored to have a cycling champion like you staying in my hotel. I read about your accomplishments a few years ago. But lately, nothing. You've been injured?"

Cal tried to pass off the compliment casually. "No. I decided to pursue some other stuff. You know, can't keep riding a bike forever. Bike riding is for kids."

Luigi moved backward as if he couldn't believe such blasphemy. "*Ma, no*. That isn't true. Coppi, a true gift from the gods, although some bastards still say the greatest Italian cyclist is Bartali, rode until he was nearly forty. No. You're in your prime."

"Well, maybe so. But racing is a part of my history. I've decided to focus on the next chapter of my life... Whatever that is." Cal punctuated the last comment with a self-conscious laugh, but the effect was lost on Luigi, who looked to Paul for an explanation. How could such a promising and noble career be abandoned?

Paul interceded to cut off the inquiry and said, "Well, we're here to ride now. So why don't you give us a hand and help us get these bags into the room?"

"Sure, Signor Paul. Are you going out this afternoon? A light spin up Monte Grappa?"

"Whoa, not so fast, Luigi. We just got in this morning. The legs aren't ready for climbing yet. Today is a day for *piano, piano,* as you Italians like to say. Slowly, slowly. Think we'll spin down toward Asolo. Ride some flats and let him get used to you crazy Italian motorists before we do anything that takes us into the mix."

"Asolo? I'll let Gianni know you're coming. He has some new designs you would like to see."

"Thanks, Luigi. Yeah, tell him that we might stop in. I e-mailed him a couple of weeks ago that we were coming, so he should know we're here. And when are you going to get your fat ass on a bike and join us?"

"*Come mai*? Why would I do something like that and spoil your trip? You go, I'll have *una pasta buona* waiting for you when you return. You take care of the cycling and I'll take care of the pasta. That way, we each stay with what we know."

CHAPTER 6

After a quick change in their separate rooms, Paul and Cal met in the courtyard and assembled their bikes. Cal snapped the case open and extracted his Colnago frame. The shop had done a good job of packing the bike, wrapping the delicate carbon fiber tubes in pipe insulation to protect against the airline's baggage handlers, notorious for the damage they inflicted on bike boxes. The components had been removed from the frame and tucked into separate bags, and his shoes and helmet were wedged into the corners of the box. He held the frame up and examined it. After all these years, he still marveled at the magic the engineers did with carbon and steel, building a frame that withstood the fury of the road, and still weighed no more than sixteen pounds, even with all of the components, the front and back derailleurs, the aerodynamic wheels, the light-as-a-feather saddle and bars, and the clip-in pedals.

And then there was the paint job. Colnago didn't just paint their bikes. They created moving pieces of art. Cal admired the rich black base coat and the blue scrolling highlights that snaked across the top tube like wisps of smoke in an evening sky. Cal had matched the blue of the detailing with blue tires and, for a finishing touch, blue handlebar tape and a saddle with a blue insert. Even the wheels had blue carbon spokes. And the components, pure Campagnolo, tapped into the well of Italian heritage. With T Mobile, he had ridden what the sponsors dictated, Shimano Dura Ace. Nice stuff, high quality, Japanese, tech advanced, but lacking the classic look and feel of Campy. There was function, yes, but there was also art. When he left the team, he rebuilt his old bike, replacing the original components with newer ones from Campagnolo. When he was finished, he felt like he had taken an old classic frame and turned it into a hot rod.

He stood back from his rolling expression of creativity and admired it. Even standing still, it conveyed efficient and effortless motion. No matter how conflicted Cal was about cycling, he had never fallen out of love with the bicycle. His bike fully assembled stirred the cool factor that had attracted him to cycling way back in high school. When other kids were tinting the windows of their cars or adding sound systems that would shake a city block, Cal was swapping steel bolts in the chain ring for titanium ones, a savings of three grams per bolt. Not economical when you considered the cost per gram saved, but shaving weight was the Holy Grail for cyclists back then. The technology had advanced, of course. Bikes were lighter now than they had ever been — so light that the governing bodies of racing had instituted a bare minimum of fifteen pounds for bikes in competition. But the simple elegance of the bicycle design? That hadn't budged a millimeter since Cal got into the sport.

Paul saw Cal standing silently, admiring his bike and nudged him.

"How does that compare to the ride they gave you on T Mobile?

"Oh, well, you know, we were sponsored by Specialized, so we rode them. And they were good. But some of the guys wanted other rides. They made their own deals for other bikes, but had them painted over to look like a Specialized. But this is my baby. Other frames come and go, but we've spent a lot of time and crossed a lot of miles together. It's been good to me, and I wouldn't want to be disloyal." Cal looked over at his father's Time carbon frame. It shone in the sun and was a statement of modern technology: integrated seat post, shiny carbon fiber tubes, $2,500 Campangnolo Hyperon Carbon wheels, new eleven-speed Campy Super Record gruppo. It was a $14,000 dream bike. He always thought it ironic that the fat cats got the fast rides, while the up-and-coming racers often made do with beaters, but then, it was the engine not the rider that made the difference, wasn't it?

"Yours isn't too shabby, either. A lot of the pros I know would be happy to be riding that."

"Well, you know my philosophy," Paul answered quickly. "If you can't go fast, look fast."

Cal looked over at his father, decked out in his Assos bib shorts, top of the line, the skin-tight jersey, his wrap-around sunglasses, and his aerodynamic helmet. He looked good. Looked strong. What the hell, he thought, his father did the work on the bike, and he had the money, so why not? Cal had promised himself that he wouldn't travel the reverse judgmentalism avenue with his father, especially on this trip.

"What say we sample some of the delicious roads Bassano has to offer?" Paul asked.

There was no time to respond; his father had already clipped in and was heading out of the driveway for the first mile of what promised to be a cycling lover's dream ride. They rolled out of the driveway and onto the road. The air was fresh and clean and it felt good to stretch their legs after the long flight. The warm, spring breeze washed away the travel fatigue. The road wound by small homes and farms and the occasional small store. Off to the side, farmers were riding their tractors grooming the fields. Time slowed to a leisurely pace as they made their way down the country lanes. When they needed to cross one of the busier routes, Cal was reminded that he was in Europe by the willingness of the motorists to give way to cyclists. A quick wave of the hand and a nod of the head was the signal indicating the need to cross; a reciprocal nod gave the go-ahead sign. It was so different from the States, where crossing traffic required a master plan, exquisite timing, high-alert vigilance, and a willingness to stare death in the face. Paul piloted a course through the back roads to give Cal a feeling for the terrain and local pulse.

The ride started slowly. Pedaling down the road, two abreast, Paul and Cal engaged in the easy small talk that is generic among recreational riders. They spoke of the terrain, their plans for the week, the promise of unforgettable meals, and Paul's hope that Cal would come to love the Veneto region as much as he had. There was no past or future beyond a few days. Maybe his mother was right, he thought, maybe his father was changing. It was a relief to not focus on training protocols, gear ratios, energy drinks, wattage output, rehashing the finish of the last race, and the latest tech advances in equipment.

Paul pointed out some of the landmarks they passed, the access road to Monte Grappa, the surrounding vineyards, and the road up to Asiago—all routes that they would explore in the next week. As the tree-lined road narrowed, they slid from a two-abreast formation to a single file. He and Cal settled into a gentle exchange of leads on the bike. The front bike broke the wind for the following rider who stuck close to enjoy the slipstream. Then they switched. Sharing the work, helping each other with the load, gave rhythm and meaning to their passage down the road. It was this give and take, borne out of a sense of cooperation, that comprised one of the things that Cal liked best about cycling. The harmony of a well-organized line of riders felt magical.

Cal reflected back to the thousands of miles he and his father had ridden together back in the States. From his earliest training-wheel expeditions down the block to his first pro-quality ten-speed, their shared rides had been a staple of his youth. He relished the times when riding was fun, before it became a form of work and racing replaced riding, training replaced exercise, and the whole nature of the experience transformed from one of escape to one of focused intensity. Reflecting on this transition, Cal felt like he was exploring the archeology of his young adult life. He tried to shut off the reflection and focus on the sensation of his legs turning perfect circles on the cranks and the wind passing across his face. He filled his lungs with the country air and felt, for the first time in too long, a quiet comfort settle over his body.

The pace was casual. No need for hard effort yet. This was a ride with a purpose, and the purpose was to stay within their comfort envelope. The idea was to stretch the legs and enjoy the passing scenery—nothing more and nothing less. Cal settled into a relaxed cadence on the bike. A sly grin spread across his face. No matter what difficulties Cal had with himself, with his father, with teammates and team organization, with racing, with goals, or with success and failure, there was one refuge for him that endured—cycling. It all had to do with the rhythmic spinning of the wheel, the tensioned arc of the pedals, the cool flow of the wind, and the floating sensation he felt as he angled his bike through a turn. These were curative. And for the first time in a long time, Cal remembered what drew him to cycling in the first place. From his first spin around the block, his first experience with the freedom of two wheels, he felt a deep connection. Cycling was something that belonged to him. This was something that he could lose himself in. It was a boundless activity. He had mastered much of cycling, but there was so much more to learn—about cycling, about himself, and about life.

After an hour, their steady pace brought them up to two other riders, a couple of young racers out for an afternoon's training session. Since the pace of the riders was fairly well matched, it wasn't long before they melded into a foursome. Then the four began to ride as one, sharing the work like a cooperative. The paceline that developed became a single, efficient machine. Each rider took his turn at the front, and then slid to the back as the line of three moved past him. No words were spoken. No words were needed. The four communicated by cadence, gear shifts, and body position. A flick of the arm indicated that the rider in the front wanted the rider behind to come around. A wave of the hand by the front rider warned of debris in the road, or a pointed finger indicated potential cross traffic. The four individuals soon began to think, move, and ride as one organism.

As they did so, their pace increased. It wasn't a conscious decision. Instead, the group moved more quickly down the road simply because, as an organized whole, their collective power outstripped what any one of them could produce on his own.

CHAPTER SIX | 55

Ahead in the distance, another small group of four riders was pedaling in their own paceline. The white script on their blazing red jerseys, Squadra Diavolo, identified them as club riders, racers, out for a training ride.

Paul turned to Cal and said, "Hey, let's see if we can chase those guys down."

Before Cal could register his resistance — he really wasn't interested in getting into a *mano-a-mano* with a group of strangers on the road — his father had taken up the pace and was off the front in pursuit. Not wanting to leave his father alone in his quest, Cal shifted gears, stood up on the pedals, and tucked in behind him. The other two riders followed suit. Now they were a eight-legged animal, chasing down the prey in front of them.

What had been an easy cadence became a whipped fury of flashing pedals. Cal and his group were beginning to breathe harder and the exertion was showing on their faces. In the back, Cal frowned.

He called forward to his father, "Hey, Dad, tempo ride. What the fuck? Let those other guys go up the road. We don't need to catch them."

Cal's complaint fell on deaf ears. Paul continued the furious push at the front. Soon, the intensity of the effort became too much for the two Italian teens. As they hit the wall, they signaled their abandonment of the chase with sighs of fatigue, bodies slumping over their bikes, and their heads hanging, mouths pulling in as much oxygen as their lungs could possibly grasp. Now the chase, what was left of it, consisted only of Paul and, so close behind him that their wheels were separated by only millimeters, Cal. Despite the effort he was putting in, Cal's ambivalence was cresting. Did he really want to be going this hard? Was it really worth it? He had had more than his share of incidents on the road where friendly rides turned competitive. There had been too many times when a basic tempo ride turned into a sadistic bloodbath, with riders throwing themselves against the wall of exhaustion, trying to bring their training partners to the breaking point and beyond. But he knew his father. Paul was going for broke and the only choice for Cal was to either throw in with him or to quit.

Cal heard the click of Paul's derailleur as he grabbed a higher gear to kick up his speed and shot forward. He could also hear his father's breathing get more ragged as he gulped down as much air as he could force into his lungs. Despite this effort, though, the gap between the chasers and the pursued refused to shrink. The thirty yards that separated Cal's group from the Squadra Diavolo group seemed fixed in stone, a seemingly permanent gap. As he reached the end point of his effort, through gritted teeth and with his last gasp of air before pulling to the side, Paul spurred Cal on.

"Go for it, Cal. Don't let them get away."

Something snapped in Cal. From somewhere deep inside, he felt a surge of energy. He rose from his saddle, flicked the lever to go to a higher gear, and felt the immediate increase of resistance as he purchased more road with each turn of the cranks. He quickly left his father in his wake, and, with an explosion of power, gobbled up the gap separating him from Squadra Diavolo. The last rider of Squadra Diavolo turned and, in surprise, found Cal closing in on him.

When Cal reached the last rider, he took some of the power out of his stroke and relaxed behind him, sliding into the last place of the train and enjoying the opportunity to rest in his draft. The last Squadra Diavolo rider, a blond, lean rider, who looked a little frightened by the American who had descended on him like a hawk, squawked out to him, "*Cosa fai? Da dove viene?*" What are you doing, where did you come from? His question had an edge that conveyed a mixture of wonder, surprise, fear, and more than a little annoyance.

"Huh?" Cal said, betraying his shortage of Italian. By now, he had slipped in line with the four Squadra Diavolo riders. "Where are you guys riding to?" He wasn't really looking for a race; rather, he was thinking that he would just jump in with some fellow riders out for a spin. But they were in no mood for a communal effort.

The leader of the Squadra Diavolo, riding in the front position, was a young man with broad, square shoulders, more muscular in the upper body than the typical racer. He sported a shock of black hair beneath his helmet, and had intense dark eyes that trained on Cal at the sound of a new voice. He craned his neck around and appraised the American sitting on their tail. He frowned. Clearly resenting the arrival of an unknown rider, he made a quick decision. With a sense of urgency, and the deliberate goal of ridding the group of this nuisance, he increased his cadence and jumped forward, dragging his teammates along with him. His message was clear.

Like a puppy intent on sticking with the bigger dogs, Cal tagged along. The increased pace struck him as rude. He wasn't sure that the Italians, especially the frowning one in front, were really trying to turn this into a race, but the audacity of someone treating him, a visitor with no ill intent, so shabbily made him angry. If it was a race he wanted, then, what the hell? It was a race he would give him. Remembering his father trailing along behind him, and the faith he had in Cal's competitive spirit, a vestige of that old kid returned and wanted to show his father his cycling strength. He abandoned his ambivalence, and like a bird freed from his cage, he flew.

The sharp increase in effort took its toll on the group. First, one of the Squadra Diavolo riders fell off the pace, then another, shaking his head in acknowledgement that the end had arrived for him. Finally, the third pulled to the side with silent acceptance that he had hit the wall, leaving only Cal and the leader of the Squadra Diavolo group. The Squadra Diavolo leader seemed more than a little surprised to see Cal still riding with him, this interloper in his generic cycling clothes, with gear that made him look like a recreational rider out on a Sunday cruise. Here he was, this stranger, this fucking *turista*, glued to his rear wheel. The rider ground down on the cranks. His intention, if Cal had any doubt before, was now clear. He was out to drop Cal off of his wheel.

Up ahead, a flashing barrier spanned the road. In the middle of the barrier was a control gate, a gap with enough space to allow only one rider to pass through. The race was going to be decided by elimination. It was a game of "cycling chicken."

In a last effort to shake Cal, the Squadra Diavolo rider jumped out of his saddle, and started sprinting. Cal anticipated his move, and with a blind fury he hadn't experienced since his competitive racing days, pounded against his pedals. He soared out of his seat and scorched past the Squadra Diavolo rider, nipping through the gate first, with less than a wheel to separate them. The Squadra Diavolo rider was forced to clamp his brakes, in order to avoid hitting the barrier. Cal glanced back to see the Squadra Diavolo competitor pound his hand on the handlebar in frustration.

Once through the gate, Cal slowed down and allowed the guy to pull up next to him.

"Nice sprint," he said with a smile. "You guys ride out of Bassano?"

The Italian looked at Cal with disdain. "What sprint? If I don't allow you to go ahead, we both crash. I don't take that chance. I have more important races to do." He blew his nose on the pavement between their bikes. "You need to learn some road manners. This isn't America. You don't just jump in with a group. You made a mess out of our training ride."

"Sorry," said Cal. "I mean, I didn't mean to mess your paceline up. Besides, it seemed to me that you were the one pushing the pace." The situation was immediately clear to him—another arrogant roadie, too cool for his own good. *Thinks he owns the road and the rest of us are supposed to just back off and give him his way.* It was true that cycling protocol dictated that you just don't jump into a training group, but Cal had been courteous and had assumed a conciliatory position at the back, where he wouldn't cause any disruption. Now this guy was up barking at him, after he had schooled him in their "sprint?" Just as on the bike a few minutes before, he couldn't let the challenge go.

"I don't mean to get you bent out of shape or anything, but if you weren't sprinting, then what the fuck do you call that death charge effort you put in at the end?" Cal leaned closer to the Italian, close enough to make out his name embroidered on the left topside of his jersey. "Rocco? So uh, Rocco. Next time, I suggest you think a little about 'road manners,' as you call it, yourself. And if you're going to try to drop someone, make sure you have the legs to make it happen."

"Fuck you. If I sprint, if this is really a race, you wouldn't even be within spitting distance of me."

Cal paused, taken aback by the sudden escalation of hostility between him and this stranger, so quick and so volatile. It was the arrogance that got to him, as if only Europeans had any right to cycling dominance. It struck a nerve, still inflamed from the discrimination that American riders experienced on the European pro tour. Granted, bicycle racing had been dominated by Europeans. Americans besides Lance Armstrong had made their mark in cycling over the years, but rarely got credit for being anything other than selfish, spoiled brats. It was the same stereotype that greeted him on the T Mobile team, and he was sick of it.

By this time, the rest of the riders — the Squadra Diavolo riders and Cal's father — had pulled up, surrounding the two arguing riders.

Paul, having caught the last of the confrontation and seeing the look on Cal's face, pulled Cal to the side of the road. He knew the look on Cal's face — the wrinkled brow, the flushed cheeks, and the fire in his eyes. If he didn't dampen things down, an explosion wouldn't be far off.

"That was a hell of a sprint, Cal. You smoked that guy."

"Yeah, that's me. Always making friends and allies on the road."

"Now, do you think you can drop it? Don't let that shit bother you. There's always some hometown hero who puts his ego on the line every time he turns a pedal."

"Fucking poseurs." Cal made sure that the Squadra Diavolo riders heard his last comment.

It was now Rocco's turn to drop the insults. Turning to his teammates, "This boy here, he comes with his daddy to protect him. Maybe next time we teach him what happens if his daddy isn't around to protect him." The other Squadra Diavolo riders laughed, mounted their bikes around, and rode off.

Cal and his father wheeled their bikes around and pushed off in the opposite direction. As they rode away, Cal looked over his shoulder and glared at Rocco. He wasn't surprised to see that Rocco was doing the same. They seemed locked together in a contest to see who would break first. Finally, Cal let it go. He was there to have fun, he reminded himself, and skirmishes like this one were all too reminiscent of a life that he thought he had left behind.

CHAPTER 7

"You still have some power in those legs, son," said Paul as they pedaled toward the turnaround point. "All it took was a little anger for you to get the competitive juices going. Remember what we always talked about, though. Use the anger—don't let the anger use you. Ride smart, not angry."

Cal hardly heard his father's voice. It buzzed somewhere in the background. In the forefront of his mind were the other riders, the chase, and his reaction. The competitive fire was burning again—or had never gone out. It set off a cascade of introspection. He had made his decision to quit. It was his career to give up. He had earned that right, hadn't he? And it was the right decision, too, wasn't it? In the three years since leaving T Mobile, he had ample opportunities to change his mind: Other teams came sniffing around, but he'd polished the art of the quick, offhand comment, "There are other things I want to accomplish." Better to make it sound like he was moving toward something, despite a lack of clarity of what that next goal might be. As his father's voice continued to drift in the background, he also heard Gerhardt's voice at his final team meeting.

* * *

Following Paris–Roubaix, Cal knew something was up when the T Mobile director asked him to come to his room after the post-race massage.

Paris–Roubaix, L'inferno du Nord, the hell of the North, was acknowledged by all who raced to be the most brutal, most punishing race in the pro circuit. Two hundred and sixty kilometers in Northern France, bouncing over twenty-eight different, teeth-rattling sections of cobblestones, this torture chamber of a race was considered a joke by some of the pros. Too difficult to be called a race, some thought. More of a death march. The small percentage who finished dragged their bikes over the finish line, covered in mud, chilled to the bone by the hateful weather characteristic of Northern France that time of year, and aching from the six-hour beating. The suffering enhanced its prestige, and winners were granted admission to an exclusive club of those who had earned the knowledge of just how much suffering they could endure.

When Cal first learned that he was going to be part of the T Mobile team competing in Paris–Roubaix, he was surprised. For a neo-pro, to be chosen as a team member for such a difficult race was a special acknowledgement, a nod to the belief that he had the ability to suffer. Even though some of the older vets considered his selection to be a form of child abuse, and even though he would be riding in support of the team's designated finisher, Franz, the fact was the same: Cal had made the cut. For a newcomer to a pro team, the acceptance was like money in the bank.

As a *domestique*, his job was support. Break the wind, chase down the attacks, ferry water bottles and food from the team car to the designated leader, stand by and help the leader catch on after he pulled over for what the pros called a "nature break," and even surrender his bike if there was a mechanical problem and the leader needed a new ride. It all came with the territory. And there was no dishonor in serving his team leader well. Franz was certainly the most gifted of all the T Mobile riders, and he was never short on the compliments or encouragement that kept a *domestique*'s spirits high. Of course, *domestiques* got a share of the prize money if their rider won, but money was not the issue here. It was the honor, not the money, that kept the rider in the saddle through monstrous conditions.

And what a day it had been. From the beginning of the race, T Mobile and Franz fought for the lead in a select group at the front, with Cal in support through much of the race. But a crash with less than sixty kilometers to go to the finish line sent Franz off the cobbles and into a ditch. He could have remounted his bike, if his front wheel wasn't twisted like a pretzel. But to what end? The lead group was far up the road. His shoulder was aching and a ride in the warm team car, sheltered from the penetrating wind, offered an irresistible appeal.

Cal had worked hard for him, taking pulls at the front of the peloton and carving a path through the surging crowds that squeezed the road down to a narrow file on the cobblestoned sections of the forest. The crash ended Franz's afternoon, but not Cal's. He put his back into the effort and continued, crossing the finish line in a time of six hours and twenty-one minutes. Nowhere near the race leaders, but not bad for a first-timer. He was the highest-placed T Mobile rider, and after the race, when Franz rolled into the hotel in the team car, nursing his road rash and bruises, he was effusive in his praise and his thanks.

"Congratulations, youngster. You must have an engine instead of a heart beating in your chest. I didn't finish my first Paris–Roubaix until my fourth attempt."

"Thanks, but I'm sorry about your crash. How you feeling?"

"Sore, but nothing broken. It's Paris–Roubaix," he said, shrugging his uninjured shoulder. "No way I was going to take the win, anyway. Pascal was up front with two of his teammates. He's one of those Belgian beasts. They thrive in conditions that make the rest of us call out for our mommies… But you, you're a, what do the Americans call it? A natural born killer. You showed strong today. And thanks for the help. Gerhardt was impressed."

"He was?"

"Yeah. We talked about it in the car just now. He wants to see you after your massage. Said to tell you to stop by his room."

Cal's heart surged. "Any idea what he wants to talk about?"

"Yes. But no, I'm not going to tell you. You guys figure it out."

It was no secret that Gerhardt had a negative attitude toward the team's non-Euro riders, and that Cal was there by the grace of the team's executive directors. In the modern era of cycling, they were convinced that a team needed to be international. It drew a broader audience for the sponsors, making them more willing to open their wallets. Still, American riders would always have to prove themselves on European teams. The hurdle was a steep one to get over, but after Cal's performance at Paris–Roubaix, he was beginning to feel confident that he could make it. Respect earned was respect valued, he believed, and he was willing to earn Gerhardt's the hard way — in the saddle.

Cal resisted the urge to go to Gerhardt's room immediately. Protocol after a race was closely controlled and parceled out: cool down, relax, re-hydrate, replace glycogen with something rich like a piece of cake or fruit, and get a massage. Miss any of these, and his body, a racing engine, would suffer for the next two days. This was no time to change the routine, even though the massage was not going to be very relaxing. As the masseuse kneaded his aching quads, he kept drifting off to imaginary scenarios with Gerhardt. "Happy to see that you didn't fuck up today, Cal. Don't let it go to your head." Or worse, "Cal, why didn't you prevent Franz from crashing today? You were there. You should have found a way to keep him from going over."

When the massage was finished, the masseuse tapped Cal on the cheek and sent him on his way. Fatigue dragged at his legs as he climbed the stairs to the third floor of the inn. On the other side of Gerhardt's door were the muffled sounds of an animated conversation.

He hesitated, afraid that he might be interrupting something important. But Gerhardt had invited him, for chrissake. Cal told himself to grow a pair, and knocked.

"*Hereinkommen*, come in," Gerhardt called out.

Cal entered the room. "You wanted to see me?" Seated next to Gerhardt, sharing the sofa with him, was a handsome man dressed in a designer suit, tanned, and in his fifties. His suit was out of place in the casual world of cycling, but he had the bearing of someone who would make himself comfortable no matter where he found himself. His face was familiar. Cal had seen him around some of the training camps, but had never been formally introduced. A telephone sat on the table in front of them, and a conference call was taking place.

"Just a second, Conrad. He's just arrived. I'll put him on the phone."

Gerhardt motioned for Cal to have a seat. When he had settled in, Gerhardt continued. He motioned to the well-dressed guest seated next to him.

"Cal, this is Dr. Steiner. He consults with the team on medical issues. And on the phone, joining our conversation is Conrad Stuller." Cal flushed. Alarm bells sounded in his head. Dr. Steiner? He had heard the name bandied about in the pro cycling circuit. There were stories and rumors about him, none proven. But they all suggested that he was involved with something that cycling had been trying to rid itself of for years. Doping. Drugs. Cheating. Some referred to Steiner as the sinister "Dr. Frankenstein" for the work he had done turning ordinary riders into monster contenders for the Tour de France and other pro races. It had become so common for mid-pack racers to transform into peloton leaders in the space of a year that it hardly raised an eyebrow any longer. No charges had ever been proven with Dr. Steiner, but the whispers spread like a virus throughout the peloton. Racers were excellent judges of talent, and when someone suddenly improved... Well, when something was too good to be true, it often wasn't.

Cal recognized Conrad Stuller's voice, too. Herr Stuller was the executive director of T Mobile, a man who was known for his "take no prisoners" approach to business negotiations. He ran T Mobile like a corporation, with the same attention to "ROI," return-on-investment, that he applied to buying equipment for one of his many factories. Cal had met him only once, when he was presented with his contract with T Mobile. After that initial meeting, Stuller disappeared and left the daily decisions to Gerhardt.

Stuller started the conversation, his voice echoing from the phone. "Cal, that was a wonderful performance today.

I watched it on the television. I could not believe my own eyes. A first year pro finishing so high? You've shown yourself to be very promising. Very strong, indeed. You have a bright future. On this matter, I feel confident."

"Thanks," Cal mumbled. He had heard his father toss out this kind of obligatory flattering in his negotiations enough times to know that there was always another shoe, and it was about to drop.

"That's what I feel, and that's what Gerhardt feels. Of course, Gerhardt can be quite the taskmaster, so I doubt he's done much to boost your confidence. That's what I love about the old bastard, eh, Gerhardt?"

Well, at least Stuller knew that Gerhardt was an asshole. No need to call a summit meeting to point out the fact.

"So you're wondering what this is all about, I'm sure. Gerhardt? Won't you explain to Cal what we have in mind?"

"Yes, Herr director." Gerhardt swiveled to face Cal. "Cal, I know I've been tough on you since you joined the team. But you know it isn't personal. That is just part of the initiation, I guess you could call it, for new riders. Comes with the territory."

Cal nodded, stifling his urge to let Gerhardt know how de-motivating his "initiation" felt. The other shoe was surely on its way down by now.

"So in the last couple of races you've shown me something that I didn't, frankly, think you had in you."

"Thanks. So?"

"Well, we signed you as a *domestique*. Our expectations were not too high, to be frank. Thought it would be good to have an American face on the squad — public relations, you know. Cycling is becoming more international and having a US rider would be good. Maybe we would have you ride in the Tour of California or some of the domestic races in your country. Would be good for the 'optics' of things. Who knows? You throw your line into the water and you never know what you catch."

Cal waited for him to continue. Inside he was beginning to boil. A risk? Is that what Gerhardt thought of him? An American face?

"But after today, we're revising what we think. You made us open our eyes. You could have quit after Franz crashed out today. Nobody would have blamed you if you stacked your bike on the team car and saved yourself from the elements. But you didn't. You finished strong and that says you have the mental strength to suffer with some of the best."

Another insult? Cal thought. You didn't know I had mental strength? How did you think I won all the races before I turned pro?

"So I won't beat around the bush, now. Your performance on the road has been impressive. I've liked what you've shown in the training sessions, too. Herr Stuller and I feel that you have the potential to be a leader of our team. Maybe not today, but soon, sooner than we would have guessed. Franz is getting older and, let's face it, cycling isn't for thirty-seven-year-old men. And today, he goes down and hurts his shoulder. Cycling can be cruel, no? Maybe a younger man would have the reflexes to avoid the crash. Maybe not. But no matter. The point is, we would like to start grooming you for a leadership role on the team."

Cal's head spun. What the fuck? Team leader, really?

"To be a leader on the pro tour isn't for everyone. There are a lot of very talented cyclists out there, but only a few special ones who have what it takes to win. Training methods have gotten very scientific. Used to be that we just rode long and hard. Now, there are training protocols, nutrition, periodization, and a lot of other things. Factors that Dr. Steiner is an expert in. So if you're going to be a leader of the team, we need to start preparing you. You won't do it on hard work alone. And that's why I wanted you to meet Dr. Steiner."

Cal nodded to Dr. Steiner, who returned his nod with a soft smile. Steiner picked up the conversation. In sophisticated English, spoken with a British accent owing to his training at medical school in Oxford, Steiner continued, "So Cal, to make a total commitment means to address training on all of the fronts: physical, technical, psychological, medical, and so on. A complete package of sophisticated training. As you're already doing, hard work, nutrition, and all the rest are important, I'm sure you would agree?" He didn't wait for Cal's response. "But there's more. I think you know what I mean?" Again, no pause for a response. "The winning riders understand that there is a science to success, and that's where I come in. To put in the training at the level you are asked to do now requires some extra help. You see, raising the VO_2 max to the level that is needed to sustain the effort required to put out the wattage…"

Stuller's voice broke through Steiner's soliloquy. His impatience was palpable. "Cal, what Steiner is talking about is that we want to make available to you some, I suppose you could call them, enhancements, to help you with your training. Make available to you the latest developments in training and conditioning science."

Cal's head spun. Drugs. They wanted him to start doping. That was the other shoe—EPO, CERA, whatever. Not that he was naïve about the doping situation in cycling.

Nobody was. Even if the racers didn't test positive, there was always the suspicion. After so much scandal and so much scrutiny, the racers joked that you only were cheating if you got caught. The cynicism threatened the profession as much as the cheating itself, and Cal knew he would face this crucial decision some day. But he didn't know his choice would be dictated to him in this way, that it would be the carrot on the end of the stick of race leadership. Gerhardt's presumption was that he would simply say yes, as simple as accepting a different type of cycling shoe. Easy. Everybody does it. It made Cal wonder, what about the rest of the team? What about Franz?

"Enhancements?" replied Cal, barely containing the sarcasm. "You mean drugs, don't you?"

"Well, yes, drugs, I suppose," replied Steiner with a tone that conveyed his boredom with Cal's outrage. "Of course, you don't have to do it. But you aren't going to make it to the top if you don't. Everybody else is doing it. I can guarantee you that. From personal experience, I can assure you that you won't be alone."

Cal felt like he was falling in space. He tucked his chin and looked down, hoping that a legitimate answer would come to him. He mumbled an inaudible response. Gerhardt leaned forward. With feigned sincerity, he attempted to discern Cal's resistance.

"There really is nothing to fear. We've made this safe. It's a science now. Not like the old days when the riders didn't know what they were doing and were raising their hematocrit ratios to dangerous levels and turning their blood to sludge. Cal, listen, we aren't talking Willy Voet and Festina here. We're talking about new, more scientific, techniques. We're really talking about things that actually help the health of the riders. Protect the riders."

Cal bristled at the mention of Voet and Festina. Voet was the masseuse for the Festina team who was caught crossing the Belgian border in 1998 with a carload of EPO, testosterone, human growth hormone, all of it to be used to help one of France's premier teams prepare for the Tour. Voet spilled the beans and the scandal confirmed what everyone suspected, that the pro peloton held more drug users than a crack house in Chicago. At first, cycling tried to maintain that it was one team, one set of bad apples, but the publicity caused by the arrest, and the subsequent scrutiny it brought, blew the roof off of the cover-up. It had taken years for the sport to repair itself, and a scar tissue of cynicism remained.

Cal felt a chill run through his body. "Performance chemistry?" Did Steiner really believe that it was just the safety issue that was a problem, that they were telling him that they were concerned about the health of the riders? What about treating riders like they were livestock, animals that needed a boost here, a supplement there? He wanted to scream at them, but feared that he would sound like a raving idiot, especially with them presenting their idea with such calm and resolve. He thought about his father. What would Paul do in this situation? Argue with logic? Call their bluff? Walk out of the room? He decided to take them on with the most obvious of their presumptions.

"Safe? It's fucking illegal. They're testing all over the place. Riders are getting caught left and right and the sport is in danger of being banned altogether. People are beginning to look at cycling like it's professional wrestling."

Steiner and Gerhardt exchanged a quick look and chuckled at Cal's indignation. As if Cal was naïve, Steiner jumped in to explain. Speaking slowly, as though he needed to translate for Cal, he said, "The ones getting caught are the ones who don't know what they're doing. Have you heard of a single one of my riders getting caught? I mean, Costello, Mitterand, Stutz, Trentnor? Have they been caught? You didn't know?"

"It isn't that I worry about getting caught," he said. "So you say, and I take it for granted that you can keep that from happening. But doesn't it bother you that doping is wrong?" Cal never had thought of himself as a particularly moral person. Maybe it was the presumptuousness of their attitude. Maybe it was the powerlessness he felt in that moment. Maybe it was all the times his father lectured him for not making levelheaded decisions in a race. He was surprised to hear the vehemence in his voice. He felt alone, isolated on an island and unsure of whom or what he could trust.

Stuller broke into the conversation through the phone again. His tone punctuated by frustration. His words snapped through the phone like rifle shots. "It doesn't matter whether it bothers Steiner or me or Gerhardt for that matter, although I don't think anything bothers Gerhardt, so long as he gets his wins. What matters is that you're going to do it if you're going to continue racing with the T Mobile team jersey on your back. This isn't an ethical question for us. The team is a business. You're a member of the team. It's a question of developing your talent for the team. And for the team, it's a matter of getting our jersey on the podium..." He choked on something, and coughed once, hard. "Sport? Definitely..." He was too angry to let himself cough again, so he started firing out words even faster. "But also a... business, and winning is the only thing that ensures the return that I need to show my investors. So there you have it. Take it or leave it. Cal, you're a promising rider, but only promising. And there are so many promising riders around these days. There is Barnard on the Sky team whose agent is asking me each day if there is room for him... There is... There is..." His coughing fit overtook him, and he still tried talking through it. "Oh well, no need to name more names. If you don't take it, you can pack your bags."

It was beginning to sink in now. The team management wasn't making an offer. They were issuing an ultimatum. Take it or leave it.

Stuller took a drink of water and continued. "If you decide not to come along, we'll draw up a press release and say you contracted a virus that prevents you from finishing the season. And if you're of a mind to go to the press about this in return, I can assure you that we'll come prepared to defend ourselves by explaining how you came to us first looking for chemical enhancement. That it was your idea. So there you have the offer, young man. What will your answer be?

Cal was crushed. He walked into the meeting feeling high after his performance today. He might have expected to be upbraided by Gerhardt for some mistake he made on the road today. But this? He felt like a train was bearing down on him and there was no escape.

Cal took a deep breath. "You say you believe in me. But if you did, you wouldn't be asking me to do this." He felt totally unprepared to do anything other than go with his gut. "My answer is no. I'm not going to do it. If that means that you kick me off the team, then do it. I can find some other team to ride for."

Stuller was quick to respond. "Maybe so. Maybe not? You don't seem to understand how close the directors of the teams are. We talk and we, well, we cooperate with each other. And you? You're a neo-pro, hardly more than a junior racer, really. But I suppose you can always go back to the States and continue racing there on one of the domestic teams, the minor leagues. That may be better suited for you. Huh? But this is a lot for you to digest in one meal. I'll do you a favor and ignore your no. So sleep on it tonight. Tomorrow you can let Gerhardt know your final answer."

By the time Stuller had finished, Cal was already on his feet grasping the knob to open the door to the room. He turned back toward Gerhardt and Steiner and caught their gaze. They looked at him like he was a lab specimen climbing off the table of their workstation. He just shook his head and left the room.

* * *

Even though it had been three years, Cal's blood still went molten when he thought about the meeting. Time had given him a little perspective, though: He could now see that there was as much hurt as anger. His bosses didn't really believe he could do it without the drugs. And what about his father? What would his father have told him to do? To take the drugs and keep his career? He wished that his father had been there with him to guide him through the forest of that decision, if only so that his father would know what he was up against.

He even thought about going public with the situation. Maybe contact *VeloNews* or *Cycling World* and spill the beans—but he loved the sport and the press was already piling on about doping in the sport. Hamilton denying and then confessing his blood transfusions? Rasmussen and EPO? Andreu telling all about Armstrong's hospital bed confessions? Landis coming out against Armstrong? Operation Puerto had spilled the beans about a certain

Dr. Fuentes, the team doctor for the Kelme team, and his blood-doping scheme. Botero and Guittierez took the fall on that one, as did a host of other riders. Did cycling really need another stain on its reputation? Did Cal want to be the one whose word was up against the defenders of the sport? He really didn't relish that kind of fight, and he never made the call. Seeing what happened when Landis went to the press about Armstrong, how Landis became the story instead of Armstrong, was enough to make any whistleblower think long and hard about going public.

* * *

Paul was still rhapsodizing about Cal's overtaking the brash Squadra Diavolo rider. "Yeah, you were on fire. When you came around him, he had nothing, nothing. That sprint reminded me of Cippolini in his prime. I once saw him leading out a sprint in Castelcucco, in a stage of the Giro. I arrived just as the peloton hit the outskirts of the city. My view was blocked by the crowd around the course, but I got a glimpse of a helmet going by and thought it was the motorcycle leading the rest of the riders. Then, it came around again and I saw it was Cipo, flying. That guy back there, Rocco? I think he will think twice before he tries to take you in a sprint again."

The two riders continued cruising across the Bassano countryside. To Cal, it felt like a suspended free fall across a horizontal plane. He shook off the tension of the flight and the annoyance of his encounter with the Squadra Diavolo riders. Back in the saddle, enjoying an effortless traverse, Cal smiled. Cycling had a mesmerizing effect on him and the opportunity to do it like this, unburdened by an agenda, freed from the oppression of goals, liberated from the pressure of prescribed wattage, cadence, and time parameters, he reconnected with the simple pleasure of the wind in his face and the kinesthetic feedback of tracing a smooth arc through a turn. The trees suspended over his head offered dappled shadows on the road. Closer to town, the farms were replaced by small country homes, which eventually gave way to little village hives of commercial activity. Cal loved the way the subtle transitions differentiated the roadside. Rural expanse one moment and then, within a hundred meters, a cluster of stands selling fresh produce, and then, the buzzing town center, the gathering spot for daily community commerce. It all seemed so natural, the pace so relaxed. His eyes absorbed the passing parade of shoppers, grandmothers with bags filled to the brim with their daily purchases of bread and vegetables, mothers pushing strollers, and gaggles of businessmen standing at the coffee shop, sipping espresso and gesturing with their hands as if no point of view could stand without a physical prop. A rider could dissolve and disappear here, he thought.

Gradually, Cal became aware of a knocking sound coming from the bottom of his bike, persistent, rhythmic, accompanied by a small vibration. Tok, tok, tok, it persisted. Nothing serious, but annoying as hell. After all the time he had spent on a bike, not to mention the countless hours fixing other people's bikes, there wasn't much that he couldn't repair with a set of wrenches and a pliers, but he didn't have his tools with him now. Diagnosing the problem was half the battle. And for that, you needed a quiet place in your mind. Bicycles are simple machines, really, but their simplicity could mask a world of complexity. He could get lost for hours trying to chase down a simple squeak or a rattle. When life got complicated, he would often seek out the quiet enclave of the bike repair stand.

They crested the top of a low hill, and Cal drew up next to Paul. He pointed to the his chain. "I'm pretty sure I bent a link in the chain in that last jump."

"No problem," said Paul. "I told Luigi I was going to stop in Gianni's shop. We can get it fixed there."

They rode side-by-side into the heart of Asolo. Through the narrow winding streets crowded on either side by shops and sidewalks crowded with shoppers, they made their way through the center of town, finally emerging out the other side. Finally they came to the shop of Gianni Di Salvo. This was not your typical, shabby, rundown bicycle shop, nothing like The Spinning Wheel back in Mill Valley. The exterior of the shop would have suited a Ferrari dealership; large glass windows covered the front offering a view into a hyper-modern interior. Behind the glass, lined up like runway models, sparkled a dozen state-of-the-art, high-tech, racing bikes. A bold sign across the front announced the owner's name, Di Salvo. Inside, the floor was surgically clean. The cabinets, curated like museum displays, displayed the latest instruments of cycling technology: derailleurs, brakes, pedals, tape, bottom brackets, and headsets. Walking through the door, Cal felt like he was entering a "clean room," and he tried to walk more softly in his cleats. Beyond the lit cabinets, racks held an array of fine cycling clothes in a rainbow splash of color.

The photographs that covered the walls sported a veritable who's-who of Italian cycling heroes: Pantani, Bartali, Coppi, Chiappucci, Bugno, and Cippolini, all signed with personal messages to Gianni Di Salvo. The classic pose, repeated in nearly all of the photos, was the rider in some state of agony, face set in a mask of pain, while pedaling in a fury of effort. One or two showed the iconic victory salute with rider's arms to the sky. In some, the elements were the star attraction—snowy mountain passes, riders layering newspapers underneath their jerseys to insulate them from the frost, or torrential rain soaking a peloton of riders as they descended a mountain pass, their hair plastered to their heads, their clothes sopping wet, and their bikes spraying a rooster tail of water behind them. The photo display was a study in devotion, an historical homage to the simple core belief that bicycle racing was more than getting from Point A to Point B as fast as possible. It was an act of courage, an all-consuming commitment to push oneself to and beyond the bounds of suffering. It was, as Cal understood, a ritual that transcended person and place. It was man and machine against other men and their machines, working against the same adversities, the elements, history, and fate.

On the opposite wall, in isolation, displayed like a shrine, was a framed pink jersey, the illustrious *maglia rosa*, the pink jersey given to the leader of the Giro d'Italia. This was no replica. This particular *maglia rosa* jersey was inscribed with the autograph of the owner of the shop, Gianni Di Salvo. Underneath the framed jersey, a bronze plaque identified the jersey as the true *maglia rosa*, worn across the finish line of the Giro d'Italia in 1983. While Di Salvo had won many races, none equaled the victory in that year's Giro. In fact, many suggested that Di Salvo never reached that level of glory again. And no surprise, really. When you fly that close to the sun, you too often emerge changed in a way that makes other accomplishments a little less relevant.

Gianni Di Salvo, even though of humble origins, looked like Italian nobility. A compact, lean man in his mid-fifties, he still had the taut physique of a cyclist. He wore dark grey slacks and a casual black, short-sleeved shirt. He sported a full mane of silver and black hair and a deep ruddy complexion that was earned from hours of pedaling in the sunshine around the hills of his native town. The corners of his eyes were webbed with lines, receipt for a lifetime of squinting into the sun.

As Cal and his father strode through the door, they saw Signor Di Salvo seated in his immaculate office, just off the main showroom. A large picture window separated his office from the showroom, and from there, he could keep a watchful eye on the floor. At the moment he was poring over a spreadsheet and exclaiming loudly about some entry that he found particularly annoying. He leaned back in his chair, removed his glasses, and rubbed his eyes, fatigue deepening the wrinkles of his face. When he replaced his glasses, he looked out through the window of his office and saw Paul clamber through the door, his cycling cleats clicking against the tile floor. He lit up and charged out of the office to greet the father and son.

"Paul, *come stai*? Luigi called me to tell me you might stop in. *Benvenuto*. Welcome."

"*Grazie*, Gianni." Paul backed up a step and took a harder look at Gianni. "You look like you could still win the climb over the Poggio. Still turning the pedals with the young guys?"

"Ah, the young guys! Yes, I still have much to teach them. But they're younger and stronger than they are smart. And thank God for that. For if they're smart, they realize that they're too strong to ride with an old man like me."

"Gianni, you? You won the Giro. You'll always be a national hero in Italy. I bet you haven't had to pay for a glass of wine since 1981."

"Perhaps so. A national hero. But in my company, just another worker. And you? Still riding?"

"Of course, but just a little, and only for fun. I gave up the competitive stuff a long time ago…"

Hearing Paul's comment, Cal stifled a laugh. The thought of his father just riding for "fun" was hard to take without a chuckle. It was one of the traditions of cycling that riders rarely admitted to the amount of training and riding they were doing. Ask any rider if he has been riding much and the answer you invariably get is, "Not too much," or, "Not as much as I'd like to." It seemed like every serious rider was just getting over a cold, or about to get one, or had been too busy to train lately. These cover stories were, of course, always in the service of setting up the inquiring rider for a beating once the real riding began. So it was in the world of cycling; cooperation transitioned into competition once the wheels started rolling.

"Gianni, this is my son, Cal," Paul said, motioning to Cal who stood transfixed by the framed jersey on the wall.

Gianni looked at Cal and strode forward, offering his hand. As he grasped Cal's hand, he looked him over from his toes to the top of his head. His eyes seemed to be making an assessment, sizing him up, calculating in a glance the length of his femur, the composition of body fat, estimating the power to weight ratio.

"Yes, Cal. *Il piacere e mio*. It's my pleasure to meet you. Your father has told me about you. Finally, you come to ride with him in Italy. And what do you think so far? How do you like riding in Italy?"

"Well, so far so good. Had a little encounter with some of the local team, Squadra Diavolo, just now that was, well, a little dicey. But…"

Hearing the mention of Squadra Diavolo, Gianni's eyes flashed in recognition. "Ah, Squadra Diavolo. Rocco, no doubt. Like I said, stronger than they are smart. He's a good boy. Has good potential. But sometimes I wonder if he has spaghetti in his head instead of brains. Rocco will be good some day. Who knows? Maybe he'll compete in the Giro. But right now, I coach him. Squadra Diavolo is my team, and I think that only 10 percent of what I say sinks in. If only there was a way to speak directly to his legs and leave out the weak part, his head."

They all shared a laugh at Gianni's assessment of Rocco. Gianni narrowed his eyes and looked directly at Cal. "I heard from your father about your experience a few years ago with the T Mobile team. A bunch of Bavarian assholes. They think the only way to win is to go hard all the time. Big volume of training miles. No time for rest. And no team strategy. Ullrich could have won the tour many times if he wasn't tied to that team." Gianni's gaze shifted to the side, as if he were searching for an image. "Ullrich, what a man! They didn't call him *The Diesel* for nothing. Much better talent than Armstrong. Stronger. He could turn huge gears. So big that they would make other riders weep. Even Armstrong, himself, said so. But T Mobile? No team strategy. They raced like gypsies trying to get out of town ahead of the police. "

Ullrich was one of Cal's favorite pros. It was refreshing to hear that someone else appreciated the big German, and Cal felt an instantaneous connection with Di Salvo. In America, the Armstrong phenomenon was so strong that it blinded many fans, even knowledgeable ones, to Ullrich's greatness. Ullrich had an up-and-down career, winning the Tour de France only once, but placing second five times and coming in fourth once. Cal fashioned his style of riding after him, turning big gears, generating high wattage, and attacking from the front whenever possible. He was a true cycling champion. And hearing Di Salvo confirm Cal's conviction that Ullrich was the man created an immediate appreciation for the man.

"So you think Ullrich was that good?"

"That good? One of the best ever. Maybe not a genius. But then, that's where the race director comes in. It is he who is supposed to be doing the thinking for the rider. Think of it. Tour de France. Ullrich goes out, establishes a lead on Alpe d'Huez, one of the major climbs in the Tour. He's on the verge of breaking the race open, dropping the peloton like a bad habit. *Dio mio*, what a talent. And then what? His own teammate chases him down! Kloden, his own teammate, pulls the rest of the peloton up to him! Only a fool does something like that. And that crazy Kazakh, Vinokourov, is on the same team and he makes the same tactical blunder, pulling the dropped riders up to close on his own man. And the director of the team? Rudy Pevenage? If a rider does something like that, I blame the director. He's on the radio with them, no? Riders are fatigued. They need a strong direction. They're in oxygen debt and don't think clearly. They think only about getting over the top. Surviving the climb and recovering on the descent. No, I blame the director on that. If that were an Italian doing that? Well, it wouldn't happen. On my team, we had discipline."

Gianni continued, "You should have signed with an Italian team. Here, we raise *ciclisti* like we grow grapes. Like fine wine, we allow for maturation. We know that time and care are the two ingredients that can't be given in short measure."

"Yeah, well," Cal avoided looking at Gianni. "It was good while it lasted. But I'm like my father now. A recreational cyclist. Just in it for the fun."

Gianni raised his eyes in disbelief.

"But you're too young to give it up. Maybe you should come here to train."

Cal laughed and chuckled his reply. "No. Thanks, I appreciate the offer. Strictly recreational now."

"By the way," Paul interjected, "Cal's bike needs a little adjustment. You have someone back in the shop who can take a look at it?"

Gianni motioned toward the rear of the shop, behind a swinging door. "Sure. Take it back in the shop. Have Dani look at it."

Cal wheeled his bike back into the repair shop. The bench, the tools, and the equipment were as surgically clean as the front of the shop. It was a place where bikes were operated on, not simply fixed.

Hunched over a bike, deep in concentration, the mechanic barely registered Cal's presence. Cal stood watching the hunched back, the bent head, and crooked cycling cap—in these, he recognized the state of total concentration that even a simple repair required. After a couple of adjustments, the mechanic straightened and stepped back, passing a hand over the bike, deep in focus. In the tall, lean frame and strong legs, Cal saw a fellow cyclist.

Cal cleared his throat to get attention, "Hi? Dani? Gianni sent me back. My bike? I got a tight link. Wonder if you can help me fix it."

Dani wheeled around.

It was then that Cal realized that Dani was a woman. Deep blue eyes, startled wide. The olive in her skin was sun-burnished, and her face seemed to glow. Like her cap, her right cheek was smudged with grease, a casualty of a careless wipe from her hand. She removed the cap and long, dark hair cascaded from the top of her head. Cal immediately felt his blood warm. In the place where her shorts stopped and her long legs took over, he saw the telltale marks of a cyclist's tan. Even her wrists and hands were pale from cycling gloves, giving way to suntanned arms that showed a strong musculature. Cal was about to stammer a quick explanation when she cut him off with a motion to bring his bike over to the stand.

Cal instinctively lifted his bike to place it on the rack by himself. Dani stopped him short and took the bike from his hands. She deftly lifted the bike with one hand, opened the clamp on the rack, and slid the bike onto the stand. Standing back, she looked at the bike, taking time to note the components, the frame, and its geometry, and the relationship between the bike's many parts. She nodded her approval. She finally approached the bike and turned the pedals with one hand placing her other hand on top of the bike. Concentrating deeply, she closed her eyes and tilted her head back, using her hand to feel for the vibration that Cal had described. She nodded her head and drilled her attention down to the noise coming from the bottom of the bike.

"*Cosa c'e' di sbagliato con la tua bici?*"

It dawned on Cal that, of course, she didn't speak English, but he surmised from her posture and the way that she looked into his eyes that she was waiting to hear his complaint about the bike. He moved to the bike and pinched the chain with the forefingers of his hands. Crimping two links together, he attempted to make the sound he had been hearing.

"Tok, tok." He pointed to the chain and waved his hand to indicate that the problem could be found there.

Dani looked at him with a grin.

"*Di nuovo?*"

Gauging by the quizzical look on her face and her

hunched shoulders, Cal launched into an explanation, speaking very slowly to help her understand, "Well, it's like this," offered Cal, forming each word carefully and illustrating the problem with his hands. "I was sprinting." He rotated his hands quickly, like pedals flashing in a sprint, and screwed up his face in an expression of exaggerated exertion. "I think I bent a link in the chain." He made a twisting motion with his wrist to convey what a crimped link would look like. Cal felt a little silly using such clumsy sign language, but the awkwardness of his gesture was clear when he looked into Dani's eyes.

Dani looked at him with a grin on her lips. She could barely suppress the giggle in her voice. She mimicked his gesture, exaggerating the rotation of her hands, with a quizzical look on her face, as if she were trying to decipher some archaic sign language. When she stopped, she looked at Cal and shrugged.

"Yes, that's it." Cal repeated the rotating hands gesture even faster. Anyone entering the room and seeing this exchange of rotating hands, excited expressions, and meaningless sounds would think that he had entered a nursery school room in which the children were playing a game of some sort. At this point, Dani broke out into a full laugh. To Cal's surprise, she said with a thick accent, "So you're convinced that the problem, the noise you're hearing, is coming from the chain?"

"You speak English."

"Yes, I speak English. I learned it watching MTV." She offered her hand to Cal. "My name is Daniella. I also am called just Dani."

"Cal. I didn't realize that you spoke English, so I was trying to…"

"I understand." She repeated the pedaling motion with

her hands, and tried, unsuccessfully, to stifle a laugh. "I thought maybe your hands were speaking some kind of international sign language."

Cal turned red. "Well, whatever. There's a tight link that's making a knocking noise." He was stammering, but he couldn't shut up. "I may need for you to replace the chain because every time I turned the cranks, it made this *tok tok* noise, and…"

"I disagree. I could feel the problem. Chain is fine," Dani said. "You have a bad bearing in the bottom bracket."

"No, couldn't be," Cal said. "I just had the bottom bracket serviced not too long ago. It's the chain. A tight link."

Daniella looked at Cal with indignation. She took a step back and placed her hands on her hips. Fixing Cal with a stare, she said, "We have a disagreement, but one of us is definitely wrong. The chain is fine. But if you don't believe me, I can put a new chain on and you can leave. Take your bike out and ride it. Then tomorrow, you can come back and tell me that the new chain maybe has a tight link. Because even with a new chain, you're still going to have that '*tok tok*' sound. Why? Because the problem doesn't come from the chain. It's the bottom bracket. It's up to you. How would you like to proceed? I can change the chain and leave the problem as it is. Of course, you will have a new chain, which you really don't need or I can fix the bottom bracket. Your call."

Cal tried to take in what Dani was telling him. It was hard to concentrate. He was distracted, thinking how foolish he must have looked with his exaggerated hand pedaling motions, and his halting, slow English. Besides, he was thrown off by the whole scene—Gianni, the *maglia rosa*, how attractive Dani was, the altercation with Rocco and his group on the road. Considering his options, he decided to stop trying to look smart because he only felt himself looking dumber.

"Okay, you're the boss," he said. "Pull the bottom bracket and we can check it out. Bad bearing and you win. Bad chain and I win."

Daniella turned to face the bike and said over her shoulder, "Is this a competition?" She motioned for Cal to approach the bike. "Come here." She took his hand and placed it on the top tube of the bike, while she turned the pedal with her other hand. "Feel that vibration? Each pedal crank, in the same spot. That's a bad bearing. A tight link makes a different feel. Sometimes, you have to feel, not think. Knowledge isn't always in the head. Sometimes, it's in the hand. Sometimes, in other parts of the body."

Most of what she said was lost on Cal. He hadn't really heard much of anything, since she had touched his hand.

With an efficient and elegant confidence, Dani grabbed her wrench and began to dismantle the bike's bottom bracket. She effortlessly removed the bottom bracket and dumped the bearings into her hand. Like a diamond merchant eyeing merchandise, she rolled the tiny bearings over in her hand, examining them one by one. Finally, she picked one up and held it out to Cal. "See here. This one is damaged. This is your problem."

Cal looked in her hand and picked up the offending bearing. He held it up to the light. He rolled it back and forth between his thumb and forefinger. He could feel a rough surface where it was scored.

"You felt this? I mean, you just felt this one bad bearing?"

"It's badly damaged. Not too difficult to feel. And not just that."

She pointed to the headset and ran her finger between the top of the frame and the headset. "Look here. Whoever installed the headset didn't tighten it properly. The gap is too large. Give me a moment to fix it."

Cal was amused by her curt conclusion and a little embarrassed that his bike was in such disrepair. He didn't want her to know he had installed the headset by himself. By now, Dani had turned from him and was busy reassembling his bottom bracket with a new set of bearings. When she finished the bottom bracket, she turned her attention to tightening the headset.

"I guess this bike needs some tuning up."

"Tuning up? Maybe. But if it were my bike, I'd rebuild it from the frame up. Look, there are a lot of so-called mechanics who can put a bike together. Some are actually pretty good. But really? There's an art to bike repair. It isn't simply a matter of placing the parts and tightening the bolts. It's a matter of creating a working, moving piece of art. All of the pieces fit together and in the end, the bike takes on a life. It becomes alive."

"You make bike repair sound like Leonardo da Vinci."

"Ah, Leonardo, or da Vinci, as Americans like to call him. Yes, another great Italian cyclist."

"You're an Italian chauvinist. Not all the great cyclists are Italian."

Daniella turned to face Cal. She had a wry smile on her face. "That's true. And sometimes, we Italians get too carried away with all of the Italian heritage stuff. But besides Armstrong and LeMond, tell me, who in America has been a force in cycling?"

Cal was about to reply, perpetuating the argument, when Paul and Gianni entered the repair shop.

Gianni smiled, "So I guess you've met my daughter, Daniella. Don't get into an argument with her. I guarantee you'll come out the worse for it. I've been arguing with her since she learned to speak her first words, and I don't think I've won one yet."

"Your daughter? I didn't know…"

Daniella raised her head from her work. "Yes, he always wanted a son to carry on the Di Salvo racing tradition. But too sad, he ended up with a daughter. And a mountain-biker at that." She smiled a saccharine smile at her father, underscoring the sarcasm in her comment.

"No sadness at all, *carina*. I have you and a racer all in one. And the best mechanic in all of Italy."

He turned to Cal and Paul. "Daniella is one of the best female mountain-bike riders in the region. Two times Veneto champion. She has her father's climbing genes. And her mother's determination."

"Female rider?" Daniella snapped emphatically. "Best riders, period. And I'll be happy to show the rest of you my road riding skills any time. If there were any other females worth racing against on the road, I'd be winning there, too."

Just then, the group was interrupted by a commotion at the front door. Led by Rocco, the raucous Squadra Diavolo foursome that Cal had encountered on the road spilled into the store as if they owned it. They were in the midst of a loud recounting of the encounter with Cal and his father. Rocco was in mid-sentence, "Yeah, he jumped me from behind. I was caught by surprise. Head-to-head? I would crush that bug…"

Rocco shouted a greeting to Gianni and then noticed Cal and his father standing beside Daniella. He nodded toward Cal.

"So I see you're making friends with all of the locals. You planning on picking something up here?" He grinned at Daniella.

Cal kept his voice even. "Just getting my bike fixed. You might want to get yours checked out, too. Maybe a brake is rubbing or something, because you didn't seem to have much acceleration back there on the road."

Hostility swirled up between them, and Gianni broke in. "Ah, I see you all have met. These are guys from my local team, Squadra Diavolo. SD, as they are known around here. Rocco, this is Cal, the son of my old friend, Paul. Rocco, Cal is a former pro. He rode for T Mobile for a season, a few years ago. He's here as my guest. You can show him the same courtesy that you would like to receive if you were riding in California and you met him there."

Rocco replied to Gianni, but kept his eyes on Cal. "I've heard about a road race there, 'The Tour of California.' Amateur race, isn't it?"

Cal, against his better judgment, rose to the bait. "It's pro." A look from Paul silenced the rest of what he wanted to say—that some of the best Euros have competed in it and none of them has done very well. Not like the major European races, where Americans were beginning to take their place on the podium.

Rocco glared at Cal, but a look from Gianni derailed any further argument. Instead, he turned to Daniella and said, "I came by to see if you wanted to go for a ride. We're heading into town. You want to come?"

Daniella was flipping through a stack of service tickets on the workbench, seeming bored with the alpha-male bantering. At Rocco's question, her brow wrinkled, and she lingered over the array of paper slips, looking for an excuse not to go.

Finally, Rocco raised his voice. "So are you coming with me or not? I don't have all afternoon to wait for you."

Daniella started putting away wrenches, obviously stalling. "Rocco, thanks for the offer, but I have plans to ride with Francesca this afternoon. You go ahead without me."

"What? You're going to choose Francesca over me? Come on. You know you prefer to ride with me."

Cal's ears perked to the tension—it reminded him of the way he and Lisa talked to each other when their relationship entered its death spiral.

"No, Rocco, I don't," she said. "Not now. Just go. So you take your guys and finish your ride. I'm going to wait here for Francesca."

Gianni sensed her irritation. He seemed fatigued by it. He ushered Cal and his father to the door and outside. In the background, they could hear the sounds of Daniella and Rocco arguing. Soon, the other Squadra Diavolo riders emerged, shaking their heads. They mounted their bikes and headed down the road, waving goodbye to Gianni as they pulled away from the shop. A moment later, the voices inside heated up and burned out, and then Rocco agrily slammed through the outer door to the parking lot and mounted his bike. He circled around and stopped in front of Gianni. "She's upset now. But she'll calm down." He pedaled off in the direction of his teammates.

Gianni watched Rocco turn the corner. He shook his head and sighed. It was a scene that he had witnessed more times than he cared to remember. He was annoyed and saddened by the antagonism between his daughter and Rocco.

"It's like an Italian soap opera every day here. Those two." Gianni motioned back toward the shop. "She has a strong will. I can't control her, and I don't know if I should."

"I can see that," said Paul, commiserating with Gianni. "But you know, nobody wins when you try to control too much. Believe me, I've tried and failed."

Cal bristled, but said nothing.

"Ah, *si, si*. Control is an illusion. The more you think you have, the harder you try to control someone, the less control you really have. The best way to maintain control is to give it up. What do you think, Cal?" asked Gianni. "You're her age. Do you have any advice for me?"

"Signor Di Salvo, I don't know you or your daughter well enough to get in the middle of this one. But when it comes to control, I've always lived my life by the words of that famous philosopher."

"Yes?"

"If you love someone, set them free."

"Famous philosopher?" asked Gianni with a raise of his eyebrow. "Which famous philosopher? Nietzsche? Hegel? Sartre?"

"No," laughed Cal. "Sting."

CHAPTER 8

The next day, following a full tour of the bucolic countryside on their bikes, Cal and his father settled in for dinner at Il Soldato, an open-air *trattoria* in the *piazza* of Bassano. They made their way through the clutter of crowded tables and were given their choice of a seat in either the frenzied outdoor patio or the quiet indoors.

"We're here for the total, authentic experience," said Paul, indicating the *piazza*, which was ringed by restaurants and *gelaterias*. In a small town, one of the only sources of evening entertainment was to watch the evening traffic.

"Good by me. Besides, we want to take in the sights."

Cal harbored a secret hope that somewhere in the constant flow of evening pedestrians, he might catch sight of Daniella. Since he had met her the day before, he had hardly been able to keep his mind focused on much else. She was beautiful for sure, he thought, but the memory of her working on his bike, the way she snapped Rocco into place, and the force that emanated from her were as attractive as her physical presence. The harder he tried to put it into perspective—that he was just there for a couple of weeks, that she was already in a relationship with a local hero, that there was no reason to believe she could be interested in him, that he was only lonely after seeing Lisa back home — the more frustrating all of these logical reasons grew. But then, he thought, she seemed to be on the outs with Rocco, so maybe…

While Paul attacked his dinner, Cal shuffled his food around his plate as though the perfect configuration of pasta across the expanse of his plate might unlock the confounding puzzle. In the background, he was vaguely aware that his father had tried to initiate a conversation with him, but he hadn't really been paying attention. Maybe it was the fatigue from the day. Or maybe he was just avoiding a conversation he knew was definitely going to appear on the agenda during the trip, or maybe it was the preoccupation with the way Daniella seemed to fill a room with confidence. No matter, distraction was small defense against his father's insistence.

"I said, you were really pushing the watts today. I'm amazed at what you can do. And you haven't even been training for the past three years."

"Well, maybe it's the payoff for the zillions of miles I rode until I quit."

"Maybe. Or maybe it's that you have an inherent talent."

Cal knew what was coming next. Still, it was better to let it come up and deal with it, rather than continue ducking and bobbing. This conversation was inevitable.

His father continued. "Yeah, talent. You had it. Still do have it. I was pretty dazzled by that sprint you put on to catch those guys from SD. You blew past them without too much trouble. I really liked the way you sat in 'til just the right time. Picked the perfect moment to drop him. That's something beyond power and training. That's instinct. Indurain had that. Great rider, for sure. Huge power output. But he rode smart, knew when to attack and when to sit in.

That's the X ingredient that separates a lot of the winners from the also runs."

"Nah, it's always easy to catch someone when you're coming from behind. They don't know you're coming. You catch up. You have the momentum, and boom, there you are…" Cal hoped that by keeping the conversation to something specific, to the catch yesterday, he could steer the discussion away from where his father was going.

"Yeah, easy." Cal's dad stifled a chuckle. "Easy when you can turn the pedals at 650 watts. Easy when you can feel the pace and sense the timing. No, son, like it or not, you still have a gift. Just that getting you to use it is a mystery. Seems like the trick is to get you pissed."

Cal looked at a pair of mothers on the other side of the *piazza*, talking over their pair of strollers. He tried processing the last part of what his father had just said, but it didn't sink in. "Maybe. Maybe I was a little pissed, but what does it really matter? You can't ride pissed all the time. Burns too much energy. Changes something that ought to be fun, ought to be cool, into a passion play. At least I learned that much with T Mobile."

"Cal, you had it all. California state champion. US Amateur champion—I'll never really understand what happened."

Paul gave him one of the long, humane, rapt looks that he used on his clients—the kind that begged a guilty party to come clean with their transgressions, for both their sakes. Cal turned his head and looked away. Paul had coached him, paid for trainers, and hooked him up with the right cycling clubs. He set an example, on the bike and off the bike, of how you win. Tenacity. Ferocity. Guile. Whether it was directly, with his lectures about sizing up an opponent and figuring out what his weakness was, or indirectly, with the dinner table stories of his accomplishments in the courtroom, Cal was supposed to inherit his father's success. Why, then, didn't he feel more grateful? Worse, why did he have this urge to spit it all out in a way that would hurt his father the most?

He wiped his mouth as if wiping away something bitter, and said as carefully as he could, "Dad, I know it doesn't make sense to you. I'm sure it seems like I threw it all away. All I can tell you is that it wasn't the right time or the right situation for me."

"Cal, I get that. Hell, I'd have to be a moron to not get that. But what I don't get, what you haven't said is what made it the wrong situation, the wrong time. That's what still mystifies me. You always wanted…"

"Damn it, Dad. You can't understand what I did, the decisions I made, because you wouldn't have made those same decisions. You can't get it in your head that you and I aren't the same person."

Cal's anger sparked in Paul's eyes. "You think I don't know that you and I are different? Hell, of course I see that. There's just no way I would have quit."

"And you can't see anything beyond the fact that I *quit*, as you call it." Cal threw his napkin on the table. "Shit. Maybe I just had it up to here…" He cut his hand across his neck, "with racing, with the whole scene, with your expectations."

"I don't buy it. If you were on trial, a jury of halfwits wouldn't buy it. If you told me, after a few years of racing, and getting no results, that you were done, I'd get that. If you told me that you'd reached the point where the competition was just too good for you, I'd understand. But you and I both know that wasn't the case. I read the race reports. I saw the results you were getting—any fool could."

"Yeah, I'll bet you did."

Paul sighed. He was his old self, at ease and unflustered again. "The sarcasm doesn't get us anywhere. Until you sort it out and figure out what the hell was going on, whether you decide to tell me or not, I'm not going to tell you that I understand."

"Maybe I don't need for you to understand."

He smiled. "Maybe so. Maybe I don't need to understand. But you need to understand. And I'm not sure you do. That's why you're stuck."

Cal paused. In his mind, there was no denying the truth of what his father was saying. He was spinning his wheels. Living at home, working at Peet's, avoiding commitments.

"Fine, you win. My life is one big dead end," he said. Cal got up and left his father sitting at the table, and walked away from the chaotic restaurant scene for the greater chaos of the *piazza*.

* * *

Once, Cal had asked one of the older, more experienced, American pro riders if a certain Spaniard named Delmondo, who had won the Tour a few years ago, was taking drugs. Cal was still a junior racer then. They were on one of the regular reservoir rides, a route that took them into the rolling hills of Western Marin.

The vet looked at him with surprise. "Let's see. Was Delmondo juiced when he won the Tour? Let me think." After a mock attempt to consider the possibility, he said, "Let's consider the factors. Okay? He's Spanish. He won the Tour after having a pretty undistinguished career until then, and not having won a major race in three years before winning the Tour. He's a professional rider. Hmmm, I guess you'd have to say he was juiced."

"So is everybody doping?

"Well, first, no, not everybody is juiced. There are still some riders who are riding clean. You just don't hear about them much because they ain't winning." He paused to let that sink in. "Think about the pressures. You race bicycles professionally? You're riding for the win. You don't win, or you don't contribute to someone on your team winning? You're fucked when it comes time for the next year's contract. You aren't riding for a hobby anymore. It's a fucking business. That's the deal you make when you turn pro. Your sponsors want results and, if you don't deliver them, they aren't your sponsors for very long."

"But what about the health risks?"

"Yeah, there's that. But your typical professional rider? He's twenty-four years old. He thinks he's going to live forever. I mean, it wasn't until a few years ago that the pros agreed to start wearing helmets. Talk about a health risk, where does splitting your dome open fit in?"

"What about getting caught? They're cracking down. The World Anti-Doping Agency is on the case. Off-season piss tests. You never know when the knock on the door comes telling you that it's time to donate a sample. Post race samples. I mean, how do they get away with it?"

"Testing? They're pushing a rock up a hill. Shit, you get the door-shakers hitting your room at all hours of the night, after a long day riding, draining you for a sample. You feel like peeing right on them. But the pee-police are always playing catch up. The researchers creating the shit and the masking agents are a whole lot smarter than the ones trying to figure out who's using. Only the stupid dopers test dirty. Use your head. Follow the money. You win? Sponsors are happy. Endorsements roll in. Hot chicks with big tits chasing you. The guys who are trying to catch the dopers? Not too much money. Always lagging behind the cutting edge chemists. Maybe a little bit of glory preserving the 'purity of sport.' But there are no groupies, or money, for the fucking pee-police."

Cal decided to ask the question that was really on his mind.

"So did you do it? Are you doing it now?"

The pro turned to Cal and scowled. "Let me tell you a story. Five years ago, I'm racing in France. Paris—Tours. You know it? It's a sprinter's paradise. Pretty flat, straight finish on the three-kilometer Avenue du Grammont. I'm out front with a group of eight in a breakaway, about twenty kilometers from the finish. We're clear and the peloton doesn't feel like chasing. They're giving us a pass. So the winner is coming out of our little group. We're on the rivet, totally buried, burning for the finish. I'm cooked. But what the hell, I figure that none of us is feeling all that hot. There are a couple of beastly sprinters in the group, Lazar from Aqua Sapone, a Russian on Katona. But I think I have a chance if I can grab the right wheel going into the sprint. I've been going pretty good the last couple of weeks."

"So what happened?"

"Here's what happened. I'm sitting last in the paceline taking a little shelter from the wind, saving what I have for the sprint, and the guy in front of me reaches into his pocket and pulls something out. I think, at first, it's a Powerbar or something. Then, right there, I see him stick his hands down the back of his shorts and stick something up his ass."

"You're kidding me."

"Wish I was. It was some kind of a suppository, probably amphetamine. Anyway, the race marshals are right there, in the fucking car, right next to us. I pull over to the car and rap on the window and start pointing. I'm waving my arm like a fucking madman. 'Hey, did you see that? He just stuck something up his ass.' I'm screaming at them. I know they saw it. They were sitting right there watching us."

"What did they do?"

"Absofuckinglutely nothing. Just stared straight ahead. I kept pointing and they kept staring ahead."

"And?"

"And what do you think? We get to the final sprint. We're all lined up and who do you think has the legs to torch the rest of us? Wins going away."

"Did you do anything?"

"Yeah, I went up to him and asked him what it was. If the race marshals aren't going to do anything, then the only thing that's fair is to level the field. I wanted to get some of it."

"Did he tell you what it was?"

"Denied the whole thing. Lied like a rug. Nothing I could do about it. But I sure didn't shake his hand. Not after I'd seen where it'd been."

"So you're telling me that everyone is doping and I should be doing it, too?"

"Fuck you, Cal. You want me to make up your mind? If I said yes, that means you should? If I say no, you don't? It's a decision you have to make on your own. And if you get faced with it, believe me, think long and hard about it, because it may be the most important decision you make."

• • •

Years later, in Roubaix, the morning after a sleepless night tossing and turning over T Mobile's ultimatum, Cal ached with ambivalence. The idea of being a team leader was so tempting. He spun the idea around 360 degrees, looking at all of the angles. He wondered what his father would tell him to do. The seduction of winning, glory, and a successful career were so compelling. His father had always stressed that he should take every advantage he could find in defeating the competition. Success was the goal, for sure. But his father also had a sense of fair play, and that meant staying within the rules.

To hell with it, he thought. Going forward with their program, independent of the racing, meant climbing in bed with people he wanted nothing to do with. The drugs and the doping were bad enough. The association with people who were so cynical and so willing to drag the sport into the dirt to win was even worse. In the end, that was what made the offer so repellant; it was the way it came down, the manipulation, the cold-hearted manipulation, and the way they made him feel so expendable. Not only was the answer no, but he had a few other things to tell Gerhardt about his coaching style, his mismanagement, and the way he was corrupting the sport he claimed to love. It would cost Cal his job. He would be finished with T Mobile, but, at the moment, it seemed like he would be winning release from the jaws of a sinister, dehumanizing machine.

The next morning, buzzing with his own righteousness, he set out for Gerhardt's room. He turned the corner to enter the hallway, and nearly bumped into Franz. The veteran had his arm in a sling, nursing a separated shoulder from his crash the previous day, and was moving sorely down the hallway. He greeted Cal with a smile and asked him if he was on his way to Gerhardt's room.

"Yeah, you know about it?"

"Yes, young star. I knew about it before you did. In fact,

hang around this sport long enough and you'll know nearly everything. You'll feel like you can predict the future."

"Predict the future?"

"Yes. Predict the future. For example, when you joined this team. When we started training in the spring. When I saw your potential, I could have predicted you were going to emerge as a force on this team. And when Gerhardt started riding you hard, and he would yell at you for making a move in a race, I could have predicted that he was going to ask you to step up to a leadership role. The offer he made you? I could have predicted that, too. It's a strange style of management here. But that's how he rolls. And now, I predict something else."

"What's that?"

"It's a prediction for me. I predict that the end is near for me."

"What? Because of this injury? You've recovered from worse."

"No, not the injury. This will keep me off the bike for a week, tops. Besides, I love the painkillers. Nothing like a little Vicodin to kill the boredom of being on the road. It doesn't actually kill the pain. It just makes it seem like it belongs to someone else. But there's something else. I've been around this sport long enough to know how the decline starts. You start to notice that you don't have the stamina that you once had. You don't recover as quickly after a race. Training rides get shortened because you don't have the burning desire to spend six hours on your bike. You make a break on the road and push yourself. You send the message down to your legs, calling for more power, and it seems like you're motoring down the road, but the competition stays with you. Maybe it's a bad day, you tell yourself. And maybe it is. But then, you have another and then another. Soon, you start to question whether you have it or not."

"Everybody has their ups and downs."

"Ups and downs? Yeah, you think so? I wish so. Finally, it goes one of two ways. Either you really begin to hate the younger ones, the ones that you can't drop anymore. Or it goes the other way. You start to appreciate them. You say to yourself, 'Okay. It's their turn on the stage now. And surprise, you actually begin to feel something other than envy toward them. You even begin to feel proud about their accomplishments."

Cal didn't know how to respond. Maybe someday he would understand how you come to grips with the inevitable decline of a sports career, but today, especially in the midst of his decision, it was difficult to separate his story from Franz's. He tried to shrug him off, but Franz put out a hand.

"Listen to me. Every team needs a graybeard to show the young guys the ropes. Now is the time for a shift of the heart. I watch you and I win when you win."

"That is pretty generous of you."

"Generous? I've seen the other reaction, the guys who hate the younger ones catching up to them. I see how it eats away at them. The hatred becomes a way of putting what they have festering inside of themselves onto someone else. It's ugly. If I can maintain some dignity, and take a little satisfaction from watching you win, then why not? It's a small price to pay for all those years we put in the saddle, no?"

Cal was knocked off balance by Franz's message. Five minutes before, he was ready to walk out on the sport he loved. He'd never thought of himself as a particularly noble guy. Wearing a green shirt for Earth Day, back in high school, was about as far as he had ever gone in support of a cause. But this was personal.

"I don't particularly care for the strong-arm tactics," he told Franz.

"So what are you going to tell them? To shove it? Or do you sweep the gold off the table and put it in your pocket?"

"I didn't sleep much last night. It's pretty tempting. But I hate the way it came down. And right now, I'm pretty much hating cycling, too."

"Hate the player, not the game, Cal. Your answer is...?"

"No. In fact, fuck no! My answer is that they can find themselves another patsy. Another rider to juice up and send to the front for the glory of T Mobile."

Franz put his hand on Cal's shoulder and looked into his eyes. He spoke carefully, slowly, deliberately to make sure that his message was received the right way.

"Cal, you have every right to tell them to fuck themselves. You can do it. Drop off the team, return to the States, go back to being the local hero in California if you want to. Nobody would criticize you. But before you do, hear me out."

Cal rolled his eyes, but waited. Franz deserved at least a final say.

"Let's say you accept their offer. You do the shit, whatever they have up their sleeves. You won't be the only one on the circuit who's enhanced."

"Right."

"So you do it. Upside? You continue with the team. You continue with your career. And I don't need to remind you, this is a career that you have been dreaming about since you were a child. Maybe you win some races. Maybe you win a lot of races. Maybe you even make it onto the podium at one of the grand tours. Picture that. You on the podium at the Giro, or the Tour."

"But..."

"I know. But you did it using drugs. You did it while you were juiced. Well, you know what? If you take the time to look to your left on the podium and then look to the right on the podium, both of those guys are probably using, too. And if you look out at the racers who are just arriving while you're getting your medals? A lot of those guys are juiced, too. And they aren't on the podium. You are. So does that mean your drugs are better? Or does that mean you're just a better rider?"

"So does that make it right? I mean, you say that everybody is using. Does that make it the right thing for me? For the sport?"

"Cal, Cal, you're so young, so, so naive. Is it right? Maybe not. But what's right? You go home and go back to work as a bike mechanic? Is that right?"

"It's honest."

"Yes, that it is. But imagine this. You go ahead and agree to work with Gerhardt. You do win. Then what? In a year, maybe two, you have enough wins under your belt, so the other teams come calling. Only now, they come calling for you as a winner, not as a promising junior with no credibility beyond potential. And now, with a tour or two behind you, some top finishes, you get to dictate your own terms. You always say you want to be in control of your destiny, right?"

"Right."

"Well, this is the ticket to get you there. Sure, going home is always an option. But what is the prize there? You're miserable and you have only your 'dignity' to keep you warm. On the other hand, cooperate with Gerhardt, not because he's a good guy. He's a dick. We both know that. But use him just like he wants to use you. Use him and his sneaky Dr. Frankenstein to get what you want."

"Which is?"

"That's for you to decide. From a position of power, as a team leader on another team, you have some influence. You pick the schedule you want to race. Hell, you even pick the teammates. I've been there and let me tell you, with the right director and sponsor, this life in the saddle beats the hell out of a lot of other options. On the other hand, you become just another American who came over here and didn't make it. No shortage of guys like that. They're hanging around every city. Mill Valley? I bet you can find a dozen riders there who thought they had the stuff to make it. You can do the weekend rides with them. Sounds attractive, huh?"

CHAPTER 9

Cal walked twice around the *piazza*'s central fountain, and realized he'd been childish in leaving his father sitting alone at the restaurant. The sun was setting behind the buildings. As he started back toward the outdoor tables, the buttery evening light fell on the cluster of umbrellas and the two cups of espresso that the waiter was setting on Paul's table — one for Paul, and for Cal's empty chair. Typical of Cal's father — argue, then make a quick peace. It made Cal feel even more like a brat.

Suddenly, Cal's attention was drawn to a commotion across the square. A crowd was gathering around a woman's shouting voice and a cluster of jeering young men. He could make out Daniella in silhouette. She was the one shouting — and as Cal got closer, he made out the guy on the receiving end of the tirade. Rocco. The group of young men surrounding the arguing couple included several of the riders whom Cal had encountered on the road the day before.

Daniella, her face rose-red with fury, was pouring a heavy stream of Italian invective on Rocco. One of the SD riders was trying to intercede, but each time he tried to get between the two, she pushed him away. Cal got close enough to make out the gist of the argument.

"You're a pig. No. I correct myself. A pig has some intelligence. You're a rat. That's what you are!"

Rocco laughed at Daniella, which only stoked her anger. "Come on. You take things too seriously. Don't be jealous. You know my heart will always belong to the 'little mechanic girl.'"

"Fuck you! 'Little mechanic girl?' Is that what you think of me? 'Little mechanic girl?' You have no respect. You think you're such a big deal. You're nothing but a small-time, small-town, rider. And not such a good one at that. And you have the nerve to call me 'little mechanic girl?'"

Rocco continued to tease, playing to his friends, "What? I should call you something else? Maybe you'd like it better if I called you 'little Gianni,' like you would be the son of your father. Because we know that he's made you into the son, not the daughter, he always wanted to have. Come to think of it, you're kind of butch for a girl. I don't know why I was ever interested in you. Maybe I'm the one who needs to be gay." Rocco turned to his friends and appealed for their laughter, and they were only too willing to appease him.

Cal had pushed to the inner ring of men. He saw the wound sink in behind Daniella's eyes, and knew what was coming next.

Blind with fury, Daniella made a lunge at Rocco. Cal reached out nearly too late, catching just the slippery fabric of her shirt. She landed a sharp blow to Rocco's chest. Cal stepped in again and wrapped his arms around her shoulders and pulled her back.

"Hold on, hold on. Hang on for a second. Calm down," said Cal. Daniella struggled against his grasp. By now, he had such a firm grip on her that he had lifted her off the ground. Her legs swung wildly, looking for purchase to pull away.

"This son of a dog. This half-wit, retard, this cunt, has no respect. He thinks he can treat me like shit and get away with it. He wins a race or two and thinks it gives him the right to treat others like they're dirt. He insults me and my family? No way. Let go of me!"

Rocco took advantage of Cal's hold on Daniella. Emboldened by the safety, he said, "Look, you and I both know that you're just jealous. And you're just pissed because you know that I'll be off racing the Giro while you're still tightening bolts at your dad's shop." His SD friends howled in delight like a crowd at a heavyweight fight witnessing a heavy right-hand blow.

Cal, however, didn't find it to be funny at all. He stepped in front of Dani and stared Rocco down, saying, "You're really an idiot. I figured maybe yesterday, on the road, you would have learned a little humility. Some guys are stupid on the road, but off the bike are smarter. But you? No. You're even more of an idiot out of uniform than you are in."

"Stay out of what doesn't concern you. You don't belong in this fight. And you don't belong here. Go back to the US."

The *piazza* and all the faces around him seemed to disappear, and in a small point of hyper-clarity, Rocco's sneering face hung before him. Cal loosened his grip on Dani's shoulder. Just as he was drawing back his fist, he heard his father's shout.

"Cal! Cal! Let it go. Not now."

His father's voice punctured the balloon of anger he was feeling. He stepped back from Rocco, feeling off-balance, and the wall of voices and faces surrounded him again. It was then he realized he still had Daniella in his grasp. He became acutely aware of the heat of her body as he held her close to him. It was a warm comfort, anchoring him. He pulled her away from the SD riders.

"What was that all about?" he asked.

His efforts to intervene on Daniella's behalf were hardly appreciated, however. She was still seething.

"Who do you think you are? Stay out of what you don't belong in."

"But I was only trying to help you."

"You think I can't deal with that worm myself? You think I can't handle this situation myself? I need you to help me? You arrogant men are all the same."

"But I…"

Around them, bystanders retreated, casting sideways glances at the new argument.

"But what?" Daniella said, loudly. "I don't need any help when it comes to that moron. I've been dealing with his insulting attitude for too long. I'm sick of it. And I don't want anyone to fight my battles for me. I can take care of it myself. Do you understand?"

"Understood." He raised his hands and physically took a step back, but couldn't help but feel that Daniella's bravado was generated from hurt as much as from anger.

Daniella abandoned him in the square and stomped off down one of the little alleyways that exited the town central. Cal stood in the midst of a crowd, many of whom lingered to hear the final burst of anger from Daniella. To them, he was the culprit and, try as he wanted to, there was no point in making them understand that he was simply trying to help. His head was hot and light with embarrassment, and adding to his discomfort, the SD riders, including Rocco, were glaring at him as if they were only waiting for an excuse to reinitiate the feud.

If there were a trap door that Cal could descend and disappear from the square, he would have gladly taken it. He was rescued, finally, by his father who had stood behind him during the whole fiasco. He broke through the crowd and put his arm around Cal and ushered him outside the circle of onlookers.

"Nice going, Gandhi. You deserve the Nobel prize for handling that one."

"Yeah, smooth, huh? Had her right where I wanted her."

"Any smoother, and I'd be posting bail for you right now. Let's get out of here before you do any more harm to Italian-American relations."

CHAPTER 10

Paul sat at the hotel breakfast table, surrounded by a Herculean plate of delicacies, so different from the celebration of austerity that marked his usual breakfast.

Luigi, the hotel proprietor, eyed Paul's plate and made his way over to the table.

"Good morning, Signor Paul. I see you're preparing for a long day on the road today. I think there's one croissant still on the table that you missed. Would you like me to carry it over to you? Maybe you'd like it packed in a — how do you American's call it? — a 'to go' bag?"

Paul returned Luigi's good-natured teasing. "Luigi, your food is so dreadful that I thought I'd save the other guests from the experience of having to eat it. Besides, it's a little windy today and we're going to do some climbing. I thought it might be a good idea to add a few pounds for ballast."

"Yes, more weight and a built-in excuse for not being the first up the summit."

"Yes. But Luigi, you forget that I'm nothing but an old man trying to hang on to the last vestiges of his youth. I no longer worry about placements at the top of any climb. I'm just happy to get up the climb in the first place."

Cal entered the room and eyed his father's plate.

"Did you save anything for the rest of the hotel guests?"

Paul laughed and motioned to his plate. "You can graze off of mine here. I was just protecting your share." He pushed a croissant and then a bit of cake onto Cal's plate, and turned to discuss the day's itinerary. "I'm thinking we should climb Monte Grappa today. Ride the Le Scale course to see what it's like. Trial run to see what the race is going to be like. You know, remind ourselves of what it's like to suffer. Departure in thirty?"

"I'm passing today, Dad. Rough night sleeping last night. I thought I'd hang here. Read a bit and maybe go out for a light spin later."

"Unh, unh," quipped Paul. "You're in for the whole thing. Remember? If I'm climbing today, you're climbing today. Departure in thirty."

Paul finished the last of his espresso, draining the cup with a satisfying pucker of his lips, savoring the exquisite bitterness on the back of the tongue, and pushed away from the table. Luigi, still standing by the table, motioned toward Paul's disappearing frame, "He never gives up, does he?"

Cal picked at his cake. "No, never. At least not without a fight."

"So young man, you're going to race Le Scale? Your father has been telling me for years about how talented you are."

"Nope. That isn't in the program. I'm here for your food, Luigi. That and a little exercise. Race? Let the racers do that."

After a leisurely morning spent by the pool and catching up on e-mail, Cal decided to go for a ride by himself. As he departed from the hotel, he cranked his iPod to Hendrix.

*"Purple haze all in my brain.
Lately things don't seem the same.
Actin' funny but I don't know why.
'Scuse me while I kiss the sky."*

"Yeah," Cal thought, "I could learn to love this sport again, if this is all I had to do."

Once on the road, Cal found himself at a crossroads. To his left, one road led sharply uphill. The other turned right, following a stream along the flat valley. He thought for a second. Ride hard, push up the climb? Climbing, throwing himself against the pull of gravity, meant a wrestling match with discomfort. When you climb, sometimes it hurts a little. Sometimes it hurts a lot. But—and this was his dilemma—it always hurts. Go right, however, and he could ride the flats all day long without ever experiencing the pulsing blood flow, the gasping for air, the aching muscles that a steep climb demanded.

His racing strength was never climbing. Racers know from their earliest encounters in competition what their forte is and what their liabilities are. For Cal, it was power. He was an eight-cylinder engine of pure, raw force. At six feet and an inch, he had the lengthy femur to provide leverage to generate big watts that translated into powerful surges and sprints. He wasn't built like the "mountain goats" that carried their 135-pound frames effortlessly over the hills. Even at a lean racing weight of 160, climbing meant suffering.

With resignation and a shrug of his shoulders, surprising even himself, Cal angled his bike to the left and onto the hilly road. He paused for a moment and stared up at the mountain pass he was about to take on. What he saw gave him chills. The road carved its way along the side of the mountain, often disappearing from sight as it hid around turns and rises. Midway, the tree line announced the break between the verdant green below and the cold, gray granite at the top. Wisps of clouds laced the summit, just barely visible behind them. In nooks and crannies, the vestiges of snowfall still lingered, hidden from the spring sun.

His studied eye told him it was going to hurt. With winding grades that looked to be as steep as 15 percent, the route he was on would afford some great views, but he was going to pay for them with sweat and tired legs. What the hell, he thought, let's just see how much pain tolerance I still have after all this time off the bike. Starting slowly, he tapped out a steady rhythm on his pedals. He stood up out of the saddle, swaying from side to side with the effort. He wasn't surprised that he fell into the rhythm so easily. But it did surprise him when he felt a surge inside his chest willing him to push himself harder.

The tendency, for most professionals, in preparation for the season was to work on their strengths. They stayed in an envelope of comfort. Cal knew better. The pre-season was a workshop during which the chinks in the armor were repaired, or at least, shored up. One winter day, the year before he signed with T Mobile, when he was in the local gym working out with weights, he was approached by a local cycling coach who had been standing at a distance, watching him burst his guts in a set of 300-pound squats. Finished with the set, legs still quivering, Cal nearly collapsed against the wall. He saw the coach approach with a smile on his face.

"Cal, what are you doing?" asked the coach.

Cal, between gasps and repetitions of squats, said, "Squats."

"I can see that," replied the coach. "Why?"

"I'm tired of getting dropped on the hills. This coming season, I'm going to hang with the mountain goats on the climbs."

The coach let out a snort of a laugh. He told Cal to put the weights down and walked him over to a full-length mirror, where he positioned himself next to Cal, facing the mirror, arm around his shoulder. "Cal, what do you see in front of you?"

Cal studied his image in the mirror, perplexed by the question. "I'm not sure what you mean. I see me."

"Right," replied the coach. "I see you, too. And what I see is a sprinter, not a climber. Good muscle mass. Big legs. Tall, I guess you probably weigh northward of 150."

"Right. About 165."

"That's about what I expected. So you go ahead and do your squats. Go ahead, prepare for the season. Improve your climbing. But between you and me? It's a sprinter that I see in the mirror, not a climber, and you can do squats until you walk around like a frog, but you still aren't going to be a climber. You're never going to drop the fucking mountain goat climbers on the big hills. True climbers are born that way. You're a sprinter, so use your head about it. Pick the events that work for you. Avoid the big climbing races. And beat the shit out of the climbers on the flats, because they sure as hell won't be waiting for you on the climbs."

"And if I can't avoid the climbs?"

"Like I said, use your head. If you're in a peloton and see a climb coming, go to the front of the group and slow down, slow way down, don't go with the climbers. Make them come around you. Become a road hazard. By the time the whole peloton has come around you, you'll be pretty close to the top. If it isn't too long a climb, maybe you're still in contact and can pick off the places on the descent."

"And if it's a long climb?"

"Shit, if it's a long climb, you have two choices. One, you can try to go out and get some time on the peloton long before the climb, hit it hard on the approach to take their legs out and gain some time, so that you have a minute or two on the climb before they arrive. Other choice? Take it down, relax, climb at your own pace, let the lead group, with the climbers, go up the road, watch them as they crest the top of the climb, if you can still see them, and then? Sit back, ride your own pace, and enjoy your shower when you get finished with the race."

"That sounds like giving up," Cal lamented.

"Maybe so. But look, take a climb like the Tourmalet in the Tour. Cavendish, the best sprinter in the world, a fucking rocket, is off the back, even before they get to the steep part, the 12 percent grade, while Contador and Schleck and all those skinny Spanish fucks from the Pyrénées are killing it at the front. Do you think Cavendish is feeling bad about himself?"

Cal paused to consider the question.

"Don't even think about it. No. Hell no. Cavendish is thinking, 'Fuck those guys. Let them climb this mother to their heart's content. When we get to Paris, I'm going to be rocking across the finish line with another sprint win.' He isn't feeling bad at all. And neither should you. Use what you have as your natural talent."

Cal was tired of riding smart, though. He could have continued riding at a more comfortable pace, but he wondered just where the boundaries of his comfort level were. He selected a smaller gear that would afford less resistance, but sat down and picked up his cadence to compensate for the lighter purchase of each rotation of the cranks. After so many years in the saddle, he needed no heart monitor to know what was happening. He was passing through the training zones: His heart moved from a comfortable 120 beats per minute, to 140, and then, before too long, to 165. His breathing, which was smooth and steady at the start, became more ragged, and his muscles cried out for oxygen. He gulped air. It was all too familiar, he thought. He simply couldn't ride in a comfort zone. Not that he didn't want to. It just seemed that riding comfortably was breaking the unwritten code of suffering that all racers embraced. Cal remembered what Greg LeMond once said, "If you aren't suffering, you aren't training." Sick, he thought. Even when he wanted to, he had a hard time taking it easy.

Was it a virtue or a vice? One thing he knew for sure as his bike rocked underneath him: he was actually pretty good at this. This ritual of self-punishment, followed by recuperation, may be what he was supposed to be doing. Then, he thought about his father. Why didn't he, couldn't he, simply come clean, spill the whole story? The easy answer was that he feared his father's disapproval. The boundary between him and his father had always been paper-thin. Sometimes, it was difficult to know where he ended and his father began, and vice versa.

He remembered his father telling him once, a long time ago, that there would be times when the right choice wasn't immediately clear, when two or maybe more choices seemed about equal. What to do then? His father's advice seemed sensible. Pick any of the avenues, and then go down it with conviction. Make the choice that you have selected a right one by investing your heart, your soul, and your energy into it.

As the mountain road circled up the valley in front of him, revealing pitches ahead that would push him to the extremes of pain, he wondered if it wasn't time to put his father's lesson about commitment and dedication into operation. As if the ideas that he had been mulling grew hands and pulled him up, he rose out of the saddle and set to the work of climbing into the clouds.

The trance of steady effort continued. He floated up, moving the world farther and farther away, until it seemed like he was passing through a void, separated from his immediate surroundings by a wall of indifference. It was something that was refreshingly familiar. He remembered how the steady cadence of his legs pumping the pedals up and down, the rhythmic beating of his heart, and the steady inhale and exhale of his breath became the only elements of his world. It was a good place to be.

Just shut up, he thought, shut up. Shut off the chatter between your ears. Just enjoy the moment. Life could be a lot worse than riding on a beautiful mountainside in Italy. Then, with a little surge of humor, he told himself that if he didn't watch it, he was going to turn into one of the faux Buddhists who frequented the coffee shop where he worked. They were the ones who seemed to be the most impatient, always asking him to hurry the order. "Was it ready yet? Could you do it over again? Hotter, colder, less foam, more milk?" There must be a special place for Buddhists who are caffeine-addicted, he thought.

After climbing for a mile, Cal caught sight of another rider further up the road. Riding can be a lonely enterprise, so the idea of sharing the pain with some company was attractive. Of course, he wasn't looking for a race, and he didn't want to repeat the experience he had with Rocco a few days before, so he decided he would approach the rider ahead of him carefully. It would be nice to have a little conversation. And little it would be, considering that his Italian was so rudimentary and his breath was in short supply. But even without the words, it would be nice to have someone to pace along with.

Within a dozen pedal strokes, he found himself closing in on the rider ahead of him. The figure was familiar. Long, slender frame. Dark hair flowing out of the back of the helmet. It was Daniella. His heart beat just a little bit faster. Maybe it was from the extra effort required to push, but more likely, he thought, it was a reaction to the idea that he was about to have another opportunity to spend some time with her. And this time, no Rocco. And this time, in his world, climbing on a bike.

When he was only a few yards behind, he called out to her:

"Hey. I thought I was the only one who wanted to suffer up this climb today."

The sound of Cal's voice startled Daniella.

Looking a little embarrassed about her last encounter with Cal, the shouting match in the square, she attempted to ignore him at first. In a vain attempt to get away, she stood on the pedals and increased her tempo, accelerating away from Cal. It was an exercise in futility, however, because Cal easily ramped up his effort to catch her. In a matter of moments, he was riding by her side.

They repeat this scenario several times. Daniella tried to ride away and Cal reeled her in. Finally, she gave an exhausted groan and fixed him with a somewhat accusing look.

Cal pulled up to her and attempted to initiate a more cordial conversation.

"Nice day, huh? I thought I was going to be doing this alone and then I saw you. I thought to myself, 'What the hell. It would be nice to have a little company. Someone to share the work with. You know, pass the time in a little friendly conversation.' A heavy load shared with a friend is a help."

"You think I need help? You think I need you to help me? I ride this climb three times a week. And I definitely don't need any help. With this climb or anything else. I'm capable of taking care of my own struggles."

"Like the one with Rocco last night?"

Daniella flashed Cal another look of irritation. It was obvious it was not a story she wanted to go into, not with a stranger. Her drama with Rocco was probably already the town staple, gauging by how public their arguments were. Maybe she wanted to start with a clean slate, he reasoned. He could grant her that much.

"No offense intended," he said. "Last night or today… or ever even, if you want to know the truth. I was only trying to stop an ugly situation last night. And today? Today, I'm just looking for a riding partner. I thought you would like some company. I know I do."

"Stop an ugly situation. You're a little too late for that one. That train has already left the station. Who are you, the Peacemaker?"

Cal reflected on her comments for a moment. "Yeah, I guess so. Peacemaker? Sounds like me. Doesn't always work though. Last night is a good example. I stepped in to help out and now both of you are pissed at me. And I think I looked like an ass in front of most of Bassano."

Daniella blew out a hard breath and settled into a more relaxed posture on the bike. She softened her tone and said, "You are the first guy I know who will admit he's wrong. Why don't we leave it alone for now? I tell you what. I'm going to show you one of my favorite secret rides. There's a back road near the top of the climb. It spins off this climb and then descends into town. I'll buy you an espresso. My treat. I owe you for last night."

"Espresso? You're on. But let's make it interesting. Last one to the bottom buys."

"We'll see about that." Daniella shot off the front like she was ejected from a toaster. She called over her shoulder, "See if you can keep up. The road gets a little steep here."

They continued up a sharp incline for another mile. The road carved a path between looming granite outcroppings. It was an extended ribbon of rider's paradise. Despite the temporary truce between Daniella and Cal, the pace on the road accelerated. Daniella was flexing her strength on the bike. And Cal was impressed by the tempo she set. For the next two miles, the two went at it. First, Daniella would accelerate and put a gap between the two, and then Cal would counter and pull even. When he did catch up to her, he would make exaggerated sounds of exhaustion to communicate to her that he was working hard to keep up. He was feeling playful and attempted to get Daniella to drop the *mano-a-mano* battle. Gradually, the mood took hold and he had Daniella laughing along with him. The ride became more lighthearted, with Daniella laughing as she accelerated, and Cal mimicking exhaustion as he hung on her tail. He hoped he was making a good impression.

Suddenly, Daniella veered to the right and turned off the main road onto a smaller back road.

"Here is where the fun begins," she said.

"Good, because I was getting tired of kicking your ass going up the hill," Cal yelled with mock bravado.

"Well, you did good just to hang on. Let's see how your descending skills match your climbing skills."

She pushed off and began a steep descent through the woods. It was here that the ride took on a grim seriousness. The road was rutted and angled steeply in a crazy zigzag pattern of left and right turns. The descent felt like a freefall. At times, they hit speeds as fast as 50 mph. At one 180-degree switchback, Daniella glided through the turn, while Cal had to slam on his brakes to keep from sliding off the road. This was her turf, and her prowess as a mountain bike rider was translating into technical skill that made high-speed descending on ruddy roads a natural. For Cal, just keeping the bike upright and his ass on the saddle took all the concentration he could muster.

The maniacal pace continued all the way down the mountain until they entered the outskirts of town. They powered their way down the main road snaking into town. Daniella led, weaving between stopped cars, running red lights, and hopping curbs to take the shortest distance across a road barrier. Cal hung on the best he could, but he was no match for her technical skills or knowledge of the town. He could only hang back and react. Still, he was impressed by her grace and fluidity on the bike. He was watching a natural, someone who had grown up on a bike. As they sailed through the gates leading to the main center, Daniella was twenty yards ahead of Cal. She threw her hands up in mock salute for her victory.

Cal pulled up next to her and offered his compliments.

"That was a great descent. You have no fear. And the way you dealt with the 'traffic furniture,' you don't let much get in your way. There were a couple of points where I thought you were going to have to call the helicopter to fetch me from the side of the road."

"You're talking to a mountain bike rider. You road riders have stamina and power. We mountain bike riders have bike-handling skills. Besides, I've been riding that route since I was old enough to go out with my father. I think I could ride it blindfolded."

Cal laughed, "There were a few times when I wished I was blindfolded. Seeing the drop off on either side scared the shit out of me. Come on. You won. I buy."

"Yes," said Daniella. "Espresso is the nectar of cyclists and a fitting prize for winning the race, don't you think?"

"Fitting prize for winning? I don't doubt it. But as for espresso, now that's an area where I excel. You're looking at a certified, licensed barista."

Daniella guided him through the labyrinthine town center and pulled up to a small café. She rested her bike against the window of the shop and motioned for Cal to put his bike next to hers.

"You don't worry about someone stealing your bike?" asked Cal.

"Are you making a joke?"

"No. In the States you don't leave your bike just hanging out on the outside of a shop. Not if you want to find it there when you come back out."

"This is Italy, and it isn't big-city Italy, like Milano. It's Bassano. Here we wouldn't think of messing with someone's bike. What a world you come from."

Daniella led the way into the shop where she was greeted with a warm embrace by the proprietor, a short, portly, middle-aged man, Claudio Ferma. With no more than a quick nod to the two riders, Claudio stepped back behind the counter. Dominating the shop was a huge, antique La Pavoni machine. Claudio set to work and began to pull an espresso for Daniella. Cal looked on with studied interest, watching Claudio's moves — the tamping down of the coffee into the filter basket, the twist of the wrist that snapped the gruppo handle into the machine, and the slow, steady pull on the arm of the machine that produced the pungent, dark brew into the steamed cup. The machine itself was a work of art. From gleaming chrome on the outside, to the copper boiler, to the filigreed, winged eagle at the top of the boiler, it was a far cry from the sleek, modern, electronic machines that Cal manned at Peet's.

"This machine, it's beautiful. It's gorgeous," exclaimed Cal, barely able to contain his enthusiasm.

"Yes, *grazie*. It's old, maybe fifty years old. It belonged to my father, who started this café a long time ago. Of course, it has been rebuilt many times, but it holds up. Lots of love and care to keep it working, but pulling espressi this way is the only way."

"Can I come back and take a closer look at it?"

"*Perche no*? You know espresso machines?"

Cal had maneuvered himself behind the counter and was lovingly running his hand down the manual pull handle of the machine. His eyes were filled with appreciation.

"Yes, well, a little. I work in a coffee shop in the US. A place called—"

"*Il diavalo*? Starbucks?" Claudio spat out the name as if he were expelling poison from his mouth.

"No, not Starbucks. A place called Peet's. It's a chain and it's big. But it isn't Starbucks."

"Okay, then. You're welcome here. Starbucks? They think they can rule the world with their coffee. Every shop the same. Every blend the same. Where's the creativity? Making espresso is an art, not a manufacturing process. You want the same all the time, no variation, no, how do you say, soul? Go to Starbucks."

"And here?" asked Cal.

"Here, you get espresso that is created from loving experience. I do it my way, which is different from how Pietro, who owns the shop next door, does it. Maybe better, maybe worse. You be the judge. Not everything should be the same all the time. Would you like to try to pull your own shot?"

"Can I?"

"Yes, be my guest," replied Claudio as he handed Cal a cup and motioned him toward the gleaming machine.

He felt like a surgeon initiating his first delicate procedure. Under the scrutiny of the espresso maestro, with Daniella smiling across the counter, Cal self-consciously filled the basket with the aromatic ground beans and slowly twisted the gruppo handle into the machine. He watched the pressure gauge edge northward into the green zone. When it was solidly in the green, he turned toward Claudio waiting for the okay to proceed. With a nod from Claudio, he gripped the ceramic handle and pulled down with steady pressure. It was a totally different experience than the button-pushing automation of his machine back in the States. The automatic, electronic sensation was replaced by a tactile feel of the handle forcing the water through the basket. What emerged was a trickling stream of amber-black. On the top of the brew, the foamy, brown crema gathered and floated, the signature of an ideal cup of espresso. He lifted the cup first to his nose to savor the aroma. Then, to his lips and sipped. The richness, the dense, robust flavor wafting up from the cup, and the bitter aftertaste on the back of his tongue identified this cup as a piece of art. He smiled at Claudio.

"Perfect. This is perfection. Your machine is a gift from the gods."

"Thank you," said Claudio. "But the machine is only as good as the operator, and you aren't bad. A little too fast with the pull on the arm, maybe. But, all in all, not bad. Pulling espresso is not for everyone. For example, only men can make espresso. Never trust a shop where a woman operates the machine."

Daniella, feigning indignation, jumped into the conversation. "*Come mai*? How come? Women can make a fine espresso."

"No, Daniella, *carina*. Women are good for so many things, and even better than men at many more. But, and I don't mean to make you angry, not for making espresso. You see, making espresso takes patience and concentration. Women? I'm sorry to say, you get distracted. You don't have the patience."

All three were laughing, even though it was clear that Claudio was only partially joking. His prejudice against women, particularly in the arena of espresso-making, was a vein of heritage that still pulsed under the surface of modern Italy. He turned to Cal, hoping to secure his agreement.

"So you. What do you think? Can women make espresso?"

Not wanting to miss the opportunity to pay Daniella back for beating him down the mountain, Cal grinned at her and said, "Well, I have to say that, and here I must present my credentials as a coffee professional, a 'coffee jerk,' as we say in the United States, Signor Claudio is totally correct. When it comes to making espresso, many are called, but few are chosen. And the primary criterion is gender."

Daniella let out a shriek in mock horror and punched Cal in the arm. "You chauvinist American! What do you know about espresso? You Americans don't even know the proper way to drink coffee, let alone make it. You order coffee that you think is espresso, but it's really some sort of watered down version of the real thing. You even have something called 'Americano.' What the hell is that? You put it in paper cups. Paper! And then you walk away. Where are you always going in such a hurry? Here in Italy, when we go for coffee, we go to sit, to think, to talk, and to enjoy. It's a time to pause, to take a deep breath, and live, maybe to share a bit of conversation with friends. And no paper cups. Paper cups are a sacrilege, an indignity to the espresso gods. Ceramic cups only. And the right size, too. Delicate. You hold them with one hand. None of those huge bowls the French like. They look like dog bowls. Come on, let's go outside before I lose my temper even worse."

CHAPTER 11

They grabbed their cups and settled into the chairs at one of the outdoor tables. Strollers, shoppers, and perambulating retirees passed by their table frequently, all of them spending the loose change of afternoon time. Anyone who could read body language could take meaning from the way Cal leaned forward, his elbows spread on the table, and from the way Daniella mirrored him. Chemistry.

After preliminaries of person, place, and statistical details, the conversation gravitated toward deeper issues. Daniella broke the ice first. "So my father tells me you rode for T Mobile. That's a pretty strong team. You had it made."

"I suppose. Things aren't always as good as they seem to be. I mean, there was a lot of it that I loved. But professional cycling has its ups and downs. And no way is it as glorious as it seems. I learned that personally."

Daniella nodded her head sympathetically. "You don't have to tell me. Remember, I grew up in a cycling family. I watched my mother sacrifice for my father. We were like a traveling circus in the early days. Everything the family did, and this was before he made it successfully, was organized around his riding. Not that we resented it. I mean, riding a bike here is part of the life force, and to do it and win, and to win professionally, is something to sacrifice for. Still, it's never easy. Even when Papa was successful, and he was away riding the big tours, we no longer had to travel and stay in shitty hotels, but he was still gone for long periods of time. And then, when he did come home, he had no energy until he started the next round of training. Meals, sleep, noise in the house... Everything was arranged to keep Papa's schedule, his routine, unchanged. Sometimes, I felt like we had a dying grandmother in the house."

"Professional riding is never easy. You think it's all about the cool equipment, the excitement of the race, the fans. But some days, you ride up a mountain pass and it's cold and raining. Then, you get to the summit and it's so cold, the rain has turned to snow. When you finish the training ride, all you want to do is climb underneath the heater of the car to get warm. But since you aren't the lead rider, when you get to the car, you find that the team leader already has that position, so you take what you get."

"And what did you get out of it?" asked Daniella.

"Huh?" Cal knew what she was asking. It was not dissimilar from the questions he had fielded a thousand times before. It was the "how did you do?" question, and he knew what was coming next, so he decided to preempt it.

"I did okay. I started slow, but then, I decided I wasn't as committed as most of the other guys on the team, or in the peloton, so I thought I'd explore some other options back in the States."

Daniella gave him a sideways look. "Some other options in the States? Like what? Like becoming a barista? Come on, Cal. I'll show you mine if you show me yours. What really happened? You had it made, a dream of yours came true and you gave it up. I smell a fish."

Cal sat back and swirled his cup. In time, he thought, maybe. But not now. "You smell a fish? People don't know about what other people want for themselves. I'm not sure I even knew what I wanted. Let's just leave it that I had my turn. I did my spin. And now..."

"And now you're a recreational rider with legs of steel, spending time tearing up the hills of Italy. Okay, I get it. But you know that I've grown up in this sport and there isn't too much that I haven't heard. This conversation? It's the opening chapter of a book, not the closing one. Someday, we'll talk about it in greater detail. Someday, when you trust me more."

The intimacy conveyed by Daniella's comment, the presumption that someday he would tell her the whole story, and her unwillingness to accept the sanitized, "I did it and got tired of it" version had a profound effect on Cal. It settled into his chest like warm liquor. In a short conversation, she had managed to get closer to him than so many others had done in three years. He didn't know if it was intentional or not, whether he was the cause or the effect of the connection between them, but he felt, for maybe the first time, that he had encountered someone who understood that realizing your goal isn't always the fairytale ending to your dreams.

It was a funny sensation. He felt torn between the urge to spill it all right now, to tell her all the details and lay open his deeper thoughts, to give her unfiltered access to his unfiled, cluttered, messy internal confusion. And right next to that feeling was the opposite, the fear that telling her everything would freeze any possibility of getting to know her better. Daniella was a creature of extraordinary strength. He could see that already. Not just physical strength, but emotional strength, too. She conveyed an eagerness, a hunger, to know more about Cal. This was both enticing and flattering, and more than a little terrifying.

Cal wanted to know more. "You said something about 'you show me yours and I'll show you mine.' Well, I've shown you mine. Let's hear yours."

Daniella crossed her arms. "Mister Cal, first of all, I don't for a second believe that you've shown me all of 'yours.' You've shown me some of it. But mine is a simpler story. Small-town girl. Daughter of the local racing hero. Papa had me working in the shop since I was seven. I switched from road racing to mountain bike racing. Won a few races, now I'm trying to figure out the next steps."

"Why the switch to mountain biking?" asked Cal.

"Road riders? You never see a smile. They always have a frown. Mileage, cadence, heart rate, wattage! Come on! It's a bicycle. Only a mode of transportation, a child's toy. And I'm not even getting into the clothes and the gear. You guys can be ridiculous, like a bunch of teenage girls at a boutique. Sometimes, I see you guys checking yourselves out in the mirror before you leave the shop. Shorts fit right? Jersey tight enough? Zipped up to just the right level? Gloves match the socks? Glasses over the straps of the helmet? Helmet sitting right on the head? Get over yourselves."

Cal couldn't deny the truth of her observation. "Speaking of 'getting over yourself,' what was the story with you and Rocco last night? Are you two a couple?"

"Were a couple. Past tense. Now, who knows? Rocco and I have been thrown together since we were *ragazzi*. This is a small Italian town. I was a winner of bike races and so was he. It seemed destined to be. We're like an Italian arranged marriage," she explained. "Worse. We're like an old married couple who has been together so long that it's a habit. You can't even remember making a decision to be together. And you don't know why you stay together."

"So what does keep you guys together?"

"Didn't you hear me a second ago? *Did* keep us together. I can't really say. I mean, of course, he has some good traits. But the way he treats me sometimes makes it clear that I'm living in his drama, and I'm not much more than a prop on the stage. I watched this with my mother and my father. I said it wouldn't happen for me. And here I am."

"You can always get out, can't you?"

Daniella smiled at the simplicity of his solution. "You make it sound like a decision to order cannelloni or fish. Which do you want today? No, if only it was that easy. We're talking about a family drama here."

"Family drama? This does go deep."

"Deeper than you may understand. In America, you think you can be anything, do anything. Here, In Italy, your destiny is too often set by the family history. In America, if your father is a butcher, you're inspired to be a surgeon. Here, in small-town Italy, if your father is a butcher, you're expected to be a butcher, to carry on the family tradition. If you want to explore your destiny, you can enlarge the shop. Maybe open a new shop. But you're still a butcher. Oh, you can move and start something new, but first you have to break the chains of expectation."

"But you still must have made a choice," Cal insisted, thinking that there had to be more to the story.

"My father would like me to continue to work the shop. He talks about retiring, and since there are no other Di Salvos around, his retiring would mean closing the business if I don't take over. My father has traveled the world, so he has seen that there are choices in how you live your life, and understands that he can't lock me into the shop.

He accepts that I need to make a choice for myself, even though he isn't good at hiding his truest wish. He also has coached Rocco since he was a youngster. He knows the darker side of his personality. So if my choice is to do it without Rocco, he would support that."

"So you do have the choice to leave or take off and try something else."

"My mother, on the other hand. She's a real case. She grew up with the belief that girls don't leave the family village. Even when my father was racing, she hardly ever left Bassano to watch him. Now, she sees me thinking about escaping and exploring the rest of Italy, forget the rest of the world, and she freaks out. She wants me to settle down, marry Rocco, raise *bambini*, and continue the family business. The idea of me doing anything else just doesn't fit into any meal she can stomach."

Daniella lowered her eyes and fell silent. Cal hesitated to comment. He had learned a few things from Lisa: Even though he thought he understood, Daniella was somewhere inside herself, processing a delicate web of feminine feelings, and anything he said would make him sound like an oaf. He drained the last of his espresso carefully, leaving the brown residue at the bottom.

"Anyway," Daniella finally said, "it's a story that's coming to a close—maybe a sad one. Maybe a happy one. Who knows? Tears are a mystery. They can refresh you or they can drown you. Sometimes, you don't know which until it's too late."

He gauged her tone, and decided that it was now okay for him to speak. "What does 'coming to a close' mean?"

"Well, in ten days, we have Le Scale, the town race. Lots of the representatives of the professional teams will be there to pick the best of the fruit. I'm certain that Rocco will place high, maybe even win it, and then he's off to the glamorous life of a big-time cycling pro, which, for an Italian boy from a small town like Bassano is the only route to fame and fortune. He'll be a star off to his glory."

"And you?"

"Me?" Daniella looked off across the street, at nothing in particular. "I don't know. I'm scheduled to race in the mountain bike nationals this fall, in Como. I'll do that. After that, who knows? I'm thinking that if I come back here, I'll make it harder on myself to leave. Maybe I'll just pack up after that and move. Maybe to Milano. I have some old racing friends who are living there."

"Sounds to me like you've made up your mind. You know what you want. You just don't know how to do it."

"If I don't leave Bassano, then I'll be just the 'little mechanic girl' as Rocco likes to call me. No, I want something more."

Daniella made a move to rise from her seat and Cal reached out to grab her arm. At first, she pulled her arm away, reflexively, as if she had somewhere to go and needed to break free, but then, she relaxed and settled back down into the chair. There was more that Cal wanted to say to her. He didn't want her to go yet. But he wasn't sure what to say, or how to continue the conversation. Finally, he released her arm. They looked at each other. Daniella smiled and took his hand in hers.

"I'm glad you caught up with me today on the bike. I say that I like to ride alone, and I do most of the time. But I also like having company. You're a good listener and a good talker. That's a nice combination. But it's time for me to get back to the house."

Together they made their way through the square, wheeling their bikes underneath the Galleria that covered the walking path. When they reached the opposite side of the square, Daniella reached over and hugged Cal. She placed a kiss on his cheek and turned to leave, but stopped short and turned back to Cal.

"Listen. I don't know what your situation really is with riding and racing. I think it's a jigsaw puzzle and I don't even know what the pattern is. But one thing I do know. You're strong as hell. And it would be a shame if you don't do Le Scale. It's a great event and you could do well."

"My father has been on my case about it. But I don't know. I mean, I haven't trained hard in a couple of years. I'm not exactly what you'd call in 'race fitness.' And…"

Anticipating what he was about to say, Daniella cut in. "And you don't know if you want to get started racing again. Come on! Don't be such a coward. All that power," she chided him. "I mean, if you can keep up with me on that climb, you must be pretty strong. Besides, it's almost all uphill. Your pathetic downhill skills won't get in the way."

They said goodbye to each other, riding in opposite directions, Cal to his hotel and Daniella off to her shop. As Cal rode away, he noticed people smiling at him—and realized that an enormous grin was pasted across his face. He smiled back. Daniella touched him, something that hadn't happened in a long time. His attraction to her had, at first, been physical. But the more he got to know her, the more her spirit intrigued him. She pushed him emotionally. She demanded that he turn back the cover of his "I'm all right, don't bother me" façade, and she made it clear that she wouldn't judge whatever he brought up. It was just like having a good training partner on the road, one that pushed you by forcing you to work on the parts you suck at, but doesn't hate you because you do suck at certain parts. Cal laughed to himself. "Good training partner? Hell, did you see the way she climbed and descended that hill?"

When he was a hundred yards away from the café, Daniella surprised him by pulling up to him on his left. She had started riding in the opposite direction, back to her home, but now she was next to him again. He looked over at her with a question on his face.

She leaned over and said, "Sunday night, my American racing star. My house. Italian family dinner. No trip to Italy would be complete without the experience of an authentic Italian family dinner. Six thirty, and don't be late. My father, the great Gianni Di Salvo, *Il Maestro di biciclette*, holds court and you need to be there to be part of it." With that, she leaned over her bike and put her arm around Cal. She gave Cal a strong kiss on the cheek, and then peeled off in the opposite direction. Cal's grin turned from a smile into a full-throated laugh. As he pedaled off toward his hotel, he shot both arms skyward into the air in the classic cycling salute of victory.

CHAPTER 12

Daniella's invitation had come on Friday, which meant that Cal had the whole day Saturday to think about his Sunday dinner invitation. Saturday morning, he and Paul went for an easy spin on the flats around Bassano.

The roads were jammed with knots of colorful riders, clubs out for a Saturday morning spin. These rides were like scripted plays. The riders, all wearing their club jerseys, rode in a carefully managed paceline, sometimes rotating the lead off of the front, but never deviating from a modest pace, until a town sign appeared in the distance. Then, like lions preparing to pounce, the pace picked up. Riders got twitchy. And finally, someone, usually one of the younger riders, could no longer contain the tension and jumped to sprint to the sign. The first attacker was rarely, if ever, the winner. The seasoned veterans waited and used the attacker as fodder, drafting behind him until the time came for a brief explosion of energy. After the sign slipped past, and because there was usually only a very narrow gap between the first and the following riders, there was a good-natured argument about who had actually taken the line. Or if the winner was clear, there was the usual bragging and barking to ensure that his dominance was clear.

Their Saturday ride ended when they stopped in the town square in Bassano and slid into a small, outdoor café for the post-ride espresso.

"What a beautiful way to spend a day, riding around the countryside here," said Paul. The afterimage of their argument the other night still hung between them, but only Cal could see it.

"No doubt," he said. "Funny, riding behind those Italian clubs today… No matter where you go, riders are pretty much the same."

"It's one of the things I love about cycling. We can speak different languages, come from different cultures, but the love of cycling is a common denominator. Speaking of different cultures, Luigi tells me that he saw you with Daniella in the square yesterday. How did that happen?" Paul made the last comment with a knowing smile.

"Just dumb luck, I suppose. I was riding up the mountain and she was, too. We ended up riding together. You should see her climb. And she's a better descender. She's hell on a bike."

"I'm not surprised. From the way I saw you look at her in the shop, I think she's hell off the bike, too."

Cal gave him a cool shrug. "We had coffee after the ride. She wins a lot of races around here. Pretty accomplished."

"I should think so. She's a Di Salvo. The genes don't lie. Hell, look at you. You have my genes and…"

"Don't get me started with that. Besides, Mom tells me that the fast twitch fibers come from her, not you."

"She would say that. But stop avoiding the question. Daniella? Something up?"

"I don't know. She did invite me to their house tomorrow night for dinner. You're on your own."

"Sunday night dinner with the Di Salvos? Nice. Sounds

like she might have fallen for the 'lost boy struggling with existential angst' story."

"Yeah, works every time. Wounded guy, works like kryptonite on the girls."

"Seriously, you interested in her?"

Cal stifled a laugh. "Interested? Who wouldn't be? She's beautiful. She can ride. She has this great spirit. Her situation is a little complicated, with her family and that guy Rocco, though."

Paul gave Cal a wry look, and then scratched at a stray mark on the table. "Look, you're only here for a couple of weeks. You might want to avoid getting involved with a family mess, a broken relationship, and all that stuff."

"I know, but she's pretty cool. She gets me going in ways that go beyond the usual shit. Besides, talking with her is so easy. I don't know what it is, but she seems really interested in what I have to say."

"Kryptonite, like you said before."

"No, I'm not talking about her just paying attention to me. I'm saying that she seems to be more genuine than a lot of the girls I meet back in the States. Seems pretty thoughtful and has a heart, too."

"Cal, you're here for a riding vacation. You're here and then you're gone, back to California. Don't fuck up our vacation by getting your head turned around chasing after Daniella. Keep some perspective." He finished his coffee and picked his gloves out of his helmet.

"Thanks for the encouragement, Dad."

"I'm just saying…"

"You just said it. Don't worry. I hear you. And…"

"And you're going to do whatever you want to do, regardless of what I say." He flipped his helmet onto his head and worked his hands into the gloves.

"Right. But just so you don't feel too bad. If I marry her, and we have children, I'll name my first boy child Paolo, after you." Cal stood up and pushed their cups to the center of the table.

"Thanks. Nice to know you still respect our relationship." Paul clapped him on the shoulder, and the two headed for their bikes, laughing.

• • •

Preparing for Sunday dinner at Daniella's house, Cal's nerves were rolling like ball bearings on a cruise ship floor. Finally, he went out to the inn's veranda, and sat away from the other guests, studying the patchwork landscape and the roads that threaded it together. He tried to steady himself with a plan, a strategy. He could approach this like it was a race, a competition, even though he didn't know what would make the evening a winner or loser.

His father saw Cal sitting alone and came over to join him.

"Mind if I sit for a bit?"

Cal motioned to the open chair.

Paul could see the furrowed brow and the glaze over Cal's eyes. "What's up son? You look like you're trying to solve a riddle."

"Oh, I was just thinking about dinner at the Di Salvo house and what you said about me being here for such a short time. I'm a little nervous."

"Look, son. You're going to the Di Salvo household for a dinner. Sunday dinner in an Italian household is an institution. Something bigger than you. Don't worry about it. Just go. Be polite. Don't get too grabby with the daughter. And be prepared to listen to hours of Gianni's greatest hits."

"Gianni is a singer?"

"Gianni considers his best races to be like hit songs. He'll sing them to you until you surrender. But that doesn't mean you shouldn't listen. This guy has won more races than you've even entered. And if you pay attention, there will be lots for you to learn."

"Should I bring something? A bottle of wine? Flowers?"

By this time, Luigi had overheard the conversation between father and son. Considering himself an expert on all matters of Italian protocol, he couldn't refrain from pushing in on their conversation. "Bring? What should you bring? You bring your heart. You bring honesty. You bring yourself." He set down two glasses of wine, on the house. "Oh, and a bottle of wine won't hurt either. And one last piece of advice. The bottle of wine that you bring? Make sure you give it to Mama Di Salvo. She's the one you need to impress. In Italy, we men like to pretend that we run the family. But it is *le donne*, the women, who run the show. And even in the Di Salvo family, a home with a national champion at the head, it's the mother who makes the policy. I've known Daniella since she was a baby. People around here say that she's fierce like her father. But they don't know. It's the mama who put the fire in her heart. Her father may channel the explosion, but the mama lit the fuse. In fact, it's the *nonna*, Gianni's mother, who put the fuse there in the first place. You, my boy, are about to take a deep trip into the archeology of the Italian soul."

Cal repaired to his room. He settled on a casual outfit of jeans and a t-shirt, the standard uniform for all situations back in California. Then, he looked in the mirror and decided to change. Maybe a shirt with a collar. He tried it. Too stuffy-looking. Back to the t-shirt. Too casual. Maybe a sweater. Too hot. T-shirt with a jacket. Too preppy. Finally, he went back to the t-shirt. Better to be comfortable, he thought. He descended the stairs, mounted his bicycle, realized he forgot the wine, returned to the hotel—then re-mounted his bicycle with the wine bottle under his arm and made his way over to the Di Salvo household.

* * *

Daniella held the lettuce under the tap and turned the head. A cascade of black flecks swirled down the drain. Just thinking about Cal coming to the house sent a nervous shudder down her spine. Having male friends to dinner, particularly if she liked them, was a rare event. Rocco was like one of the family. She knew her father would take to Cal, but what about her mother? She felt her mother's presence at her shoulder, one eye on the basil she was chopping, another on her daughter's face.

"*Carina*, you've already washed that same lettuce twice. Let it be. You're as flustered as a schoolgirl before her first day of school. What's going on? This American, Cal, who is coming to dinner, is that what has you so agitated?"

"Mama, I'm not worried about him coming to dinner." She shook out the lettuce and grabbed a handful of the fresh-picked spinach. She paused. "Yes, I am. Of course, I am."

"Why, dear. You're afraid that he won't like us?"

"I'm afraid that you won't like him."

"Because he's American? You forget that his father and your father are good friends. I'm sure he's a nice boy." She settled back into the rhythm of her knife on the cutting board, and swept heaps of basil into the old ceramic bowl.

"Man, Mama. He's a man, not a boy. And I don't know. He's very different from the boys, or men, who have been around here. He's very different from Rocco, for example."

Her mother *tsk*-ed. "Dear, you're too hard on Rocco. His way in life hasn't been easy. He tries too hard sometimes, that's all, because he has a lot he must overcome."

"Mama, you don't know Rocco like I do. And I just want you to understand that this guy, Cal, has something about him that I like a lot. He's smart and he's cute, and he laughs easily. He even can laugh at himself, which is something that's good in a man."

She lifted Daniella's pile of lettuce and began dismembering the leaves into another bowl. "So you like him because he laughs at himself? Maybe you have a soft spot for comedians." The way she snapped through the greens was dismissive.

Daniella dried her hands and threw the towel on the counter. "Don't make fun of me, Mama. The fact that he can laugh at himself tells me a lot about him. He doesn't have the edge that Rocco has. He thinks about things and doesn't want to fight about everything. He doesn't insist on being right all the time. He has a good heart. I can tell that from the conversations we've had. The other day, in the shop…"

"So I see. And he's here to do the race? He's come to race Le Scale?" She pointed her knife at the remaining spinach. "Wash it all."

The hiss of water from the tap interrupted them for a moment, and Daniella's *nonna* shouted in a reminder to bring up more wine from the cellar. "Yes, yes…" Her mother answered, and the conversation was in jeopardy of being forgotten.

"Papa wants him to do the race," Daniella said, stopping her. "His own father wants him to. But he doesn't say yet. He's an independent guy. And I like his soul, and the way he looks at me." She turned off the water, and met her mother's eyes. "I feel like I'm a real person to him. Like he cares about what I think."

Her mother shrugged and pointed for the spinach to go into the bowl, and turned for the cellar. "Darling," she said over her shoulder, "I'm happy that you've invited Cal to dinner. I'm looking forward to meeting him. I won't scare him. He'll meet our family and we'll meet him. There. Does that make you comfortable?"

"You make it sound like you're just going to tolerate him for the evening."

"What? More?"

"No more. It's just that I feel like you're humoring me. Like you think I'm still a little girl and my desires and my wishes mean nothing."

Her mother stopped in the stairwell and rolled her eyes to the ceiling. "Ah, so that is it? Milano? Everything we talk about—could be about going to the market, could be about your racing, could be about the weather outside. It all comes back to you wanting to go to Milano. Milano, Milano..." She made an elaborate shooing gesture, as if she was pointing a gun to her own head. "I'm tired of talking about it. If you want to go, go. Go. I don't want to be the one you look back on when you're older and think your own mother deprived you of your life."

"Mama, it isn't that I need your permission, your approval, to leave. I want you to be enthusiastic about it. I want you to want it for me. Some excitement, maybe. Is that asking for too much?"

Her mother was down in the cellar now, and her voice was muffled. "How can I give you approval for something I think is wrong? You have a life here. You have the shop. You have your family. What, tell me, what do you have in that city?"

"I don't know, Mama," Daniella shouted, "but, whatever it is, it's something different from what I have here. And I know what that is. Every day I know what it is. I want to not know what it is that I have in front of me."

"Daniella, the young people in Bassano leave the town now when they get the first chance." Her mother reappeared with two dusty bottles in her hands, and tread heavily back up the stairs. "It wasn't always that way. You're drawn like a fish to a bright object in the water. Maybe you already have your bags packed. But if you want permission, then I give you permission. If you want me to actually want you to go, that will never come." She blew the dust off the bottles and coughed. "So don't hold your breath waiting for that one."

"Ah, Mama. You make me want to scream." Daniella gave up, and sighed as she tossed the heap of salad, the chaotic mixture of lettuce, spinach, and green onions. "I get so frustrated with this old-school thinking. Papa is okay with it, so why can't anyone else be?"

A cork popped. "Your father is a man. He thinks you have the skills of a man." Another cork popped. "There's no amount of riding fast or knowing how to turn a wrench that will teach you how to survive in a city like Milano." She shook her head emphatically and looked outside the window. "If you feel like screaming, though, I suggest you hold it in. Your visitor is walking up the path."

* * *

The Di Salvo home stood like a monument to the wealth of a successful Giro champion. It rose out of a vineyard situated on the shoulder of the Monte Grappa, and was surrounded by the more modest bungalows of more modest families. Cal propped his bike against the stone wall bordering the yard and made his way up the long cobblestone driveway. The sounds of Italian opera spilled out from the open front door and the raised windows. Behind the music, Cal could hear the voices of several people mixed together in a stew of discussion. He took a deep breath and paused before approaching, steeling himself for what he might find across the threshold.

The porch was obscured by six-foot tall sunflowers. Behind the flowers, he heard someone laughing. Emerging around the flowers, he saw Daniella standing in the doorway. She was casually dressed in worn jeans and a v-neck t-shirt that flattered her strong arms and broad shoulders. She stood in sandals. Cal looked down and noticed that her toenails were painted a bright red. Nice touch, he thought. In jeans and a t-shirt, Daniella looked much more female than he had seen her before, either in the mechanic's garb or her cycling kit. She had even applied nail polish to her fingernails. Cal was looking at a more self-conscious Daniella than the one he had met in the shop or on the road. The attention she gave to her appearance, clearly in preparation for his arrival, was a comfort. Nice, he thought—she's as nervous as I am.

Daniella had witnessed his hesitation at the gate of their yard and seemed to find it charming. "You look lost. Don't be afraid. Nobody is going to hurt you in there."

"You clean up nicely."

"So do you. I see you put on your dress t-shirt."

"It's the only thing I had that wasn't too...."

"Don't worry." She brushed her hands over her t-shirt and pointed to her jeans. "There may be some judging of you that happens here tonight. But I can guarantee you it won't be about your clothes. Come on in," she pulled him more forcefully. "I'll see that you don't get too beat up."

Daniella laced her arm inside Cal's and tugged him through the door. She looked more beautiful than he could have imagined. She moved with a flowing elegance and comfort that blended with the opera emanating from the interior of the house, and on her arm, Cal felt like he was descending backward in time to a slower, more comfortable, and sensuous time.

A riot of chattering and raucous family surrounded him. He was greeted warmly by Gianni Di Salvo and his wife, Isabella. Daniella had the physical stature of her father. But her black hair, blue eyes, and olive skin were a genetic gift from her mother.

Isabella grasped Cal's hand warmly and looked him in the eye. "I'm happy to have you in our home. Gianni and Dani have said much about you. And your father has been a long-time friend of Gianni's. I hope you'll make yourself comfortable in our home."

Daniella stood, watching her like a hawk.

"Of course. And I brought this for you." Cal handed her the bottle of wine. She glanced at the label and quickly rendered an evaluation.

"Bardolino Superiore. You have good taste in wine. You're already a popular guest." She glanced at Daniella, nodded approvingly, and carried it off in the direction of the dining room.

Daniella moved to his side and whispered in his ear. "I didn't know you knew wines, too."

"I don't. I can only tell the difference between white and red if the lights are on. Thank Luigi."

"*Grazie*, Luigi," said Daniella in mock hushed tones.

With Daniella leading him from cousin to cousin and from aunt to uncle, he felt afloat in a sea of names and enthusiastic welcomes, and disoriented by it all. Each time he met another cousin or aunt or uncle, he did his best to punctuate the greeting with a little Italian. "*Il piacere e mio*," he said. "The pleasure is mine." He knew he was fracturing the language. His hosts knew it, too. Of course, many of Daniella's family spoke English pretty well. Unwilling to embarrass him, however, they kept their English to themselves until Cal reached a point where his Italian failed. This usually wasn't too deep in the conversation—he would start out in full stride Italian and then hit the point where his vocabulary or conjugation or idiomatic knowledge petered out. Then, the person he was talking to would wait expectantly until they saw the silent pleading in Cal's eyes. A rescue operation would follow, either with the listener providing the missing Italian link or, with a generous wave of the hand and a clap on the back, they would take over the conversation in English. Either way, Cal was relieved to get the help.

He had met girlfriends' families before, and he believed this one was going okay, even if he had to keep reminding himself that he was just Dani's friend. After making his way through young and old Di Salvos, he finally felt that he was done. But Daniella had one more introduction to make.

"And now, for the *prova finale*, the final test."

She led Cal across the room and the crowd around him parted. Seated in a rocking chair was a bit of Italian history, Daniella's grandmother, known in the family, in fact all of Bassano, as Nonna Di Salvo or just Nonna D. The matriarch of the family, she sat nobly in the corner, scrutinizing the proceedings. She had been watching him like a hawk since he walked into the room and had expressed her doubts about him with a series of grunts, groans, and sighs.

Daniella took the lead and introduced Cal. In rapid Italian, she introduced him. *"Nonna D. Questo e` Cal, da Gli Stati Uniti. E` venuto qui per andare in bici."* She turned to Cal and pushed him forward, murmuring that she had simply told her grandmother that he was here from the United States to ride bikes.

Nonna D peered at Cal through glasses as thick as Pellegrino bottles. She squinted and asked in Italian, *"Quest uomo e` Lance Armstrong?"* Daniella started to laugh, and Cal recognized the name "Lance Armstrong," but looked to Daniella for translation of the rest.

"Nonna wants to know if you're Lance Armstrong."

Laughing, Cal looked Nonna D in the eye and said, "I'm not Lance Armstrong, but he's a good friend of mine."

Not missing a beat, Nonna D replied, *"Dirgli che avrebbe dovuto restare in pensione."*

Cal turned to Daniella for translation, and she responded, laughing, "She says, 'Tell him that he should have stayed retired.'"

"I agree, Nonna D. And to tell the truth, I think he'd probably agree with you, too."

By now, the whole family was gathered in a scrum around Nonna D. Finally, Nonna D asked Cal to pull up his pants leg. He was perplexed. Was this some kind of joke? But eager to please, he raised his pants leg to his calf.

"Non, piu alta," Nonna said, motioning up higher with her hands palm-up. Cal was in no position to resist. He self-consciously raised his pants leg a little higher, exposing his leg to the thigh.

"*Basta,*" spat Nonna D. Then, she leaned in closer and wrapped her bony hand around Cal's thigh, kneading the muscle. She released her hand and sat back in her chair for a moment. Then, momentarily satisfied with what she had just felt, she motioned for him to turn around. Cal complied. She leaned forward and clenched his butt in her extended hand. Tilting her head upward and closing her eyes, as if she were appraising a fine linen by feel alone and didn't want sight to contaminate the verdict, she mumbled something inaudible to herself.

Daniella leaned forward to better capture what her grandmother was saying. "What do you think, Nonna?"

"*E` forte,*" replied her grandmother with certitude.

Cal's eyes begged for an explanation, from Daniella or from any one of the family, who were gathered around, nodding their heads in unison like ducks bobbing for bread in a pond.

Daniella explained to Cal, "You see, my father may be the resident cycling hero, but Nonna Di Salvo is the source of all of the cycling wisdom in the whole region. She just used her own educated hands to evaluate you. Her method may be crude, but it rarely fails. Her hands can tell the muscle definition, and through the touch, she can measure the strength in your legs. She could probably tell you the percentage of body fat just from her grip. As for your heart? She'll make that judgment as dinner rolls along. But don't let it freak you out. If I bring you here, you're already three quarters of the way home."

"And how did I do, muscle wise?"

Before Daniella can answer, Nonna D interrupted. "*Grado A. Superiore.*"

"You've passed the test," Daniella says. "Grade A, quality specimen."

"Geez, too bad the pros with all their equipment and water tank tests and VO2 measurement and lactate threshold testing don't have a Nonna D to cut to the chase."

"Yes," said Daniella. "Too bad. You know all the numbers and measurements in the world are no substitute for an educated eye when it comes to evaluating quality." She flashed a look at Cal's eyes when she said that. There was more in her comment than what sat on the surface, but he was too disoriented from the noise and attention to think it through.

Over the course of the next two hours, a riotous, raucous juggling act of bowls, plates, glasses and, of course, bottles of wine, took place. The conversation was loud and as is often said, "two Italians, three opinions." Through it all, however, an undercurrent of good nature and playful challenge cushioned the blows from the more contentious points of view. There was a cacophony of opinions, beliefs, and facts ventured on topics ranging freely, and without rhyme or reason, from politics to art to religion, and finally, when all were settled and nearly spent, to racing. Daniella brought the conversation to a pause by asking her father who he believed would be the winner of this year's town race, Le Scale.

A hush settled over the table as Gianni considered the options. Whereas opinions were offered freely before, now, the table waited for Gianni to declare his position first. Gianni started with a quick review of the course, pointing out that, with the particular terrain of this race — a long lead in and the final extended miles of climbing — it was a course that favored endurance over sheer power. That meant that it was to the advantage of riders who were efficient, had a strong power-to-weight ratio, and — here he paused and looked around the table — were prepared emotionally and physically to suffer like their lives depend on it. The Di Salvos listened to him as if they had never heard these facts before.

"Le Scale is no ordinary bike race," Gianni said. "Many years you start in the sunshine in town, only to finish in the snow on the top. Even on the warmest of days, Monte Grappa only surrenders its glory to the fiercest. To win takes strong legs, yes, but it takes a strong heart, too. Because when you get to the top part of the mountain, the last ten kilometers above the tree line, where there's no shelter and the road seems to run vertical, the mind will need to convince the legs that there's reason to go on. And then, there's the wind. The noise alone from the wind can drive you crazy. Lots of the best *ciclisti*, true champions, guys who made it to the Giro, have come to Le Scale thinking that it's just another local race. They leave thinking that a joke has been played on them. This 'little town race' becomes a trial of will and courage. But for those who do make it through, win or not, there's pride to have simply participated. We have here the saying, *la vergogna e solo di non correre*."

Daniella, seeing that Cal's knowledge of Italian didn't extend that far, interjected the translation, "The only disgrace is not to race."

By now, the table was as silent as a church. All who were seated around the table were waiting for the final prediction. "So" Gianni went on, "this year's race will be an interesting one. I believe that the winner will come from the local boys, hopefully a rider from our SD squad. And among them, none is stronger than Rocco. He may be stubborn, and coaching him has been a trial, but there's no doubting his strength. And he knows that if he wants to get out of this town and onto the professional circuit, he has to impress the directors from the professional teams who will be there to watch. So for my money, the bet is on for Rocco."

The table broke up into fits of dispute.

Gianni's wife, Isabella, interjected her opinion. "I have heard that Nove Colli, from Mussolente, has a very strong squad this year. They're always a good team. What about them? And what about the climbers who always seem to show up from Trento? You can't count them out."

"Yes, Nove Colli always brings something to the race. And this year, they have a new junior that they have elevated to the senior team, a young guy, Stefan. He's a superb climber. Dances on the pedals like Pantani used to. He's young, though, and with the young ones, you never know for sure how they'll react when they're thrown into the mix of a strong field. We'll mark him, definitely. Nove Colli likes to come in and eat the meal off of our plates, here in our own town, and they're good. The guys from Trento? They come strong every year, but the party in Bassano the night before always seems to take some of the strength out of their legs."

Isabella continued. "And that's it? There are no other threats?"

"Isabella, *carina*, you've watched enough racing to know the truth. The reality is that any competitor who shows up at the start line with a bike can always be the first one to cross the finish line. That's what makes racing such a glorious event. That's the mystery and the excitement. So nobody is counted out as a potential threat."

"And that's why team tactics are so important," added Daniella. "The surprise racer is less of a surprise if you have the eyes of a whole team watching the peloton. It's a chess game."

Gianni laughed. "This is my real advantage." He turned to Cal. "In the Di Salvo household, I may be the one that won the Giro, but I have the craftiness and the cunning of a whole family in reserve. Still, if I had to bet money on the race, I would put it on Rocco. At least that's what I'm betting today. Tomorrow? All bets can be changed."

Daniella jumped in. "But Papa. You're not really objective. You coach Rocco. You coach SD. Of course you think they'll win. And you think that Rocco will win."

"Just making my guess on the strength of the competition."

"Strength? Yes, Rocco is one of the best racers in the valley. And he certainly has the strength. But you've always said that racing is only partially determined by the legs, that the legs only take you so far, that what's in a racer's heart and in his head is just as important. Maybe even more important. Now you're calculating the victor on the basis of the wattage he can turn?" She turned her gaze to Cal, who was trying to decipher what fire was burning in her that would make her confront her father.

She continued, "There are other riders in this race who have their opportunity, too. Some of them are experienced and will want or need this race enough that they're willing to push themselves beyond their limits — way beyond their limits — to win. You can never, never, be certain of the outcome of a race. Otherwise, why bother lining up at the start? Why not just give the trophy and the prize money to the guy who has the best training numbers?"

Gianni smiled at his daughter. "Yes, everything you say is true. And everything you say is something that I believe. So who do you pick, *Signorina*?"

"Maybe there will be a mysterious challenger this year," she declared, shifting her eyes in the direction of Cal.

Gianni followed her gaze, and speaking to the table, but making it clear that he was talking to Cal, said, "Yes, there's always room for a surprise winner. But only if that surprise winner has entered the race. And only if he has committed himself with the intention of winning. And finally, only if he wants it bad enough to turn himself inside out to reach the summit first."

With this final pronouncement, dinner reached its conclusion. Cal rose from the table, said thank you to Signora Di Salvo, and was about to leave when Gianni grabbed him by the elbow. He motioned for Cal to follow him. Together they left the main house and crossed the yard to another building, a faded, rickety garage that stood behind the main house.

CHAPTER 13

The garage was an Italian classic, built of old stone with two large central doors that opened outwards. The walls were a foot and a half thick, and ivy sprouted from the mortar.

The exterior was old world Italy, but the interior was a gleaming, shining, space-age laboratory. Everything was glass, chrome, or white tile. The large, central room was stacked with equipment of all sorts, all in the service of cycling training and assessment. There were computers, treadmills, stationary bicycles, water tanks, and cycling equipment of every shape and form. The walls were covered with charts and graphs. A quick scan of the charts revealed what looked like progress graphs for each of the SD riders. This was where Gianni ran his tests, kept track of his team, measured their progress, and prescribed their training routines. It was as advanced and state-of-art as any facility Cal had ever seen, and that included the top secret, inner sanctum of T Mobile's training and assessment facility in Munich, where he had spent days being prodded, poked, weighed, and analyzed from a dozen different perspectives, including the psychological testing that was part of every team's seasonal preparation.

With eyes as big as saucers, Cal turned to Gianni and

stammered, "This is amazing. You've got enough equipment here to measure a pro team."

"Yes," said Gianni. "Nonna D's method of assessing riders is good. Hands on. But me? I like to rely on science. I think I have a good eye for talent. I watch someone on the bike and I can learn a lot. But the science of cycling, the exercise physiology evidence, has grown, and only a cretin would ignore that information. Come over here. Let me show you what we have."

Gianni led Cal across the room to the far side where several bikes were mounted on stands. "Over here we have the computrainers." He motioned to another room visible through a glass wall. "In there we do the VO2-max. Over in that corner is a tank for measuring body fat." Stepping back into the main work laboratory, he approached a series of computers and some handheld digital assessment devices. "This is the brains of the operation. We keep a detailed database for each rider. When you train, you wear a heart monitor. We equip your bike with a power meter. After each training ride, we download wirelessly and put the data into the computers. Then, I can analyze it with software that some exercise physiology geeks at the university developed for me. I can then give each rider a specific set of workouts for the week. Each one tailored for his particular need. The days of 'one size fits all' are over. And over there, is my latest installation." Gianni walked Cal over to a side room. At one end of the room stood a giant fan. In the middle of the room was a platform with a stand for a bicycle. Video cameras were mounted at strategic locations around the room, and a giant monitor filled the rear wall.

"A wind tunnel?" asked Cal in disbelief? "You have a wind tunnel here?"

"How else to work on aerodynamics for the time trial?"

Cal was flabbergasted. What he was seeing was as advanced as anything he had ever encountered. He had pegged Gianni as one of the old-school cyclists, the kind who rejected anything that hadn't undergone the test of time. If the old pros didn't do it, then those Luddites would reject it as a fad and downplay the possible benefit. Those were the guys who still insisted that hydration should consist of nothing more than water, and only when needed. Their idea of nutrition on a bike was a ham sandwich, and when it came to training, you simply did as much as you could, going all-out for as long as you were able. Those dinosaurs still existed in the world of racing, although they were a dying breed. Scientific training techniques and nutrition were simply too powerful to ignore. The technology that went into the bikes alone, not to mention the riders, moved the sport light years away from its pioneers. Those guys had heart, for sure, but heart alone, although necessary, was not sufficient for triumph in the modern era.

Gianni moved across the room and motioned for Cal to have a seat with him. After a moment's pause, he started in, "So your father has told me your story. He told me of your experience with T Mobile. Too bad. Their *director sportif*, their manager, Gerhardt, he's an idiot. He's ruined more riders than he's ever created. Besides, most of his stars have been riding dirty EPO, CERA, steroids. Who knows what they're on now that the testing has gotten stricter?"

Cal shifted in his chair. He was about to speak up when Gianni held up his hand to stop him.

"I'm not asking you to confirm or deny that T Mobile was doping. Every one denies. That's the way it is. And then, some riders produce some amazing results, and a year later, their pee turns up dirty. What you might have done with them, or didn't do, is between you and them, and between you and your conscience. All I'm saying is that my riders are riding clean. And we're getting results without drugs. If you do it right, if you train right, and you train smart, and if you have talent and your soul is in your effort, you get results. Maybe it's a longer road, but that only makes it more rewarding. No shortcuts. No gifts.

"Now for you, Cal. What is it that you want? I've had a long talk with your father. You know, he's your biggest fan. Not sure how realistic he is about your potential, but that's the way all fathers are. Me included. That's our job. And your father has done his faithfully. But you? What is it that you want out of cycling?"

Gianni regarded Cal down the length of his aristocratic nose, and waited. He wasn't a man in love with the sound of his own voice, despite all the attention Bassano lavished on him. He seemed interested in what Cal had to say.

Two weeks before, the answer to the question would have been easy. He was over it and ready to move on with his life, whatever that meant. But to tell the truth, nothing he had encountered since leaving racing had held a faint resemblance to the thrill of the race, or even the simpler thrill of being on a bike again. Gianni was inspirational, but would that translate into desire for the hard part, the work that professional cycling demanded?

"I wish I could tell you, honestly," Cal said.

"Are you interested?'

"Interested? In what?" Cal knew exactly what Gianni was asking him, but used the question to stall a bit. He wasn't sure how to put into words his hopes, and his fears.

"In racing? In joining my team? In racing Le Scale."

"When I left T Mobile, I was so damned done," Cal said. "I was convinced that it was a kids' game. That we professionals were expensive toys of rich team owners. They used us at their pleasure, and then they chucked us to the side when we weren't fun anymore. I mean, how important is bicycle racing, anyway? In the scheme of things? What does it amount to? You, Gianni, you've dedicated your life to cycling. Does it make for a meaningful life? Do you feel like you've contributed?"

"You ask me? That doesn't matter to you. The question I'm asking you, Cal, is a simple one. Do you want to give it a try again? Maybe just for Le Scale. The expectations will be realistic. You've been out of training for too long to make a charge at the top. But you have talent. I know how you did in your stay with T Mobile. These things I know. What only you know is whether you have the guts to suffer again."

Gianni continued, "You question the importance of cycling in the larger scheme of things. Life is about challenges and how you deal with them. It could be school, or work, or being a baker or a plumber. None of them is all that important in themselves. It's the value that we place on these daily, mundane things. We create our own value system. They're only worthy endeavors because they provide a stage on which you come to know yourself."

Cal expected that Gianni, in the tradition of all great, veteran cycling pros, would dismiss his ambivalence about resuming his career as faintheartedness. Instead, Gianni's willingness to accept his confusion made him realize that the onus of the decision was truly his and his alone. Not his father's. Not his coach's. The question was only for him, and was a much more profound and existential one than simply Le Scale.

In the room, the only noise came from the lights and a motor somewhere behind the water tank.

Cal said, "In all honesty, I do love the sport. Winning, when it came, was fun, but then it got out of hand."

Gianni nodded in agreement.

"You're asking me to jump back into the pressure cooker. Knowing what I know about me, and what I know about the commitment that sport takes, and about the world of professional cycling, I can't say yes, at least, not at this time."

Gianni sighed, voice thick with fatigue.

"Ah, I think it's too bad. But it's your life… and your decision to make." He stood up and offered his hand to Cal. "Well, if you change your mind, you know where to find me. And having seen the way that my daughter is looking at you, I have a strong suspicion that we'll be seeing more of you. As for now? It's been a pleasure talking with you."

He walked with Cal to the door and saw him out. When Cal had gone a few steps out of the door, he suddenly stopped and turned to Gianni, who was watching him leave from the doorway.

"Wait. What if we struck a deal. What if I said that I wanted to sample it again. I can say yes to training. It was the part that I always enjoyed best, anyway. If you can accept that as a yes, then we're on board. If you're asking me to make a commitment to return to full-time, professional racing, that's a leap that I just can't make yet."

With intuition borne out of experience and empathy. Gianni abruptly declared, "Ordinarily I'd make no such deal. With me, you're either in or out. No sampling. This isn't a *trattoria* where you can try the soup to see if you like it. But I have a funny feeling about you—So. No more discussion. Tomorrow we start. Full day of evaluation. We assess your fitness and complete a training program for you. We have only a short time before Le Scale, so you'll need to work hard. We won't have you in prime shape in such a short time, but it's only a one-day race, so that won't matter. Be here at eight sharp. You'll start evaluation tomorrow and you'll start riding with my team, SD."

Cal laughed. "I think I'm only afraid of the suffering that you're going to inflict on me."

Gianni responded with a laugh of his own, "Listen. In bicycle racing, pain is inevitable. But suffering is optional. You have strength, talent, and experience. What we have to work on at the same time that we make your body tough is to make your mind tough. Pain, yes. Suffering? That's up to you."

* * *

For the first time in longer than he wanted to admit, Cal felt like his train was back on the tracks. He wasn't sure where it was heading, but at least he felt a sense of progress. After he had shaken hands with Gianni and returned to the house, Daniella offered to ride back with him to the hotel. "It's dark now and you don't know the roads. It could be very dangerous for you. I'll make sure you make it home safely."

Hearing this, Nonna D spoke up from her rocker.

"He might be safer going home alone than he is going with you."

CHAPTER 14

Winding down country roads lit only by the moon, Daniella and Cal slowly navigated to the hotel, laughing about the events of the evening. Nonna B, the arguing amongst the cousins, the tumult at the table, were so different from anything Cal had ever experienced in his own home, and so much more fun. Still grating on his mind, however, was the conversation he had with her father, and the commitment, however ambivalently it was made, to his own.

"So you told him you'd race?"

"Not so fast. I told him I'd train. We'll see how it goes. Make the decision about racing when we get to that point."

"So you made a commitment to train, and maybe, maybe not, to race."

"That pretty well describes it."

"Some commitment," Daniella chuckled. "Let me tell you how I hear it. You made a commitment, but you're holding the right to renege on that commitment. Is that it?"

"Yeah, I guess so."

"Very strange."

"Yeah, that's how we roll in California. Welcome to the new definition of commitment."

"And in your relationships with others. This is how you make commitments? To a girl, maybe?"

Cal turned and looked at Daniella, slowing the pace on the bike to make sure he got her attention. "To tell you the honest truth, I've never made a commitment to a girl."

Daniella picked up the pace and started to pull away. "And that's how you 'roll' in California? Men, all over the world, it seems, 'roll' exactly the same way. You'll fit in perfectly here."

Cal laughed and chased after Daniella. "But…" His words were wasted because when she decided that she had the last word, she stopped listening.

• • •

At the hotel, Cal invited Daniella in for a last glass of wine. "This may be the last drink you have for a long time if you're going to train with my father," Daniella offered. "So you shouldn't have it alone." She led the way into the hotel—it was still familiar to her from the banquets Luigi hosted for the Di Salvo family weddings, baptisms, and funerals.

Tonight, his hotel was hosting a local wedding party in the courtyard. The bar was crowded with wedding guests, floating in and out of the courtyard, and the strains of the wedding band filled the bar. In the midst of the wedding whirlwind, Daniella and Cal sought out a quiet corner of the bar and slid into a booth where they could find a bit of privacy. They shared a glass of wine, and then another. What started out as a short nightcap chat turned into an extended conversation. They talked of racing, of their hopes for the future, and about their past. Over the course of the next two hours, a couple of glasses turned into a full bottle of wine, and the distance between the two dissolved. By the time Luigi came over to announce the closing of the bar, Daniella had worked her way into Cal's arms, and enjoyed the sensation of his warm skin through their thin summer clothes.

As Cal walked her to the door of the hotel, he suggested that since it was so late and so dark, it might be dangerous for her to ride her bike back to her home.

"What's my choice?"

"Well, you could spend the night here. Here, with me."

Cal's invitation raised Dani's heart rate higher than it had been in any mountain bike race. She hesitated, caught her breath, and slipped one hand around his waist. "Yes, riding home is a little dangerous. But is it any more dangerous than spending the night here, with you?"

"I thought you were the one who laughed in the face of danger," Cal chided. He slid his arm around her and pulled her even closer to him. His lips brushed hers, tentatively at first. She slipped her hand into his hair and pulled him against her. It was she who led the way upstairs, giggling, to his room.

Cal fumbled with the key to the door. Dani sensed his nervousness and took control. She pulled the key from his hand and inserted it into the lock, turned the handle, and pushed the door open. She kicked the door closed with her foot. Once inside, she explored the room with her eyes. She wandered over to a window that overlooked the hotel's interior courtyard. From the overhead view, the wedding party looked like abstract patterns changing shape in a kaleidoscope of colors. The band played enthusiastic but off-key renditions of wedding classics. The bride passed from groom to best man laughing and dancing, spinning, her head thrown back, lost in the excitement of the evening. The dancers were surrounded by a circle of people clapping in time to the music.

"You have a great view from here."

"The view from right here isn't too bad, either," replied Cal, looking at Dani. They both broke up laughing, not because what he said was so funny, but because they were both as nervous as high schoolers.

Dani walked over to Cal and took his hand. She knew where they were going to end up, but she was uncertain how they were going to get there. She guided Cal over to the bed and they both sat sideways facing each other. They kissed for what seemed like hours until she made herself pull away. She could sense the building urgency, hers as well as his, and she wanted to say some things, to carve a path through her layered feelings before they arrived at a place where there would be no turning back.

"This is the place where I'm supposed to tell you that I don't do this all the time," she said.

"You don't need to tell me that," Cal murmured. "I know that. I wouldn't be here with you if I thought that."

"No, don't stop me. Just listen for a moment. I have to say some things. Even if it's only because I need to say them out loud."

"If you tell me you're a virgin, I'm not believing it," replied Cal with a twinkle in his eye.

"If I told you I was a virgin, and you did believe me, I'd leave the room right now. This isn't about my sex life. Or yours, either. You need to know what the situation is." Dani took a deep breath. She placed her finger against Cal's lips to keep him from speaking.

"When you first showed up in the shop and we disagreed about your broken chain, I wanted to fight with you. I needed to prove that you were wrong. I thought a lot about that later. Why was I so willing, so ready, so damned determined to make you wrong?"

"Because I was wrong?"

"No, you don't see. Even if you were correct, I was going to win. You could have been spot-on, and I would have found a way to make you wrong. I see that I've been fighting for so long that it seems like the only way out of the box I'm in. I don't even question it. Now, I get to know you and I see someone who's willing to listen to me and not put me down or squash me for his own purposes. I feel like I'm undressed."

"It may not be my place to say this, but you've been dealing with Rocco too long."

"Yes, you could say that it's Rocco. But it doesn't matter, because by now I'm also part of the problem. Can you understand how different it is for me to feel something for someone and know that the person I'm feeling it for isn't using me in some way? I can trust you."

Cal reached out and pulled Dani close. He stroked her hair and lifted her downturned face. There were tears in the corners of her eyes that she didn't want him to see. He kissed the tears away and caressed her neck.

"I can be so fucking tough. You've mostly seen me in the midst of fights. I fight with Rocco. I fight with my father. You saw me in the *piazza* the other night and I'm like a crazy woman. And you don't seem to find that repulsive? Don't you worry that I'm going to fight with you, too?"

"Fight with me? Probably, but it doesn't scare me off. Hell, I love the part of you that insists on fighting, that won't back down. Rocco is a bully. He'd never stop bullying you if you didn't stand up to him. Honestly? I wish I had more of that fight in me. I feel like I've lost it. Lost the instinct to fight. But I admire it in you. I want to learn it again from you."

Cal's words caressed Dani's body at the same time that his hands were busy stroking her face, her shoulders, her arms, and her legs. She felt the armor melt away, revealing a softness she had kept hidden for so long that she wondered if it still existed. Was it that he came from another culture? Were American men just simply less macho? She pushed the idea out of her head. Saying he was from another culture negated the reality that he had touched her, not just with his hands, but with his heart. The feeling she was experiencing, the name of which had escaped her, now popped into her head. Safe. She felt safe with Cal.

She moved closer to him and placed her hand on his belt buckle. Cal looked down and watched her hands as she attempted to free it. An electric charge surged through her body, and when she fumbled, he took over. He jumped from the bed and urgently yanked his jeans down and stripped off his shirt. He was wearing no underwear, so there was nothing to hide how turned on he was. Dani laughed at his impatience. She followed, pulling her sweater over head, pulling off her jeans, and stepping out of her bra and panties.

They kissed for a moment before they fell back into bed, testing the feel of their bodies touching again. First Cal lay on top of Dani, and their lovemaking was slow and tentative. As the passion built, she arched her back and legs and flipped Cal over and guided him inside her. She set the rhythm of their motion, gradually taking him deeper and deeper inside of her. When she came, she let out a stifled groan and collapsed on top of Cal. He waited for her climax to finish and then came inside of her.

The two lovers rolled over, deeper into each other's arms, exhausted.

Cal had a sweet smile on his face.

"What are you smiling about," she asked, mostly to fill the space between them.

"Well, you know, I've seen you climbing on a bike. I've watched you tear up a hill. And now, now I've seen what you can do in a bed. You're a cardio animal."

"Nice, Cal. Very sexy. Nice to know you think of sex in the same terms as you think of cycling. You're a true cycling nut. But since you're already there with the cycling idea, what about endurance? I'm good at that, too." Dani smiled as she said that, and reached over and began to stroke Cal's cock. In a matter of moments, the two were locked together for a second round.

* * *

Later, after Cal had fallen asleep, she rose from the bed and wandered back to the window. She looked down at the remnants of the wedding party. The bride and groom were dancing slowly, barely moving, but holding each other tightly. The band had stopped playing and only a few of the guests remained, a few stragglers, too tired or too drunk to negotiate their way home. The lack of music made no difference to the couple. They were oblivious to everything around them.

Dani's eyes shifted back to Cal deep in sleep, wrapped in the covers. He looked so calm and peaceful. She had tried to fall asleep, but the unfamiliar room, the strange bed, and the power of the intimacy with Cal set her mind spinning. So much had happened in such a short time. She struggled to understand, to put a name to the feelings that swirled in her head. She knew that Cal had guided her over a threshold that she had faced before, but had never dared to cross. Now, there was a way forward. She was uncertain what that meant, but the idea of returning back to the shop, back to Rocco, back to her life as it had been, were all steps backward. Full stop. It would mean leaving her family, too. She would need to explain that to her mother. Her father would understand. Her mother would not.

She studied Cal. Where did he fit in? Did he think his life included her? These two questions were either mirrors of each other, or a very sharp break between expectations. The answers were impossible to guess, and the harder she considered the future, the heavier her eyes became. She stifled a yawn and slid back into bed, feeling the warmth from Cal's slumbering body. For the present moment, this was all the certainty she needed to quell her tension and drift off to sleep.

CHAPTER 15

The next morning, Paul came down to breakfast early. Cal was already up, and spooning a helping of fruit onto his plate. Daniella sat by his side, their chairs nearly touching, sipping a steaming cappuccino. "Well, good morning," he said as he settled his plate on the table and motioned for the waiter to bring the coffee over. "I hope you had a restful sleep."

"I did. Rested well. Thanks," said Cal.

Paul turned to Daniella, trying his best to not look judgmental about her being there. "And you?"

"Me, too. Very restful." Daniella blushed.

They rummaged around in the awkward conversation until they could find a topic that struck just the right note of engagement, without being too personal or too loaded with meaning. Finally, Daniella asked Paul how it was that he knew her father.

"Oh, your father and I have known each other for twenty years," he said with relief.

"Twenty years? And how?"

"Well, I met him here. I used to come here every year to ride."

"You rode here? Did you race or was it just for fun?"

Paul laughed. "Well, I'd like to think that the two

aren't as dissimilar as it seems. Yes… well, it started out as fun. And then, I met your father on the road. He was a young pro at the time, just starting his professional career. And I was an American amateur racer and had heard about Le Scale."

"And you just met?"

"Yes, on the road, one day. I was out there busting my tail trying to get acclimated to the climbing, and he passed me going up Monte Grappa like I was standing still. Well, I considered myself to be a pretty good climber, and I had some pride. So I chased after him."

"Hmmm, you're a brave man to try to chase my father down."

"Well, I didn't say I chased him down. I chased *after* him. For the next fifteen miles around every turn on that damned mountain, I chased him. When we got to the switchbacks, your father was on the road above me and could look down across the switchback and see me. He kept slowing down to let me think I was catching him, and then accelerate just as I thought I was gaining ground. He finally completely dropped me. And then, when we finally got to the top and into the lodge, there's your father sitting reading the newspaper with a beer in front of him. There's another beer on the table. He motions for me to join him, pushes the beer toward me and says, 'Here. This is for you. You looked like you could use it.'"

Daniella was laughing. "That's one of my father's favorite games. He calls it 'trolling for trainers.' He lets you catch on and drops you again. On and on, until you give up in frustration. It's rather cruel, I think. But you became friends?"

"We became friends. Of course, that didn't mean that we stopped trying to beat each other's brains in on the bike. And to tell the truth, I'd still fall for his same old tricks. Some things never change."

"And have you ever beaten him up the climb to Monte Grappa summit?"

"No, not yet. But I'm not done trying."

Laughter filled the room. Having finished breakfast, Daniella rose from her chair to leave. She gave Cal a peck on the cheek and he walked her across the dining room to the door. When he returned, his father was sitting with a huge grin on his face.

"Home game last night?"

"Yes, I guess so," Cal mumbled.

To change the subject, he announced that he had decided to race Le Scale and that he was going to train with SD and, more importantly, was putting himself under the tutelage of Gianni. Paul wasn't surprised that Gianni had made the offer. Gianni had said on several occasions that Cal should give it another go. Paul seemed a little surprised, though, and more than a little pleased that Cal had accepted the offer. "Perfect," said Paul. "I can't think of anyone better for you to work with. And nobody knows Le Scale better than Gianni. I wouldn't want you working with anyone else."

"So you aren't jealous?"

"Jealous? Of what? That you decided to race Le Scale because Gianni inspired you? Because you're going to train with him? I couldn't have asked for a better plan for you. You're in the best hands I could think of."

"Well, it was my choice," Cal insisted.

His father shrugged. He was beaming.

"Look, I'm telling you something," Cal said. "Listen. You've been pushing me to return to racing ever since I left T Mobile. And I haven't exactly been very receptive to you. In fact, to tell the truth, I've been pretty negative about your advice. About you, too, to get down to it."

"Yeah, I've noticed," replied Paul.

Cal ignored his sarcasm, and the hard edge in his smile. "Working with Gianni might be exactly what I need to do now," he offered. "But I don't want you to think that my agreeing to work with Gianni means that I'm going back into pro racing or anything like that. I'm racing the Le Scale. It's a point in time, an event. Not a continuing story. And if it were a continuing story, it would be *my* story. Are we okay with that?"

"Your call. Just one thing…"

"What's that?

"If you're going to do it, do it right."

"Which means?"

Paul gave Cal his best cut-the-bullshit look. "Do I have to spell it out for you? Daniella? Rocco? The whole scene here in Bassano. It's a triangle, son, and in every triangle there's a hero, a victim, and a villain. Right now, you're the hero and Daniella is the victim to Rocco's villain. But the roles shift. Today's hero is tomorrow's villain. It can happen in the blink of an eye."

"Dad, I think the time to warn me off of getting involved with Dani has passed. But I hear you. I'll keep my eyes open." As Cal pushed away from the table to leave for Gianni's lab, his father continued to eat his breakfast.

"One other thing," Paul called.

"What's that?"

"Gianni isn't one to tolerate tardiness. So you better hit the road. I'm going out for an easy day spinning. Going to sample some of the local wines. Eat some of the cheese that Asiago is known for. Maybe stop for lunch up there.

That's my plan. You, on the other hand, are entering another world of training. Enjoy the suffering."

"Thanks a lot. I'll be thinking about you eating and drinking, while I am puking my guts out in Gianni's torture chamber lab."

CHAPTER 16

Once the physiological evaluation started, Gianni was as thorough as Sherlock Holmes. He started with physiological assessment: height, weight, leg circumference, flexibility, and body fat percentage. When he recorded a number, he would punctuate the data entry on his computer with an audible sigh or a "hmmm." A couple of times, he looked up, peering over his glasses, and stared into Cal's eyes as if he was assessing something beyond what the numbers were telling him, something deeper that only an artist could discern.

Gianni performed all of these measures with a practiced efficiency. Watching him work gave Cal the distinct impression that, despite the high-tech, space-age quality of the hardware, he was in the hands of an experienced craftsman. Yes, it was all in the numbers, but the interpretation, the reasoning that held all the data points together, was an art. And in that, Cal saw an application of science that far surpassed all the testing he had undergone before.

Stepping off the scale, Cal was relieved to see that the reading put him at 170 pounds. This was seven pounds more than his ideal weight, but several pounds less than he feared the number would reveal. Too many *biscotti* and not enough miles. It was a simple ratio — work vs. calories taken in. And Cal knew that he had been on the losing end of that ratio for some time. On a frame of just over six feet, his ratio of height to weight was passable, not great. Cal knew he would easily drop a couple of pounds once he started training in earnest. That would be easy. In fact, once he started training, with the extended time on the bike and longer mileage, keeping weight on would be more of a problem than taking weight off.

After assessing body composition, Gianni escorted Cal over to the station for the VO2-max assessment. The apparatus was familiar: a simple bike mounted in a stand with the rear wheel placed against a smaller rotor to provide resistance. Then came the "snorkel," a mouthpiece slid between Cal's teeth, sealed with his lips. And the final touch, a nose clamp, to ensure that the gas exchange of oxygen to carbon dioxide was measured. This test measured his lung capacity, how much oxygen his body was capable of processing at its max, and how efficient his body was in processing oxygen. It was like measuring the size of an engine and its fuel efficiency.

As Gianni slid the snorkel into Cal's mouth, he felt the first, vague twinges of anxiety. He anticipated what was coming. With the mouthpiece between his lips and his nose clamped shut, a claustrophobic sensation enveloped him. He drew in a deep breath through the mouthpiece and settled into the frame of the bike. He told himself to relax, but the words just bounced off his brain. Connected to all the gear, wired and enclosed, relaxation was a distant wish. Cal focused on his breathing. Slow and steady inhale. Extended exhale. Repeat. Try to bring the heart rate down. For the next few minutes, he turned the pedals of the bike with the least possible resistance, 50 watts, the power that it would take to barely stay upright going down the road.

"Are you ready?" asked Gianni.

"Aaa-haaanh," garbled Cal. He knew the protocol. For the next half hour, the apparatus would measure the intake of oxygen and compute it against the resistance of the wheel he was turning. The result would be graphed on the computer facing both Gianni and Cal. Every three minutes, Gianni would raise the resistance 50 watts. The first efforts would be easy. Going from fifty to one hundred watts would hardly move the dial on the perception of exertion. In fact, he knew from past experience that he could stay comfortable all the way up to three hundred watts. And so he was. At each increase, Gianni would look to Cal to see if he wanted the next dose of pain. Cal signaled yes with a nod of his head, and the resistance jumped to the next level. It was a primitive form of torture. But all for a good cause. A man needs to know his limitations, he thought. Or maybe that was a line from Clint Eastwood. No matter, it was only a matter of how hard, how long. A suffering measure, pure and simple. Perfect preparation for racing.

From 300 to 350 and then on into the 400s, the effort to turn the cranks began to produce some real hurt. His jersey was soaked with sweat and beads of sweat were dripping off of his nose by now. The feeling of being oxygen-deprived descended on him like a wet blanket. At 450, he started to wonder just how long he could continue. The end wasn't in sight, yet. But he knew it was out there. At 550? At 600? He wasn't in prime shape, so he knew he wasn't going to break the power meter bank. But how long before his lungs surrendered?

He made it through 500 with his breath coming in great gulps. He pulled in so hard on the mouthpiece that it stung against his gums. And he exhaled with such force that spit and drool cascaded down his chin. On to 550, and the light in the room was beginning to grow dim and his field of vision narrowed. He kept an eye on the computer screen in front of him, begging the timer to move faster. It seemed to be frozen. Three more minutes, he told himself. Or at least two thirty, or two twenty-five. Was the clock even moving?

With ten seconds left before the next jump to 600, he hit the existential zone. What the fuck was he doing? Could he continue? Here's where it gets interesting, he told himself in a futile effort to turn pain into curiosity. Every fiber in his body knew the end was coming. He tried to calm himself and focus on just getting the cranks around at a reasonable rate. He wanted the 600 number. It was a matter of pride, not to mention a critical threshold he needed to cross to even think about racing again. Even if he couldn't hold it for the full three minutes. When Gianni looked him in the eye, asking if he was ready for the next increase, he wanted to say no, but knew that a yes was in the cards. He nodded his head, even though he wanted to jump off the bike.

Gianni punched in the number on the computer and the resistance increased. Cal lifted his body off of the saddle to gain more leverage and cranked down as hard as he could on the pedals. The trick was to keep the cadence up. If he slowed the pedal speed down, he was cooked.

And then, the inevitable happened. His body made the decision that his mind wasn't prepared to make. It just quit. Like that. He collapsed over the handlebars and spit the mouthpiece out. His frame convulsed as he sucked in air like a drowning man. He stopped pedaling and lay across the frame of the bike, totally drawn out.

"Nice effort. You're still very strong. I'm impressed,"

said Gianni as he handed Cal a towel to wipe away the spit and sweat that dripped from his face.

Cal didn't even try to speak. He simply nodded his head and smiled. Yes, he thought. Nice effort, but they both knew it was good, not great, certainly not good enough to win anything on the pro circuit. But considering that he really hadn't trained in three years, it was a damned good place to start.

Besides providing baseline measures, the test was good for pitting Cal against the pain again, to make him experience it vividly and force him to recall some of the battle strategies he would need to deploy against the pain. Running from pain never worked, he remembered. You can't outrun it. You have to bring it close. Embrace it and detach from it emotionally. Be a scientist studying your own pain. That had worked for him before, but he feared he was too out of practice to be able to do it again, on Le Scale.

Still soaked in sweat, but breathing a little more comfortably, Cal took a seat next to Gianni, who was scrutinizing the numbers on the computer printout. Numbers on a graph never won a race, but they told a story. For riders, they were a map of sorts, and would guide the protocol for the next block of training. Cal scanned the charts with an anxious feeling in his chest. The charts wouldn't make or break his day, but they would tell him where he stood and what he would need to do to get to a competitive level.

Cal studied Gianni's face for a clue. Gianni was pouring over the charts like they were sacred texts. He punctuated his study with frequent grunts, "ums," and "ah-has." Finally, Gianni lifted his head and looked at him with a big smile.

"Very impressive. Very impressive. Let's see. Height, 1.8 meters, a bit tall for a rider, but your weight is good, seventy-seven kilos. You should get down to seventy-three or seventy-four to be effective, but that will come with time. Your body fat is at 16 percent, a little high, but we can watch that decline as you ride more. From now on, the diet is strict. Pasta in limited portions, no bread. Lots of protein. You'll need it."

Cal was not surprised to hear the prescription about his diet. In the past three years of his "retirement," he had come to enjoy the normal diet of a healthy, young adult. Eat what you want, when you are hungry, and stop eating when you are full — nothing like the austerity that cycling pros have to endure when it comes to calorie intake. Professional riders watch their consumption like anorexics. Cal remembered one of his first professional camps and the look on the other riders' faces when they saw him commit the crime of putting mayonnaise on a sandwich. Finally, one of the team's older riders asked him, "What are you doing?" and pointed to the mayonnaise like it was poison. Before Cal could offer a legitimate answer to this seemingly obvious question, the pro interjected the information that the little spread of mayonnaise was adding 300 calories to the sandwich and did he know what that would translate to in terms of weight that he would have to drag up the hill that afternoon? Like a physicist with a mental calculator, he went on to break it down to power output, calorie consumption, time, and finally, with no mercy, pain. This kind of scrutiny took place at every meal.

Visions of heaping risotto danced in his mind. "Shit. This is Italy, land of pasta and gelato. You might as well tell me that I'm going to prison."

"Prison will seem like a holiday for you when we get into the serious training. Don't worry, though, you'll see results and you'll be happier. Skinnier, but happier."

"What about the power ratings and the other measures?"

Here, Gianni began to get truly enthusiastic. "These numbers are good. Your peak power is high. Of course, that's perhaps only a measure of your pain tolerance. You know the formula; it's all about the ratio of power to weight. You're an engine pushing mass up the hill, down the road. To be competitive with the big boys, you have to be able to sustain seven watts for every kilogram you're carrying in the mountains. On the flats? Another story, there you can push some mass without worrying about carrying it up the side of a hill. But Le Scale is a climb. So do the math."

Cal was already calculating. Seventy seven kilos. Times seven. Northward of 535 watts. For how long? Cal had seen the numbers. He could hit that wattage, but holding it? He knew that kind of effort. He had experienced it before. It was a form of death. It made you delirious. It made you beg to quit.

Gianni saw Cal's face. "Be calm. Five thirty is for climbing in the Alps or the Pyrénées. This is a local race and the group you're competing against isn't world class. You aren't going to find a Pantani in the group, and by the time you hit the line, you'll be down from seventy-seven."

"Yeah, that's what I was afraid of." Cal imagined plates of pasta passing him by.

"Maybe you drop one or two kilos. But not too much in too short a time. You don't want to lose muscle. You have the ability to power through the pain. I just saw it. But here's the real story. It's in your VO2-max. It's innate, God-given. Some have a talent for processing oxygen. Others aren't so lucky. There've been gifted winners with low VO2-max ratings, but not many. Having a high VO2-max is like admission into a privileged fraternity, a pass into a special club. Yours is interesting."

"What's so *interesting* about it?"

"Well," Gianni replied, "sometimes, we put too much attention on the numbers, as if they make the rider. But let's consider. Lance Armstrong, a rider many consider to be one of the best of the modern era, had a remarkable VO2-max. His peaked out at eighty-five. One of the highest ever recorded in a professional cyclist. Rocco's is quite high, too. He comes in at the low eighties, 80.7 to be precise. Sometimes, I think that's his IQ, not his VO2-max, but that's another story."

"And mine?" asked Cal.

"Well, I'd want to check it again to be sure, but right now it reads at 83. Cal, you have a gift. How you will use it is up to you."

Cal thought back to the same tests he took with T Mobile. Gerhardt took many of the same tests, but the results, particularly on measures like VO2-max, were guarded like state secrets, for fear that they would unduly influence their efforts. Gerhardt in particular believed that it was better for riders not to know what their potential was. He feared that the riders with strong profiles would rest on their numbers and the riders with low numbers would give up. Most of the riders considered this to be a little patronizing, but it was the team rule, or more accurately, the director's rule—so, it was law. And keeping information like your VO2-max private reinforced Gerhardt's control. Cal immediately liked the idea that Gianni was willing to share the information.

"What all this means," Gianni said, "is that you're going to work like hell for the next sessions, which you were going to do anyway. We can't expect miracles in such a short time, but you have a reservoir of experience that will help you get up to speed. Your body will react quickly as you remind it of what is demanded in the saddle. You'll ride with the SD team, starting tomorrow. These are controlled rides. It's training, not racing. I'm going to install a wattage meter on your bike. You can't ride without knowing what your body is doing. Each day. You'll get an outline of what you're to do. Follow it. No two riders are the same, so, no two daily schedules are the same. You ride to the numbers, to the wattage, and the zone that's recommended — not to compete with each other. You're a team member now. No cowboy efforts, as you call them in the US."

Assured that he had made his point, Gianni crossed the room to a closet and pulled out a package. He tossed it to Cal. Cal opened the wrapper and pulled out the SD kit, the flaming red shorts and red jersey emblazoned with the Squado Diavolo name and logo. Cal looked at the gear with mixed feelings. Nice to be part of a team again. But this team? With Rocco and his crew? He felt no loyalty to anyone but Gianni. Ambivalently, he turned the jersey over and made a show of examining it. Then, he looked down at the funky shorts and jersey he had worn for the testing session. What a contrast, torn jersey, baggy shorts, and mismatched socks, one blue and one black. He couldn't have looked less fashionable if he had tried. Any uniform would be an improvement.

Gianni observed Cal's hesitation and jumped in. "What? You expected to be handed the leader's jersey? Just to start with? Maybe you'll get it. But first you earn it." He laughed and motioned to the door. "Now, let's get on with it. Today is yours to do with as you please. Tomorrow you belong to me. First morning session at seven thirty. Get to bed early, so that you're refreshed. And getting to bed early means getting to bed to sleep. No company, if you know what I mean." Cal flushed with embarrassment. Before he could say anything, though, Gianni answered his question.

"Bassano is a small town and Italians are one big family. Yes, I know about you and Daniella. And even if the network hadn't picked up the news, the look between you two at my house told me all I needed to know. You're both adults. What Daniella does and what you do, and what you do together is your business. Just don't be stupid about it."

Cal could feel the heat creeping into his forehead and the heat rising from his collar. "So you don't mind that I'm seeing your daughter?"

"Seeing? That's an interesting word. And if I did, would it make a difference?"

"Probably not," admitted Cal.

"That's what I thought. But what I think isn't the most important thing. There's Rocco, too."

"Rocco?"

"Rocco? Don't play dumb. Of course, Rocco. Rocco hasn't been given anything in his life. He knows only one way of winning, and that is by taking, sometimes with force, what he needs. He probably looks at you as a spoiled kid whose father handed him the world."

"That's not true," Cal protested. "Right, I may have been fortunate in some ways. My father provided well for us. But I earned every fucking thing I got on the bike. In a bike race, and you know this, privilege doesn't count for a thing. I've never been in a race where they checked your wallet to see who wins." He tucked the kit into his bag, thanked Gianni, and then headed out to meet his daughter for lunch.

CHAPTER 17

The morning wake-up call shattered Cal's sleep. Since leaving the racing circuit, he had enjoyed his late nights and extended mornings in bed; and in keeping with the barista lifestyle, he took the afternoon shifts whenever possible. After a groggy stretch and a yawn, he dragged himself off to the bathroom. Brushing his teeth, he leaned on the windowsill and surveyed the terrain. The sky was a steely blue. Off in the distance rose the imposing, granite gray face of Monte Grappa. His eyes traced the course as it carved its way up the mountain. He started to count the switchbacks, but gave up after he reached twenty-five. This, thought Cal, was going to be a bitch.

At seven thirty, he rolled up to the Di Salvo shop and joined the cluster of Squadra Diavolo riders. There were nine in total, gathered in a circle, shifting from foot to foot as they waited for the morning training ride to get underway. Rocco was in the center, regaling the group with a tale of riders from the neighboring town of Trento who had the audacity to try to out-sprint him in a recent local race. Cal recognized some of the other riders from the encounter on the road with Rocco the other day. One, in particular, a weedy, angular rider with a crew cut, hung close to Rocco's side and laughed too hard at Rocco's story. Cal looked at his jersey and saw his name inscribed on the right hand side. Paolo. He made a mental note to keep an eye on him.

The group's attention shifted his way, and he could feel their eyes on him. He felt self-conscious, and his discomfort was made even more powerful when he looked down and caught sight of the bright red Squadra Diavolo jersey. Nothing like a quiet entry, he thought.

All conversation had stopped and their eyes tracked him as he approached. Cal started to introduce himself. "Hi. *Mi chiamo* Cal. I'm here from the States and I'm going to be training with you guys for Le Scale. Gianni invited me to…"

Rocco interrupted Cal and turned to the other SD riders. "What our friend here isn't telling you is that Gianni has added a new rider to our team. He's strong. But he's sneaky like a thief. A couple of us met him on the road the other day, so be sure to keep an eye on him. Also," and here Rocco made sure to look Cal in the eye, "he likes to win. He has ridden professionally for T Mobile, so he's just dropping in on us amateurs, honoring us with his presence." And then, with a smirk, he added, "We all know the race up Monte Grappa should be nothing more than an easy training spin for Captain America."

The sarcasm in his voice hung like a cloud over the valley. At first, the other SD riders stood in silence, eyeing Cal. Slowly they made their way over and introduced themselves.

"*Benvenuto, mi chiamo* Lucca. Welcome to our team." He reached out and shook Cal's hand. Lucca was fair and had a slight build—the typical climber's body, narrow shoulders, skinny arms, no body fat, and legs like tree trunks. Probably someone who will kill me in the mountains, Cal thought.

"Hi, Lucca. Thanks for the welcome."

Lucca stood to the side and one by one introduced some of the other riders.

"That one is Filippo," he said, motioning to a shy, dark-haired rider. "He's your lead-out man in the sprints. We call him the Generator because of the power he puts out."

Cal waved a greeting to Filippo.

Lucca continued, "Marcello, say hello to Cal." Marcello, a tall, lean rider with a serious look on his face, moved forward and made a formal greeting.

"Signor Cal, *il piacere e` mio*." Cal knew enough to intuit the spirit behind the greeting and responded.

"*Grazie. Non e` vero. Il piacere e` propro mio.*"

"Don't worry about Marcello, Cal," Filippo chimed in. "His name is *il professore*, the Professor. He's serious and old-school. He thinks that by being formal with you, you will take mercy on him in the sprints."

"No worries, Marcello," Cal responded. "I'm just here to try to get some fitness for the race. I'm not here to hurt anyone. In fact, I'm a little worried about the hurt you guys are going to put on me."

"Well, if it's hurt you're worried about, then avoid this one," Filippo said, motioning toward a muscular, broad-shouldered rider, whose helmet bore the scratches and gouges of more than one crash. "This one is Pietro. He has a philosophy of racing. If you can't out-sprint someone, you knock him down. Right, Pietro?"

Pietro feinted toward Filippo, hand cocked as if for a punch. "If you don't like hitting the deck, then you should stay away from me. You're too delicate." At the last minute, he pulled back and laughed.

"I'll show you who's too delicate," Filippo said. "When we get to the top of today's climb, you'll be weeping like a little girl, trying to hang on to my wheel. I hope you don't mind peeing in your pants on the descent."

"Both of you are writing checks with your mouths that your bodies won't be able to cash," said one of the riders still standing off to the side. He moved forward to Cal. "My name is Tomas and this is my brother, Giorgio." He motioned to a younger rider standing beside him. "We're the Swiss contingent here. And the rest of these guys think they know how to descend in the mountains, but, real mountains, not these mounds around here, which used to belong to Switzerland. Their roads belong to us still. If you're looking for the fastest way down, I suggest you get on my or my brother's wheel for the express route."

Cal immediately recognized their Swiss heritage in their fair skin, blond hair, blue eyes, and strong jaws. He nodded hello and extended his hand.

Rocco had moved to the side and busied himself with a brake adjustment, and now made his way into the center of the group. "Very nice. Now that we're all best of friends, maybe we can get some training in. There's a race coming up and joking doesn't win anything but popularity contests. That isn't of much interest to me."

Cal stood off to the side. He was well versed in the subtleties and nuances of joining a new group of riders, especially a group as bonded together as a racing team. You took your time. You proved yourself with your legs, not your mouth. And you earned your way on the team by putting in the work on the road. Then, and only then, after the foundation was established could you take the liberty of considering yourself to be a part of the team.

Cal noticed that one of the SD riders had not introduced himself. He was younger than the rest, maybe only sixteen or seventeen, slight of build with a baby face. A shock of blond hair stuck up in the air from the top of his helmet giving him the appearance of a rooster. Like Cal, he stood apart from the other riders and shifted from one leg to the other. Cal circled behind the collected riders and approached the young rider.

"Hey, how are you doing? I didn't catch your name."

"My name is Carlo. Welcome to our team."

"Thanks, Carlo. I'm Cal. I'm happy to be here. I think."

"Yes, me too," said Carlo. "I just moved up to the team from the junior team. It's a little scary. Once you're on the road, these guys aren't that friendly. You have to prove yourself to be a part of the group. I'm still working on it."

Seeing the tension in Carlo's eyes, and remembering what it was like for him when he joined his first pro team, he felt a pang of compassion for the young rider. "Look, Carlo. You and I are the newcomers here. We need to stick together. You watch my back and I'll watch yours. And don't worry about being the new guy. Everybody goes through it at least once. Some guys bounce from team to team and keep repeating the same experience. Anyway, before long, you'll fit in, so keep your mind on your cycling and you'll do fine."

"*Grazie*," replied Carlo, not looking any more relieved despite the support that Cal had tried to provide. Seeing the concerned look on Carlo's face, Cal clapped him on the back. A gray Audi A4 slid into the parking lot and edged its way over to the cluster of riders. Out of the driver's side, Gianni emerged. He was all business, now. "All ready for the ride today?" Without waiting for a reply, he walked away from the group and entered the shop through the back door. In a few moments, he reemerged, wheeling a Vespa, and drove it over to the group to dole out the instructions for the day's workout. He was joined now by two other coaches, each on his own scooter. In formation, they approached the riders like hawks descending on their prey. A hush settled over the riders. All heads turned toward Gianni.

"Okay. So today we start the final set of training sessions for Le Scale. We'll have some tough days this week, so I don't want anyone complaining. This week you'll work so hard that the race will seem like a pleasure ride. By now, you all know what's expected of you. Are there any questions?"

The riders responded with silence.

Finally, Gianni gestured toward Cal.

"Good. Some of you have met Cal before. Some of you haven't. Anyway, this is Cal. He's the son of one of my closest friends and is here to race Le Scale. Cal is an accomplished rider, with a lot of podium finishes, so treat him with the respect due to a professional rider."

Cal took the opportunity to address the whole group, using the cover of Gianni's presence to try to smooth things over. "Thanks, Gianni. We all just met. Anyway, it's been a while since I competed, or even trained hard, so try to be gentle with me."

The last comment brought a quiet chuckle from the group. There were smiles and nods of agreement. A couple of the riders signaled their approval by giving Cal the thumbs up gesture. All but Rocco, who glared with a smoldering intensity.

After a quick review of the map for the day's ride and some minor adjustments of the gear—jackets off, helmets tightened, glasses adjusted, and water bottles inserted into cages on the frames, the team was ready to begin. Gianni divided the ten riders into two squads of five, an A-group of stronger riders, and a B-group that was not as strong.

He made a point of separating Cal and Rocco. Rocco was assigned to the A group and Cal in with the B group.

Gianni delivered the day's itinerary. "*Bene*. Today we're going to ride the river route up to the *alti piani*, the high plateau. Let's keep it down to a tempo ride. If you're going so hard that you can't carry on a conversation, you're going too hard. When we get to the road up to Foza, we'll regroup for the climb, which we'll do together. Try to stay loose on the climb. Remember to alternate between climbing in the saddle and out of the saddle. You need to give the alternate muscles a break. Keep the cadence high. Don't let your cadence drop below 60 rpm."

Cal was surprised at the level of detail Gianni was offering. For years, he had been his own coach. Later, as he began to win races and joined his first teams, the coaching consisted of little more than housekeeping details: arranging transportation to the races, ordering uniforms, and organizing rides. As the teams became more competitive and more professional, the training became more disciplined and detailed. It wasn't unusual, at the pro level, for riders to have their own personal coaches in addition to the team coach, which often caused friction. What was best for the development of an individual rider did not always match what a team coach thought, or needed from that rider. But the premier riders, the stars of the teams, were usually given a free rein over their own training protocols. At the highest levels, it was assumed that the training and the conditioning were the riders' responsibility. Gianni's detailed instructions reminded Cal that he was truly riding with amateurs, not pros. Oddly, he found it refreshing. The amateurs still were learning and still had an enthusiasm that was too often lacking in the pros, who were more often focused on the contracts, the dollars, the benefits, and the girls who followed the professional teams.

With an assistant coach monitoring their efforts as he rode beside them on his Vespa, the A-group set out at a brisk pace. A couple of minutes later, accompanied by Gianni on his scooter, Cal's group, the B-group, followed. As they descended to the road that followed the river, they passed through the narrow streets and lanes of Bassano del Grappa. The homes that lined the streets were small, many in the Bavarian style that hinted back to the time when the region was the southern part of Austria. They passed the market, crowded with the daily shoppers picking out the pasta, vegetables, chicken, fish, and bread that would fill the dinner tables that evening. Some pedestrians—young females—called, "Ciao," as they passed. The SD riders had grown up in Bassano. Their victories and defeats were the source of pride, and disappointment, for the whole town, and their popularity reflected the town's loyalty.

On the outskirts of town, the riders began to pass the green fields that fed the region. Cal rode in his pack like a fish in a school. At this point, the riders rode two by two. Cal's limited Italian kept conversation short and superficial, but nevertheless pleasant. He settled onto the saddle, keeping one eye on the wattage meter and the speedometer. Although the pace was casual, he still needed to monitor how much work he was putting out to maintain the easy pace. His heart rate was the best measure he had of his fitness. He was relieved to see that his heart rate was a very comfortable 127 beats per minute and that he was staying with the group by cranking out only 175 watts. Let the hard part come when it does, he thought. For now, I'm doing okay.

He mentally reviewed his position on the bike. His bike, the old Colnago, dated to the pre-T Mobile days. He was still riding a machine with only ten gears on the rear cassette. The new bikes had eleven, and more recently, the manufacturers of components had started making bikes with electronic shifting. Technology advanced with lightning speed: it developed lighter, stiffer materials in the frames, smoother shifting with a greater gear range, redesigned seats, and new composite tires. Average speeds for all the pro races had increased noticeably year by year. Some said it was the drugs. Others said it was better training programs and better equipment. Cal knew it was the jockey, not the horse, that made the difference. Even with all of the technology, the heart monitors, wattage meters, GPS systems, and speedometers, nothing really changed the basics of riding a bike.

Cal leaned into a turn and bumped shoulders with the rider next to him, the lanky, young Marcello. Marcello smiled at him and offered a quick, "*Scuzzi.*" Cal waved it off. Suddenly, the two riders in front of Cal started talking excitedly and pointing to the side of the road. Cal looked over and saw the object of their attention: a beautiful, blond young woman, walking by the side of the road. "*Ciao, bella,*" yelled out one of the riders and made a gesture of blowing her a kiss. She turned her head in embarrassment, attempting in vain to hide the smile on her face. Marcello called up to the rider who had yelled out the hello, "You should be paying more attention to your riding, and less attention to the scenery." Unabashed, the offending teammate countered, "I'm good enough that I can ride and flirt at the same time. You don't do either one very well." This set the tone for the next five minutes as the riders cruised down the road, joking and teasing each other to pass the time.

Over the course of the next two hours, the group rolled together through small villages and up mountain roads of staggering beauty. Once they reached the river route, they settled into an efficient paceline.

The pace picked up — not to race speeds, but brisk. Each rider stayed at the front, breaking the wind for the group for a couple of minutes and then rolled to the back, leaving his spot to the next rider in the group. Occasionally, Gianni maneuvered his Vespa to the front and spurred the group on to a faster pace, or cautioned them to ride *piano*, or slowly, to take their effort down. He studied Cal's pedaling action carefully, checking his position on his bike. He positioned his Vespa close to Cal's side and suggested a deeper bend in his elbow, an adjustment that lowered Cal's riding position and flattened his back, allowing him to get more of his glutes into his stroke and giving him a more aerodynamic profile on the bike.

After two hours of steady riding, the B-group pulled up to a small roadside café, where the A-group was already waiting in a loose group, a couple sipping espresso, others pulling on their water bottles to rehydrate.

Gianni strode up to the group. "Okay. So far, so good. From here we'll turn up toward Asiago. Now we ride as a group — A and B together. Keep it in control. Keep your pulls at the front short. I don't want anyone pushing himself into the red zone."

As they remounted their bikes, Rocco turned to the B riders.

"So are you losers ready for the next section? From here the real riding begins. We start the real climbing for today's session. No more tempo riding. Now, we see who's ready and who isn't." The comment may have been addressed to the whole group, but Cal felt a personal challenge in the ugly tone of his voice. As the riders clipped in, Rocco steered his bike next to Cal, and leaned in close. "I hope your heart belongs to your mother," he sneered, "because for the next hour, your ass is going to belong to me."

The collected riders let out an uncomfortable chuckle. Although he appreciated the humor in the comment, Cal's temperature rose. Confidence is one thing, he thought, but this was a challenge. He had enough experience to know that this kind of chest-thumping self-promotion was a cheap trick, a sign of weakness. The truly great cyclists refrained from making light of any competitor. They all knew that the strongest rider on any given day is vulnerable to a collapse on the next day.

The merged group moved off from the rest stop ensemble. For the next fifteen kilometers, the road zigzagged its way to the summit. The pace started out slow, with the silence of the mountains punctuated by the clicking of derailleurs to easier gears and the humming of skinny tires against the asphalt. Cal stayed in the back of the group, cautiously saving whatever energy he had left in his legs. He had done well in the morning's roll-out, but the next half hour was going to be a much stiffer test.

It wasn't long before the group started to sort itself out, with the stronger riders setting a more challenging pace, and the weaker riders falling behind. Cal was uncertain where he should place himself. Sit in with the slower riders and take it easier, or push to stay with the lead group and be at the front? It was important to stay in contact with the leaders, but at what cost? The road pitched upward. Cal locked his vision on the rear wheel of the rider in front of him. He tried to relax and focused on his breathing, which, despite his efforts to marshal energy, was now coming in shorter, more powerful gulps.

Rocco and two other riders rose out of the saddles in concert and kicked the pace up. An attack. Chains clattered to stiffer gears as the riders put their backs into a stronger push.

Rocco's acceleration was in direct contradiction to Gianni's directions. Cal knew what he would do on his own turf — he would let the lead riders go, secure in the knowledge that this wasn't the time or the place to prove himself. But this wasn't his turf, and this wasn't the time for modesty. He was new to the team and felt like he had to show some balls. Maybe a preemptive tactic would work. He rose out of the saddle, took up his cadence to increase his speed, and pulled even with Rocco.

"Hey, did a bell go off or something? What's up with the attack?"

Rocco turned his head and simply stared at Cal. His silence spoke volumes.

Cal continued. "I mean, I thought this was supposed to be an easy push up to the top. You're dropping the rest of the team." He motioned behind him to point out that several of the team were being spit out the back of the line, unable to keep the pace. If nothing else, Cal hoped that appealing to Rocco's responsibility as a team leader would temper his effort.

"To hell with the rest of the team. If they can't hang on, that's their problem."

The abruptness of the comment came as a shock. Cal felt the urge to school him right there and then about the consideration a team leader needs to have for the well-being of the whole team. This wasn't the time and place, though. He could see in Rocco's eyes that winning the climb to the summit was the only thing in his mind and that with his single-minded focus, nothing was going to deter him.

He decided to take another stab at it. "If you want to save something for the race, you should take it down a bit. I mean, you need to have fresh legs when it comes to the real thing."

Rocco flashed Cal a sneer and snapped back, "If this is too hard for you, take it down for yourself. For me, this is normal. I don't need you to tell me how to train. Either you come with us, if you can hang on, or go back with the caboose." It didn't take more than a moment for the insult to sink in. Despite his better instincts, Cal was hooked.

He dropped back from Rocco's side and surveyed the situation. At the front of the group was Rocco, followed by Lucca, the designated climber, and Tomas, the Swiss rider. Next in line was Filippo, but from the posture on his bike, and the clumsiness of his cadence, Cal could see that Filippo was in danger of being dropped. He was strong on the flats, but as the road pitched upward, he was beginning to move beyond his comfort zone. The gap between the three front riders and the rest of the group was widening. They had made a clean separation. Cal made a quick decision to put in as much effort as he could to catch on. He was prepared to turn himself inside out, if necessary, to close down the gap. If he let Rocco go, he might never see him again. Perception and reality, Cal thought. It was time to start making a statement to Rocco.

Rocco's pace was relentless. Got to hand it to him, Cal thought, the guy is strong as hell. Riding through tree-lined roads that soared up at a hideously steep pitch, Cal wondered how long he could hold the pace. Filippo suddenly reached his limit and pulled out of the paceline, opening a small gap between Cal and the two riders trailing Rocco. Cal reacted instinctively, quickly accelerating to close the gap. Immediately, he felt the effects of his push. He was breathing hard, but the acceleration worked, and he closed in on the wheel of Tomas, the last of the three in front of him.

He cautioned himself to remain calm. The fear of blowing up, the recognition that he couldn't sustain an effort, was the preamble to quitting. The mind plays tricks in that circumstance. You have to be clever, and convince yourself that you can keep it up, ignoring the gnawing fatigue in your legs, the feeling of suffocation as your lungs struggle to provide the oxygen the muscles demand.

Watching the lead trio carefully, he studied their form on their bikes, looking for the signs of fatigue. Did their shoulders slump? Were they rocking their bikes back and forth to gain more leverage? Were they able to maintain a brisk pedaling cadence, or were they grinding the pedals around? Rocco appeared as strong and fresh as he had at the start of the climb, but Tomas and Lucca were beginning to look fatigued.

The sign on the side of the road announced that the summit was only one more kilometer ahead. Now, the games began. Rocco actually slowed down the pace and slid to the back of the train of riders, falling into the fourth position. As he slowly passed each rider on his way to the back of the group, he studied faces, reading expressions. He stared them down, taking a reading of what they had left. He was also playing with them, sending a message. Just the fact that he was making contact and showing them that he had the wherewithal to look them in the eye, said, *I'm still strong, how about you? Ready to go for it?* Rubbing it in and softening them up for the final push.

Finally, Rocco slid next to Cal. Cal felt the intensity of his stare, but avoided eye contact. Acknowledging Rocco's game, in his current condition, would be like a poker player turning his cards over at the table.

His reconnaissance completed, Rocco was convinced that none of his teammates had much energy to put up a resistance. The time was right. He rose from his saddle and charged past the group to the top, hammering like he was pounding nails into the lids of their coffins. Lucca and Tomas tried to stay with him, but quickly fell back. Cal tried to hold Rocco's wheel, but the acceleration was too much for him to match. Rocco pulled away. The separation grew from five meters to fifteen and then twenty-five. As Cal and the other riders struggled to close the gap, Rocco looked behind him and grinned. He called out to them, "Come on, *ragazzi*. What's wrong with you guys?" Bad move, Cal told himself, winning a summit was one thing, but pissing off the other riders, particularly your teammates, was dangerous. Riders are like elephants when it comes to memories and pain on the road. There would be other opportunities to settle the account. But today, no doubt about it, Rocco had the legs to just motor away from the group. When Rocco slid over the top of the summit, the gap had expanded to thirty seconds. If the climb had continued past that point, he would have been clean out of sight.

Seeing Rocco disappear over the top of the summit, Cal switched to Plan B. Catching Rocco on the climb was no longer possible. But the descent? That was another story. Sheer physics dictated that a group of riders would outdistance the best efforts of a single rider on the descent. And damn it, he thought, the guy must be getting tired.

At the summit, Cal herded Tomas and Lucca together and they slowed, allowing Filippo to catch up. One more rider made the group that much stronger for the descent. No words needed to be shared. These guys were experienced enough to know that any chance they had of finishing with Rocco depended on a cooperative effort. Cal glanced down the road across the sets of switchbacks. Several turns down, he caught the flash of red. Rocco was bent over his bars, making every effort to be as aerodynamic as possible. Catching him wasn't going to be easy, but with some cunning, courage, and cooperation, it could happen.

One turn after another, Cal's group slalomed down the road. They worked as a unit, with Cal leading the way, careful to pick the best line through each turn. He swung wide approaching the turn, and then cut the apex, sliding through the turn and readying his bike for the next turn. His heart was ripping with excitement. This wasn't supposed to be a race. It was supposed to be a training ride, but Rocco had transformed it into something different, a test of wills, and Cal wasn't about to let him get away. Even though his heart was about to pop out of his chest, he made a conscious effort to slow his breathing. Stay alert, he reminded himself. Stay calm. Mind the road and keep the group together.

Gradually, like a chisel carving away stone, Cal's group ate into Rocco's lead. Cal glanced down at his speedometer as he worked his way down the mountain. Fifty kph, sixty kph, seventy kph—the digital display became irrelevant, though, as he hit terminal velocity. At one point, as they hit a straightaway between the switchbacks, the numbers on his readout hit eighty-five kph. Fast yes, but under control. Cal's tires buzzed over the pebble grain of the road and the wind whistled in his ears as he screamed down the mountain. By now the group was linking turns like downhill skiers.

As they approached the last switchback before hitting the road that led back into town, the gap between the chasers and Rocco had narrowed to fifteen meters. The catch was inevitable now, and Cal was savoring the satisfaction of looking at Rocco eye-to-eye. He turned to his accomplices and laughed. Good job, he gestured. They had worked together and spoiled Rocco's victorious entry into town. His partners nodded back, sharing the same sense of accomplishment and relief that the dangerous part of the ride, the treacherous descent, was now behind them. Cal pulled even with Rocco and glanced over. Rocco's face was a mask of determination. He showed no inclination to work together with the arriving group.

Under ordinary circumstances, on a regular training ride, this would be the time when the riders backed off and sailed into town on the momentum gained by the descent. The road into town would be a place to rest, relax, and share a few jokes with the teammates. But this was no ordinary ride. Rocco poured the power on intent on making a statement.

In a last attempt to ratchet down the competition, Cal leaned over to Rocco and offered a compliment, hoping that it would take some of the edge off.

"That was a pretty good climb. I'm impressed. But you know, putting in an effort like that at the summit, with a downhill finish, doesn't make a lot of sense. If the race ends on the summit top, okay. Then you win. But with a long downhill following the summit, you always get caught. No matter how hard you work, we had the numbers."

Rocco listened to Cal's attempt to call a cease-fire and sneered, "Not so stupid if you can win the sprint into town." He exploded out of his saddle and charged ahead. A quick calculus took place in Cal's head. Tempting to call it a day, but, then, hadn't he just about killed himself chasing this guy? He wasn't about to give up now. He saw the town sign up in the distance and recognized it as the impromptu finish line that Rocco was heading for. Fuck it, he thought, if it's a race he wants, then it's a race he'll get. He snapped the lever on his handlebar, moving to a higher gear, and slammed down on the pedals. His bike responded with a sharp increase and he pulled into Rocco's slipstream. As they approached the town sign, Rocco made his final lunge. Cal could do no more than stay on his wheel. Rocco flew past the town sign and looked back at Cal with satisfaction.

Cal knew he had been bested. Rocco was too strong—today, anyway. Coasting back to the shop, though, he mulled over what had just happened. He didn't win the sprint, but he had seen Rocco's cards. The guy was predictable in both his mentality, always going for the win, and his tactics, always trying to sprint from the front. The guy was strong, but he wasn't crafty. He rode exactly how Cal had ridden in his teens, before Paul drilled it into him to race with his legs *and* his head. Right now, Rocco had the advantage in strength, but Cal was going to get stronger as he rode himself back into shape. On the other hand, Rocco wasn't going to be getting any smarter. That was going to be Cal's best chance.

The two spent riders pulled into the parking lot in front of Di Salvo cycle shop, trailed by the others who had followed them down the slope. The final sprint had taken all that they had to give, and they bent over their bikes gasping for air to fill their lungs. They were soon joined by the remaining riders who cruised into the lot. Finally, Gianni pulled in and skidded to a stop on his Vespa. His eyes flashed with anger.

"Tempo ride, *ragazzi*! Don't you know what that means? Training ride. If you go out like that for the next week, before the race, neither one of you, or any of your teammates, will have anything left for Le Scale. Rocco, you charge to the top like the fight is today instead of in the race. How many times have I told you about pacing? Look what you're doing to the ride. What about your team? What in the hell are you trying to prove? *Pazzo*! Are you crazy? You are like a dog that never knows when to go and when to hold back. You can't push all the time. It simply isn't done."

Cal couldn't keep from smiling as he listened to Gianni blister Rocco. His pleasure was short-lived, though. "And you, Cal, your first ride with this team? You want it to be your last? You don't know these roads? You descend like a maniac? And then, you want to sprint for the finish? And you don't even know where the finish line is? Didn't you learn anything with T Mobile? I took you on as a project. Don't make me drop you from the program before we even get started!"

Gianni wheeled away, shaking his head. As the team split up to go their separate ways, a few nodded their heads as they cycled past. A couple offered compliments. Carlo, the recently promoted junior, approached Cal and could hardly contain his enthusiasm.

"That was fantastic. You nearly had him. Nobody around here is able to out-sprint Rocco. If you had a few more meters, you might have taken him. Shit, you're good. Unfuckingbelievable!"

"Thanks. But Gianni is right. It's stupid to turn every training ride into a race. I got caught up and I'm sure that my legs are going to be screaming tomorrow."

"Maybe so," replied Carlo, still nearly breathless in his

praise. "But today, they were screaming fast."

Rocco was stewing over Gianni's comments and the praise that some of his teammates had offered Cal. He slammed the top of his bike and pointed to each of them.

"Look. This guy shows up one day and thinks he's taking over the team? Not now. And fuck you guys. You're too fucking disloyal. Remember that I'm the one who leads this team. If you don't like it, then you better look for another team."

Cal got back on his bike and headed out of the lot, leaving Rocco to continue the tirade outside his hearing. Nothing would ruin his satisfaction, or the returning excitement of racing. He couldn't wait to tell Daniella and his father.

Deep in thought, he didn't hear the bikes approaching him from behind. He suddenly found himself riding with company. Marco and Paolo were at his side. He sensed they weren't there to offer congratulations, and his fears were confirmed when Rocco pulled up on one side. Rocco positioned his bike next to Cal and leaned to the side, so that his shoulder was firmly against Cal. He continued to force Cal over to the side until they ran out of road and Cal was forced to pull up before he tumbled down into the ditch. He clicked his shoe out of the pedal and put his foot on the ground to regain his balance.

"Is there some problem?"

Rocco was in a state. His face was as red as his jersey, and the cords of his neck were pulsing with fury. "You need to understand something. I didn't become *capo* of this team only to turn it over to you because you come in like some visiting dignitary. Di Salvo may be your father's friend, and you may have been a big-time pro, but there are no gifts on the road. Not today. Not tomorrow. And definitely not on Le Scale. This is my team. These are my teammates and, in case you need to be reminded of it, Daniella is my girlfriend. So stay away. Don't be giving her any crazy ideas."

Cal started to reply, but was cut short by Rocco. "Since you've come around, she's been filled with crazy ideas. Just keep in mind, Captain America, these can be dangerous roads and people unfamiliar with them can take painful spills."

Cal was taken aback. "Are you fucking threatening me? Listen, today I started to develop a little respect when I saw the way you took the climb. I thought to myself, 'The guy is good. He's spent his time in the saddle and he has some talent. He's done his work, and props to him for it.' But this shit? Talking to me that way? Who the fuck do you think you are? I've been squeezed off the road and ridden into the dirt by riders who were a whole lot better than you."

He continued. "I'm not looking to take your place on this team. At least, I didn't think anything of it until now. But after this, you don't deserve the respect of this team, or any other team." He had momentum, and he opened his mouth to carry the argument back to Daniella. But in his mind was Paul's voice, *Fight with your head.* Also, Paul and Gianni's warning to be careful. He pulled off his sunglasses and looked Rocco straight in the eye. "So take your *domestiques* here and turn the fuck around, because I don't scare that easily."

He and Rocco glared at each other, neither willing to blink. Cal wondered where it was going to end. Pushing? Fists?

Suddenly, Cal's phone rang—the tune rang out the old War song,

Why can't we be friends?
Why can't we be friends?

Cal laughed at the irony and shook his head in disbelief.

"Come on," Rocco said. "Captain America is clearly a social butterfly, and we have more important things to do." He snapped his cleat back into his pedal, and pushed off, trailing his henchmen behind him down the road. Already, they were laughing.

Cal dug out his phone, and caught it on the last ring.

"*Ciao*, Daniella! *Come stai*? No, you aren't interrupting anything. I was just having a little, friendly chat with some of the SD guys. What's that? Yeah, they've been great. Real welcoming." Daniella made a happy squeal, and sounded so glad that it went well that Cal was embarrassed by his sarcasm. He played it off. "Your father took us on a tour of the hills today and it felt pretty good. Tonight? Sure, I would love to. Grappa Antica Pizzeria? What time? I'll see you there." Cal ended the conversation and jammed the phone back into his jersey pocket.

He wheeled his tire out of the gravel and rode off, knowing that Rocco would find out soon enough.

* * *

The last encounter with Rocco sat on Cal's shoulders like a weighted pack as he pedaled to the hotel. He couldn't shake the dread of a near miss: He had actually come close to hitting Rocco. The idea of him getting into a physical confrontation struck him as both laughable and upsetting. The last actual fight he could remember was with his best friend. When was it? Junior high school? He searched for the details. Maybe it was an argument over a foul on the basketball court? And hadn't the two of them ended up rolling in laughter after Cal had tried to throw a punch, missed and slipped, and had fallen on his ass? So what was it about Rocco that had gotten under his skin? Why couldn't he just let it pass?

Cal understood that Rocco was frightened, threatened, and immature. Someone whose world was getting rocked by a newcomer, an alien. Of course he would protect his turf. But Cal should have stayed cooler. His father had taught him that. You use another person's rage against him. You stay calm, detached. It was kind of a code that the family lived by. Cool won. Heat lost. Cal needed to keep that in mind.

He tried to shake the heavy feeling as he pulled into the parking lot of the Villa Palma. He rolled his bike into the garage and hung it on a hook. He saw his father's bike hanging there, which meant that Paul was already in the hotel. In his agitated state, he wasn't looking forward to dealing with his father. He just wanted to be left alone. Maybe, he thought, he could just make his way up to his room, take a shower, and get some rest before going out to meet Daniella for dinner. That thought alone, dinner with Daniella, was enough to take some of the edge off.

Any thoughts he had of slinking off to his room were squashed as soon as he opened the door to the hotel. Paul was standing at the reception counter, a glass of white wine in his hand, laughing with Luigi, who was busy shuffling papers on the business side of the reception desk. Paul turned his head at the sound of the door opening. His face brightened at the sight of his son.

"Hey, Cal. I've been waiting for you. Let's grab something to drink and you can tell me how it went today."

Cal bristled. The shower, cooling off, both physically and emotionally, was what he wanted more than anything else. He craved the sensation of the cool water washing away the grit from the day's ride. He wanted to be alone.

"It went well. You know, hard training session. I'm pretty beat. How about we meet in half an hour. I really need a shower." He turned to walk toward the stairs. "I'm going to have dinner with Dani in town tonight. I need to get cleaned up."

"Dinner with Dani, huh?" Paul was still wearing a public grin, but his eyes were suspicious. "Are you sure that's a good idea? You're supposed to be here for the riding, not playing the dating game. I mean, that's what I'd say if I were Gianni."

The comment was like fingernails on a chalkboard. He shifted his eyes away from his father and took in a deep breath. "Don't know how Gianni feels about it. Dani is an adult. I think she keeps her own schedule."

Cal tried to slip away to his room.

Paul was undaunted. "Come on. I'm meeting Gianni for dinner in town in a few minutes, and I definitely want to get the 411 on your training today before I meet him."

"Half an hour…"

"I don't have that long. Come on. I'll make it short."

Cal's shoulders slumped. There was no getting out of it. He followed Paul across the lobby and into the bar. His body was so tired from the day's training that each step felt like he was walking through sucking mud. Typical, he thought. The old man wants to talk, so everything else needs to stop. Cal knew his nerves were shot, and he made a mental note to keep the conversation focused, not to say anything he would regret. They sank into chairs in a corner of the lounge. Luigi appeared at the table with a tall bottle of Pellegrino sparking water. Cal loved the green bottle, the classic Italian script, and the perfection of the carbonation. At least that part was going to be good.

"So tell me about the training session. How did it go?"

"Fine. It went fine." The shorter the answers, Cal thought, the sooner the shower.

"Did you have enough to hang? Were you fit enough?"

"Had enough, I suppose. Enough to hang, but just barely." He sighed. His father was giving him the classic dad-coach look, a staple of their relationship when Cal was in high school. Old habits die hard. He shrugged. "These guys are amateurs, so they aren't that experienced. But they're in the prime of their season. They're race-ready. It's tough. Particularly with that guy Rocco. He's a beast."

"I'm sure it's just a matter of time before you get your legs ready. You're going to come around real quick. Just give it some time and remember what you're here for, right?"

Cal could feel the anger rising. He hated it when his father behaved like a naïve cheerleader. Did he even really know what it took to race at that level? "Dad, I've been off the bike for a long time. It ain't coming back overnight. I'm going to do what I can, but I don't want you expecting miracles." The reference to "remember what he was here for" was a low blow to warn him off of Dani.

"I'm just saying," Paul continued with a hint of apology. "If you want it bad enough, then it's right there for the taking. You'll be back in form in no time."

Cal's voice rose an octave. "Want it bad enough? Is that what you think? That the difference between winning and losing is just 'wanting it enough?' Do you think that's the magic ingredient?" He shook his head with annoyance and downed the glass of sparkling water.

Paul pleaded his case. "It's part of it. Not all of it. I know that. But it's necessary."

"And you're wondering if I want it. Is that it? Why don't you just go ahead and ask me?"

His father gave him a yesterday's-news shrug. "Well, I mean, you did walk away once, but you've said yourself…"

"Dad, yes I did walk away. But it had nothing to do with a lack of desire. There were other factors. Stuff that you don't know about." Cal's eyes floated across the room and returned to his father's face. He fixed his father with a stare. "Don't *ever* think that I left the team because I didn't want it enough. Don't go there."

Sensing Cal's anger, Paul switched focus. "Ok, I get it. Sorry, didn't mean to annoy you." He let a moment pass and then asked, "What do you think about training with Gianni? You're lucky to have the opportunity. There are a lot of riders who would like to be in your place."

"Gianni's fine. Knows his stuff." Again, brevity was the strategy he was counting on to keep him from going off. The urge to leave the table and go to his room was so strong that Cal had to physically grab the arms of the chair to keep from bolting out of the seat.

Paul leaned forward and placed his hand on Cal's forearm. "I understand that you've had a hard day. But don't shine me on. Don't patronize me. You owe me this much."

There it was again, thought Cal. The balance sheet. He was so fucking tired of being reminded of the debt that he owed his father. It would never be paid off. Not unless he did something huge. Something like winning the Tour. Shit, he thought, even then, Paul would want to know what it was going to take for him to win two, three, how many major Tours? Seven, like Armstrong? Eight? Would that be enough?

Cal's tone turned sarcastic. "Don't worry, Dad. I keep the same ledger you do. I won't forget that I owe it all to you. In fact, sometimes, when I was out there, when I was racing, and my legs felt like shit, and I was hanging on to the back of the peloton by my fingernails, and it was cold, and I was getting hammered by some knucklehead who was pushing the pace at the front, and I knew it was just a matter of time until my grip gave out and the pack moved on up the road ahead of me, I'd say to myself, 'Cal, you feel like shit, you're a worthless dog, hoping that the peloton is going to drop you. So then, you can suffer in peace, on your own, in private.' But then, I'd say to myself, 'No, you can't give up. You *owe* it to your father.' Yeah, that's what kept me going. We both agree that I owe it all to you. Can I go now?"

Silence filled the space between the two. Finally, after what seemed like an hour, Cal rose and left the table. Paul slumped back into his chair and followed Cal out of the room with his eyes. He made no further effort to keep him there.

Cal stood under the showerhead. The pulse of the stream was deliciously refreshing, the hot water stinging his shoulders and neck. His mind played a loop of the day's events, the ride, the climb, the confrontation with Rocco after the ride, and then the phone call from Daniella inviting him to dinner. He reflected on the conversation with his father. He had snapped, he knew it. He had overreacted. Shit rolls downhill. He hated losing control like that. He was still pissed that Rocco had won the sprint into town. That marked the second time in one day, first with Rocco, and then with his father, that he had lost his balance. He needed to settle down. He took a few deep breaths, nearly inhaling the stream of water. Hell, he thought, I'm like a boat without a rudder, moving erratically whichever way the wind is blowing. Then, it occurred to him. Maybe this is a good thing. Maybe feeling all this shit is just what I need after three years of living in the doldrums.

Cal stepped out of the shower and dried off. A quick glance at the clock next to the bed and he saw that he needed to hustle if he didn't want to make Daniella wait. He snapped a clean t-shirt over his head and hopped into his jeans. He looked out the side window of his room, and peered into the driveway. He saw his father getting into his car to make the trip into town to meet Gianni.

He pushed the window open.

"Hey, Dad."

Paul looked around, startled by the sound and unsure where it was coming from.

"Up here," Cal called out. He waved his arm to catch his father's eye. Paul looked up and waved back, but didn't smile. "What?"

"Have a good dinner with Gianni."

"Thanks. You, too."

"I will. And I just want to say that I'm sorry. I was a dick down there. I know it. Just really tired. Sorry for snapping at you."

Paul nodded his head and waved his hand as if he were batting away a fly. "No matter. I get it. Just have a good time tonight and make sure you get some rest." He slid into the driver's seat and piloted the car across the cobblestones of the driveway and through the gate. Cal watched the outline of his father's head in the rear windshield until the car was too far away to distinguish. He closed the window and thought, "Yeah. Just tired." In his heart, he knew the truth of it; fatigue was only the catalyst. Fatigue was a convenient excuse. Both he and his father knew the truth of their relationship, and changing it was not going to be easy.

CHAPTER 18

Gianni embraced Paul with the warmth characteristic of Italian friends. They ambled across the cobblestone square, toward Da Silvano. As a town celebrity, Gianni commanded deferential treatment in every corner of commerce in Bassano, but Da Silvano was special. It was not the most elegant restaurant, but the glow in the windows and the aromatic, northern Italian food made it his favorite. The meals were delivered to the table by the proprietor's extended family — his sons, daughters, sons- and daughters-in-law, nephews, cousins, and grandchildren — and they encouraged Gianni and his guests to linger for hours. As Paul and Gianni made their way through the wooden door and strode into the noisy dining room, Massimo, the proprietor, called out a greeting.

"*Buona sera, Dottore. Come stui?*"

"*Sto bene,*" replied Gianni. "*Ma perfavore, stasera, Inglese.* Tonight English, because this is my good friend Paul, from the US, and his Italian is as bad as the food served by your neighbor, Antonio, at Il Frantoio."

Massimo ushered them to Gianni's favorite table, a sheltered spot in an alcove near the kitchen. There, Gianni and Paul could share a quieter conversation undisturbed by the commotion and clatter of silverware hitting plates and the buzz of lively discussion that filled the restaurant. Before menus had arrived at the table, Massimo approached with a bottle of Gianni's favorite Amarone, and poured two glasses. Ordering was not necessary. Massimo knew Gianni's favorite choices, and as for his guest, Paul was to be served whatever Massimo felt was the best thing coming out of the kitchen.

"I see that you continue to milk the glory from a few *insignificant* victories on the road," joked Paul.

"Yes, and why not? I earned them with my sweat? No? Sometimes, I wonder how my life might have been different without cycling. I'd probably be working as a butcher in my father's shop if I hadn't fallen in love with the bicycle. Sometimes, I think my greatest fortune was that I had nothing to fall back on other than the butcher's apron. It wasn't like my cup was overflowing with opportunities. And to tell the truth, cutting meat made me a little sick. I was always afraid of cutting off one of my fingers? So for me, it was cycling, and once the commitment was made, I had no choice but to win."

"Yeah, sometimes I think the choices kids in America have is part of the reason they can't make a decision," replied Paul. "And you give them an opportunity, and they still do whatever the hell they want."

"Yes, opportunity can be a problem as well as a solution. We parents bear the responsibility for making their lives too easy, I think." Gianni shrugged graciously. He took a deep sip from his wine, savored the taste, and asked, "Paul, as your friend and not as Cal's coach, I can't help wondering what happened with Cal. The world of professional cycling is so small. He was getting good results with T Mobile, and then he's gone. There's something that doesn't fit."

"The kid is like the sphinx. And more stubborn than I am." Paul accepted the plates of bread and olive oil that the proprietor's son placed between them. "I guess he got that from me."

"Paul," Gianni said, "you probably know what I'm going to ask. Did he get busted? Was he doping?"

Paul watched the waiters at work and the lighthearted conversation at other tables. The possibility that Cal was doping sat like a stain in the clean values he'd been raised to practice. Paul sighed past a lump in his chest. "I asked myself the same question. I can only reassure myself that if he had, it would have made it into the papers. I would hope he couldn't hide that from me."

Gianni put some bread on his plate. "Here, eat. We can only deal with facts. Gerhardt, their director, has a very naughty reputation for juicing his stars. I don't know that for a fact, but this is something that I hear."

"But I don't think Cal would do it. I really don't."

"Paul, don't be naïve. The boy you sent out into the world isn't the same boy who came back. And in the pro world, results are king. It's hard to resist."

"Whatever, if he did it, it's over now." His anger tipped toward doubt. "Do you think he did?"

"Paul, Paul," Gianni said, patting the air for him to calm down. "For me, it makes no difference. My situation is different. Squadra Diavolo is an amateur team. These boys still ride for the love of the race. They haven't been exposed to the shit yet. And Cal? If he's riding with us, he's riding clean."

"If I found out that Cal was doping, it would be the end between us. That would be the end. It's so hypocritical."

Gianni laughed. "You instilled in this boy the desire to win. You taught him how to use his legs to punish other riders, push them into submission. You made winning the only thing that matters, and you'd ex-communicate him for the sin of taking drugs? Who's being the hypocrite now?"

The question cut, partly because it was true, and partly because it was incongruous with Gianni's laughter. "I know," Paul said defensively. "I know. I just want him to get back on the tour. I want him to catch on with another team. He's wasting his talent. That's what I'm hoping you can do for him."

"You want him back on another team? But, is it what Cal wants? You have to back off." A smile lingered in the remark, as if there were a joke Paul didn't understand.

"Back off? I've tried. But if I do…"

"If you do, what? You have to let this boy find his own path."

"And?"

"And life will go on. In my opinion, Cal is a 'diamond in the rough.' He has all the gifts that a professional rider needs, except one — a belief that he belongs on the winner's podium. You know, every rider faces a crisis in his career. We all entered the pro ranks thinking we were winners. But for most, that's an illusion. And how you dealt with the reality of losing made all the difference. Some give up. Some work harder. Some find a niche as a role player, a *domestique* on a team. It takes time. During the winter training rides, with boots on and gloves, it would be so quiet that I could hear my tires crushing the snow, and I'd have long talks with myself about what I was doing. I loved the training and the work. But it was cold and all I wanted to do was go home and thaw in front of the fire, not take the turn on the road that meant another hour or two of riding in the cold, fingers freezing, cold biting my cheeks, and eyes tearing from the wind. But I talked myself into it. I had only myself to answer to at that point. Today? Would I do it again? I don't know."

Paul let the argument die. He knew when he was losing. "So I should make Cal make that same kind of commitment?"

"Paul, my good friend, you still insist on thinking in obsolete terms. '*Make* him make a commitment?' No such thing. Cal is a young man. He's seen the world of pro racing. He isn't a novice. And for you? It's time to let go of Cal. It's time to let him fly on his own, for his good, and yours. Or maybe crash. It's time for him to choose." Gianni's eyes lit up. "Ah, now. Look at the choices that have already been made for us: *penne arrabiata* and *fusilli con pollo!*"

CHAPTER 19

While Paul and Gianni were finishing their dinners with coffee and *biscotti*, Daniella and Cal were just getting started at Grappa Antica on the other side of the *piazza*. Grappa Antica patrons were decidedly younger and louder than the Da Silvano crowd, and more colorful, too. The conversational din rose as voices competed with the music, mostly Euro hip-hop that tried with little success to match the driving rhythm of the American version. The bar was packed with the evening regulars, some drinking beer, others sipping on the local offerings of *grappa*, for which the town was known. Daniella glided through the door with Cal in tow. Like a snake she slid through the crowd, searching out her best friend Julia, the *maitre-d'*, a fixture at Grappa Antica door. Daniella raised a hand and called out her name. Julia flagged them over with a "come here" gesture, and directed Daniella to a table she had just finished wiping.

After a quick kiss on the cheek, Daniella introduced Cal to Julia. She grabbed his hand enthusiastically, pulling him closer. Not satisfied with a simple handshake, Julia offered her cheek for a kiss. Cal responded with a kiss on her cheek and was about to pull away when he saw that she had swiveled her head to offer the other cheek. She was just hanging there with her cheek exposed waiting for his attention. Oh yes, he reminded himself, a little embarrassed. Europe, two kisses, sometimes three, although the distinction between two and three was one that he still didn't fully understand.

"So you are Cal. I've heard a lot about you."

"You have? Good things, I hope."

"That depends. From Daniella, yes good things. But from some of the local *ragazzi*, not so much."

Daniella jumped to his defense. "What have those *bastardi* been saying? Who's been talking?"

"Who?" replied Julia. "Well, around here, who hasn't? You know how news travels in this town. If a glass is knocked off a table on one side of town, the people on the other side of town know about it before it hits the floor. With Italians, gossiping is a national sport. Especially when it comes to the things that we love the best."

"And those would be?" asked Cal.

"Well, first is gossip about who's 'hooking up,' as the Americans call it. The second, in this town, anyway, is cycling. Or it could be the other way around—first cycling, then gossiping. Either way, you two have hit the jackpot."

"Julia, my business is my business," said Daniella.

"Here?" answered Julia with mock incredulity. "You have to be joking. In Bassano, your business has always been everybody's business."

Daniella wrinkled her face in annoyance. Taking the cue that the couple wanted to be alone, Julia swept away from the table. As she passed, she reached over and placed her hand on Daniella's arm and gave it a squeeze. Daniella seemed to understand the meaning behind the gesture, but Cal could only hope that it was favorable to him.

The waiter arrived to take their order. Before Cal could open his mouth, Daniella told him their pizza order without a pause to even consult with him. She handled it all with such grace and charm (including the smile at the waiter to ensure quick service), that it struck Cal as kind of sexy, and he simply fell back into his chair with a resigned grin on his face.

"You invite me to dinner. You choose the restaurant. You order the pizza. Next thing I know, you'll be telling me what time I should go to sleep and when to wake up. Do you treat all of your men that way?"

"Just the ones who need to be told what to do," she replied with an exaggerated nod of her head. "Why, do you have a problem with women on top?"

"No, no problem. It actually makes me a little turned on."

"Well, I eat here all the time. And I thought you might have a hard time with the menu. So I just thought…"

"Pizza is international," laughed Cal. "We do have pizza in the US you know. And sausage is sausage, even if you do call it *salsiccia*."

"I'm sorry," laughed Daniella. She seemed to get his innuendo, but wanted to string him along. "If it makes you feel better, more manly, you can order the beer."

"Lucky for you, ordering beer is my second-best skill on a date." Cal made his way over to the bar and returned with two frosty draught beers, foam spilling down the sides and light flashing through the amber ale. "Here you go," he said as he placed them on the table. He sat down, so that he shared a bench with Daniella. He could feel the warmth of her body as she scrunched over to make contact with him. It felt good. She pushed over closer until their shoulders were touching. Cal had nowhere to put his arm, so he guided it around her shoulders, which only pulled her closer. He could pretend that they needed to be that close to hear each other over the noise of the restaurant, but the truth was that there was a magnetic pull drawing them together. Cal could smell the fresh scent of vanilla on Daniella's neck.

"I heard about your little fight with Rocco," Daniella confided. "He's so ignorant."

"I get what's bugging him," says Cal. "I mean, it's hard. Cycling is really competitive and you get tired and irritable out there. You've been on the bike for four hours. Your ass hurts. Your legs are cramping. Your body is totally depleted. Anyone who crosses you is likely to get the full fury. That is, if you have any energy left to fight."

"Well, don't take it too lightly with Rocco," cautions Daniella. "His venom is of a nature that goes beyond fatigue on the bike. I've heard about some ugly talk between him and some of his boys. You need to watch your back."

"And. that means…?"

"It means that Rocco will do anything to win this upcoming race. It's a basic part of his plan to move on to the next level of racing. He needs to get a fat contract and move out of here. There will be a lot of scouts at the race. And a lot of careers have gotten their start on the slopes of Monte Grappa." Daniella gave him a look that went beyond the subject of Rocco and Rocco's dreams.

Cal pondered the comment. "I know. This has all happened so quickly. One day, I'm a tourist in Italy on a trip with my father. An ex-rider and damned happy to be done with it all. The next, I'm on some team with a bunch of amateurs with big hopes and I'm back training for a race. I'm not sure whose plan it is.

"You wouldn't be back in the saddle, training if there weren't a feeling for *ciclismo* in your heart. My father doesn't take on losers, or even those who don't have winning in their blood."

Cal pondered Daniella's comment and replied, "I like the racing program, exactly because it's an amateur one. It's made me do a lot of thinking."

Daniella kept silent. She sipped at her beer. She knew there was more to come and waited for Cal to continue. He felt the tug of trust in his heart, pulling him through a claustrophobic little space that he had blocked off for years. His eyes drifted upward, as if there were more safety above, and he started pulling words out of that little space, stringing them together in a line that might lead them both around to the truth.

"You know, cycling has always been a part of my life. Even when I stopped racing, after my T Mobile blowout, I didn't know what the hell to do with myself. I just put a lot of energy into making it clear to everyone that I wasn't a racer anymore."

"That's not much to build a life story on."

"I know that now. I guess I even knew it back then, but didn't know what else there was for me. And then there was my father. I knew how disappointed he was. And I knew that his disappointment and my disappointment needed to be kept apart. But I didn't know how to do it."

"And now?" prompted Daniella.

"And now, I think it's easier somehow. I think this trip has been a good experience for us. We're fighting, but it feels strangely good."

"How?"

"I can't say exactly. Nothing too dramatic, I suppose. But training with Gianni and SD is a start. You know, your father never insisted that I had to race Le Scale. It just was a kind of, I don't know, seduction. And that's what I think I needed to have, a seduction."

Daniella smiled. "You need another seduction? I think I know just the person to provide this 'seduction.'" She pressed her leg against his and molded her body against his side. "My father tells me that you have all the tools to make it on the pro tour. I Googled you and found that you had some pretty good results with T Mobile. It seems like you were going to make it on their Tour de France team. It's all very mysterious. You know, someday when you trust me enough, I still hope you'll tell me the story."

Cal grew silent. He weighed the truth. Did anyone really understand the pressure? If anyone would, it would be her. She had grown up in the world of professional racing. And he wanted to believe that she cared about him.

"I do trust you," he said.

She squeezed his leg, and took a casual sip of beer. He twisted his glass on the uneven wooden table a few times, gauging the pocket of silence in the noisy restaurant. It was intimate, and he felt her giving the silence to him. It was his to do with what he chose—break it, push it, or waste it on more excuses.

"The professional life of a racing cyclist is..." He struggled for words. "It just is that you kind of lose your sense of who you are, what's important to you. You start taking shortcuts to get to the top. It's so fucking competitive. And then, once you're on the verge of winning some of the big races, you know you have to reach a little deeper, work a little harder, which is okay, really, because you haven't gotten to that point without doing the work. Suddenly, like overnight for me, it all seems so close, but you know..." His voice drifted off. He heard himself rambling.

"You know, what?" prompted Daniella.

"You know, well, you know that, for example, not everybody you're racing against is playing with the same deck. Some of the guys are taking shortcuts. Some of the best riders, and some of the mediocre ones, too, are fucking cheating. You know that, and you wonder, 'Well, if they're doing it, maybe I need to do it, too.' Because if you don't, you aren't going to get the results, and if you don't get the results, you're going back to the States, back to a shitty job. And you aren't going back as a winner, either."

Daniella tilted one shoulder. "So the drugs. I thought the teams were making it harder for riders to use drugs. I mean the testing."

Cal laughed. "The teams? Making it harder? Hell, the teams are as responsible for the doping as the riders. Who do you think sends the riders to the doctors? Who pays for the doctors? Who do you think makes the stuff available? Who do you think helps the riders avoid testing dirty? No, if it were left up to the teams, there would be no controls at all. They use the riders like horses. Look at Astana, when Vinokourov tested positive. Phonak when Landis tested positive. Virenque and Festina. The teams wash their hands. They say, 'We didn't know.'"

Daniella could see the anger flashing in Cal's eyes. "What about the World Anti-Doping Agency? I thought they were cracking down."

"Yeah, they try. It's gotten harder to get away with it, but you know what? That only means that the teams with the best system, the best doctors, are the ones that are getting away with it. You want to know who's still doping? You want to know who's still juiced?"

Daniella raised her eyebrows.

"I'll tell you who is doping. Look at the podium. See who is consistently placing high in the standings, week after week. Then, you'll know who's doping. The whole fucking sport is turning to shit."

"But you...?"

Cal grew silent. He thought of that morning when he was ready to charge in and confront Gerhardt, to tell him that he was done. No. He was ready to quit. And then Franz had stopped him on his way in. He made his case. After all, hadn't Cal been working toward being a champion his whole life. If he threw it away now, then what?

"My dad used to tell this story," he said. "Remember when LeMond won the Tour in 1989?" Daniella shrugged. She was young then, but she'd heard of it. "Well, it's like this. Going into the last day, a time trial, he's behind a French rider, Laurent Fignon, by fifty seconds. No way is he going to make up fifty seconds in a time trial on Fignon. Fignon is celebrating his victory before the ride even begins. The fucking French are toasting his win, sure that he is going to wear yellow on the podium. But the day of the time trial, LeMond shows up with aero bars and an aero helmet. First time anyone had used them in a Tour. Fignon laughed his ass off. He thought the bars and the helmet were stupid-looking. Fignon loved his look, the long hair and round glasses. Looked like a professor on a bike. Cool. The Euros thought LeMond's kit was goofy American stuff, that it defiled the Tour. So what happened? LeMond goes out, with his silly aero bars and long aero helmet, beats him that day by fifty-eight seconds. Wins the tour by eight seconds. Know what they calculate the aero bars and helmet saved him? Yeah, eight seconds."

"And your father's point was?"

"Take whatever advantage I could get, because a lot of riders had legs as strong as mine. Use whatever you can to win."

Daniella frowned. "Are you saying...?"

Cal sighed. His glass was empty, but he kept twisting it on the table. "Look, it's like this..."

* * *

Cal knocked on Gerhardt's door. It was only seven thirty, and he had hardly slept a wink the night before. His eyes were gritty and he hadn't taken a shower yet. But if he didn't get this over with, he wasn't going to rest anyway. Behind the door, he could hear Gerhardt shuffling closer. The door clicked open and Gerhardt peered out.

"Ah, Cal. Yes, come in." He pulled the door open wider. "Had your morning coffee yet?" He offered an empty mug to Cal and motioned to a pot brewing on the counter.

"No. Let's cut to the chase, Gerhardt. Let's get this over."

Gerhardt raised his eyebrows. "You're so impatient. Well, we do it your way. Have a seat." He and Cal sat down on opposite sides of the coffee table that served as a centerpiece in the cramped hotel room. "So okay, Cal. You have slept on the decision. By the way, you look like hell. Did you sleep at all last night?"

"Not much. What I'm about to tell you is something that doesn't come easy."

"The hard decisions are never easy," quipped Gerhardt. "If they were, they would never be called hard." Gerhardt laughed at what he thought was a clever turn of the phrase. Cal sat stonily silent until Gerhardt stopped chuckling.

"If I understand your position, and Stuller's position right, the only way I stay on this team is if I start doping. And if I do…"

Gerhardt interrupted Cal. "Cal, Cal… you're being too, damned, American, too confrontational. What we said, what we meant… "

"Please, Gerhardt, don't bullshit me. I know what you meant." Cal was beginning to feel the heat rising from his chest as his anger grew. "You said that it's your way or the highway, and your way is EPO or CERA, or some other shit. If I don't do it, then *adios*. Right?"

"If that's the way you see it. I suppose you could interpret it that way."

"Fuck, Gerhardt. What other way can I interpret it? I'm not stupid. Don't play me. So here's what I've decided."

Gerhardt leaned forward and studied Cal's eyes. Cal was a promising rider, but he didn't really have any leverage, so any negotiation would run on the strength of his ability to bluff.

"I'll do it. But only on the condition that…"

"Condition? Wait a second, Cal," Gerhardt reacted in mock surprise. "One day, you're offended at the offer, and the next, you're agreeing, but you want conditions?"

"Gerhardt, I'm not trying to make this difficult. But you want me to lead this team, right? Okay. Then, I actually will get a chance to lead the team. I'm not running the risk of a suspension or of being barred from competition forever, without a guarantee that you're willing to deliver on what you say you will."

"Which is, what?"

"That I'll get a chance to race with the first team. That you'll pick me for the Giro and the Tour. That, if I'm in the position to win, you'll have the team work for me. You'll designate me as the team leader. You know, the number one on my jersey. You'll put the team resources behind me. That's all I'm asking."

"That's all?" Gerhardt laughed. "Your idea of a modest request is unique. But all things considered, not unreasonable. Before Stuller and I even made the offer to you last night, the decision was made. T Mobile needs a win. Sponsoring a team costs millions. You guys don't come cheap. Anyway, I need a win to keep my job. Stuller needs for T Mobile to win or the shareholders begin to ask what the fuck he's spending six million Euros on a cycling team for. Franz is tired and old. We need to line up his successor. And right now, you're it. So of course, you agree with us and we agree with you."

"And for the Tour and the Giro?"

"Yes, of course, for the Tour and the Giro. You get on the program, you cooperate with us. Do what Dr. Steiner says to do, and we'll be behind you 110 percent."

Cal knew what it meant when a manager told an athlete he was behind him "110 percent." It usually was a code phrase for "you keep performing and everything is great. You fail? You're on your own."

"So it's agreed," sighed Cal. "When do we start? What do you have in mind? EPO? CERA?"

Gerhardt looked at Cal and grinned. "Cal, you're so behind the times. EPO? CERA? They're so yesterday. No, Steiner has been working with a new boost. Something called HemAssist."

Cal's head spun. HemAssist was a rumor on the circuit. Some of the riders claimed to have used it. Others insisted that it was a hoax, that it was no more than the pipe dream of underachievers, hoping for the boost that would take them from the middle of the peloton to the top of the podium.

"HemAssist? I heard that that shit doesn't even exist. Or that it did and wasn't on the market anymore?"

The smile of satisfaction spread across Gerhardt's face. "I'm glad to hear that."

"Hear what?"

"That the riders don't think it ever existed or that it did once and isn't around anymore. That's the point."

The conversation was moving too quickly for Cal. He held up his hand, motioning for Gerhardt to slow down. "So what exactly is this shit. And do you really have it??

Gerhardt adopted a professorial tone and sat back in his chair. "Okay. Let's start with the first question. HemAssist was developed in the late '80s as a substitute for hemoglobin in cases where blood was needed, but not available. Like an emergency room or a battlefield. Like all of the HBOC substances…"

"HBOC?"

"Hemoglobiin based oxygen carrier. A blood substitute that helps the blood carry oxygen. Gives the blood an added boost in bringing oxygen to the rest of the body. Shelf stable, short half life, does its job, and then disappears, like a superhero. But I'm not a scientist, so you'll need to ask Steiner for the details of how it works."

Cal nodded his head. "So it clears quickly and is hard to detect. I get it. Sounds like it's ideal for athletes looking for the extra bump. But from what I heard, it was taken off the market."

"It was. The clinical trials didn't work out as well as the manufacturer hoped. People in emergency rooms died with HemAssist at the same frequency that they did with regular blood transfusions, so they stopped the trial and, poof, no more manufacture of HemAssist. But that left a stockpile of it and the product that wasn't destroyed made it out."

"How?"

"Not important. Just accept that it did. I'm a director of a professional team. Acquiring the necessary supplies is part of my job."

"But if it didn't work in the emergency rooms, how's it going to work with riders?"

Gerhardt smiled. "I didn't say it didn't work in emergency rooms. I said it didn't work any better than ordinary blood. That made it a marginal improvement for medical situations, but now, we come to performance on a bike. A whole different story, no?"

Cal shook his head. "I don't know. It just seems too risky, too much reliance on technology."

Gerhardt jumped out of his chair and started to pace the room. His impatience with Cal was palpable. "HemAssist is just the latest scientific advance at our disposal. Why not use it?"

"And is it safe?"

"Of course. We wouldn't do anything that would endanger you."

"And the doping police?"

"They have no test for HemAssist. They look at your hematocrit level, the percentage of red blood cells in your blood. Over 50 percent and you're declared ineligible. But come on, 49.9 percent and you're good to go. We won't let you go above that level. We aren't stupid, and we don't want you to die, like all those Dutch idiots who never woke up because their blood had gotten so thick that their hearts stopped in their sleep."

Cal's eyes widened. Gerhardt, seeing his alarm, tried

to make a joke out of it. "Come on, Cal. You have nothing to worry about. You're no good to us dead. Eh?"

The conversation and the details made Cal's head light. The whole 'scientific advancement' argument reminded him of his father's admonishment to "use what you have." But hadn't his father always made a distinction between legitimate resources and ones that crossed the line? Where was the line? In the pro peloton, the line between legal and illegal seemed to be changing daily. While Cal pondered what his father would have him do, Gerhardt seized the moment to make his move. He crossed the room and picked up a business card.

"I'll call Steiner this afternoon," Gerhardt said. "He's in Paris right now. Working with a couple of formula one racers. He'll take it from there."

"Formula one racers? You must be shitting me. Race car drivers are doping?"

"Why not, Cal? They have to win, too. Don't they?"

Cal sat numb. Gerhardt reached out to him with the card he had picked up. He handed it to Cal. It was contact information for Dr. Steiner. Cal slipped the card into his pocket and got up to leave. Gerhardt made his way to the door, but Cal motioned to him to stay where he was. He could show himself out.

As Cal left the room and headed back to his own, he felt the sun shining on his face. The warmth felt good, erasing the chill that had come over him when he was sitting in Gerhardt's room. So the deal had been made. He wound his way down the stairs and was about to enter his room when his phone buzzed. A text message. He pulled out his phone and saw a text message had arrived from his father. "Check *VeloNews*. Breaking story. T Mobile announces that Franz has retired from competitive racing."

CHAPTER 20

"So you decided to do the drugs?" Daniella was quiet now, her disappointment barely disguised by her question. "You had no choice, right?"

Cal was touched by her attempt to spin it. He swiveled in his seat, uncomfortable with the direction the conversation was taking.

"Sure, I had a choice to make. I mean, I could have walked in and told Gerhardt and Stuller and the rest of the team that I was done. They would have made up a story, explaining that I was leaving the team for one phony reason or another. I could have gone home. Fine. Done. End of story. But I didn't. Next chapter."

Daniella placed her hands on the table, palms down, as if she were studying her fingernails for a manicure. The hurt expression on her face lingered. "So go on. The next chapter?"

"Are you sure you want to…"

"And the next chapter was?" she said, sharply.

"And the next chapter was fucking glorious." He waited, and she didn't react. So he went on. "First, I went to Paris and met with Dr. Steiner. Beautiful office on the Champs du Mars. I go in and first thing I see is he has all these pictures of famous athletes on his wall. He's with

Bjarne Riis. He's with Indurain, Ullrich. He's with soccer stars like Zidane and Viera, and track guys. And the pictures are all inscribed and signed with, 'Doc, you saved my career.' And 'Thanks, you're a great partner," and this testimonial and that endorsement. So I'm thinking that he must know what he's doing, and I'm feeling a little bit better about the whole thing. Not that I think that it isn't a little shady. I'm not that stupid. But if all these guys are doing it, and they're willing to put their faces on the wall, then how bad can it be? And that's where I should have kicked myself in the ass and gotten out of there."

"Why?"

"Because you don't make decisions for yourself based on other people's sense of right or wrong. But I didn't listen to myself then. I went ahead and got the first injection of HemAssist. I was still saying to myself, 'It's not a big deal.' So I took the first injection of HemAssist and Steiner laid out a schedule for follow-up injections every couple of weeks. He drew what seemed like a gallon of blood that he was going to spin and save, and then inject it back in at the right time, not too close to the actual races, but close enough for it to give me a boost. He even told me not to worry about coming into his office. He'd meet me at the events or send someone from his staff for the injections. Sweet. How convenient. In fact, I felt pretty flattered. I was getting the same treatment that some very heavy superstars were getting. In a way, it made me feel like I'd arrived. All very above board."

"And, did it work?"

"At first, I was expecting a pretty dramatic boost. I thought, well shit, I'll just go out and start powering higher wattage, climbing like Pantani, and sprinting like Cipollini. But it doesn't work like that. It's more subtle, and at first, all I noticed was that I was feeling a little stronger on my training rides, and that I could do hard training rides on back-to-back days. And that my max power increased about 5 percent. I mean, nothing like what I thought would be the bang you're supposed to get from this kind of shit."

"So were you disappointed?"

"Maybe a little, at first. But then, give it a little time, and the improvements start to roll up. You train harder. You recover faster. You turn higher wattage for longer. Before long, you're riding like your engine is turbo charged."

Cal paused for a moment. Daniella was watching his face now, and he could see that some of her judgment had made way for tentative curiosity.

"So I had a couple of races coming up," he said. "These are some of the spring classics. You know the ones you dream about when you're a kid and bicycle racing is all you want to think about. You read about this stuff in *Cycling News* or *VeloNews* and think that if only one day you can be in the pro peloton, flashing down the cobblestones in Belgium or flying down the coast of the Mediterranean...

"The next race of the classics rolls around. Flèche Wallone. A dream race really. And now, all of a sudden, I'm one of the guys. I have a team working for me. And Gerhardt makes it clear that I'm the team leader. The rest of the team follows orders. They figure if Gerhardt makes me the leader, he must know something. So they work their asses off for me. Now the thing about Flèche-Wallone is that it's a real killer, an endurance test to see who has been training during the winter and who has been getting fat, drinking beer, and sleeping in. I'd done my work, and now I had the juice, which by this time is really kicking in. So combined with the team working for me, my new 'enhanced' legs, I hang with the peloton. And I'm there at the finish."

Daniella arched her eyebrows in surprise. "Your first Flèche Wallone, and you're with the lead peloton? That's very impressive."

"Yeah, I mean, just to be with the lead peloton after five hours in the saddle was way beyond what I would have expected. Anyway, the sprint takes off and I miss the break. No problem, I'm just on cloud nine because I'm not totally off the back. And in spite of a brutal pace, I still feel okay. I finish with the rest of the lead peloton a couple of minutes off the lead. I'm totally stoked. I'm floating on air. I think, 'This is the greatest sensation ever.' I'm so stoked that I don't even think, could it just be the drugs?"

"Do you think it was the drugs? You were the one who did the pedaling?"

"Daniella, I was so pumped at the finish. I didn't even ask myself the question. And that, I think now, was another turning point. If I'd thought about what had just happened, thought seriously about it, I might have taken the drug thing more seriously. I mean, come on? My first Flèche Wallone and I'm in the hunt? Really?"

Daniella motioned for Cal to pause. She saw out of the corner of her eye that Julia was returning to the table with two fresh glasses of beer. She wanted to protect Cal, so she placed her forefinger on her lips, motioning for Cal to hold the conversation. When Julia had left, she offered an open palm to Cal, indicating that he should go on. Cal looked at Daniella, scouring her face to see if she really wanted him to continue. What he saw in her expression told him there was no stopping now. And he didn't want to stop. The rest of the story had been building inside of him for too long.

"So from there, it just continued. I do great at Liège-Bastogne-Liège. Each race I find that I'm doing better. I'm hanging at the front longer. And finally, I'm feeling like I'm a force. I'm thinking that it isn't enough just to finish with the lead peloton. I need to start looking for some good finishes, some placements, you know, grab a spot on the podium."

"What was going on with the team management during this time?" asked Daniella.

"Oh, well, Gerhardt, Stuller, even Dr. Steiner, they were all thrilled. This is what they'd mapped out. They knew that it wouldn't look good if I were to start winning races without having been a contender before. That would raise suspicions. So they wanted me to progress gradually. So in a way, I was like their Frankenstein monster. Gradually doing better in each event. I mean, we all know about the guys who are *domestiques* one year and lead the peloton the next. It's a dead giveaway."

"But you're being too hard on yourself," interjected Daniella. "Cal, you weren't the only one out there who was using. You have to know that. And to deprive yourself of the satisfaction that comes from doing so well is, I don't know, it's unfair."

"Look, I appreciate it. But we both know it was cheating."

Her expression darkened.

"I've tried every excuse. I even tried to blame my father, at least in my mind. His 'winning is everything' approach. Every time I come close to accepting the choices that I made, the voice in the back of my mind says, 'You used, you were dirty.'"

"So the guilt got to you, and you decided to quit. Is that how it ended?"

Daniella's face was sweet, open, and calm. Now, he thought, now comes the real hard part.

"So no. I was doing real well. Feeling great, actually, and I don't want to give the wrong impression here. It's not like I'm losing sleep each and every night over the drug thing. The funny thing is that once you start taking performance enhancements, it becomes a part of your training program. You just do it. You don't think about it any more than you think about what kind of recovery drink to slug down after a long day in the saddle.

"We were getting ready for the Tour of Romandie. It was supposed to be the final shakedown before the Tour de France. Gerhardt had decided to pass on the Giro d'Italia because he didn't feel the team was together enough. I think it was because he wanted more time for the HemAssist to do its magic.

"Anyway, Romandie is the race that Gerhardt is using to make his final selection for the Tour team. He puts me in with the rest of the guys he's picked for the Tour. But there's one new guy. Another first-year pro, a young Frenchman, Yves Drummond, who he brings up from the junior team. Dedicated guy. He was willing to sacrifice himself for the team, even though he wasn't going to be making it to the Tour team. To him, though, that was okay. He was just happy to be getting a paycheck for riding his bike. We were the young guys on the team, so we spent a lot of time together. Both of us felt that Gerhardt was full of shit. We both knew that Gerhardt didn't give a fuck about the riders."

Cal paused for a second and took a deep pull from his beer. "So when Gerhardt picked me as the team leader, Yves was a little jealous. I mean, who wouldn't be? But he was focused on the team. He figured he was a *domes-*

tique, a support rider, so he should show his strength and be the best support rider he could be. The night before the first stage of Romandie, Gerhardt has a team meeting and makes the call. 'Cal is the team leader for the tour. The rest of you guys will ride in support of him.' Afterwards, Yves comes to me and says he really believes I have the goods to make it on the podium and that he's willing to give it everything he has to put me there. I mean, the guy was so genuine, so earnest, and so clear that he was willing to push himself to see me succeed that I started to feel bad. After all, the reason I'm getting the leader consideration, the reason he's sacrificing his chances for me is that I'm getting the star treatment, which included the HemAssist, the blood transfusions, and who knows what else. Now, I don't know if he knows that I'm using. And I don't know if he is or not. The guys on the team don't talk about these things."

"So the Romandie starts and I'm doing fine. Hanging with the lead peloton, making my moves, and the team is working together beautifully. Yves is hammering at the front each day, just exhausting himself until he can hardly turn a pedal, and then going even further on guts, just to keep me up front. Each night at the dinner table, we all joke about how Yves is my 'bitch.' But the guy doesn't even complain. Each night at the end of dinner, he tells me in his sweet way, 'You sleep good tonight. Nothing to worry about tomorrow. I'll lead you to victory.' And in the meantime, he's getting no love from Gerhardt. He works his ass off, and Gerhardt treats him like he's expendable. In fact, he and I used to joke about it. He would say, 'Me? I'm the invisible man out here.' That's the way he felt."

"Well, that's the life of the *domestique*, no?" said Daniella.

"Not exactly. You'd like to think that the team management knows how important the *domestiques* are to the success of the team. But Gerhardt, he thinks that you motivate guys by breaking them down." The memory was painful to him, and he took a pause. Their food had arrived, but neither of them touched it. She waited for him to resume.

"We get to the third stage of the race. There are five in all, but the last day is a time trial, so there's no help that the team can offer there. And the fourth day is pretty flat. But the third stage is the queen stage. The big one. Huge climb up in the Jura, hellish steep part of the Alps. It's the day when the race is going to be decided. The route is a gradual but steady climb for the first couple of hours, with a last hour of brutal, 15 percent climbing up to the summit. Then there's a killer chase down the other side for thirty kilometers until you get into town and hit the finish. But the descent, it's really technical. Lots of switchbacks and the road is a disaster zone, narrow, potholes, cracks. And there's a lot of exposure. The drop off the side of the road is like falling down an elevator shaft."

"I know the route. My father has talked about it. It's very dangerous."

"Going into the third stage, I'm sitting in fifth place in the general classification. I'm in striking distance, though. Maybe not for the lead, but I'm within a minute of the guys in fourth, a German named Krabbe, on Quick Step, and the guy in the third spot, Sorenson, Dutch rider on Saxo Bank. I'm totally focused on pulling in the time on these guys — if I get enough time on Krabbe and Sorenson, I'm on the podium. And this is the day it's going to happen, or not."

"It sounds like this is the make it or break it stage," said Daniella.

"Exactly. Make it or break it. And this is the shot for me, my first podium finish, if I can make up some time on the guys in front of me. So as we hit the summit, Yves is pulling like a madman. I can hear his breathing and it sounds like a jet plane intake. We reach the top, and I'm thinking that maybe we take a blow and catch our breath, then apply the hammer on the flats into town. Yves isn't thinking about backing off, though. Yves is still working and I'm just sitting in behind him. We hit the summit ahead of the fourth position, Krabbe, by twenty seconds, and I can see Sorenson about one hundred yards ahead. I've got him in my sights. But the road down to town is so fucking steep that it makes your skin crawl. I want to take it carefully. Not push it too hard. A crash and the whole tour is over for me."

"And your descending skills?" asked Daniella.

"You saw them. Good, but not great." murmured Cal. "But Yves is a hawk. He leans over to me when we crest the summit and says, 'Cal, don't be afraid. Just grab onto my wheel, and I'll guide you down.' Which he does. And we're descending like a rock in freefall. My eyes are tearing from the speed. I can't see anything beyond Yves' jersey in front of me. There's no scenery, as far as I can tell, because I don't want to take my eyes off the road. Yves is pulling me up to Sorenson. I can see that we're going to catch him on the next switchback. And then, shit, it all happened in a flash."

"What happened?" asked Daniella.

"Yves went into the switchback too hot. Too high on the turn. I don't think he ever touched his brakes and he just..."

"Crashed?"

"Yeah, crashed. Flew off the side of the road and disappeared. Airborne, over the side of the road. I thought about stopping at first. But I was closing in on a podium position, so I just continued. I didn't know how badly he was hurt."

Cal dropped his head and saw the table blurring—the beginning of tears. Daniella put her hand on his arm and gave it a squeeze. "How bad was it?" She knew how these types of stories ended too often. Injuries, and even deaths weren't that unusual.

"Skull fracture, three broken vertebrae, emergency surgery, a craniotomy to relieve the pressure, and chest tube for the collapsed lung. I didn't find out about it until after the finish. I caught Sorenson and gapped him on the run in to town. I caught enough time, so that I was on the podium for the first time as a pro. I was feeling so good. I just thought Yves was somewhere in the back of the pack, still making his way down. I figured he got back on the road and was pedaling in with the stragglers. Gerhardt said nothing to me, but I could tell that something was up. When I finally came down from the podium and asked him where Yves was, he told me he was in the hospital and they were taking him into surgery."

"That bastard, Gerhardt. He said nothing to you before the ceremony? Left you in the dark?"

"No, not until the award ceremony was over. And then, we all went down to the hospital, but we couldn't go in the room. He was in a coma. I didn't see him until a couple of days later, after we finished the tour. I can still remember the smell of the hospital. You could smell the blood and the antiseptic. I went into his room and the sight was awful. He was all bandaged up. His head was swollen like a melon. His eyes and his face were black and blue. His mother was there holding his hand. He could hardly speak. But when he saw it was me, I could see a smile beginning on his lips. He was trying to say something, but it was so hard to understand. I leaned over him to put my ear closer to his mouth, so I could hear him."

"What did he say?"

"He asked if I caught Sorenson. I told him I'd moved into third position on general classification and I'd held the position all the way to the end. Finished on the podium. He smiled and gave me a thumbs up. I'll never forget that."

"And did he recover?"

"Well, he made it out of the hospital. The doctors told him he couldn't risk another crash. The fracture in his neck vertebrae was so close to the spinal cord that another millimeter and he would have been paralyzed. So his racing days were over."

"So he sacrificed his body for you?"

"Yeah. And this is a guy who lived for cycling. He had nothing to fall back on. It wasn't like he could go home and go to college, become a lawyer or something like that. Cycling was his profession, and his family was pinning their hopes on him. And the day after he gets out of the hospital, he gets a text, *a fucking text*, from the team management telling him that they're dropping him, terminating his contract because he isn't going to be able to race. Now, I can understand not renewing his contract for the next year, but dropping him then. Right at that point? The guy has just given it up for his team. And they couldn't even continue his contract to the end of the season? He's a farm-kid and he needs the money to support himself and to pay for the therapy. They just fucking cut him off."

"That's cruel."

"Cruel? Yes, I guess you could call it cruel. But it's just another example of how this business—and I do mean business, because when you see something like that you wonder if it's really a sport at all—works. Anyway, that was pretty much it for me."

"It? The end? Because of a crash? You have to be kidding."

"No, not because of the crash. I know that crashes are part of the sport. I get that. But what I couldn't accept was that this guy, Yves, had sacrificed himself, literally put his body on the line, for me. And I'm juiced to the gills. The only reason I'm getting that kind of support from a guy like him, total dedication, is because I'm so juiced. It just was so wrong. And it all hit me. I felt dirtier than I would have if I'd tested positive. So the next day, we're supposed to start training for the Tour. But not me. The idea of getting on my bike, of putting on the jersey, made me sick. I quit. I stopped at the hospital on my way out of town. Yves was doing better. He was more alert. We talked about the crash. He didn't remember it. The last thing he remembered was telling me to grab his wheel and follow him down. I told him I was leaving the team. He tried to discourage me. Told me I shouldn't let his crash scare me off."

"A lot of riders can't make the images of terrible crashes go away."

"Right, but it wasn't the fear that put me off. It was the fact that this kid had given it up for me, and the idea that the whole sport was turning to shit. And that I was part of it. I left his room and was waiting for the elevator when I heard his mother coming up behind me, calling my name. She had a package in her hand. She told me that Yves wanted to give me something before I left. I opened it and there were his cycling gloves. His name was written on the inside. He wanted me to take his cycling gloves because he knew he wouldn't be able to use them anymore. I left the hospital, packed my shit, and called Gerhardt from the taxi to the airport."

Daniella raised her eyebrows in surprise. "Pretty dramatic, no?"

"I didn't want to see Gerhardt. He could be so persuasive. I was afraid that if I told him face-to-face, he'd talk me out of leaving. You know, all that stuff about the history of the sport, and the promise of wins, big contracts, and fancy cars."

"Did he try to talk you out of it?"

"Well, first he tried to make it seem like this was something I'd get over. He told me to take a day or two to think it over. You know, the same old bullshit. Just tough it out."

"And did you?"

"I left the team hotel, went to the airport and waited for the next plane to Paris, so I could get back to the States. When Gerhardt realized I was in Paris, he called me. Tried to talk me out of leaving again. Threatened me, actually. Told me I'd never get hired by another team, that my career was over. It was as good as singing to the deaf. He didn't realize it, but telling me I was done was actually a relief in the state of mind I was in."

"But to quit? Like that? Yves was doing his job. He knew what he was getting into."

Cal shrugged. "It may have been his job. And it may have been mine to take the drugs. But I freaked out. I didn't want anything to do with cycling anymore."

"And that was the end?"

"Pretty much. I got a few calls from Gerhardt and from Stuller, trying to get me to come back. I even heard from some of the domestic US teams, but I wasn't in any state of mind to listen to what they had to say. I moved back in with my folks. Nice, huh? Twenty-five years old and I'm living at home."

Daniella smiled patiently. "You're talking to an Italian woman. Italian men stay at home until they have another woman to take care of them. And even then, they bring their laundry home and stop by for *mortadella* sandwiches. Your mom took you in because she loved you."

"Or because I was such a mess that I didn't have any other plans. Anyway, I took a job in town. Didn't even unpack my bike for another two months. The checks stopped coming in the day I left. So I guess that was the end of my professional career."

"And your family? How did they take it?"

"I never told them the story. My mother was supportive, of course. That's what moms do. My father? He would just come home and look at me like I was an alien living in his house. Total disconnect."

"He must have been disappointed."

"Sure. It would crush him if he knew I was doping. I'm just so embarrassed…"

He opened his hands, as if he could take the whole story in his hands and crush it into a ball and throw it aside — but the truth was there, huge and immovable. Daniella sensed his pain and pulled him into her arms. She placed a kiss on his cheek and whispered into his ear. "What happened is over. What you did is in the past. The thing now is to look at the present. You have a chance to start over. And putting yourself into the here and now, training for Le Scale, giving it your best, these are the things to do that would honor the commitment that Yves made for you. That's the way to move forward and let the past stay where it belongs."

"Move forward? Yeah, I'd like to… if I knew what it meant."

Daniella turned and faced Cal. She put a piece of pizza on his plate, and it was still hot enough for the cheese to stretch. She waved to Julia for more beers. Then, she put her hands on his, and smiled. "I have one request for your future, and it's a simple one."

"And?"

"I'm racing tomorrow afternoon, a small regional mountain bike race. Not much, considering what you've seen and been in, but I'd love it if you'd come to watch."

"Argh. Your father has a long training ride scheduled. Another four-hour slog through the foothills north of here. I don't know if I can make it, but I really, really want to."

"Come on. Talk with him. It will be fun. And since I've watched you work your magic on the bike, I'd like you to see some of mine." She guided the wedge of pizza into his mouth. "I'll talk to him, too. Trust me."

* * *

Cal met with Gianni early the next morning to plead his case before the team gathered for their training session. He wanted to, needed to, watch Daniella in her race. Gianni was skeptical at first, but Daniella had already worked on him, and he eventually relented with a compromise. Instead of doing the full ride with the SD team, Cal would cut off from the primary route an hour early and take the direct route over Monte Grappa via Feltre instead of the planned route around it. The fierce climb over the mountain seemed like a fair concession for the opportunity to watch Daniella's race. The climb would be punishing, but it also offered an opportunity to get a little extra time on Monte Grappa before the race.

Several of the riders, sensing an opportunity to shorten a long day in the saddle, "volunteered" to accompany him, but Gianni silenced them with a look. When the turn-off for the short cut appeared, Cal slid off from the back of the pack, hoping to make a quiet exit.

"See you on the other side. Hope you don't get lost going over the top," called out Filippo. He was joined in his teasing by several of the other riders, including Marcello. "We know where you're going. Give Daniella our best. Maybe you should enter the race with her and pull her to victory."

"Are you kidding?" shouted Tomas. "If he entered the race with Daniella, it would be her pulling him, not the other way around. I don't know if this roadie has ever put his butt on a mountain bike."

Cal took the teasing in good nature and set out on the climb. He settled in for what he knew would be a long pull up grades that topped out at 14 percent in spots. Riding by himself was a pleasant departure. One of the things Cal had always enjoyed about riding was the opportunity to spend solitary time and take in scenery and places that were only blurs from a car window. Dropping his chain onto the smaller chain ring and shifting to the lowest cog, he settled in for a leisurely climb. He spent the next hour winding up the shoulder of Monte Grappa.

It was a clear day in the Veneto region, and as he climbed, he was able to see all the way to the city of Vicenza, almost seventy-five kilometers away. The vista before him was dotted with small towns, notable for the clusters of red-roofed homes. Between the clusters of homes, small family farms and green fields filled the space. There was no automobile traffic. He lost himself in the sounds of his tires against the road, his chain rolling around the gears, and the steady inhale and exhale of his respiration. It was an enchanting way to spend an hour, even if it did tax his sore legs to power up the hill. After hitting the summit, he raced on the descent, hoping to catch Daniella before the start of the race.

Below the tree line and around the bend, a gathering of a few cars and a cluster of riders filled the roadside by a bright blue tent. Cal saw Daniella just as she was leaving the registration table, headed toward her teammates. He rode his bike over to her.

"Whew, I didn't know if I was going to make it on time. Your father made me climb over the mountain in exchange for leaving the ride."

"Yes, I know," replied Daniella. "I talked to him last night. We both decided that it was a fair tradeoff. Did you enjoy it?"

"You arranged that? You're as bad as your father when it comes to training regimens. The truth? I actually did enjoy it. Great views. Nice road. No traffic. And a killer descent."

"Well, the idea wasn't for you to take a scenic spin. The idea was to make you work for the pleasure of watching me race. But it doesn't hurt that you had a good time."

"Thanks," said Cal with exaggerated gratitude. "But I'm glad I made it over here before the start. There's something I want to give you—for the race, for good luck." Cal reached behind him into his jersey pocket and pulled out a small package. He handed her a newspaper-wrapped bundle tied with string, protected from his sweat in a plastic bag. Daniella looked at it with surprise. She accepted the package and slowly unwrapped it, shifting her eyes from Cal to the package, with a hint of curiosity mixed with suspicion. When she finished unwrapping the newspaper, what she found inside puzzled her.

"Gloves? Riding gloves?" She turned the gloves around and studied them. They were white gloves, perforated calfskin, with a velcro closure at the wrist. At the fingers and thumb, the white was smudged with streaks of gray, worn down against handlebars and shifters.

"Yes, but look inside," urged Cal.

Daniella took one of the gloves and turned it inside out. On the inside she saw a name inscribed. She slowly read the name written there, "Yves Drummond." She was speechless for a moment, then reached up and put her arms around Cal and hugged him. "You're giving me Yves' gloves. But they were given to you. I can't..."

"Take them? Of course you can. I want you to race with them."

"Yves wanted you to have them. It wouldn't be right for me to have them."

"What Yves wanted was for these gloves to continue racing. He wanted a connection with the sport to continue. Besides, he loved mountain bike racing. And I can't think of a better use for them. Go ahead, wear them."

Daniella slipped her hand inside the glove and flexed it, feeling the tight fit and the way the glove hugged her fingers. She turned her hand over and admired the white gleam of the leather and the supple feeling against her palm. "Okay. I'll take them. But just for today. They're yours, and I can't keep them."

Daniella hustled off to the start line, taking her place in the front line of the racers.

* * *

As the race director gave them instructions, Daniella looked down at the gloves and then over to Cal, who had taken a seat on the grass near the start line. She smiled and waved at him, twisting her wrist to make sure he saw the white glove on her hand. Her heart was beating fast, partly from the excitement of the start of the race and partly from the proximity of Cal. In all of her racing days, Rocco had never, not once, shown any interest in her racing. He was like most roadies. He looked down on mountain bikers as outliers, rogues, hobbyists without appreciation or reverence for the sport. If he came to one of her races, it was only to gather with his friends and make fun of the riders. For him, female riders were the sideshow to real competitors — men.

The loudspeaker buzzed on, and the organizer spoke. The announcer called out her name and she stepped forward and acknowledged the applause of the audience.

She rolled her bike back into the lineup, where the other competitors deferred to her, clearing a space at the front in the middle of the first row.

The starting gun fired, and she hung close to the front to make sure she was first onto the single-track. The course was a twisting roller coaster, covering six laps of a five-kilometer trail up and down the nasty shoulder of the mountain. Along the way, there were obstacles of all sorts — boulders, sharp drops, transitions from deep ruts to steep inclines, and a foray across a stream, followed by an angled series of switchbacks that led to the top of the hill. Daniella's climbing strength, combined with her handling skills, kept her in the front position.

As she began the final lap, Daniella looked behind and saw that only two girls were hanging on to her wheel. Right behind her was her teammate, Bianca, whose compact size—she was only five feet and one inch—was an advantage in making her way through the twists and turns of the course. At seventeen, she was one of the most promising riders, having placed in the top ten of nearly all of the races since the middle of the season. Daniella had taken her under her wing and helped with training, race strategy, and all of the secrets of race preparation. She showed her how to pre-open the energy bars in her pocket, showed her the right mixture of electrolytes to use in her water bottle, and even made adjustments to the straps on her helmet to prevent it from falling over her eyes on the bumpy terrain of a mountain bike course.

Behind them was a third girl, Donata, a veteran racer from Trento. She had played a savvy hand, allowing Daniella and Bianca to do the work up the last hill, and was poised to compete for the finish in a downhill dive that would carry them down the face and into a flat sprint to the line. As they approached the summit, just before the sprint to the finish, Daniella motioned for Bianca to move up next to her. The trail was narrow, affording room for only two riders abreast. The coordinated move between Daniella and Bianca closed off the trail to Donata, who, if she wanted to come around to gain the advantage on the downhill, would be forced to leave the trail for the weeds on either side.

Daniella could hear Bianca sucking wind like a bellows next to her. She glanced over at Bianca and smiled, and with her eyes, reminded her to push through it and keep her cadence high, because momentum was essential. As they reached the top of the hill, just before the descent, she reached out and placed her right hand in the small of Bianca's back with practiced precision. She steadied herself on her bike, gripped the bars with her left hand, braced herself against her seat, and pushed Bianca forward, sending her flying down the trail toward the finish line. Bianca exploded over the top and streaked out in front, catapulted by the helping hand of her teammate. She power rocked her bike from side to side, searching for a gap between her and the trailing riders. The transfer of energy robbed Daniella of momentum, causing her to slow dramatically. The tactic of sending Bianca forward had worked.

Taking advantage of Daniella's stall, Donata came around and sped off in chase of Bianca. She struggled to catch the flying rider, throwing all of her weight and power into each pedal stroke. Bianca crossed the line with a five-meter advantage over the closing rider. Daniella took her time down the finishing straight. She saw Cal in his bright SD jersey, jumping around like a madman and grinning like a fool. She was beaming when she skidded across the finish line in third place.

Cal tossed her a bottle of water. She quickly grabbed it before Bianca and Donata gathered around and embraced in a cluster of sweat and dust, laughing and buzzing about the hotly contested finish.

* * *

Cal shook his head in disbelief. It was so different than men's road racing, he thought. Daniella's move would have caused an argument at the least, maybe even some fighting at the finish line. There had been times when a head-butt and a fist were the only things that could settle such an action. But here, these girls, fierce competitors a moment ago, were now rehashing the finish like school kids after a test. In fact, they were making plans to meet for a coffee later that afternoon.

He caught up with Daniella as she was leaving the course, heading toward her car. Bianca was walking with her bike next to her.

"Great race, you two. Nice move at the end," he said.

"Thanks to Daniella, I got the win. You're most generous." She made a mock curtsey.

"My pleasure," answered Daniella.

"It looked to me like a setup," interjected Cal. "If something happened like that in a men's race, there would be a lot of woofing and shouting afterwards."

"Nothing illegal. No cheating." Daniella giggled and put her arm around Bianca.

"Yes, nothing that doesn't happen all the time," Bianca chimed in.

Bianca jumped on her bike and took off, leaving Daniella and Cal alone.

"So what was that? You had a great shot at winning that race. You had the jump at the top of the hill. You gave it away for her? I don't get it."

Daniella looked Cal in the eye and smiled. She was slowly stretching her hamstrings and twisting. "Yes. An easy win, actually. But Bianca needed the points in this race to qualify for the regional race coming up in the fall."

"So you gave her the points, instead of taking them for yourself?"

"Right. It was our plan. Donata, the girl coming up behind us, is right there with Bianca, and the points she would have won would have moved her above Bianca in the standings. Couldn't let that happen."

"And you think Bianca couldn't get the points on her own?"

"Maybe yes, maybe no. But I need Bianca in the regionals riding for our team. I've got enough points, so I can be generous now. Bianca is on the fence. Points now, and she qualifies for the regionals. She rides for me. Had Donata's teammate been in my place, the same thing would have happened. It's just how it works. You understand that, don't you?"

Cal shook his head in disbelief. "I understand it, yes. But I'm surprised to see it. In men's racing, something like that? Dutch World Champion Hennie Kuiper once described cycling this way, 'It's a sport where you eat the other rider's lunch first.' I guess women don't always see it that way."

"Sometimes, it goes that way. But today, I decided to give her my lunch first, to make sure she was well fed. Donata? She didn't take a pull in the last three laps. She didn't deserve the victory, or the meal."

"And then you were all making plans to meet them for coffee? Can I jump in with you?"

"Sure," Daniella answered. "But don't bring that macho pride with you. This is going to be a lady's coffee, and we don't want you infecting us with your manly chest-thumping."

CHAPTER 21

The next several days brought more of the same — long days in the saddle, lots of hills, and a vitriolic understanding between Cal and Rocco that, while teammates, they were competitors for the prize of Le Scale. The psychodrama was wearing morale thin on the SD squad.

As Cal developed more fitness, the gap that Rocco had over Cal on the steepest of the climbs began to diminish. By the last day of hard training before the race, they were virtually equals in nearly every aspect of riding, except one. Cal knew Rocco's vulnerability — his fragile ego. It manifested in the way Rocco would back himself into a place where the options disappeared in the heat of his desire to win at any cost, and where he was blind to any vulnerability of Cal's. In Rocco's eyes, Cal was a fallen star, but a star nonetheless, someone who had hit the big time and, even though he was three years out from his professional glory, he had at least made it to pros. What he couldn't sense was Cal's ambivalence about cycling. Every visit Cal made to the hurt locker on one of their training rides brought into relief the same old questions — did he still have it? How motivated was he, really, to do the work? Was he even interested in making it back? Had Rocco known the inner dialogue playing in Cal's head, he might have been able to exploit it. As it was, despite the rancor and dispute between the two riders, Rocco secretly held on to a secret reverence, an admiration, for Cal. He might try to assassinate Cal's character; he might resent his presence all the way down to his bones; but he could never dismiss the fact that Cal was a "made man" in the world of professional cycling.

Cal rode from a position of growing strength, and continued his mind games with Rocco. He deferred to him when they came to those places where they went head-to-head. He didn't want to rouse his fury and he didn't want to corner Rocco, knowing that he could be dangerous if he felt like he was losing. The effect was not unnoticed by the other riders on the team. And as Cal improved and showed himself to be a reliable and generous teammate, he gained their respect. The SD team recognized and admired his talent. They also recognized his courage in sticking out the competition with Rocco without backing down or escalating the conflict. All this, and a native appreciation of a gifted racer, made them warm to Cal despite Rocco's efforts to keep his teammates in line behind him.

After their last hard training ride, two days before Le Scale, Gianni announced that there would be a team meeting that evening at the shop. Cal arrived a few minutes early, expecting the rest of the team to straggle in as they usually did. He was surprised to see that the whole team was present and seated. Although the usual chatter was subdued, their energy was intense. Le Scale had turned all of Bassano into a buzzing hive with teams arriving from all over Italy. Trailers filled with bikes crowded the narrow streets. The roads blossomed with teams on training rides, reconnoitering the climb, and checking out the rolling hills that led to Monte Grappa.

Sensing the level of focus, noticing the hush in the room, Cal could feel some of the old juice coming back. Maybe Le Scale was a local race. Maybe it wasn't the Giro or the Tour de France, but for these guys, it might as well have been. There would be no going through the motions. This was real racing, and the buzz he felt in the room was a familiar and invigorating sensation.

Gianni eyed Cal. He motioned to an open seat in the back row and began. "So *ragazzi*, you've trained hard and you're as prepared as you're going to be. Tomorrow, a light ride on your own. Nothing too hard, maybe two hours in the saddle at the most. Keep the legs loose, and your blood warm.

"So, we all know the course by now. Flat roll out from town for the first fifty kilometers until the bottom of Monte Grappa. Then comes the climb itself. In total, the climb is sixty kilometers. Most of it is about 5 percent, up to 11 percent in a couple of spots. In the beginning, it's an easy climb. But it gets steeper as the course climbs Monte Grappa. Patience, *ragazzi*, especially at the start. Too many riders have blown themselves up trying to separate from the pack from the start. But *piano*, slow. Here you ride as a group and set a steady, but demanding pace. The first selection will happen over the course of this section. We'll see what riders emerge from the other teams, and from ours. You can count on there being lots of company at this point. Riders from Nove Colli for sure. Others too. At the end of the first fifty kilometers, the real race begins. Then comes the climb. And finally, comes the last selection. The last ten kilometers, the road goes up. By the time you get to the finish line, there will be some sections of 15 percent—real ball-breaking stuff. Here's where the real winner will emerge. Above the tree line, at altitude, the air is thin and the road is steep. Any pretenders will be exposed there."

Although the riders all had years of experience on the course, the description of the climb, complete with numbers, produced a palpable discomfort. The room went silent.

"Now, for the last ten kilometers. Here's where the team will show its strength. We work for one rider at that point. Whoever is left in the pack at this point, we'll see who on our team is the strongest and has the best chance at the podium. Right now, I'm saying that we'll work for—" Gianni paused, letting the tension build. Finally, he shrugged dramatically and finished, "Whoever looks like he's the strongest and has the best chance to win."

Murmurs of confusion filled the room. Not to name a rider as leader was a breech of protocol. The various team members turned to one another with puzzled looks on their faces. Filippo leaned in toward Rocco and shrugged his shoulders. Rocco pushed his chair back and rose to his feet.

"No!" he pleaded. "It's suicide to leave it to the road to determine who's the strongest. I just don't understand. I've been leading this team since the beginning, and now..."

Acknowledging Rocco's frustration, Gianni addressed him with a kind but firm look and said, "I know what we usually do. But this time, we have unusual circumstances. I struggled over this decision, and I feel it'd be wrong to clip the wings of anyone in this situation. Let the ride and the race, and the slopes of Monte Grappa, decide who's the leader this year."

Gianni clasped his hands together and looked out into the gathered riders. His eyes were fixed and his posture indicated that he would take no more questions. Unsettled by the decision, the riders broke up and moved toward the door in groups of two and three. As they filed out to the parking lot, Rocco stood, pleading his case with the riders as they passed, attempting to convince them that he was the genuine team leader and that they owed him their allegiance. Some stopped, but a few brushed past him and exited the shop. Cal stood outside, watching the men casually over his shoulder.

In frustration, Rocco slammed the door to the shop and stormed across the parking lot. Before he reached his car, Paolo caught up with him. "Fuck! Rocco, you're getting fucked by Gianni. This guy comes in and…" Cal missed a few words, but Paolo's voice rose again, carrying across the lot. "And I think Gianni's daughter is making up his mind for him."

Rocco wheeled around to face Paolo. Daniella's name grated and stung like road rash. "No, amico, this isn't the last of it…"

"But, Gianni has said…"

"Fuck, Gianni. And fuck this team. If they want to ride for the American, then let them. I'll tell you one thing, though. I'm not going down without a fight."

"But you don't think you can win without support, do you?

"Maybe not, but maybe the last chapter of the race is still open. There's something that I want to talk to you about."

Rocco glanced over his shoulder to make sure that no one was within earshot. He put his arm around Paolo's shoulder and ushered him over to the side of the parking lot. The two put their heads together in conversation. Rocco was gesturing vigorously, his hands executing choreography of emphatic expression. Paolo nodded his head in agreement. When they were done talking, they shook hands and went their separate ways.

CHAPTER 22

Daniella turned her head away from the work stand in the shop when she heard the door to the shop open. Hearing Rocco greet her father sent a chill down her spine. She had not been face to face with Rocco since the argument in the *piazza* and was dreading the encounter. What was there to say? Or more accurately, what *more* was there to say?

Hearing the door to the shop open, Daniella lowered her head and bent herself over the bike stand, holding the frame she was repairing. She grabbed a balky brake and flexed the mechanism. Maybe, she hoped, if she pretended that she was busy, Rocco would go away. No such luck.

"So the bike whisperer is at work. Maybe I should come back some other time. I don't want to distract you." Pausing for a moment, he continued in a mocking tone. "Oh, I forgot, nothing distracts you." Daniella tensed. She gripped the edge of the workbench tightly.

"Hi, Rocco. What's up? I'm pretty busy. I promised Geraldo this bike this afternoon, and it's going to be tight."

"Yeah, you seem to be busy all the time these days. Busy girl. Busy girl. You haven't been around much lately. I didn't see you at Da Silvano last night. I thought you would show up. I tried your mobile, but no answer. You didn't get my message?"

"No, I got the message and I was going to call, but then things got real crazy at the shop. I'm trying to get all of the SD bikes ready for the race. And I have a bunch of bikes from a tourist group that's in town." The excuse was flimsy, Daniella knew it before it even came out of her mouth, but she was playing a defensive hand, waiting to see where Rocco was going.

"Yeah, I hear you're very popular with the tourist crowd. One tourist in particular."

So there it was. The slap she knew was coming sooner or later. She took a deep breath and wheeled around to face Rocco. When her eyes met Rocco, she saw the smirk on his face. Maybe he did have reason to be hurt, she thought, but cruel? No, not this time.

"I don't know what you've heard. But it's true that Cal and I've been seeing a little bit of each other."

"A little bit? I'd say more than a little bit. Did you think Antonio wouldn't tell me about your visits to the hotel?"

Daniella blushed. She put her tools down and stepped toward Rocco. She placed her hand on his arm, hoping to avoid the inevitable flash point.

"I was going to tell you myself. I just…"

Rocco pulled away abruptly. "Just what? Were waiting until the rest of the town told me? Were waiting until I looked like a fool in front of everybody?"

"No. It's not like that. I didn't know how to tell you." She took a deep breath and let it out. "Come on, Rocco. We both know that this situation between us isn't working out. Not for a long time. The other night in the *piazza*, I felt like I was a piece of trash that you were throwing away. You were making fun of me, humiliating me. And you didn't seem to care that it hurt me."

"A little fun, that was all. You can't take a little joke? That's the way we've always been. Now, all of a sudden, you're growing too sensitive?"

"If you paid closer attention, you'd realize that my 'sensitivity,' as you call it, is nothing new. Once, a long time ago, we were like children, making fun of each other. And back then it was something that children did. Now we're grown and the time has come for you, for us, to take it all more seriously. You take me for granted. What did you think? That I'd just take it from you forever? That you could go on making fun of me in front of other people, and make it up to me by apologizing in private?"

Rocco had no answer for her question. Instead, he shifted the line of discussion. "But we've been like brother and sister. We fight. That's what brothers and sisters do. Daniella, you're like family to me."

"We do fight like brothers and sisters, and that's fine — for brothers and sisters, not for lovers. And it makes me so tired. Can we really have a life together that goes like that? Is that what you want?"

"And this American, Cal? Can you have a life with him?"

"That's for me to decide, without your help."

"So out with the old one. Gone Rocco. Hello, Cal. Is that it?"

"It isn't that simple."

"It feels that way to me."

"I know it does. And it may look that way. But it isn't that way."

Daniella crossed the shop and pulled off her cap. She started to put her tools away, busying herself to allow a moment to think before she spoke.

She looked at Rocco with ferocity in her eyes. She had had enough. "It doesn't matter how it feels to *you*. Not anymore. This relationship between us is a drama with no final curtain in sight. So I'm drawing the curtain myself. What matters is that whether Cal came into town, or it was someone else, or I just left this town, the time has come for us to put an end to this relationship."

Rocco's gaze fell to the floor. He stammered, unable to find the words to express his rage. His body tensed. Daniella recognized his anger and humiliation—his fury was predictable. The words were out, but her resolve was faltering—it always did, and in her deepest heart, she resented herself for the cruelty she was capable of inflicting on Rocco. She knew too well the circumstances of Rocco's life and why he was so emotionally arrested.

When he finally found his voice, he was so angry that his words came tumbling out, one on top of the other. "Now who is throwing the other away like a piece of trash? To hell with you! You're nothing but a racing groupie, following the race to get in on the good times. You're right when you say that it didn't have to be this guy, Cal. It could have been a lot of different guys. Just so long as he was someone who would make your father happy. If you can't make it big yourself, then you find someone you can bring home to daddy, a racer, a big pro. Or if you can't get a real pro, then someone who's an ex-pro."

"Is that what you think? That I'm hanging around like a teenage girl at a concert, trying to get with the star of the show? If you truly think that, then I only wish you'd said so a long time ago. It would have saved us both a lot of wasted time."

"You and I are so different. You have it made here. You can always hide behind your family tree. So you win your little, local mountain bike races, or you can run your father's shop, or you can walk anywhere in this town and find a place to put yourself."

"And you, Rocco? Don't you have a future?"

"Me? Did you forget where I come from? Am I going on to the university to study? Do I have a father's business to go into? Is there a skill that I can turn into a profession? No. I have one thing. Cycling. And you know as well as I do that the only way to move on in cycling is to move up. And the only way you can do that is by winning."

Rocco's reiteration of his circumstances softened Daniella. "And so, you make every ride a fight to the death. You work against everyone, including your teammates. You'll understand one day that no one rides alone. You get to the top by working with your team, and without their support, you suffer like a rider pushing against the wind on his own. You can't fight all the time. Work as a good teammate."

"A good teammate? Teammates are easy to find, and easier to forget. Come Saturday, Le Scale, it does me no good for SD to win and for me to be a support for the winner, a cog in the machine. I'm going to take it to the next level. This train leaves now. And your Cal better get out of the way."

Daniella saw a customer enter the store, and brushed past Rocco. She shut the door hard, and in the sudden quiet of the workshop, turned around to look Rocco in the face. His face looked twisted with pride, like a ghoul's mask.

"If you weren't so fucking involved with your own story," she said, "you might learn something from him."

Rocco crossed his arms, scoffing. "I know he was a pro with T Mobile and he quit. And nobody quits unless they're made to quit. Something happens to them, or they don't have the heart to do the work."

"You don't get it. You don't get it now, and you never did. Never! You can't win on Saturday because you don't have the heart, or the brains, for a big win like that."

The force of Daniella's anger surprised Rocco. He turned to leave. When he got to the door, he wheeled around to have the last word with her. Hurt and anger flashing in his eyes, he spat out, "I never really cared about you. If not for your family, your father, I would've had nothing to do with you. When the race comes on Saturday, I'll win. And I'll do it with or without the team. As for your boyfriend, he'll be wishing he was back in America."

Daniella followed him out through the shop door and into the main showroom of the store, past Gianni, who was startled to see Rocco blowing across the floor, heading toward the main door. As Rocco shoved the door open, Daniella was about to shout after him, but a group of tourists had entered the store and were browsing happily through the cycling clothes. She bit her tongue and saw her father standing in front of the counter with a sympathetic smile on his face. What Rocco had said was intended to hurt Daniella, but the overflow of venom had hurt him, too.

He stepped out from the counter and guided her back into the workshop. She dissolved into his arms and began to sob.

"Papa. Papa. I hate him. I can't believe I was ever with him. He's an idiot!"

"*Carina, carina,* be still. You and Rocco? Well, this has been coming for a long time."

Daniella looked into her father's eyes. Between her father and her, there were no secrets. She was well aware that he had been hoping for the end of their relationship — once, a long time before, he had offered to send her to boarding school to get her away from him. Were it not for her mother's veto, maybe their relationship would never have gotten so out of hand.

"Rocco will be fine," Gianni murmured. "It will take time, but he'll get over it. In fact, you both will be fine. This break between you and Rocco? It's like the chain on a bike. It can only take so much tension before it gives out. Let it go."

Daniella pulled away from her father and turned. "I don't know. I don't know." She paused for a moment. "Papa, I want to leave Bassano. I want to just get the hell out of here. I want to move to Milano."

"I know you do. So go. What's stopping you?"

"Mama, and you know it. She's so damned set against it. She's so determined to make me stay."

"Your mother is afraid for you. She thinks you're not ready. She thinks you'll be unhappy if you leave."

"Mama is afraid for me? Come on. I think she's afraid for herself. That she'd be unhappy if she left Bassano. Not me."

"Perhaps. But listen, *carina*, you can't wait for it to be the right decision for your mother. You sound like you're looking for her permission."

"I don't need her permission," she snapped.

"I know that. You can't worry about her approval or her acceptance. If you go, then you go. The only thing we ask is that you be smart about going. Be sure you're making a good decision."

"And you, Papa. What about…"

"Di Salvo Cycling?" Gianni swept his arm around, his gesture embracing the larger enterprise that represented his cycling empire. "The shop will continue. You think I'll retire just because I lose a good mechanic?"

"Good? The best mechanic in the valley."

Gianni smiled. "Yes, the best mechanic in the valley. But I'm not worried, about the shop, that is. What I've done here stands on its own. And if it ended tomorrow, if I had to close, I'd be sad, but it wouldn't change the fact that I, we, really did something here. Something pretty damn good. I can live with that."

"And what about Cal?"

"What about him? If I said to end it, would you?"

"No."

Gianni chuckled. "And that's exactly what he told me. Now. Enough for today. Go and put your cycling clothes on. I think it's too beautiful a day to be in the shop. Let's go out and do some riding."

CHAPTER 23

The moonless night provided cover for Rocco and Paolo to sneak across the Villa Palma driveway. They crept across the gravel, stepping as lightly as possible to avoid making any noise. Rocco motioned for Paolo to grab the handle of the sliding door that opened into the garage and together the two pulled the door just enough to allow them entry to the inside. Once inside, they quickly closed the door. Rocco reached into his pocket and pulled out a small flashlight. He shined it around 'til he found what he was looking for, the mesh locker that held the bikes. Seeing that there was no lock on the cage, he smiled and winked at Paolo. "*Vede, amico.* This is going to be easier than I thought."

Rocco examined the bikes, one after another, until he found what he was looking for, the distinctive Colnago frame that belonged to Cal. It wasn't hard for him to identify. After all, he had been looking at it, or more precisely, at Cal sitting on top of it, for the past ten days, more than enough time to know every distinguishing characteristic — the chips in the paint on the frame, the color of the tires, the shape of the saddle.

Rocco rolled Cal's bike over to Paolo, who held it upright while Rocco set to work. They worked silently. Rocco reached into his pocket and drew out a small piece of sandpaper. He rotated the tires until he found a section where the tread was already wearing thin. Once he had found his spot, he applied the sandpaper in a fluid motion, back and forth. Back and forth, wearing the remaining tread down to wafer-thin thickness. The acrid smell of heated rubber filled his nostrils. It took only a few minutes. Finally, when he was satisfied that he had done as much damage as he could to the tire without totally compromising its integrity, he shifted his focus to the rear wheel tire. Paolo brushed his thumb across the results of Rocco's labor. "I've seen you select tires for best performance," he whispered. "Now I've seen you destroy a tire. You're good at both."

"Tomorrow there will be a little surprise for Captain America," said Rocco.

"Yes. Too bad we won't be there to see it. I'd love to watch him hit the deck."

Finished with their work, the two conspirators replaced the bikes, closed the garage and stole across the driveway. When they reached the street, Paolo raised his hand in a high-five gesture, but Rocco just looked at the hand and left it hanging. "We don't celebrate until the job is finished. This is just preparation. When Cal isn't at the starting line, then we'll celebrate."

• • •

Cal awakened the next morning and looked at the clock — seven. He instinctively searched the room for his cycling clothes. Then, he remembered. Rest day. Yes, he thought, sweet chance to roll over and get an extra rotation of deep sleep. When he finally awoke again, it was to the sound of a persistent knocking at his door. He groggily looked at the clock, which was showing nine-thirty.

"Oh, shit," he said to himself. He shuffled over to the door and cracked it open. There, standing in the doorway holding a steaming cup of espresso and a plate stacked with croissants and fruit, was Daniella.

"Come on, sleepy head," she said as she pushed the door open. Cal scanned her body and saw that she was dressed in cycling gear. He remembered they had set a date for a ride that morning. It was to be an easy spin day, enough work to keep the legs loose and relaxed, but not so much that there would be any lingering fatigue when the race day arrived the next day.

Cal sat down on his bed and wolfed down the croissant between sips of coffee. He watched with amusement as Daniella picked through his pile of cycling clothes to find a jersey and shorts that were clean. She picked up one pair of shorts after another, held them aloft between her thumb and forefinger, and wrinkled her nose in mock disgust.

"You have someone at home who does your laundry?"

"Aw, come on, Dani. I'm on vacation." Cal turned the corners of his mouth down in a pout and hoped he sounded just needy enough to warrant some loving attention. As he looked at her trim figure in her cycling garb, he was taken by the impulse to pull her into bed with him. When she passed in front of him, holding the last clean pair of shorts she could find, he made his move. He reached out and grabbed her arm in a playful attempt to pull her closer. Daniella fell onto the bed and reached over to Cal. She placed a kiss on his lips and looked into his eyes.

He swung his leg over hers and leaned closer to get another kiss. Daniella pushed him away and laughed. "As your trainer and coach, I think it's very unwise for you to fool around the day before a race. You know what they say about sapping a rider's strength."

"But what about my mental state? You don't want me racing with too much sexual frustration do you?"

"Frustration is good," she countered. "It turns to power, and that's exactly what you're going to need to get your lazy ass up Monte Grappa tomorrow. Now, finish your breakfast and get your shorts on. I don't have all day."

With Daniella standing nearby and tapping her foot with impatience, he slid off of the bed in his boxers and made his way to the bathroom. As he brushed his teeth, he heard the murmurings of her talking with someone in the hallway. He peeked out of the bathroom and saw Daniella and his father engaged in conversation. His father leaned around the doorway and called in to Cal.

"I was going to suggest that we go for a ride today. You and me, but I see you already have plans."

"Today, we're putting the final touches on Cal's assault of Monte Grappa," offered Daniella. "Would you like to join us? It's going to be a gentle climbing day."

By this time, Cal had slid into his cycling shorts and was pulling his jersey over his head. He popped his head out of the neckline and said to Daniella, "Just a minute. What's this about a 'climbing day?' Your father said it was a light day today. Not to get too burned out for tomorrow."

"It's going to be a light day. It's just that it's going to be a light day spent climbing. Don't be a wimp," laughed Daniella. "Save your whining for tomorrow."

For the next hour, the three rode casually through the Italian countryside. Despite Daniella's threat to haul him up the mountain, he found he could actually talk and spin at the same time, and the ride turned into a smooth spin at an easy pace. As they made their way down the road, riding three abreast, Cal clowned on his bike, rolling from one side of the road to the other like a spastic beginner. Daniella imitated his balky style. Then, looking serious, she went to the front of the line and pulled out her water bottle and squirted it over her shoulder, sending a shower of pink energy drink heading toward Cal. The lighthearted fun reminded him of how much he loved the floating sensation that a good ride provided. It was a place and time when things moved more slowly, and all that mattered was the fluid sensation of spinning pedals and wheels humming against the pavement. It was good to be back. Good to be on better terms with his father. He even felt good about the coming event. No expectations. No pressure. He would do what he could and if it worked out, fine. If he got slammed? Well, what could anyone expect? After all, he was three years removed from competition. He was racing, in love, at peace with the sport that he loved, and riding the sweet spot in time and space. Its temporary nature was part of what made it so precious.

After an hour on the road, Cal decided to stretch his legs a little. He accelerated out of the saddle, looked back at his companions, inviting them to take up the pace a bit. Daniella and Paul just looked at him. "You go ahead," urged Daniella. "I'm going to sit in with your father and enjoy the ride." Cal nodded his head. "Okay. I'll meet you up the road."

* * *

"Your son is a remarkable person," Daniella said. Paul pedaled softly next to her.

"His mother and I have always thought so," he grinned.

"I mean it. He's been thrown into a very difficult situation — with my father, with the team. Even with me. And he's taken it on like just another rise in the road. Still, it's not an easy transition, hmm?"

"And tomorrow in the race?" asked Paul.

"Tomorrow in the race?" She clicked into an easier gear to keep from pulling ahead. In the distance, Cal's white helmet disappeared over the next roller. "Tomorrow is going to be another test for him, a chance for him to taste competition again. Unfortunately, I doubt he can win it. The legs don't lie. If he does well, it will be on heart and soul, alone. There will be other riders from all of Italy who want to go home with the honor of conquering Le Scale. The local competition see this as their backyard."

"So, he has no chance?"

"Always a chance. Otherwise, why show up? But, he isn't riding with a team that has a deep love for him. Rocco in particular."

"Cal knows his way around characters like him. I'm not worried." Paul's voice rose a few decibels, and Daniella could see in his tone the tendency to brag. "Besides, I know your father. He's got control over his guys."

Daniella shrugged. She had heard, but never experienced, Paul's cockiness. No wonder he has so many Italian friends, she thought—he fits right in.

Her silence finally got to him, and he said, "What, you don't think so?"

"Well, once the riders are on the road, they're like mad dogs. They make promises on the fly. They break promises just as easily. Their head and heart may say one thing, but then they find themselves with a chance to win. And loyalty? That was something that was established miles ago, which in racing is another lifetime. The pain in the lungs, the burning in the legs, the ache in the back—these things have a voice of their own and they can change the picture in a moment."

"But, none of this is anything Cal doesn't know."

Daniella nodded. "But then, as if the riders aren't ruthless enough, the directors of the teams are riding in the cars and talking to each other over their radios. And they're making deals like they're trading livestock. 'You give me this guy to work with our leader now and we'll give you our guy when we get to the last stretch.' In the big races, a lot of Euros change hands behind the scenes. 'If you work for our team today, we'll give you five thousand Euros.' Or teams will agree behind the scenes to share a winner's prize. I've heard all the ugly stories from my father."

Daniella withdrew in thought for a moment and seemed to contemplate the opportunity for Cal. "Cal is good. He won't go unmarked, unnoticed, in this race. But he is an outsider. He'll be turning the cranks on his own, unless something unusual happens."

"Such as?"

"Who knows? It could be that…"

Daniella stopped short when she saw that Cal had circled back and was descending the hill, coming back at them. "Enough talk of racing. Let's see what happens tomorrow. Today, we enjoy a beautiful day in the Italian countryside." She pushed away the lingering discomfort from the conversation with Paul, but even as they all bantered together happily, it wouldn't go away entirely — and it left a stain on her expectations for the ride, the race, and the day itself. It was bad luck to break off in the middle of a warning. Some believed it would bring the danger to pass.

She clicked into a harder gear and stood up on the pedals to clear her head. Stop it, she told herself. You're just being superstitious.

• • •

Over the course of the next several miles, the three riders continued their playful approach to the work at hand. Mock accelerations, chases, and good-natured bumping took the place of gut-busting, sweat-generating hard work. The sight of Daniella with her tawny arms, muscular, long legs, and hair flowing beneath her helmet, added to Cal's appreciation of the day. If this could go on forever, he thought, it would still be too short.

He slipped behind her and studied her form on the bike. Her broad shoulders tapered to a narrow waist. She sat on the saddle of her bike like she was born there. Her cadence was perfectly balanced as her legs rose and fell in a smooth, metronomic cadence. Cal understood, finally, the meaning of the old expression, "Poetry in motion." And being in love made for the best poetry of all. He had fallen for her, there was no doubt about it, and, for him, at this moment, the next day's race was a million sonnets away.

* * *

"Let's finish with a little climb up to the notch and then back to town for an espresso," Daniella suggested, pointing to a crag that stood out about a mile away.

With a goal, the ride grew more intense. The three riders gathered themselves into a bunch with Cal leading, Daniella minding his wheel, and Paul closing up the rear. The quiet of the mountain road was punctuated by the clicking sound of derailleurs shifting to higher gears. The jump in effort claimed their lungs, and conversation was no longer possible.

When they arrived at the notch, all three riders clambered off their bikes for a rest. Daniella swept her arm across the vista and pointed out the landmarks. Monte

Grappa, his gray face reflecting the sun, glared back at them. The race route traced a path along his cheek like a complicated scar, jaw to hairline to frigid crown.

"From the distance, it doesn't look tough," Daniella offered, as she traced the course for Cal and Paul. Her elegant hand followed the road to the midline. "Where the tree line ends," she pointed to the place on the massive face where the green border ended and the bald granite began, "that's the place where things get really interesting. It's about ten kilometers from the finish. You can always tell it by the little café, Il Piccolo, that marks the beginning of the last long climb. If tomorrow is anything like the past years, you can expect that there will be a small group, maybe ten riders, still together at the front at that point. Most of the other riders will have dropped off by then. If you're with the group at that point, be prepared for the surge that's to come because from there to the finish is where the real selection happens."

"If I'm still with the lead group at that point," said Cal.

"Yes, if. But if you are, you need to make sure you've saved something, because this is where the winner is determined. The last ten kilometers are a dogfight, and if you have any allies with you, use them well, because you'll need all the help you can get."

"Allies? If Rocco is there, and I'm expecting he will be, I'm thinking that I'll need to watch my back."

"Right, don't count on Rocco for any help. My dear, you have to be smart here. Don't think you'll drop anyone easily. Any riders still in the lead group at this point will have done their training. Only the strong will still be there. Now, if you have any team members there, work together. If they're willing, let them pull for you. Don't try to be a hero. Save what you can for the final push at the top."

"And Rocco?"

"Rocco? Who knows? What Rocco lacks in emotional control he makes up for with his strength and knowledge of the terrain. But for sure, don't expect that he'll work for you."

Cal frowned back at Monte Grappa. His eyes followed the road upward. In his mind, he was looking at the course, imagining what it would be like to ride in a peloton again. He recalled the Tour of Romandie. Yves. The crash. Visiting Yves in the hospital. In a moment, he was standing there at the foot of his hospital bed. Then, he came to the real underlying question: Was he truly ready for all that again? He knew he hadn't made a clean break from the sport, not really. His father knew it. Gianni knew it. Maybe they had planned this whole thing to get him back into racing. Maybe, he thought, even Daniella. Was she in on this?

Daniella placed her arm around his waist and leaned her head against his shoulder. "You look worried. What are you thinking about?"

"Oh, nothing, really. I was just asking myself what the fuck I'm doing here."

"What do you mean?"

"I'm going to get my ass kicked."

"So?"

"So? I guess that's the point, isn't it? I'm going to ride tomorrow and get my ass kicked. And the answer to the existential question of 'why' do it is... What, exactly? 'So?'"

"You don't have to do it. You can drop out. Nobody will hold that against you."

"Nah. I'm a glutton for punishment. But I'm the kind of glutton who needs to have a reason to explain why I'm being punished."

"Well, nobody can give that to you but you."

Cal turned to face Daniella. "Tell me. If I didn't race tomorrow, what would you think of me? I mean, between us? Say that I decide to 'no show' tomorrow. What then?"

"Then..." and Daniella smiled slyly. "Then, I'll come over later in the morning and we'll eat croissants and drink espresso. And we'll do that until we decide to go out for a nice ride. And maybe when we're finished, we'll make love. It will be a glorious day. And if you like, we'll never speak of Le Scale ever again."

"Thanks," he replied and gave her hand a squeeze.

"Thanks? For what?"

"For letting me ask stupid questions. For nipping my stupid conspiracy theories in the bud."

"For this," she smiled, "you're welcome. Any time you need someone to answer stupid questions, you can count on me. But look, stop spinning your wheels with 'what if' and 'what about' questions. You go tomorrow. You race. You finish as well as you can. What happens after that — with you, with me, with us — let's leave that 'til tomorrow. Daniella broke off from Cal and clapped her hands, "*Allora*! About that espresso. It's time for the end-of-ride ceremonial cup of espresso."

The three riders remounted their bikes and set off down the road for town. Descending, they continued their playful ways, caressing the road and gliding through turns like water coursing through a ravine. At times, their speed hit northwards of sixty kph, but their grace in descending neutralized the velocity. Daniella's bike handling was breathtaking. She sliced through the turns, linking one after another in graceful arcs. Cal hung on her wheel. The two pushed each other to faster speeds as they carved their way down the hill.

On a straight section, Cal saw his opportunity. He surged past Daniella and, as he slid by her, he reached out and patted her behind. She looked over and yelled. "Be careful!"

"Careful of what?" Cal yelled out from over his shoulder.

"Careful of whose ass you grab as you go by. And be careful that you don't end up in a ditch on one of these turns. This is my town and you don't know the road." She let out a little laugh and jumped on his tail, following him into the next turn. As he rounded the turn, setting his tire's edge to bring him around, he yelled back, "This may be your town. But this is my turn to finish first. So just sit in and relax."

"Relax? You're the one who should relax. I'll relax when I'm at the bottom, waiting for your sorry ass to finish this descent."

Suddenly, as Cal banked through the next turn, his bike made a noise like a gunshot. The sound echoed off the pavement, and the bike began to shimmy. It registered immediately that he had blown a tire, and at this speed, the next few moments were going to be critical. He feathered his brakes in a vain attempt to control the bike. The bike was riding him now, instead of him riding the bike. Like a drunk in a parade, the bike lurched across the road, over the guardrail and headed toward the bordering ditch. Cal clutched the drops of his handlebars. Crashing was inevitable. The only question now was, how bad?

His trajectory had him headed for the ditch; the front tire hit the gravel sideways, dispersing only a fraction of his momentum. He struggled to control the slide with his weight, but could do little more than hold on to the bars and try to free his shoes from the pedals. The rear tire lost all traction on the dirt and the bike slid out from underneath him. He hit the ground head-shoulder-hip, and in a clatter of bones and metal, rolled to the bottom of the ditch and came to rest in a heap. The bike continued on, tumbling and spinning until it came to a dusty stop against a tree fifteen meters down the hillside.

Daniella and Paul's brakes squealed and screeched to a halt as the two dismounted their bikes. They scrambled down the steep ditch, their cycling shoes slipping in the loose gravel. By the time they reached Cal, he was in a sitting position bent over in pain, wind knocked out of him. He had a glazed look in his eye. His jersey and shorts were torn and he was bleeding from his elbows and knee. An ugly red stain appeared behind the torn fabric at his right shoulder and a welt was forming over his right eye. His helmet was still on his head, but pieces of gravel were embedded in the front and side.

Daniella rushed to his side and stopped him as he tried to rise.

"Shit, shit, shit," Cal moaned as he rocked from side to side cradling his right arm. He tried to rise, but Daniella stopped him.

"Be still! Just sit for a moment! Don't move. Let's see what you've done."

Paul had also made it over to Cal's side. "Don't move. Just take a deep breath. Are you okay?"

"Shit! I guess so. I think I must have blown a tire."

Daniella clasped his hand to her chest. She squeezed hard. "You could have been killed. That was awful. Are you sure you're okay?"

"Yeah, I think so. I don't think I broke anything. Damn it!" Cal said as he rose unsteadily, leaning on Daniella. He slowly rotated his right shoulder forward. "How's my bike?" He directed the question to his father.

Paul offered up Cal's bike, whose front tire was bent into the shape of a taco and whose carbon frame was broken behind the headset. "Don't think this bike is going to be seeing any more races." Paul examined the front wheel and peered closely at the shredded tire. He ran his fingers across the scarred rubber. Holding it up to the light, he peered in for a closer look. With a furrowed brow, he moved his attention to the rear wheel, repeating the process. He spun the wheel back and forth and ran his hand over the tire, feeling the texture.

After studying both tires for a few moments, he silently offered the tire for Cal's inspection.

Cal squinted at the tire and passed his hand over the worn spot on the tire. "What the fuck," he said under his breath.

Daniella looked in. "What?"

"Here, take a look at that." He gave her the blown front tire. Then, he held out the rear tire with the sanding marks on it.

"They're both worn the same way?" asked Daniella.

"They weren't worn the same way. It was just made to look that way. This is no fucking accident. They've both been sanded down. Somebody did this on purpose."

Daniella exhaled in exasperation. "That weasel! He knows he isn't winning anything with you in the race, so this is his idea of leveling the field."

Cal and Paul exchanged knowing looks and simultaneously said, "Rocco."

CHAPTER 24

Daniella fretted around Cal. When she was finally confident that nothing was broken and that he was able to stand and move around, she remounted her bike to fetch her car for Cal and his broken bike. Paul stayed behind with Cal.

Cal sat on the ground and shook his head. He wasn't sure what hurt more, the road rash that made hamburger out of his right elbow, knee, and hip — and burning with a pain he knew from a dozen falls just like it — or the idea that someone would do something so slimy and potentially murderous. That pain and fear was new.

Paul looked at Cal and said, "You must be more fit than you thought you were."

"Why?"

"Because, if you weren't a threat, Rocco wouldn't have pulled this stunt. This is low."

Cal shook his head in disbelief. "You always find a way to see the silver lining."

"That's my specialty. Finding the good in situations. You should try it."

"Yeah. I'll keep that in mind next time I find myself airborne over my handlebars. In the meantime, I think I have a new agenda for tomorrow."

"What's that?

"To make that asshole pay for what he did to me. I've been around racing a long time, and I've seen some ugly shit. I've seen guys team up to keep someone from winning a race. I've seen guys ride other guys into a barrier to win a sprint. I've even seen guys hook a rider on a descent to close the door on the inside of a turn. But this? This takes the cake."

"Just remember to keep a cool head. Remember what the godfather said about revenge."

"Which was…?"

"He said, 'Revenge is a dish that's best served cold.'"

Cal nodded in agreement.

"Listen, revenge is another of my specialties. He's going to be expecting you to get even right from the start."

"And?"

"And like Dani says, the race doesn't really get going until the last ten kilometers. That's what I mean by cold. Make him sweat as long as you can. You don't have to do anything to him, other than win the race. Slip over the line in front of him and you'll have all the revenge you could ever want."

Cal struggled to his feet. He examined the spots where the road had shredded the material of his shorts and jersey. The mealy red bottom layers of skin glistened through the fabric. He gingerly placed a hand on his hip and felt the sting. Remember this, he told himself. You'll need this tomorrow for motivation.

He heard the distant roar of Daniella's Fiat straining its way up the hill. When it finally pulled into sight, Cal saw that she wasn't alone. Behind her car was another. At first, Cal couldn't make out who was in the following car, but as it approached, he saw Gianni's profile.

CHAPTER TWENTY-FOUR

Gianni emerged from his car and strode over to Cal. He looked Cal over from head to toe with the experienced eye of a racer and team manager who had seen more than his share of crashes. He turned Cal around like a tailor examining a fabric. "You're a lucky rider. Lots of road rash and tomorrow you're going to be stiff as hell. But no bones broken. And..." he gestured to the tree Cal had nearly hit, "this could have been a lot worse. A lot worse."

"Thanks," responded Cal. "It always makes the pain a little more tolerable thinking that I could be dead." The attempt at humor fell flat. Paul approached Gianni sternly, holding the mangled wheels of Cal's bike. Gianni took them from Paul and turned his attention to the story that their tires told. He studied them closely, holding first the front wheel and then the back wheel. He fingered the place where the front wheel had blown out, and then examined the frayed texture along the rubber. When he'd finished his examination, he shook his head.

"No question about it. This is the work of someone who didn't want you in tomorrow's race."

"What do you mean, 'someone?'" snapped Daniella. "You know there's only one person with a heart dark enough to do something like this."

"And you think it's..."

"You know who I mean! He's had it in for Cal since he first showed up. You don't want to admit it, but you know it. I'm going to deal with this!" Daniella turned to walk back to her car. Gianni grabbed her arm in a vain attempt to stop her, but Daniella yanked away.

"*Ragazza*," Gianni called out. "*Calma*! What are you going to do? You have to think this through. You can't go off on just what you think."

"*You* think it through, Papa. You figure out what to do about this, this, criminal. I'm going to settle this on my own." She broke loose and climbed into her car, slamming the door behind her. She pulled away, spinning her wheels and scattering pebbles in her wake. Gianni, Cal and Paul stared after her car as it sped down the mountain road.

Finally, Gianni broke the silence. "No sense in trying to stop her. Once she gets something in her head, nothing can deter her. Better to let her handle this her own way."

"I'm not sure I'd want to be Rocco right now," said Paul.

"*Hai ragione.* You have that right. Nothing is worse than dealing with a lioness protecting her loved one. But what's done is done. Right now, let's load up the bikes and get Cal down to the hotel and clean out those wounds."

"Shit, nothing hurts more than picking the gravel out of road rash," moaned Cal.

"No matter how much it hurts, would you rather be in the position of dealing with an angry Daniella? Like Rocco is about to experience?"

"Come to think of it, no. Let's go scrub." And in spite of his pain, he was reeling around Gianni's choice of words: Daniella was protecting her *loved one.*

* * *

Daniella drove furiously down the mountain, tires screeching as she careened around each turn. In her mind, she rehearsed what she would do once she found Rocco. Finding him wouldn't be hard. Bassano was small and Rocco was a creature of habit.

Once in town, she flung her car into the first parking spot she found near the town center. She slammed the car door shut and pushed off across the square. Her shoes staccatoed across the cobblestones. In the distance, she saw a gaggle of SD riders hanging out in front of the café.

"Slow down, Daniella," called out Paolo. He headed straight toward her.

"Have you seen Rocco?"

He stammered and dissembled for a moment, half-denying that he knew where Rocco was. In the face of Daniella's anger, he looked like he would deny knowing Rocco at all, if he could.

She cut him off. "Just tell me where."

"Rocco? *Si*, he's over at the *gelateria*, maybe. It was quite a few minutes ago."

Daniella turned and caught sight of Rocco. He was perched on a bench surrounded by his usual posse. He held a cup of gelato in his hand and was gesturing broadly, mid-story. His pleasure at being the center of attention was written in his posture. When he looked up, Daniella was storming across the square at a reckless pace. He tried to stay focused on his story, but as his eyes darted to the side, watching her approach at a near run, the ease in his body closed down and shrank. She knew he saw her. Not breaking her stride, she nearly collided with him, stopping just short of bouncing him off his bench with her chest.

She screamed into his face, "What kind of pig are you? You're a moron! You think you can get away with this?"

Rocco stifled a laugh and said, "I have no idea what you're talking about."

With a quick swipe of her hand, she knocked the cup of gelato out of Rocco's hand, spilling the contents on his shirt. "Shut up. Just shut up and listen and pay close attention to what I have to say, because I'm only going to say it once." She swiveled her head and motioned to the rest of the group to make sure they were listening as well.

"You all know that there's a code amongst riders. You all want to win. You work your hearts out to win on the road. You push each other. You train and live and breathe cycling. It's part of our heritage. Nothing is more important, am I right?"

Although they were shocked into silence, the group nodded in agreement.

"And you give anything to win—but to win with honor. And win on the road. That's the thing you work for. What Rocco has done shows what a coward he is. I don't know who helped him, but if any of you did, you'll pay, too. He sliced up Cal's tires. Cal just crashed coming down the mountain. His tires were slashed, and I want to know if any of you helped this assassin do it."

The collection of riders was frozen in silence. Most shifted their eyes downward, studying shoes and crumbs and the *piazza*'s stonework. Finally, one of the boys said, "None of us would do anything like that. Are you sure it wasn't just a blow out? That happens all the time."

Daniella glared at the defender. "You think I can't tell when a tire has been messed with? I've changed more tires than all the rest of you combined. No, this was no accident. I'm telling you what I know, and know for certain, and you all know it, too. This jerk is responsible. And maybe he had some help. How can you have respect for someone who would do such a thing? What if one of you were the challenger to him? Do you think he wouldn't do the same to you?"

Rocco attempted to break in, "You have no proof that I did anything. And you can't come here and say things that make me seem like I have no honor."

Tapping her chest and thrusting out her chin, Daniella spat out her response. "Proof? I have proof here, in my heart. You think I don't know you? I've known you since you were sniveling to wear the SD jersey. And honor? Well, what honor is involved when you try to take another rider out of a race, so that you don't have to compete?"

Rocco was laughing, putting on a display to show that she hadn't affected him. He brushed the ice cream off of his shirt.

But one of his teammates was asking, "Is it true? Did you fuck up his bike?"

"What, am I responsible for everything that happens on the road around here?"

The question hung in the air unanswered. Rocco looked from one teammate to another, searching their eyes to see if he had made his case.

"Come on, you guys. This is shit... You take her word over mine?"

Finally Filippo spoke up. "The *deal* here, Rocco, is that we don't know what to believe. But if you did what she says you did, you should be ashamed of yourself. And we'd all be ashamed to be racing in the same SD jersey as you."

Rocco gestured to the group, attempting to plead his case. Hands open, he went from one rider to the next, seeking confirmation in their eyes. Seeing the blank expressions on their faces, he raised his plea a notch. "This is bullshit. You guys are accusing me of something that I had nothing to do with. You're like a group of little old lady gossips. I don't fucking need you guys. You can all go and fuck yourselves as far as I'm concerned."

Rocco pushed himself up from the bench and shouldered past his teammates. Behind him, his teammates gathered in heated discussion. Filippo was jaw to jaw with

Paolo. "If Rocco did it, I don't think we should ride for him tomorrow."

"Filippo, who are you to tell us what to do? Rocco doesn't need to take Cal out of the race. He has us to work for him. We'll deliver the race for him."

"You would work for him after what he did?" Daniella interjected.

"*If* he did it," Paolo said. "*If.* You don't have any evidence. And you saying he did it doesn't mean that he did. It's your word against his."

Filippo turned to the gathered teammates with his hands open in a gesture to appeal to the group. "I don't know about the rest of you guys, but I don't trust Rocco. We've all seen how he treats us. Come tomorrow, if Cal makes it into the race, I'm willing to work for him if he has a chance."

Paolo laughed. "You work for whoever you want to tomorrow. But be careful. The race tomorrow will be over in the afternoon, but your reputation here will live on long after the finish line."

Filippo stared at Paolo and shook his head. "I'll take the chance. And if anyone wants to question my loyalty, I'll be happy to answer that I worked for a teammate that deserved my sweat."

He cast a neutral glance at Daniella. She could tell he and the other riders respected her, but didn't wholly trust her word, not after her breakup with Rocco and definitely not since siding with Cal. The impulse to keep arguing Cal's case was strong, but finally, she let it go and headed back across the *piazza* to her car.

CHAPTER 25

Gianni cornered his car into the parking lot of the hotel. Cal and Paul popped out of the passenger side and met him at the bumper. Strapped to the rack were the three bikes, one of which hung from it like a mobile. Cal lifted it. "You know, I loved this bike. It may not have been one of the Pegorettis we rode for T Mobile, but I paid for this one myself, and it has been with me for a lot of miles. I don't want to get too sentimental about it, but shit. I don't know what's more fucked up, my body or my ride. Both the frames are a mess."

Gianni lifted the frame and studied it. "*Your* frame is going to recover. But this one?" He held up the twisted remnant of Cal's bike. "Well, I guess we could probably salvage the components. But the rest is useless."

"What now?" asked Cal. "Even if my body recovers from hitting the deck today, I don't have anything to ride tomorrow."

"I'd let you ride my bike," offered Paul. "If you can stand feeling a little crunched up."

"Thanks, Dad. But the race is going to be difficult enough, on top of being hurt. Riding it with a frame that's too small sounds like torture."

Gianni waved off Cal's stress with his typical proprietorship. "I'm heading to the shop and will check my inventory to see what I have that might fit you. Let me see what I can come up with. Go fix yourself up."

Dinner that night was subdued. Cal had taken his shower, bandaged the raw spots on his shoulder, hip, elbow, and knee, but it hurt even to sit. His father looked on in sympathy as he watched his son squirm, first leaning forward, then sliding backward in futile attempts to ease the pressure on the wounds. There was something familiar to Cal about this pain. Not that he liked it, but crashing and losing skin on the road came with the territory. When the whole enterprise of bicycle racing was one extended trip through pain, a knock on the ground is no more significant than a single snowflake in the middle of a whiteout.

"Dad?"

"Yes."

"What would you think if we packed our bags tonight and just took off tomorrow? Caught the next flight out of Venice for home."

"Is that what you want to do?"

He pushed at a heap of linguini. "Well, hell, I don't know. I mean I have to ask myself what the fuck *am* I doing here. I'm banged up. I don't have a bike. And even if I did, I'm jumping into a race tomorrow that's going to be a suffer-fest. I'm not all that conditioned. And I'm not even factoring in the notion that someone, someone on my own team, is trying to kill me."

Paul gestured for Cal to eat more. "Like I just asked, is leaving what you want to do? Because if it is, I understand. If you want to enjoy one last meal of Luigi's cooking, and pack up tomorrow, I won't try to talk you out of it."

"Why not?" Cal studied his father's tanned, angular face. It was the face of a competitor, but this time, he didn't see any of the old determination in it. His father meant it. "Any time I doubted myself, you were there to push me through the doubts."

"Maybe I'm changing. Maybe I just feel that it's important for you to make up your own mind. You decided to enter this race. You put the time and miles in on the road. It's your decision. Call it a change of heart if you want to, but don't consider it a lack of heart. I love you. And part of loving you is making sure you decide for yourself what you want to do. If you want me to push you past your doubts, you'll have to ask me to do it."

"Tough love?"

"Not exactly, son. Tough love would be making you suck it up and go for it."

"But then, there's Daniella."

"And Daniella fits in how?"

"Well, I'm a little embarrassed to say this. But I want to show her something tomorrow. I feel a little like a kid who wants to prove something to his girlfriend. Just show her that I'm somebody. You know, win the big race. Run off with the beautiful girl. It's a cliché, but what the hell. It might be true."

"Son, I've seen the way she looks at you."

"And?"

"And the look in her eye has nothing to do with the way you ride a bike. You may think you have won her over with your tight shorts and cut muscles, or the wattage you generate in a sprint. But she called you 'a remarkable person,' and I don't think she said it just to impress me."

"Are you sure of that?"

"I have a built-in bullshit meter. And do you love her because of the way she rides a bike? After all, she's a hell of a rider. What if she didn't ride at all?"

Cal let the question sink in before answering. In his mind, he was remembering the warmth of her body as she leaned into him the other night when he was telling his story about T Mobile. He thought about the sparkle in her eye when she greeted him at the door of his room, hands offering the coffee and croissants. He flashed back on the fire she showed, the disagreement over the bearings in his bike, when he first met her in the shop. How she was willing to go to the wall because she was so convinced that she was on solid ground.

"No. If she didn't ride at all, I don't think it would change the way I feel about her. Riding with her is nice. And it's nice to have that to share. But only part of who Daniella is comes from her cycling. The rest of it is her character, her heart. I love her confidence."

"So there you have it. You don't have to ride tomorrow for Daniella. You don't have to ride tomorrow for me, or for Gianni, or for SD. If you ride tomorrow, you do it for yourself."

Cal wrapped a few noodles around his fork and lifted it. A kindling of pain from his hip made him put it back down again. He hurt so much he couldn't eat.

"So what's it going to be? If you want to leave, we go. I'll check flights tonight. We can be in Venice tomorrow morning, back in the States in a day."

Cal flashed back to the last flight he took home from Europe. He had just visited Yves in the hospital, left the team, and landed in San Francisco, feeling like he had left something unfinished—something important. He had been impulsive, furious at the T Mobile team, and sick about his role in Yves' crash. He was hiding from his responsibility and unwilling to accept his role in the whole doping scenario. Now, Cal felt a cold, quiet anger in his gut. Rocco was an example of what was wrong with cycling. The lack of honor, the willingness to do whatever it took to win, the sneaky, corner-cutting strategies that placed a podium spot above the history and tradition of the sport—it was an insult to the sport he used to love. He wanted to make a statement, for himself, for the sport. Why not begin with the starting line tomorrow, he asked himself. And then, the finish line. This time, I'm seeing it through to the end, he thought, whatever that end might be. I might get shelled out of the race tomorrow, embarrassed, dropped like a stone, but I'm going to finish.

Cal set down his fork. "No. Tomorrow I'm going to be on the starting line. I don't know what I'm going to be riding. But if I have to ride a tricycle, I'm going to be there."

Paul reached across the table and put his hand on his son's arm. "Whatever you decide is okay with me. If you want to leave? We leave. But if you want to give it a go tomorrow, I'll be there to support you every way I can."

Luigi's voice boomed in the next room, greeting someone. Gianni's voice answered, and in a moment, he appeared in the dining room door. He called out to Cal and Paul and motioned for them to come outside.

"I have something out here that I want to show you."

Paul and Cal pushed away from the table, crossed the dining room, and headed out to the circular drive in front of the hotel. Gianni had already buried his head in the back of his van. He emerged cradling a bicycle. He shouldered it and carried it up to the front steps, and then lovingly set it down in front of Cal. With a sweep of his hand, he caressed the top tube of the bike.

"Your ride is broken beyond repair. But you aren't. I took your bike back to the shop and took the measurements. This is the last bike I ever rode as a professional. It's yours for tomorrow."

"Are you serious?" replied Cal incredulously. "Seriously? I mean, I'm flattered and grateful, but are you sure you don't mind?"

"I'd be honored to have you on it. I have a bicycle shop and there are many that I could have brought over. But this one is special. The bike that a rider retires on always has a deeper feeling attached to it. Climbing off the bike for the last time is like the end of a marriage. I'm happy to see it get back on the road. Of course, it's a little bit dated. I swapped out the components for you, though. The frame is a little heavy, but it will fit you well, even if it will require a little bit more power to climb. Go ahead and use it. Take it to the top tomorrow."

Cal took the bike and ran his hand over the frame in silent appreciation. The bike was a classic, double butted steel frame, elegantly painted in the bright yellow of Mercatone Uno, Gianni's last team. He looked closely at the handlebar and noticed a small picture glued onto the stem. Peering down at it, he realized it was an old picture of Daniella, taken when she was just a child.

Cal looked up at Gianni. Pointing to the picture, he asked, "Is that...?"

"Yes. In Italy, when we race, we often bring along a memento or a charm or something to help us when the pain starts to take over, something to remind us why we do what we do. I had a picture of Daniella placed there when I was finishing my career. It reminded me that I had a reputation to protect for my daughter and, even though

I was getting to the end of my career, what she would hear about me would live long after my retirement."

Paul bent down to take a closer look at the bike. He turned to Gianni. "Damn, isn't this the same bike you rode to your win in the Giro?"

"The same. Yes. This is my old bike and it served me well."

Cal approached Gianni and gave him a huge hug, and then stepped back to admire the bike one more time. "This is your Giro win bike? I can't believe that you'd let anyone ride it. I don't know how to thank you."

"You're right. I wouldn't let *anyone* ride it. But I'll let you ride it. You've earned it. Putting up with what you've endured, you've shown me that you have the heart to mount this ride." Gianni shrugged. "It has a strong racing tradition. Sometimes, I thought the bike had a soul of its own. I can tell you one thing for sure. This bike knows these roads well, and if you trust it, it won't let you down. You say you don't know how to thank me? Yes, you do. Tomorrow, some time in the race, there will be a point when your legs will ache and you'll feel you can't go any harder than you already have. You'll be thinking you've reached your limit, and you'll be fighting the urge to quit. When that happens, you'll know how you can repay me. Do it by taking one more stroke with the pedal, and then one more, and then one more until the urge to quit has passed. That will be all the thanks I need."

CHAPTER 26

Cal eased onto his bed, situated the ice pack around his shoulder, and tried to relax. Salve was lathered so heavily on his hips, knees, and elbows that he risked sliding off the bed. He carried on a minute-by-minute dialogue with his condition. How bad? What would the pain prohibit him from doing? How would he handle it when he saw Rocco tomorrow? Rocco was a snake, and Cal fantasized about taking him down in a turn, riding him off the road. But Paul was right: Cooler revenge was better. He'd take care of Rocco when the time was right, maybe later in the race.

The knock on the door brought Cal out of a fantasy that was getting bloodier by the minute. He groaned as he pulled himself upright on the bed. "*Chi e`?*"

"*Sono io*, your father. Cut the Italian. Let me in."

Carefully, he swung his legs across the bed and placed his feet on the floor. There, done. Legs still working. Feet still connected. He stiffly unbent his frame and sucked in a deep breath. These first steps, he knew, were going to be the most painful ones. He shuffled haltingly over to the door and unbolted it. Just pulling the door open sent a flash of pain rocketing up his arm to his shoulder.

Paul smiled. "You know, I have a strong aversion to people trying to speak a language that they haven't mastered. If you can't do something well, why do it at all?"

Cal flinched and let out another groan. "Because there aren't enough curse words in English to describe what I'm feeling."

Paul shook his head in sympathy as he stepped through the door. After surveying his son from toes to head, he said, "Doesn't look too bad. A little road rash, nothing that time won't heal. What about the shoulder?"

"Stiff. Sore. It hurts to straighten, but I can reach far enough for the brakes and the bars. I think I can do it. Most important thing is that my hips and knees seem okay."

"Yes. A good thing that you pedal with your legs and not your arms. But Le Scale is a climbing race. There will be a lot of torque on the bars. Are you going to be able to get any leverage?"

Cal had shuffled over to the window and looked out at the racecourse. "Yeah, I suppose. I've raced through worse. Maybe I'll get an MRI or something when we get back to Mill Valley — but for now, it's fine."

"You young supermen," Paul sighed. He eased himself onto the edge of the desk and motioned for Cal to get back in bed. "I want to talk with you. There's something on my mind."

"No thanks. Getting up once was hard enough." Sensing the gravity in his father's voice, Cal flushed the sarcasm from his voice. "I'm fine here, really."

Paul got up again and cautiously touched Cal's arm. "So I want to talk to you about a couple of things."

Cal waited. His father had the habit of prefacing important stuff with a long preamble. Cal was in no mood for it. "What is it, Dad?"

Paul turned and sank down on the desk chair and put his elbows on the table. He fiddled with a pen that sat in front of him. It looked like he was about to start writing something, but Cal knew this was just his father getting warmed up.

"I've been thinking a lot about tomorrow. I've given a lot of thought to it. Not just the race. But to you and the race. And I want to talk to you about it."

"Ice and rest, Dad. I'll be fine."

Paul was gnawing at his lip. "No, it's not that. Well, I don't know another way to say this, so I'll just come out and give it to you..." His brow furrowed. "You asked me earlier if you should drop out of the race, and I told you that it was up to you."

"Right..."

"Well, I've been giving it some thought. I wondered if you were asking me for permission or something."

"No, I just wanted to get your idea on the whole crazy thing."

"Well, either way. I came here to tell you that I don't think you should race."

"Are you serious?" Cal reacted incredulously.

"Yes. I've thought a lot about it..." Paul was prepared to continue, but Cal cut him off.

"I'm sure you have. But what in the hell are you thinking?"

"It comes down to a few things. First, you're hurt. What's the point of going out and busting your ass if you aren't 100 percent?"

Cal jumped in to interrupt. "One hundred percent? Dad, this is racing. When is anyone ever 100 percent. Fuck! If I only raced when I was 100 percent, I'd do the first race of the season and then pack it up. You yourself know that you play hurt. A racer who isn't nursing some kind of injury hasn't been in any kind of competition. No. I may be hurting, but I'm still going out tomorrow. Is that it? That's what you want to talk about?"

"When I rode up on the crash yesterday and saw you lying on the ground, my heart stopped. I thought you were hurt, really hurt. And I said to myself that if you got hurt like that because I'd pushed you in some way, I couldn't live with myself. Seeing you in the ditch there, I wondered if I wasn't responsible…"

"You? Responsible? How do you figure? I got into this situation on my own."

"Yes, you did. But you wouldn't be here if I hadn't dragged you over. I introduced you to Gianni. And to tell the truth, I had a secret hope that Gianni would figure out the puzzle. Figure out what it would take to get you back on the bike, back into competition. I'd tried and failed, so I thought maybe he could do it. I just thought it would be good for you. I don't know. Probably it was my program, not yours. And now, looking at you all busted up like that, it makes me rethink the whole thing."

Cal felt his heart quicken. His father was circling around some touchy issues, and now was not the time to pick at the scabs.

"Dad. You think I didn't know you had a plan in introducing me to Gianni? Please don't underestimate me. I wouldn't have decided to join SD, train with Gianni, and ride the race, if I didn't want to do it. It was my decision. Not yours, or anyone else's for that matter."

"But son, is it the right thing to do? I mean, that shit that happened. Let's say it was Rocco who slashed your tires…"

"*Let's say*? Dad, Daniella has her finger on the pulse of everything that happens in this town. If she says Rocco did it, he did it. But so what? He's an angry little pissant who's afraid that someone has come into town and taken his toys away."

Paul nodded his head in agreement. "But the thing is, if he can pull that kind of trick, what else does he have up his sleeve for tomorrow? What about the rest of the team? You're never going to be an accepted member of that team. Not really. How are they going to deal with you tomorrow? Ride you off the road? Sabotage any chance you have for a placement? You can't trust these guys. The rest of SD may not be as dirty as Rocco, but they're frightened of him. And frightened people do frightening things."

"I figure that some of his boys are going to need watching. Paolo is definitely one of his 'guys.' I don't know about the others. But what the hell? It's a race. A competition. So they try to do me in. It's not like they're taking a gift away from me. I still have to earn the placement on the road. Nothing ventured, nothing gained. You taught me that."

Paul's face said he had at least one more card to play. He went for it. "Okay. So you can handle yourself on the road. You have the experience. There probably isn't much these guys will pull tomorrow that you haven't seen before. But think about it. Are you really ready to race? You're hardly race fit. Why throw yourself into this? Pick another event somewhere down the road, and give yourself a chance to get ready."

Cal grimaced as a bolt of heat shot up from his shoulder. Or maybe it wasn't his shoulder that hurt. Maybe it was the feeling that his father was backing away from him and expressing doubts about his ability to compete the next day. He turned away and crossed the room from the window to his bed, where he eased himself down.

"Too late for that, Dad. I've done what I could. Now it's up to me to do what I can tomorrow."

Paul came right back. "You were the one who always talked about doing '*Le Metier*,' as you call it. Being a professional. Doing the work. You haven't done enough work to win this. You aren't ready. Give it up. Come back to the States and sign on with one of the domestic teams. Maybe you start locally, and then rebuild your career."

Cal shook his head in disagreement. How was he going to make his father understand? "Dad, it isn't really about how much training I've done. Sure, it'd be nice to come into this race with months of hard work under my belt. But I don't have that. And I'm not going to get it by tomorrow. So I've done the work that I've done. And that's it."

"So there's nothing I can say that's going to deter you from lining up tomorrow morning, is there?"

"Nope. Nothing."

Paul started to move to the door. Before he reached it, he turned and gave it one more shot. "Cal, I just don't get why it's so important to do this. You gave up racing three years ago. You dropped it altogether. Now you're like a man obsessed and nothing makes any sense. What's going on?"

Listening to his father try to make sense out of his commitment to complete in Le Scale hurt almost as much as his shoulder did. He had spent so much of the past few years parrying his father's inquiries that he could evade his best lines of questioning with ease. That didn't mean he didn't feel something, though. His father came to him with the best of intentions, and Cal was being coy. It was time to come clean.

"Dad, before you go. Sit down. There's something I want to tell you."

Paul made his way back across the room and returned to his chair. Finally, Cal turned and faced him. His eyes burned, and his lips pulled downward as he made the effort not to let the tears flow. He felt a catch in the back of his throat.

"Look, Dad. When I raced with T Mobile... I didn't quit because I wasn't doing well or because I wasn't getting along with the team, or anything like that." He took a deep breath. The words came a little easier. "All of the bullshit I've been spilling about leaving, it was just that — bullshit."

"So Cal, what?"

"The truth is that I was doping when I rode with T mobile."

Paul stared at him. He said nothing, but waited for him to continue. Cal's tears were coming back, and every time he took a deep breath to clear them, his shoulder sent pain screaming into his neck. He squeezed his eyes shut.

"When Franz started to fail, when the team was looking for a new leader to groom, they came to me and made me an offer. They told me I could be the team leader if I agreed to use some new drug they had, HemAssist, and do the blood doping thing. They signed me up with a doctor they used to administer the shit. I didn't want to do it, at first. At least, I didn't think I wanted to do it, but they told me I was going home if I didn't."

"And so you went along with it."

"No excuse, Dad. What the hell, I wanted to win. Gerhardt gave me some shit about using every advantage, and I could only think of that story you told... That you told me about LeMond —" Cal dragged his hand across his eyes, smearing away tears. "It was wrong, but I was over-thinking it. I did it for most of the spring classics. All the way into the Tour of Romaine. I'm not proud of what I did, Dad. I'm pretty ashamed."

"You should be," said Paul in a quiet voice.

It was the worst thing he could have said, because it was the truth. Cal sat down on the bed and sobbed, once. He scrubbed his hand over his eyes again and tried reining himself in again. He'd made the choice to bring it up. Stick with it. No self-pity. "Well, it's something I think about all the time. It's one of the reasons I never wanted to go back and try again."

"Why did you stop? Why didn't you continue with the juice?" asked Paul. His voice was neutral, non-judgmental.

"It's a long story. But the bottom line is that I saw guys, my teammates, putting themselves on the line for me, and giving it up for me, and I was dirty. I was getting results, and I felt like I was a phony. I just didn't want to continue. The whole process made me sick. And I'm feeling pretty sick just standing here telling you. I don't know what else to say except that it's one of the reasons I have to race tomorrow. I have to go back and race clean. I guess it's a way to make up for what I did, and to wipe away some of the bad taste in my mouth about racing, about myself. If I get my ass kicked tomorrow, I deserve it."

A silence grew between them, filling the gap. Finally, Paul spoke up.

"I knew."

"You knew? What did you know?"

"I knew you were doping. At least, I was pretty sure, even though you never said anything about it."

Cal was incredulous. "You thought I was doping? You thought I was juiced? How did you know?"

"Son, put the pieces together. You were really good. You had huge potential. But potential? That's one thing.

To start cashing in on it, and to do it so quickly? That's another. When I saw you moving up so quickly in the ranks. I had my doubts. When you got the podium finish at Romandie, I was pretty sure. I never said anything to you or your mother, but I was pretty convinced. Hell, first year on the tour and you're putting up results like that? I wanted to believe the most of my son, but when I thought about it logically..."

Cal leaned his head on his hand, clutching his hair. The revelation was almost too much. "So you're saying you knew, or were pretty sure. And you didn't say anything. That's not like you. What were you thinking? What did you think of me?"

"Son, I didn't know what to say about it, and, besides, I'm a lawyer, so I look at the evidence. There was no smoking gun, but it was all pretty fishy. Franz leaves the team. You start placing in races your first year? Come on."

"But, you must have been furious."

"First, I figured out, like you said, that it was coming from top down on the team. And it's no secret riders feel they have to do something to stay competitive. Longer stages. Killer pace. Huge training loads. No time to recover. It's brutal. But it broke my heart that you were getting pressured like that. I hoped you would only do it if you had a gun to your head. And I wondered if I wasn't part of the problem. That you couldn't just say no, walk away from cycling, because you feared what I'd think of you."

"Well, I did worry about that. Once I quit and came home, I couldn't tell you the real reason why. It just looked like I was quitting and that I was a loser. For the past three years, I've been waiting for a chance to wipe some of that away."

Cal bowed his head. The sadness he felt settled into his chest, and he watched tears drop down from his eyes, and break against his bare knees. His face grew warm from the embarrassment of crying in front of his father. At his side, he felt his father's weight sink into the mattress. Paul was extending his hand to Cal. Cal bypassed it and reached around his shoulder for an embrace. He winced from the pressure on his shoulder.

When they separated, Cal asked, "So now you know. What do you think?"

"Son, it's complicated. I've turned this over in my head a thousand different ways since you came home. And I'd be going too easy on you if I didn't admit that I am, was, a little disappointed. But not shocked. And I'm pissed? Hell yes, I'm pissed. But not at you. What you did is nothing to be proud of. But I'd like to rip Gerhardt's fucking head off."

"You and me both," interjected Cal.

"But there's something else. Whatever you did, whatever you took, whatever pressure you felt, there's something else you did that's just as important."

Cal motioned to his father to continue. "And that is?"

"You stopped, left the team, didn't continue with it. Now, normally, you know me, I don't support quitting. But in your case, it was a matter of honor, leaving the team felt like the right thing to do. And that makes me proud. Proud that you'd give up something you valued so much—and something that was in your blood—rather than continue to do it under false pretenses. I guess that says all I need to know about you. Taking the juice to win? That will never be right, whether you got caught or not. Giving it up and taking a stand and walking away? I've got to respect that. My only wish now is that we'd had this conversation three years ago."

"Yeah, me too," replied Cal. After a while, he added, "So do you get now why I have to do the race tomorrow?"

"Look, Cal, I do get it. It doesn't change the fact that I worry . But I don't want you to think that tomorrow is some kind of magical journey and that whatever happens… you win, you lose, you get your ass kicked, whatever, is going to make the whole episode with T Mobile go away. Life doesn't work that way."

"I think I know that, Dad. But it's a start. Maybe a finish, too."

CHAPTER 27

The morning of the race broke crystal clear. Cal's stomach was churning and his heart was beating with a tempo that made his chest feel like it was vibrating. Pre-race nerves. Anxiety. He actually liked the feeling. The bottom line was that it was energy. And energy was easily translated into force, and that translated into power.

Cal took himself through the mental checklist. Tempo at the beginning, get comfortable. Read the pack and size up the competition. Who's the real thing? Who's just pretending? Be an opportunist. Wait for the chance. Let the race come to you. Use your experience. And if someone beats you today? Make sure he does it by outworking you. If he can do that? He deserves the win.

Cal's pre-race litany was soothing. He knew races were unpredictable and staying focused and ready to seize any opportunities might make the difference. The pain didn't scare Cal. Pain was a familiar part of racing. Hurt was spread around. The peloton was a brotherhood, and they shared the pain, even if it looked like they were creating it for each other. So let the pain come. He had felt it before and would relish the opportunity to see just who had the highest pain tolerance today.

He heard the starting line before he saw it. The sound of

engines, voices, and the public address system marked the starting line. Riders calling out to one another. The crowd sent up a buzz of excitement. He fell into cadence with a few other solitary riders, making their way toward the town square. Around the next corner was the line, with all its colorful kits and bicycles and all the pandemonium of last-minute coaching sessions and riders warming up for the race.

Cal found the race registration desk and took his place at the back of the line, behind a dozen riders. The riders waited in silence, shifting from foot to foot, their nervous energy infectious, as each one clambered up the platform to the official registration desk. They walked stiffly in their cleated cycling shoes, and signed the register. They received their racing numbers from the race official. The riders helped each other pin the numbers on their backs. This was, for most, the last bit of cooperation they could expect. Cal smiled to himself. Funny, he thought, how we trust each other and have such camaraderie here, before the race starts. Now we're a fraternity. And then, at the crucial moments of the race, when the breaks are made and the hammer is dropped, the guy who helped you with your number becomes the guy who tries to beat your brains in with a leg-burning acceleration.

Registration accomplished, it was time to find the rest of the SD team. He scanned the crowd, trying to pick out the distinctive flash of red. His senses were bombarded by the noise, the smells, and the sounds of festivity. Italian racing crowds were loud and festive, with music, food stalls, and promotional vehicles hawking everything from bicycle components to clothes to beer. The town party was already in full swing.

As he made his way through the maze of riders, fans, and promotional vehicles, he heard someone call his name.

"Cal. Cal. Over here."

He strained to see over the heads of the milling crowd. When he focused his eyes across the square, he spotted Daniella standing in the midst of a red sea, waving her arms for him to come over. Just seeing her made him smile.

He slalomed his way across the square and melded into the SD cluster. Gianni faced the group, focused on a map of the racecourse that was fluttering on the hood of his car. He knew the course like he knew the back of his hand. But still, there was something about looking at a course on the map, calculating the spots where the road pitches up, where a little break in the effort can be expected, where the road narrows, and where the turns might afford an opportunity to get away from the peloton, that can only be established by looking at the map. His forefinger methodically traced the course from the beginning in the square to the top of Monte Grappa: 125 kilometers, more or less. With his fingers climbing the course, he recorded the notes in his mind. Go here, rest there, push, no, hold back, he seemed to be saying to himself.

Daniella was sporting the SD jersey and tight black leggings. On her head she wore a bicycling hat turned backward. She left Gianni's side and made her way over to Cal. Not wanting to make a big display of her affection, she reached down and placed her hand on top of his. It was a casual brush of the hand. She didn't want to fire Rocco up, for fear that he would make a scene or cause a distraction that would hurt Cal. Very discreetly, she leaned over and whispered in his ear, "This is it. You're going to do great."

"You sound pretty confident. I think we'll need to wait to see how it turns out."

"Now is not the time for lack of confidence. Remember, I'm a great judge of talent, and I know you're going to be strong. Besides, I'll be waiting for you at the top and you don't want to keep me waiting long."

"Well, bring lots of warm clothes," Cal laughed. "Because I hear it can be pretty chilly at the top, and you might be waiting up there for a long time."

"Are the warm clothes for you or for me?" she laughed.

"Both of us," he replied.

Gianni looked out at the riders and began in a serious voice, "Today is a day for you to show yourselves and demonstrate to the other competitors that you've prepared to compete for the summit of Monte Grappa. You represent your town, your team, your family, and yourselves. In that order. The responsibility is heavy, but you've prepared for it. Go out and work together. Be a team."

Cal was anxious to get started. He had been here before and didn't feel like he needed a pep talk. He noticed several of the riders making the sign of the cross on their chest. He glanced across the collection of SD riders. The whole team was here, Filippo, Carlo, Lucca, Marcello, Paolo, and the Swiss brothers, Tomas and Giorgio. Out of the corner of his eye, he saw Rocco. Unlike the other riders, most of whom were solemn, even prayerful, Rocco was a blur of anxious motion. He shifted from one foot to the other as if the ground was burning the soles of his feet. His eyes careened across the crowd in a frantic scanning motion. Finally, they lighted on Cal — and did a double-take. They darted to Daniella's face and back to Cal's like dice rattling in a cup. That's right, Cal thought, here I am, asshole. You're going to have to work to beat me.

Instinctively, Daniella leaned in closer, and Cal reached down and gave her hand a tight squeeze. Rocco ignored them.

Gianni continued in his pre-race address. "There will be a number of professional scouts on hand, who'll be watching you. Some of them will be looking for riders to sign to professional contracts. They'll be looking for the winners, of course, but they'll also be looking for the workers, the riders who are willing to sacrifice themselves for their teammates. Keep that in mind, *ragazzi*. Try to put away your rivalries and save your energy for dealing with the rest of the pack."

The riders dispersed into smaller groups and made their way over to the team car to retrieve last minute stores of water bottles and food. Around the car, in an area cordoned off by cones, were the stationary bikes, ready for the riders to use in preparation for the start. Their legs had to be warm for the hills that lay ahead. Cal swung his leg over the saddle of Gianni's bike, already mounted onto one of the trainers, and began to pedal. Slowly at first, he gradually picked up intensity. The warmer he got, the looser his shoulder got. A twinge in his lower back made itself known, but he disconnected himself from it. The bike and its new components hummed on the trainer like smooth, frictionless extensions of himself — he put his focus there, on what didn't hurt. He inserted the earphones of his iPod into his ears and made his selection. He searched through his playlists for something that would give him a lift. Otis Redding, he thought. That should do it. He dialed in "Try a Little Tenderness," and waited for the tempo to pick up at the end of the song. He started to mumble along with the lyrics, withdrawing from the surrounding distractions.

"*You got to hold on,*" sang Otis. Yeah, thought Cal. You got to hold on.

He was so deep into the music and his effort to warm up that he didn't immediately notice Rocco when he appeared at his side.

"I heard you had a nasty crash yesterday. What happened? Had a blow out with your tire is what I heard."

"Yeah, you heard right. Ugly blow out. Hit the deck pretty hard. Really surprising, though. I mounted those tires new just before I left. Strange that both of them would go."

"Yeah, strange. Bad luck. I thought maybe you wouldn't be here today, after crashing."

"Thought? Or hoped?"

"Whatever. I'm sure that it's going to hurt a lot, trying to pull through with all that road rash. It won't help your chances today, huh?"

Cal made a move to dismount from his bike. Rocco, fearing Cal's approach, took a step backward. He raised his hands in a defensive position.

"You don't need to worry about me hurting today, Rocco. The only thing you need to worry about is handling your own pain."

Daniella witnessed the whole encounter from a distance. She was prepared to physically intervene if the argument had gotten physical. She was relieved to see Rocco turn and walk away. She made her way to Cal on the trainer.

"What was that all about?"

"Just a little pre-race strategy session."

"Seriously. What did he say?"

"You know. The same old bullshit."

"Yes. But enough. No more distractions before the start. Are you ready?" she asked.

"Ready as I can be. At this point, anyway. Ask me that in a couple of hours."

"Is there anything you need?"

"Yeah, an extra lung and a new set of legs," he joked. "It wouldn't hurt to have some riders working for me, too."

"I think you're in this one alone. Filippo will be strong until the hills. Hang onto his wheel to carry you there. Remember what we talked about. The race is a long one. The reason they call it Le Scale…"

"I know," interjected Cal. "Le Scale means 'the stairs.' You've told me this before, Dani."

"You'll know the last ten kilometers mark when you see the café, Il Piccolo, on the way up. Hang near the front of the peloton. Not the lead, but close to the front. If anyone goes off the front, you want to know about it. And catching up takes a lot more effort than going with the initial attack."

"Thanks, coach," Cal replied with a laugh. "You think I haven't done anything like this before?"

"I don't know. Not banged up the way you are now." Daniella reached out to touch his shoulder, but stopped short. She could see the bulge underneath his jersey where he'd placed extra padding.

"I'll be okay. It's funny, but the pain in my shoulder and the bruise on my hip just seem to fit the whole idea of this race."

"Racing injured? I don't get it."

"Not sure I can explain it, but if I were 100 percent, if I were perfectly conditioned, it just wouldn't seem like racing. But thanks for worrying about me."

Daniella paused and looked at Cal. The sweat dripped off the end of his nose. His legs tapped out a metronomic rhythm, like an engine. His focus matched the intensity of his cadence. Watching him, Daniella's eyes were filled with admiration. Her expression shifted minutely, and she approached Cal and placed her hand on his forearm to get his attention. He looked up and nodded.

"I have something for you."

Cal was puzzled. He put out his hand. Daniella reached into a backpack she was carrying and pulled out the white leather gloves that Cal had given her before her race. She had kept them safe, waiting for the right moment to return them to their rightful owner. She placed them in Cal's hand with an emphatic thrust.

"Yves' gloves? I gave them to you. They were a gift for you," Cal protested.

Daniella raised her hand to stop him. "The gloves belong to you, not to me. They actually don't belong to either of us. They belong to Yves. The power of the gloves isn't in the ownership. That's an illusion. The power of the gloves is in what they represent. Commitment to the race. Take them and wear them today."

Cal worked the gloves on his hands and smiled at Daniella. When Yves' mother gave them to him as a parting gift in the hospital, it seemed tacky to check the fit, and besides, he planned to never race again. Now, here he was, and the fit was perfect — tight, classic. He leaned over and placed a kiss on Daniella's cheek.

"Thank you. I'll see what I can do to deliver these gloves to the finish line with the honor they deserve."

Both Daniella and Cal shifted their gaze to Rocco who was warming up on his own trainer a few yards away. Daniella gave Cal a final kiss and made her way out of the circle of racers, passing by Rocco on her way out. As she passed, Rocco leaned over and sneered, "So a final good luck kiss for your boyfriend? What about me? No final kiss for good luck? Just for old time's sake?"

"You deserve shit, Rocco. I wouldn't waste my time on you. You and your group of clowns have disgraced the jersey you're wearing. You've dishonored the legacy that my father passed to you. As far as I'm concerned, if I never see you again, it would be too soon."

"Yes, well, then you better close your eyes at the finish line. Because if you're looking, you'll see me crossing first."

As Daniella walked away, Cal turned up his iPod and pretended he hadn't heard.

CHAPTER 28

A distant horn pierced the morning air, calling the riders to the start line. They coalesced into splashes of color as the teams assembled. The riders exchanged last minute chatter, warding off the start line nerves. Conversation came to an abrupt halt when Signor Palmero, the local racing official, climbed onto the elevated platform by the start line. He stood proudly, flanked by the mayor of Bassano and a dark-haired beauty, the town's entrant into the Miss Italia contest.

Signor Palermo began in his booming baritone, "The first five kilometers will be a 'procession under control' until you reach the outskirts of town. Then, when I drop the flag, you'll begin the actual race. You all should know the course, so I won't waste your time with any directions. I expect that you'll obey the race marshals and you'll race respectfully. There's no neutral support, so if you have a mechanical failure, you'll have to wait for your own team car. We'll be strictly enforcing the rules on team cars pulling riders back up to the peloton. So if you have a stop, be aware that we'll be watching. Other than that, only one thing—*buon fortuna*."

Signor Palermo retreated to his lead car, a gleaming red Audi. He reemerged, standing straight as an arrow with his head and shoulders protruding from the sunroof. In his right hand, he held a white flag. In his left hand, he held an air horn aloft. He pulled the trigger and sounded the start of the race with an ear-splitting blast that echoed off the walls of the square. A roar rose from the crowd. The bass note of the crowd was punctuated by the clicking clatter of hundreds of cleated cycling shoes clipping into pedals. Like a living, breathing animal, the peloton stirred to life and organized itself into formation behind the race director's car.

Close behind the racers, a parade of team support vehicles started their engines. The cars fell in behind, easing forward like a mobile bicycle store. Inside each car was a full stock of equipment—wheels to replace those that broke or went flat and extra clothing to ward off the chill or to keep the rain from soaking the racers' jerseys. And most importantly, because riders race with their stomachs as well as their legs, food and water. These emergency rooms on wheels trailed the riders, ready to minister to any need on the road.

With the race well underway, Cal made a conscious effort to control his enthusiasm and settle into a comfortable rhythm. He allowed the crush of the riders to move ahead of him. His experience told him there would be "rabbits," the racers too excited, too enthusiastic, and too unsure of their ability to hang with the pace, and would push too hard, too soon. Even if he were inclined to go with them, his body was still too sore from yesterday's crash to jump out early. He used the first few miles to ease the stiffness from his shoulder and back. He stood on his pedals to stretch his lower back and then settled down on the saddle, seeking a comfortable position. His hands floated lightly on the bars.

CHAPTER TWENTY-EIGHT

He pedaled safely in the middle of the group, keeping his teammates in sight. He kept his gaze soft, his focus diffuse, taking in the whole of the group. Only centimeters separated his front wheel from the rear wheel of the rider directly in front of him. On either side, his elbows and knees brushed against his competitors. He was engulfed by the whirring sound of chains turning gears, of wheels humming against pavement, and the clicking of gears as riders adjusted their derailleurs to find just the right combination of cogs.

The parade of riders moved like a wave through town, eventually reaching the outskirts of Bassano, waiting for the flag to drop. The crowd noise continued to buffet them from either side of the road. Cow bells rang out, rising above the roar of the crowd as the fans shouted out to their individual favorites. Not too far in the distance, Cal saw one of the local riders dismount by the side of the road and place a kiss on his wife's cheek. She held his son, a newborn infant, in her arms, and he picked the baby up and rocked him for a second. Cal smiled at this European tradition. Local riders often encountered family and friends on the route stopping and dismounting for a quick kiss on the cheek, a clap on the back, even a glass of champagne. The peloton was never more of a fraternity than at these times. It was defintiely bad form for a rider to attack another rider by accelerating and taking up the pace during one of these interludes. What a difference from American racing, thought Cal. In the US, such a stoppage would be more likely to initiate an attack, and the rider observing this charming tradition would be mocked as sentimental and "uncommitted."

The town limit, marked by the familiar sign bearing the name, Bassano, with a red line crossing through it, loomed ahead. Here's where the race started in earnest. The race director dramatically waved his white flag from side to side and then lowered it. The fuse was lit. Cal felt his heart jump into a higher rhythm as he rose out of the saddle and kicked the pedals into action. Along with a hundred fellow riders, he flicked the levers on his bars in search of a larger gear to match the upcoming surge.

With the race finally underway, the peloton's mood churned like a thunderhead, and the profile of the pack changed shape, transforming itself from a broad blade to a pointed arrow. Several of the teams sent riders to the front to lift the pace, testing the waters to see who was prepared to work and who was just along for the ride.

Suddenly, three riders exploded out of the group. The force of their effort catapulted them off the front of the peloton. Out of their saddles, their bikes swaying from side to side for leverage, they hammered their pedals. Toward the back, from the safety of the main group, Cal watched to guage the peloton's reaction. It didn't take long. Within moments, three others joined the escaping trio. That made six in total, doing their best to separate from the rest of the group. Working as a unit, they quickly organized themselves into a model of efficiency. They gained ten meters, then twenty, and more, until the gap had grown so large that the select escapees disappeared from sight. Cal watched them slide away and was tempted to join them. His style of racing had always been to race from the front. He liked being in the lead group. But that was when he was race-hardened. Now? Too much, too early. Besides, if the rest of these guys weren't worried about the breakaway, and they knew each other so well, then it couldn't be too much of a threat. Cal took in a deep breath and settled into the pace.

More than a hundred kilometers remained, most of it on the steep hills of Monte Grappa. Cal didn't know the riders in the breakaway, but he knew the type. Riders who emerged from the peloton early, grasped a lead and tried to make it hold. The pack behind them gradually, excruciatingly, narrowed the gap, using the whole length of the course to execute their catch. The final elimination of their lead was made more cruel by the fact that it typically occured in the last kilometer of the race, just when the escapees might be harboring a hope that this time they might be fortunate enough, or have worked hard enough, to defy the calculations of the chasing group. It was most often a futile, even masochistic, effort, one destined for failure from its inception. So why do it? Cal knew the answer. For some of the breakaway riders, it was a lark, a chance they were willing to take against the long odds that the peloton would miscalculate, either through lack of care or overt mistake, and they would have their win. For others, the move came from an executive dictum, directed by team or sponsor tactics. In these cases, the message usually came from the top, the race managers or the sponsors: Get out in front, get a little publicity, a little exposure for the sponsor's logo on the jersey. And for some, it was a grab for a moment's glory, the opportunity to tell future generations, "Yes, I was in the lead, pushed the pack to the limit, led the race for 40 kilometers," leaving out the ignominious part where they were chased down like antelopes on the African plains. If you went that route, taking a flyer on the early break, mused Cal, all you usually had at the end was the glory of leading for a little while, and some tragically burned-out legs. And then, of course, there were the riders who truly believed, delusional or not, they had the strength to hold the lead for the duration. Whether they really did, only time would tell, but rare was the rider who could win the day on a solitary breakaway from the front.

It wasn't long before Lucca edged over to Cal and, raising his voice over the buzzing peloton, said.

"Rocco wants us to go to the front to work for him. We pull for the next twenty kilometers or so and see what the rest of the peloton has to offer."

"Rocco says?" replied Cal with a grin. "Is he the team strategist? The brains of this team? What does Gianni say?"

"Well, Rocco is the team captain," Lucca said apologetically.

"Okay, I get the message. But I think it's too early to start working that hard. None of the other teams seemed concerned about chasing down the breakaway. Why do we want to do so much work now?"

Lucca shrugged his shoulders. "You might be right. But Rocco wants us to start pulling."

Cal shook his head. It was too early to chase, but it was also too early to start bickering over tactics, so he followed Lucca's wheel to the front of the pack. The rest of the SD riders fell in with him. They now formed a linked chain seven strong. Lucca at the front, followed by Cal, then Filippo, next Marcello, and finally Rocco. Close behind, separated by a few bike lengths, Giorgio and Tomas pulled up the rear of the SD team. Paolo had fallen off the pace earlier on, and was nowhere to be seen. The rest of the peloton offered little resistance. They were more than happy to have SD put in the effort at the front and provide shelter from the wind.

The pack transformed into a living entity. Providing background to the hum of chains and cogs, there was a symphony of breathing, the cacophony of clicking shifters, and the warning shouts of riders on either side. The spectators gathered six-deep on either side of the road, roaring out their support. Cal felt enveloped by the fans. He was thrilled to see the support that racing received in Europe. In the US, he reflected, bicycle races were held in out-of-the-way, back roads early in the morning when the disruptions to traffic would be minimal. Often, the only attendees were the racers and, sometimes, friends and family. Not so in Europe. There were the inevitable costumed fans, like the guy who dressed as Superman, and the ones who wanted to participate in the race and ran along with the riders, hoping to get an extended look at their heroes. Those people lucky enough to be living by the course decorated their homes, even themselves, in celebration of the passing race. They stood by the side of the road for hours, ringing bells, shouting encouragement. They staked out their posts long before the racers were in sight and lingered long after the peloton passed. It's ironic, Cal thought—we watch them, they watch us, each thinks the other is the entertainment.

Surprisingly, his legs felt light and loose. He checked the heart monitor mounted on his handlebars: 137 beats per minute. He was breathing easily and his back hadn't begun to scream yet. I could do this for hours, Cal thought, and then he laughed, remembering that he was going to be, indeed, doing it for the next few hours.

The pack accelerated and he reacted, taking his effort up to hang on. No more daydreaming. A lapse in concentration was all it took to separate the competitors from the also-rans. If he had his old form, if he was truly race fit, he would have a greater margin of error. He could use his legs to make up for the mistakes his mind might make.

Not today. "Hang on or drop off" was his mantra for the rest of the ride.

Once the SD team was organized at the front, Rocco pulled up to Cal on the right hand side. "We're going to take the legs out of some of these guys before we hit the steeper parts. Be prepared to do your share of the work in the paceline."

Cal bridled at the suggestion that he needed reminding to do his "share of the work." Who the hell did Rocco think he was talking to? A rookie? A slacker? His impulse, short-lived though it was, was to shove him away. It would have sent Rocco to the ground, and given Cal partial revenge for the grief Rocco had caused him. It would be sweet payback for the sabotage. Instead, he grimaced and grinned. In a vain attempt to stay civil, he responded, "You don't have to worry about me doing my share of the work. But don't you think it's a little early to be pressing so hard?"

"Afraid that you won't last? Maybe your late night adventures with Daniella took too much out of you."

"No, it isn't me that I'm worried about. It's you. But from what I heard, there was no danger of you ever wasting any energy in late night adventures with Daniella. She told me you never brought much in the late night encounters… in the way of energy or anything else, for that matter." As soon as the insult passed his lips, Cal was embarrassed that he had dropped down to Rocco's level to deliver the insult. But it was too late. Rocco rose to the bait.

"Fuck you, Cal. Just do your share of the work and keep your mouth shut, and I may let you finish with the lead peloton."

The comment pushed Cal to respond. He swiveled his head, showing Rocco the full strength of his fury.

"*Let* me finish with the lead peloton? I didn't know I needed your permission. I've been racing at levels that you're only dreaming of. So don't try to tell me what needs to be done. Start acting like a man, like a team leader, and give up your *prima donna* act. Grow up!"

While Rocco and Cal argued, the Nove Colli squad took advantage of their dispute to pull their team to the front of the pack. Their arrival signaled a shift in the tenor of the race. The climb up Monte Grappa, the real beginning of the work, was rapidly approaching. Dressed in sky blue uniforms, the national color of Italy, the Nove Colli guys were known as fierce racers and strong competition in any race. They were the premier team from the neighboring town, Mussolente, and their rivalry with Bassano's SD team was fierce. They were also accomplished. Nove Colli had placed a rider on the podium in each of the last three races. Stefan Bianco, a nineteen-year-old racing machine, had a growing reputation as a regional hero. On weekend rides, when the SD riders would often bump elbows on the road with the Nove Colli riders, it was usually Stefan who initiated, and finished, the attacks. He was known as an accomplished climber, and with a strong team, was considered a threat for the win today.

The Nove Colli were playing it smart, thought Cal, by letting the SD team go to the front and do the early work. Cal made a mental note to keep his pulls at the front of the peloton short. Better to keep something in reserve. Rocco's strategy of pulling hard at this point in the race was a dangerous one, particularly for Cal, since he knew he really was on the border of fitness and his body was still reeling from the aftereffects of yesterday's tumble.

He glanced over at Stefan. He looked fresh and powerful. With bulging quads and the lean chest, characteristic of cycling pros, he had the look of a winner. He was youthful in appearance, but his concentration on the bike was intense. He seemed to sense Cal looking over in his direction and nodded his head.

Stefan turned to Cal and offered in nearly perfect English, "We heard you were going to be in the race."

"You heard? I didn't know it would be a topic of conversation."

"These are small towns here. Bassano? Mussolente? Sisters living right next to each other. You should have come to train with us."

"Why's that? SD seems like the squad to beat around here."

"No, SD is a powerful group, Don't get me wrong. But a bit *pazzo*, crazy, if you know what I mean."

Cal played dumb, not wanting to give anything away. He raised his palm and screwed up his face to prompt Stefan into telling more.

Stefan nodded his head in the direction toward Rocco. "That one. He rides only for himself. He isn't exactly someone you can trust. Everyone around here knows about him."

"Knows what about him?"

Stefan was finished with the conversation. He pulled his bike away from Cal, but as he was pulling away, he turned his head and looked Cal in the eye.

"Heard about your crash yesterday. I'm glad you're all right. It could have been much worse. The roads around here are scenic, but they can be dangerous. So can the riders. Be careful, especially with those you think are on your side."

Cal pulled in a deep breath. Stefan wasn't the first person who had warned him about Rocco. And he had certainly experienced Rocco's sneakiness firsthand. But the idea that the guy was known as a snake throughout the whole of Northern Italy was chilling. Cal reflected on Stefan's suggestion that he should have joined the Nove Colli team. He was beginning to wonder if he had made a mistake.

CHAPTER 29

For the next thirty kilometers, SD and Nove Colli took turns pulling the peloton from the front. Their temporary alliance was working, and their cooperative effort propelled the pace to a speed higher than either team would have been able to accomplish on its own. The steady work yielded an average speed of over fifty kilometers per hour. At this rate, the breakaway was doomed and the devastation behind them was piling up. Riders fell off the pace and settled into survival mode, just hoping to finish in whatever shape they could.

Cal felt a measure of compassion for those who were suffering. Falling off the pace in a race like this was water torture, slow, relentless and, before long, crushing. Life wasn't much better for the riders ahead of them in the breakaway. He knew when the catch was imminent, the cooperation of the breakaway would collapse, along with their efficiency. The stronger riders in the breakaway, the ones who still harbored the hope of staying out in front of the peloton, would argue with the ones who were too cooked to contribute much to their endeavor. Once the catch appeared inevitable, when they could feel the peloton breathing down their necks, one or two of the riders might try a last gasp acceleration to preserve their lead. It was futile exercise, though. Without the collective force of numbers, they were doomed. The breakaway group was now little more than a carrot dangling in front of the hard-charging peloton. It was heartbreaking, Cal thought, but it was also the law of the road. If you take it out and you can't hold your lead, you're little more than a road hazard by the end of the day.

When the final catch took place, the execution came with little fanfare. With hardly a passing nod to acknowledge their failed effort, the lead group accelerated past the first breakaway rider dangling off the back. He turned his head and glared at the group and made a desperate effort to merge with them, but the passing group's pace was too fast for him to hold. And like a falling leaf, he drifted out the back of the main pack. The lead riders never broke stride. They moved past the next rider, then another and another. Finally, the peloton pounced on the two remaining breakaway riders, gathering them up and spitting them out the back. Cycling protocol and sportsmanship dictated a few words of encouragement to each of the riders as they were passed.

"Nice job. *Calma. Forte,*" he called out.

It was an ironic kind of sportsmanship, Cal thought. Set them up. Knock them down. Move on down the road. Who's next? That was just the way it worked. These guys were history anyway, and they probably knew it, which is why they tried to get away before the race headed uphill. Now, heads down, slumped over their machines, they just hoped to finish. The symptoms of the cooked rider—the ragged breathing, the grunting and groaning, the shoulders slumping, the cadence moving from fluid to balky, and the pedaling moving from circles to squares—were sweet sensations so long as they belonged to someone else and not you.

Midway into the race, the terrain and surrounding countryside had changed. The gently rolling roads heading out from Bassano gave way to the steeper pitches that introduced the foothills of Monte Grappa. The traditional Italian homes that lined the road closer to town were replaced by bucolic farms and the occasional country café, feed store, and *trattoria*. Tractors rolled through their daily routine on the fields they passed. The drivers paused a moment to watch the passing race, then returned to their work. The course reminded Cal of the routes he regularly rode back home in Northern California. Roads that took him far away from the suburban buzz and traffic.

The knowledge that the climb up Monte Grappa wasn't too far off pulled Cal from his reverie about the scenic beauty. The crowds on either side of the road had thinned. Smaller in numbers, but no less enthusiastic, the fans still called out their names. Overnight, the more committed fans had spray painted the road with their favorite riders' names along with encouraging words. "Bravo Carlo!" "Coraggio, Paco." "Vincere, Stefan!" Cal envied that kind of recognition. As an American racing in Europe, he had never had that kind of support. At least, he thought, he had Daniella. The thought warmed him and gave him a well appreciated boost of energy.

He glanced down at her picture mounted on the handlebar of Gianni's bike.

The support car, piloted by Gianni couldn't be too far behind them. Hell, he realized, she might even be watching me right now. Just the thought that Daniella could be so close and that she might be witnessing his ride, made him sit up a little straighter on his bike. It quickened his pedaling cadence and put a little extra snap into his stroke. It didn't make the fatigue go away, but it made it seem less of an insult. This, he realized, was better than any performance-enhancing drug he had ever consumed with T Mobile. How to make it last?

For the next twenty kilometers, a slow attrition took its toll. The numbers diminished. The lone wolves were gone. Each of the teams had suffered some casualties, losing numbers. SD remained mostly intact. As did Nove Colli.

Somewhere in the middle of a race, it becomes clear who is going to be there at the end and who is not. It's like a sixth sense, an intuition gained from hours in the saddle. Cal took a hard look at Stefan and Rocco. He could see they were going to be the horses that fought it out to the end.

Cal made every effort to detach himself from the growing fatigue. He had seen firsthand what happened to riders who thought too much about the "why" of suffering. Too much thinking was a distraction, an energy sapper. The truth was this—the work never stopped and the agony was an essential part of the racing experience. The only question was "how much and how often?" At some point, in every race, most competitiors would decide they had had enough, leaving the finish to those who, through some combination of strength and will power, were able to hang in there. Cal wondered about his own fortitude. Did he have it in him? Was today going to be one of those days when he entered the fog of fatigue and came through the other side, or was the end for him only a matter of choosing when he surrendered?

A sign appeared on the side of the road. Cal craned his neck to get a good look. Several riders blocked his view, but as he got closer, he made out the letters. "Monte Grappa. Cine al 50Km." Monte Grappa. Summit in fifty kilometers. Shit, thought Cal, it's here.

Responding to the implicit message in the sign, the riders rose out of their saddles in concert like a choreographed dance troupe. The cadence of their pedal strokes dropped precipitously, but the power they pressed through each revolution soared. Shifters clicked in search of lower gears. A sense of determination saturated the group. Here was the beginning of the end for many of them. Several of the SD riders and Nove Colli riders fell off the pace immediately. Cal looked around and saw that Carlo was gone. No surprise. The last few kilometers had taken a toll on the young rider, and the last time Cal had seen him, he looked like hell. Also gone were Marcello and the Swiss brothers, Tomas and Giorgio. The Nove Colli group was also weeding out some of its own weaker riders. Like hair thinning on the top of a head, the once-dense peloton was a leaner and sparser organization now. It was selection time.

SD and Nove Colli tightened their hold on the lead, driving the pace and putting the hurt on the riders behind them. The peloton had shattered into smaller pieces, survivors looking for companionship. Each of these smaller groups became a functioning community, working together, pacing each other, and fighting for dominance inside their separate worlds. This balance of allegiance and competition was a constant dynamic, always fluid as some riders recovered and made the push to join a group up the road, and others slipped off the back. The experienced riders knew to hang in, despite the growing gap between them and the leaders. Races are unpredictable that way. A crash, a change in the heart of the leaders, a hidden store of energy discovered in recovery, and the profile of the race could change. Smart riders, experienced riders, knew that giving up was a state of mind, as well as a body state, so they hung in, waiting, hoping, and enduring.

Once he had passed the initial surge, Cal settled into a more comfortable cadence. More than ever, he wished he knew the terrain better. Staying with the front group was essential. But for how long? And what surprises might be around the next corner, or the one after that? It had been at least twenty kilometers since the last sign. Quick calculations told him he had at least thirty kilometers left to go to the finish. The café Daniella had told him about, Il Piccolo, the marker for the start of the final steep climb, was ten kilometers from the top. That meant another twenty kilometers before he reached it. He began to feel more confident. If the pace didn't accelerate too fast, he could hang in for another twenty kilometers. At that point it was anybody's race.

He took a survey of the survivors so far. Rocco? Check, still here. SD support riders? Marcello, Filippo, and Lucca were still there, although they were looking a little ragged. No matter, it was still nice to have them pedaling in support. Nove Colli riders? He stared across and checked out the expression on Stefan's face. Young Stefan looked strong. No sign that he was flagging. And to make matters worse, he still had several of his team members at his side. There were going to be no breakaway winners today. The race was going to be decided in the last few kilometers.

Knowing it was going to be a gut-wrenching climb to the finish, Cal shifted to a lower gear to give his legs a little break. He rose out of the saddle and arched his back to stretch out the muscles in his lower back. In his prime, in this type of situation, he would have felt the urge to force the issue, and push the pace to send his competitors to the point of exhaustion. But not today. Only *if* and *when* he had the strength would he try to make his break.

Lucca pulled up next to Cal and leaned in, speaking out of the side of his mouth to keep the Nove Colli riders from overhearing him, said. "Rocco says this is the time to go. Turn up the pace and 'break the legs' of the Nove Colli guys. He'll sit in and wait, and then counter somewhere up the road."

Cal understood the trap Rocco was setting. "Tell Rocco that if he wants to 'break some legs,' he should go out on his own. I'm not attacking yet. I'm not going all-in just so he can rest and then ride my wheel to pull him on the podium. Fuck that."

Lucca looked at Rocco with annoyance and frustration. Like the rest of the SD riders, he wasn't comfortable disobeying his longtime leader. Still, he understood Cal's resistance. He just didn't want to be the one to deliver the bad news to Rocco.

"But…"

"No buts," Cal cut him off with a firm wave of his hand. "Not now. I'm not gassing myself for Rocco."

Lucca was at a loss. "I'm just saying… Rocco wants…"

Cal cut him off again. He pulled his bike sharply to the left and separated himself from Lucca. As he did so, he moved closer to Stefan, the young Nove Colli rider, who had heard the whole exchange.

"So. You're too independent for that group. You disobey the team leader and you might get punished."

"I'll take that chance," snapped Cal. "I know what Rocco has in mind. And I don't think he has my interests, or anyone else's, in mind."

"Good. You're smart. Like I said before, you should work with our team. What the hell? You're out of here in a couple of days. You don't owe SD anything. Why not work with us? We'll make sure you make it to the top."

Cal laughed. "Yeah. Like you guys are going to help me? Stefan, do I look that naïve? You guys would just use me, too. Thanks for the invitation, but I'll stick with my team and see how this plays out."

Cal was used to this kind of horse-trading and cut-throat strategizing at the pro level. But at the amateur level? These guys were supposed to be in it for the love of the sport. First, his own team leader tries to get him to blow himself up to help his own chances. Then, the leader of the other team tries to seduce him into their fold. No, his best option was to continue with his plan, hang with the lead group, wait as long as he could, shorten the race, and then see what he had left in the tank when he got to the final surge.

The lead pack slogged upward for the next hour. No one seemed strong enough to take and hold the lead. The result was a complicated and subtle prisoner's dilemma, an alliance to work together while still trying to come out ahead. Despite the implicit truce to stay together, they watched each other like hawks, waiting for the signs of fatigue that signal vulnerability. If any rider in their dwindling pack smelled blood in the water, he would attack.

Cal knew Rocco was still steaming about his insubordination. Almost on cue, Rocco appeared next to Cal and snarled, "When I say to pull, you should follow my direction. You need to do what you're told. I'm still the captain of the team and you're working for the team."

"Rocco, you may be the captain, but use your head. Attacking now, before the last climb, is suicide. So we go now and what happens? Nove Colli sits in behind us, forces us to do the work, and then eats our lunch when we can't hold the attack. It's too far out. Even if we do drop them with an acceleration here, which I doubt, there's too much time left on the climb for them to reorganize, recover, and catch us. So we waste a lot of effort and what does it get us? Tired legs, and a lost race."

"We can break them now. I know it. If you'll put in the work, we can do it."

"You think so? Look at Stefan over there. He looks like he could hold this pace for a week. He's just waiting for you to do something stupid. Go ahead and attack if you want to. You can even sacrifice some of your teammates if you want to. Take Marcello and Filippo. Maybe they can go with you. But I'm figuring that the winner is going to save his legs until the end."

"You mean you're afraid to try."

"Why does everything always come down to macho pride for you?"

"And for you it doesn't?"

"No, not everything. That's a lesson for you, Rocco. But I can't teach you now. I've got a race to ride."

The two riders moved apart. Cal just shook his head. Rocco was behaving like a petulant, little tyrant. Cal may not have known the particulars of this mountain, but he was confident in his knowledge of race tactics, and he was certain that the best way to tackle this climb was to hang in with the protection of the group, not to decimate it with an attack. The incline was taking its toll. A deep fatigue was setting into his quads and his butt. His back ached and his neck felt like a vice was clamped on the base of his skull.

One switchback up, about a quarter of a kilometer away, Cal saw a cluster of people gathered by the side of the road. He saw the different team colors and realized they were entering the feed zone, where they would be able to gather up their feed bags and pull out the nutrition bars, fluids, and any other foods they needed to refuel. The riders slowed and maneuvered to the right side of the road. The support team members, positioned on the edge of the road, thrust the bags into the passing riders' hands. Once secured, the riders slung them over their shoulders, working smoothly and quickly to avoid a break in the pace. They hungrily reached inside, desperate for the energy the contents might provide. The next kilometer was a blizzard of torn energy bar wrappers, discarded water bottles, sandwich wrappings, and fruit debris. Cal, like most of the Americans pros, tended to favor the gels and energy concoctions, like the hydrating electrolyte drinks. The Europeans were more traditional, preferring "real" food—croissants, sandwiches, and pastries. To Cal's mind, those things looked a lot more appealing than the gooey mess that he was trying to suck out of a sticky container, but he didn't think a croissant would do more than sit in his gut like a load of sugary glue. He slammed down the last of his energy drink and pitched the empty bottle to the side, where it was set upon by a swarm of kids who were hungry for souvenirs. He replaced the used canteen with a fresh one and pulled the bag off of his shoulder. The empty bag followed the empty canteen to the side of the road.

The fuel hit the spot. Maybe it was psychological, but he thought he could actually feel it making its way into his legs, his back, his heart, and lungs. He felt stronger than he had before the food station. Now, was the time to bear down and plan his finishing push.

Cal wasn't the only rider who was revived. Once the impromptu lunch on the road was finished, the pace accelerated. By design, the heightened pace was calibrated to kick the pretenders out of the back. Gradually, one after another of the racers found the pain too much to bear. Two more of the Nove Colli riders dropped off the pace. The last, a veteran named Claudio, patted Stefan on the back before he pulled his bike to the left and allowed the pack to pass him. Cal couldn't make out the words, but the message was clear — you're on your own, take the team to glory.

With the loss of Claudio, the Nove Colli team was down a rider to protect and shelter Stefan. The loss of one of his lieutenants left him more exposed, vulnerable. Sensing this, Rocco and Marcello made a quick move, accelerating up the road. The Nove Colli riders let them go. A slight gap grew wider, separating them from the rest of the lead pack. It looked like the peloton was going to splinter. The sense of danger permeated the peloton. A lead peloton without organization is unpredictable.

"Oh, shit," thought Cal. "There's a long way to go and these guys are taking it out now?" He made a snap decision. Move now or get dropped. He quickly accelerated and caught up with the riders at the front.

"What are you guys doing," he asked the first SD rider, Marcello.

"I'm just doing what I'm told."

"Look behind you," commanded Cal, motioning to the trailing peloton, including the re-consolidated Nove Colli team. "Do you see what you're doing?"

Marcello looked behind him, down the road, not understanding what Cal was referring to.

"What?"

"The whole of the Nove Colli team is sitting in on your wheel. That's what. And you are pulling for all of them. Soft pedal a bit. Take it down a notch and let them come to the front. Make them take a pull. Save a little. What you use now won't be available later."

"Can't do it," said Marcello between gasps for air. "Rocco wants to go."

To no avail, Marcello continued his slamming effort until he could persist no longer. Then, with head bowed, sucking air like a drowning man going down for the last time, he steered his bike over to the side to allow the remnants of the peloton to swing past. He was done for the day, used up, and discarded. Cal shook his head in dismay. He had no problem with a rider sacrificing himself for the team. That's the burden the teammates were expected to take on. It was the timing that bothered him. It was a rogue effort, and it would leave the team's leaders exposed, without any support when the final ten kilometers arrived.

Marcello's surge had splintered the peloton as Cal predicted. As he approached a sweeping right hand turn, he looked ahead and saw a crowd of onlookers gathered by the side of the road. The cluster must have numbered at least a hundred. These were the die-hards. Getting to this vantage point took dedication, and their enthusiasm bled across the road. They screamed their support, rang bells, and jumped up and down as if their energy could be transferred to the passing racers. Behind the crowd, he saw Il Piccolo, the café that announced the final assault up Monte Grappa.

The final push had arrived.

Cal dropped back to the car to make sure he was correctly identifying the landmark. As the gap between him and the car closed, Daniella leaned out of the passenger seat. Her eyes sparkled with excitement. She screamed out over the noise of the crowd.

"Ten kilos more! Just ten. You got it! Just dig deep, Cal. These guys can't stay with you!"

He grinned back at Daniella. Over-the-top optimism was exactly what he needed to give him heart. Even if the other riders weren't as doomed as she seemed to think, the spirit of her belief buoyed him like an elixir.

CHAPTER 30

Cal swung around to the driver's side of the car to confer with Gianni, who was a picture of manic motion. He had a map spread out on his lap, was punching keys on his GPS system, and had a clipboard hanging from the mirror with the roster of the SD team. He held tight to the steering wheel, but his head was on a swivel, keeping track of all the action around him. Cal looked at Gianni, searching for some pearl of wisdom, some hint or strategy that would give him an edge in this last section of the race.

"How do you feel, Cal?"

"I've definitely felt better. Wish I knew the road better. I think I'm sitting in a good place. I need fresh bottles. Hydration."

Reaching into the back seat, Gianni pulled several from a full cooler. "Here you go." After Cal had secured the two bottles on his bike, Gianni gave him another. "Here take this one, extra for the *ragazzi*. See who needs it."

Cal smiled as he tucked the extra bottles into his shirt. "Now, I'm a *domestique*? A water carrier?"

"On this team, there are nothing but *domestiques*," replied Gianni. "Go ahead. Push it at your own pace. We don't know what Nove Colli has left. But it doesn't matter now. You give it what you have. Ten more kilometers. All uphill."

Daniella leaned over from the passenger seat and offered her own send off. "You look strong. I'll see you at the finish line."

Her encouragement had the desired effect. His legs felt lighter. If he didn't make it across the line first, after all the support she had given him, it wasn't going to be because he didn't bust his ass trying. Pushing off from the support car, and giving a wave, Cal shifted his gears into a higher cog and took off. He looked back at Gianni, hoping for a last-minute piece of advice or strategy, something to give him an edge over the next ten kilometers. Gianni just looked at Cal with a knowing smile. He simply flicked the wrist forward and mouthed, "*Vai, vai.*" Cal felt a pang of sadness leaving the team car, a little like a child venturing into the ocean, leaving his parents on the shore. He was certainly on his own now.

Cal pulled up to his SD riders and prepared to hand the extra water bottles to his teammates.

"I've got two extra. Who needs them?"

Lucca reached out to take one of the bottles from Cal's extended hand. Before he could wrap his hand around it, Rocco intercepted it, snatching it like an eagle pulling a mouse from the ground. He turned to Cal and snarled, "I'll take that. He doesn't need it. His work is almost done. He's finished."

Rocco's abrupt dismissal hit Lucca like a rock. After pulling for the last hour, he was in desperate need of hydration. More than the fluid, though, Lucca was astonished that Rocco would discard him in such a cavalier way. Rocco was pulling the plug on him. He wanted desperately to hang on longer, to finish with the lead group, if possible. But without water he was doomed.

His voice was pleading. "But I'm out of water. Just share it with me. Let me have half of it, so I can stay with you longer."

Rocco dismissed him with a wave of the hand. He opened the nozzle of the water bottle greedily and drained a quarter of it. He then settled the water bottle into the cage on his bike. His selfishness was staggering to Cal. He decided, then and there, that this was the place to make a stand. He pulled his bike closer to Lucca. Taking one of his own water bottles out of its cage, he gave it to Lucca and let him finish most of it.

"Thanks," he said, with some of the water still dripping off of his chin. "Rocco? I don't know. He gets like this."

Cal was done with excuses. "It's not right. You work for the team and the team should work for you. Oh, fuck it," he said, and pounded his handlebars. "Let's kick this mule and take up the pace."

Rocco had seen Cal offering his bottle to Lucca. Cal was glad he had seen it—he was done with diplomacy, too. Giving the water bottle to Lucca made strategic sense. The race was heading into the final stages, and having a teammate along, even for just a few kilometers, would raise the chances of keeping a teammate in the race to help him. Besides, Lucca had earned the right to sit in with the group for as long as he was able. It boiled down to respect for the effort made.

Cal took stock of the survivors: three remaining SD riders, Lucca, Rocco, and Filippo. Four including himself. The Nove Colli team, had their designated leader, Stefan, and was also four strong. Two other riders, interlopers riding without any support rounded out the group. They might fall in with either the SD or Nove Colli team, an alliance on the road, but without teammates to help them, their chances of taking the win were slim. It was clear now. The day would belong either to SD or Nove Colli, and victory would hinge on the strength, the ability to tolerate the pain, the conditioning, and, not the least, teamwork.

The riders were cresting the tree line, and pine forests gave way to barren, mountain pastures. Off in the distance, the peaks of the surrounding Dolomites sparkled with snow, and the view stretched all the way to Trieste and Venice. The road narrowed and roughened, buckled by years of freezing and thawing. Cracks along the shoulder kept the riders in the middle, effectively limiting the space to an arm-span for passing which raised the danger of crashing. Above this treacherous path, eight kilometers away, the summit face of Monte Grappa loomed. It seemed so close, so dominant and overbearing, that Cal imagined, just for a moment, he could reach out and touch it.

Those eight kilometers were going to pitch the riders up another 750 meters in elevation, a ten percent incline for most of the climb, steeper in some spots. Lung bursting steep. A quick glance up to his left revealed a tortuous series of switchbacks carved into the rock. There must have been at least twenty of them. Even though the top of the mountain, and its beckoning finish line, seemed so close, Cal calculated that the next eight kilometers would take at least half an hour, maybe a little more, maybe a little less, depending on how much fight the riders had in them—for each other and for the road. This was going to be an epic finish.

He entertained the idea of throwing in a little surge—just to see what his companions might have left. But it was suicide to do it alone. He would need a committed lead-out from at least some of his teammates. He might get Lucca and Filippo to come to the front with him. It was worth a try. He kicked his bike up a gear and stood on the pedals.

He slid past Rocco and pulled even with Lucca, who was ticking off a steady pace at the front. The two riders exchanged glances. Lucca cranked his head to the left and stared into Cal's eyes. He nodded his head in agreement and quickened his pace. Cal responded with a nod and flicked his wrist forward, indicating that this was the time to make their move. Cal brought his fist up and touched Yves' glove to his lips. "Here we go," he murmured.

Rocco watched the exchange between Cal and Lucca and reacted. He jumped to make sure Cal wouldn't get the drop on him. Close behind him was Stefan and the rest of the Nove Colli team. A bungee cord seemed to connect the riders. The group moved in concert. Who was going to make the move that would snap the band?

Lucca pulled even and motioned for Cal to follow him. He charged in front of Cal and began a furious charge. Quickly Filippo fell into the gap between Lucca and Cal, and the three riders coalesced into a powerful engine chewing its way up the pavement. Cal doubted the wisdom of the move. Would Lucca be able to continue his pull? Filippo? What were they doing? It was almost too good to believe, Cal thought, but Lucca and Filippo were willing to work for him, to pull him, and, more surprising than anything, to help him take the prize away from Rocco.

The intensity of Lucca's charge caught Rocco and the Nove Colli riders by surprise. They had been so focused on Cal that they missed Lucca's move and were stalled in their reaction. It allowed a gap to open on the road, and deserted by his teammates, Rocco had no choice but to jump in with the Nove Colli riders. Cal dared a look backward. Rocco's face bore the look of a child unexpectedly punished.

Cal turned to Lucca and mouthed the words, "What are you doing?" He tilted his head back in the direction of Rocco.

"Stop asking questions," grunted Lucca between labored breaths. "Just hang behind us and let us pull as long as we can."

"But Rocco?"

"Fuck Rocco. He'll have to do work on his own."

"But?"

"Italian road honor. Rocco is getting what he deserves. It's payback for what he did to you, and to us."

Pedals turning at a furious pace, the threesome assaulted the road. The dearth of oxygen, combined with the steep angle of the road, and the bumpy road conditions made for a struggle. Lucca was the first to go bankrupt. His head hung. His mouth gulped in air. When he hit his limit, he pulled to the side. That left Filippo to lead Cal, tucked into his sheltering draft—at this point in the race, the benefit of a teammate's draft was immeasurable.

They continued for another two kilometers like men on a mission, their bodies bent in exhaustion, and their minds captured in mental calculations, titrating time and effort against the resistance the mountain offered. Cal was awed by Filippo's pulling power. Now he knew why they called him "the Generator." He had seen Filippo work in practice sessions, but never with the fierce determination he was showing now. Cal had to dig deep just to hang on to his wheel.

Finally, though, Filippo turned his head to Cal. "Fifty more."

CHAPTER THIRTY

He counted out fifty more rotations on the pedals, standing out of the saddle, with his bike rocking from side to side as he wrenched every last ounce of power he had into the pedals. When he reached the count of fifty, he dropped his head and turned to Cal. "*Basta*. I'm done. You go." He pulled to the side, exhausted. "*Buon fortuno, amico.*"

"*Grazie,*" replied Cal. "Thanks for the pull and thanks for the help." He adjusted his grip on the bars and looked up at the empty road.

CHAPTER 31

Perhaps Gianni's bike had given him wings. Or maybe it was Filippo and Lucca's sacrifice. Whatever the source, Cal had more strength left in his legs, than he thought. In fact, he was surprised to be feeling as strong as he was. Coming in the distance, he saw the five-kilometer flag, waving overhead like a homecoming greeting. His legs churned harder. Five kilometers, he thought. Under normal conditions, pedaling around home in the hills of Marin County, five kilometers would be nothing. Under the current conditions, road pitched uphill, pace accelerating, his heart beating at a furious pace, his legs aching, and his lungs burning? Hunted down by a pack of riders? A lifetime of suffering could fill the five kilometers.

Cal recognized that he was at a crossroads. Fillipo and Lucca had sacrificed themselves, giving him the gap that he now enjoyed. But they were history now. He looked at the options. Keep putting the hammer down and try to hold his lead? Or was the wise move to let the chasers, the isolated pockets of riders behind him, catch up and lead him to the finish? Both strategies carried their risks. Trying to win from the front was attractive and certainly would be glorious. But it was risky. If he blew up and failed, the chasers would beat him mercilessly when they caught him, passing him like so much debris on the road. Which left, what? He could back off. Sit up and let them catch him, rest a little bit, and save something for the finish. Danger there, too. If he let his little lead evaporate and went in with the group, would he have any legs left for the final sprint? In his current condition, what chance did he stand in a one hundred-meter death-dash to the line?

A quick hairpin turn came up, and, as he rounded the turn, he stole a glance down the road, underneath and behind him. What he saw sent chills down his spine. Storming up the road, a mere fifty meters behind him, two riders had dropped the rest of the chasers and were closing in on him. They were churning their pedals, out of their saddles, and were eating up the grade, rocking back and forth to gain further purchase with each rotation of their pedals. Cal didn't need to see the blue of the Nove Colli team or the flashing red SD jersey to know who the riders were. Stefan and Rocco were closing fast, on their way to pay him an unwelcome visit.

Their progress made his choice an easy one. From the way they were working together, Cal could see that Rocco and Stefan had developed an alliance with the sole intention of pulling him in. If their alliance held, it would be two against one. Cal knew Rocco would make a pact with the devil to beat him. Cal's only hope was to let them catch him and go for the win in a sprint. Sprint? Cal's mind flashed back to the last time he and Rocco had gone head to head in a sprint on a training ride, and how Rocco had easily grabbed the win in that joust. A sprint finish was definitely *not* in his favor. Strategy was Cal's only hope. Rocco was predictable, but what about Stefan? What would he do? At the moment, it looked like he was marking Rocco, so whatever Rocco did, Stefan would follow. Good, thought

Cal. Let the two of them stick together. Cal knew instantly that there was only one tactic that might win the day and he put it into play immediately. He wasn't sure that it would work, but it was the only card he had left to play. "Here goes nothing," he whispered to himself.

He slowed his pace and dropped his head. He collapsed his upper body over his bars and slowed his cadence. He flipped his sunglasses up onto his forehead, all the better to allow his soon arriving competitors to get a good look into his depleted eyes. He took on the posture and visage of a whipped dog, a rider in the death throes of collapse. Within moments, Stefan and Rocco pulled even with him. Stefan came first, moving past Cal, with Rocco in tow. As they passed, Cal turned to face them, in order to give them full exposure into his mask of fatigue. From the smirk on Rocco's face as he passed, he knew that the message he was sending had been received. Rocco was convinced that Cal was cooked.

Rocco's pleasure at Cal's distress was unbounded. "If you can manage to hang on, you might make it to take third. Not bad for a tourist. But you took my lieutenants from me, and for that, you have to make it on your own."

Cal studied Rocco and made a quick assessment. Rocco still looked pretty strong. He still had his legs. He was feeling confident. Cocky, even. And his comments, about taking his lieutenants away and "managing to hang on?" Managing? That kind of bravado could only come out of the mouth of someone who considered the race to be over. Rocco, Cal thought, was ripe for a lesson in humility.

But what about Stefan? Stefan had been strong all day, probably the strongest of the three remaining contenders. But his youth was his vulnerability. The fact that he had attached himself to Rocco, instead of trying to drop him on the climb, when he had better climbing skills than Rocco, told Cal all he needed to know. Stefan was not emotionally ready to go for the kill. He didn't know his own strength or was too cautious to use it. Too bad for him.

The situation stuck Cal as amusing. If it worked, it was like taking candy from a baby. These guys, Rocco and Stefan, were strong as hell. But they were green. Neophytes.

Cal further softened the pressure on his pedals and slowed the pace, allowing Rocco and Stefan to build a slight gap. He measured out the stretch of open space between them like a fisherman doling out his line. Fifteen meters, no more, no less. He was playing with fire here. If the advantage grew too large, more than twenty or thirty meters, he would never be able to close on them. If he kept it too narrow, they would feel pushed, and ramp up their effort to the finish.

The three riders entered the final straightaway to the finish line. The barriers on the road leading to the finish line kept the screaming fans from crushing in on the riders and closing the road. The ear-splitting noise worked to Cal's advantage, preventing the two leading riders from hearing what was going on behind them. Their focus would be straight ahead, on each other, and on the finish line.

Cal focused on the fifteen-meter gap. Ahead, Rocco and Stefan had begun a cat and mouse game, toying with each other to see who was going to lead out the sprint. Cal slowed to match their easing of the pace. Fifteen meters. No more, and no less. It was the perfect distance for a surprise dash to the finish line. He desperately needed the element of surprise. Cal marked the leaders, a predator silently stalking its prey.

And now the game in front of him began in earnest. A hundred meters from the finish, Stefan softened his stroke and sat up. He slowed his pace. He maneuvered behind Rocco, trying to manipulate him into the lead-out position. It was a wise move. He was positioning himself to win.

Rocco, unwilling to play the engine to their two-man team, countered by slowing to a near stall. For a moment, the two riders seemed like they were prepared to come to a complete stop, hanging in suspended animation. Neither was willing to be the lead out rider. Cal had hoped this would happen. Rocco and Stefan were circling each other like hungry hawks. Fifteen meters gap, no more, no less. Just a few moments more. Let them completely lose their momentum. They were digging their own graves.

Fifty meters to the finish. Rocco and Stefan were locked on each other, oblivious to the strategy unfolding behind them. Cal kept his distance. Steady. Perfect. Cal eyed the finish line. Stefan and Rocco seemed almost hypnotized by their tactics. Their heads were craned to the side as they eyed each other, wondering who was going to be the first to make the charge.

Forty meters from the finish. It was now or never. He lept off his saddle and exploded into his pedals, wrenching his bike to the side, forcing all the torque his body could possibly produce down through the pedals and into his wheels. He gripped his handlebars and ripped through with his shoulders and arms. The pain in his right shoulder roared, snatching his breath away. A couple of revolutions and a quick shift of the derailleur to a higher gear. He snapped up his cadence, pulling furiously at the cranks, and slipped his bike into a bigger gear yet. The gap closed in a blur. He hit them hard, without warning. He was past them before they knew what hit them. Twenty meters to go to the line.

Ahead, he saw the finish line banner. His acceleration had caught them by surprise, but could he hold on? What was left? Maybe forty more revolutions? Could he do it? His quads were screaming for mercy. His back was seized into a knot. Each pedal stroke felt like it should have been the last. In the background, he heard Rocco scream out. *Testa di merda*! Cal's Italian was rudimentary, but he knew the term "shithead" when he heard it. It brought a smile to Cal's lips. He heard Stefan and Rocco mashing their derailleurs, searching for higher gears to chase. They never had a chance. Caught napping, and tricked with one of the oldest tricks in the book, they gave it all they had, but were relegated to a struggle for second place. Rocco slammed his fist against his handlebars and let out a scream that rang across the gathered fans.

The last ten meters were a blur. Cal rocketed across the line, raised his hands in a victory salute and pounded his chest. He looked back to see if Rocco and Stefan were still behind them. What he saw made his heart beat faster. The two had their heads buried and their legs were pumping furiously as they tried to out-sprint each other to finish second.

He had done it, won the race. Six seconds behind him, Stefan crossed the line and celebrated his second place finish. He raised his arms to salute the fans around him before he was engulfed by the Nove Colli team handlers, who were waiting at the line. He was followed closely by Rocco, who chased him across the finish line in third position, his face wracked in pain. Rocco dismounted his bike immediately after crossing the line, and in a display of pique and disgust, flung his bike to the ground and let out a roar of frustration. The anger in his cry paralyzed the crowd around him. None moved to help him. He was left standing alone, dejected, defeated.

* * *

Cal fell into an ocean of caring hands. Team handlers, friends, and fans swarmed him. For a moment, he felt a wave of panic. He was gasping for air and the crowd was suffocating him. Race officials intervened, rushing to his side, ushering him, still on his bike, to a cordoned-off area for finished riders. The press was waiting. Microphones were thrust into his face. Their questions came rapid fire, a salad of language that he wasn't able to decipher. It made no difference. He was delirious with joy and fatigue. All he could hear were the calls of, "*Bravo, bravissimo.*"

Cal's eyes skimmed across the throng looking for Gianni, Daniella, and his father. Even if they had been standing directly in front of him, the crowd was pressing in on him from all sides and the tumult would have made spotting them difficult. Still, he knew they had to be near. Daniella had promised she would be waiting at the top.

Suddenly, cutting through the commotion of the teaming crowd, an arm reached out and encircled Cal's shoulder. He fought it off at first, fearing that he was being pulled off of his bike. Its grip was insistent, and he looked over and saw Daniella's beaming face. She pulled him close. He was sweaty and dirty, and his mouth felt crusted with salt and sports drink, but she placed a long kiss on his lips. He leaned into her and felt his body surrender to an overwhelming fatigue. He was now completely and totally spent. For the first time in three hours, he felt safe. He put his shoulder against Daniella's body for support and slowly unclipped his right leg from his pedal. He put his foot on the ground and unclipped his left leg. Daniella had hold of the bicycle now. He flipped his leg over the top bar and pivoted to face her. He realized now that what he thought was sweat on his cheek was actually tears. He had been crying. So had Daniella. The two collapsed into each other. As he buried his face in her soft neck, the roar of the crowd slipped away, replaced by the sound of his breathing as he nestled against Daniella's chest.

"You did it! You won Le Scale."

"I did, didn't I?" wheezed Cal. He meant for it to be an exclamation, but between his fatigue and his incredulity, it sounded more like a question. He let Daniella lead him through the pressing crowd, aiming for the winner's podium. Over the heads of the crowd in front of him, he heard his father calling out to him, "Cal! Cal!" Paul was leaping up and down to be seen above the crowd. Finally, he broke through the fans surrounding Cal and rushed to embrace him. Cal had never seen his father cry before, not once in all of the victories he had achieved in his career. But now, there was no doubting that the glitter in his father's eyes came from tears of joy.

"Shit, Dad! Can you believe it? We did it!"

"No, son," Paul shouted to Cal. "*You* did it. Congratulations! I'm so proud of you."

"Thanks, Dad," replied Cal. He lowered his head to put his forehead against his father's shoulder. Endorphins coursed through his exhausted body, and he felt drunk with happiness and generosity. "Thanks for getting me back on the saddle."

"I may have gotten you on the saddle, son. But it was *you* who put yourself first across the finish line."

"Yeah, I fucking did it. I fucking did it!"

Gianni stood next to Paul, beaming. He was stoic as usual, but he had a youthful light in his eyes that made him look, for a moment, like the Giro champion in his prime. He clapped Cal on the back, and they both stood with a hand on the handlebars of his bicycle.

"One hell of a ride, *ragazzo*. One hell of a ride."

"Thanks to you. I couldn't have done it without you."

"Well, true. You are riding my bike," Gianni chuckled. "But that trick you played. Letting them think you were done. That was classic. The perfect bluff. I fell for it once when Fausto Coppi beat me in a final stage of the Giro. I haven't seen it played so well since then."

"Maybe I wasn't faking," said Cal. "Maybe I really was done."

"Never done," interjected Daniella. "You were never done. Even when you 'quit' racing, you were never done. Not really. Not deep inside. That's what my papa and your dad and I always knew about you. You were never done, not with the heart of a winner beating in your chest."

Their victory celebration was cut short by the race officials, who barged through the ring of cheering spectators and flashing cameras, and ushered Cal to the victory podium. Cal was floating on air as he approached it. Already there were Stefan and Rocco—Stefan waving to his fans with adolescent glee, and Rocco with his head bowed, looking ready to leave. A set of stairs led to the podium. He hesitated. Did he have the strength in his legs to get up these stairs? He looked up on the podium itself, and saw his spot waiting for him. He set one shaky foot on the first step, and climbed.

CHAPTER 32

Cal's legs felt like they were filled with concrete, but he strode across the front of the podium stage. Stefan grasped Cal's hand, placing his other hand on top of Cal's, in a sincere two-handed shake. Admiration shone in his eyes. He pumped Cal's hand enthusiastically and smiled broadly. "Good race. Bravo, *amico*," he said.

"And you, too," replied Cal. "You're a strong rider. You'll have a lot of victories in your time."

"Yes, *grazie*, thank you. I guess I learned something today."

"What's that?" asked Cal.

"Never trust a dying rider."

"Yeah, well, you were too preoccupied with Rocco to know what was going on behind you. That worked to my advantage."

Stefan smiled. "We all know Rocco around here. I figured that it was better to keep my eye on him than on you. I won't make that mistake again."

Cal returned his smile. With his hand still holding Stefan's, he said, "If I taught you that, then my work is done."

He offered his hand next to Rocco.

Rocco just stared at it. "You rode a good race," he said,

not meeting Cal's gaze, staring off into the distance. "I thought you were cooked when we jumped. I guess you were just playing us. You made me look like a fool." His eyes were lifted upward as if he could find solace somewhere in the clouds.

"Look, Rocco, it hasn't exactly been fun riding and training with you. But the race is over and we both did what we could to get where we are. I'm damned happy to be here, and you should be, too. Let's let it go."

"Happy? With third place?"

"Yeah, happy with third. Just like I'm happy to be in first and Stefan here is fucking ecstatic to be in second. Third place in a race like this? Come on, you should celebrate."

Cal was cut short by the announcement of the awards presentation. The race director moved first to Rocco and placed a bronze medal around his neck. The ceremonial flower girls, the beauty queens representing the Veneto region, placed a bouquet of flowers in his hands. The race director repeated the same gesture with Stefan, who celebrated the moment with a shy kiss for the beauty queens, and raised his arms in salute to the crowd. He launched his bouquet into the sea of outstretched arms. Finally, the director stepped up to Cal.

Cal's heart was beating as fast as it had during any moment of the race. The depth of feeling for the victory, in a little town race, after all of his big-time pro experience, surprised him. He bent down, extending his neck for the gold medal, and clutched the bouquet. With the medal swinging from his neck, he thrust his hands skyward. He brought the bouquet to his nose, and inhaled its sweet, fresh perfume, and then flung it into the audience. It sailed across the space to the gathered crowd and landed in Daniella's outstretched hands. She pulled it in and clutched it to her breast with one hand, and blew a kiss to Cal with the other. For a moment, their eyes locked together in an electric connection. She mouthed the words, "Congratulations, *caro.*"

Once the medals had been distributed, Cal eased himself off the podium, stepping gingerly in his cleats. The fatigue from the day's effort enveloped him. It was a sweet receipt for the work he had done. Working his way through an adoring crowd of cycling fans, he crossed to the side of the finish line and joined the other SD riders, some of whom were just now crossing the finish line — some thirty minutes after his furious assault had won the day. The team was jubilant. They jumped and shouted and held their index fingers up, claiming their position as the number one team. They gathered around Cal and put him in the middle of their impromptu circle. Filippo stepped forward and embraced Cal.

"Our champion. You did it," he said.

"I couldn't have done it without your help. You pulled like a mother…"

"Yes, that's true. But you earned your victory. I pulled, but in the end, that trick at the end. *Dio mio,* if I'd only been there to see it. To see the look on Rocco's face."

The rest of the SD team clapped their approval.

Cal slowly turned in a circle and looked each of the riders in the eye. He raised his gold medal and said, "This is for all of you. I may wear it around my neck tonight. But tomorrow? It goes on the wall of Di Salvo Cycling."

Lucca stepped forward and reached out to examine the gold medal more closely. After lofting it in his hand to feel the weight, he said with a grin, "So we get to keep the medal and you get the girl?" He looked over Cal's shoulder and nodded toward Daniella who was standing to the side.

Out of the corner of his eye, Cal saw his father and Gianni in deep discussion with a well-dressed man, whose dark, tailored suit, deep blue shirt, and shiny shoes stood out from the casual garb of the cycling fans. Gianni took the man by the elbow and steered him toward Cal. Cal tracked their progress as they approached. He didn't know who the man was, but could tell from the way Gianni was behaving, so deferential, so attentive, that it had to be someone important.

"Cal, I'd like to introduce you to Signor Riccardo Parisi. Signor Parisi is the director of the Banca d'Italia racing team. He'd like to talk with you."

The director moved closer to Cal and looked him in the eye.

"Signor Cal, I watched what you did today. Le Scale is very difficult, no? Maybe not like a stage in the Giro," he said glancing over at Gianni, "but still quite an accomplishment. We Italians don't surrender our local races to outsiders without a fight."

"You can say that again. But I did have the help of a great team. And Gianni. His training. His team. His bike, even."

"Yes, I know about that. I heard about your crash on the ride yesterday. It takes, how do you put it? Balls? To get back on the bike the next day and compete. You aren't a typical amateur. You've had some experience. I can tell."

"Well, I…"

"I know about your experience with T Mobile. You're not the first rider who reached out for the top tier of racing and was spit out the back. Gerhardt? Well, let's just say that Gerhardt, and his tactics, and his approach to racing, and the way he, shall I say, *uses* talent are different from what I believe in." He shrugged his shoulders and raised his palms up to indicate a disdain for something he felt strongly about. "But what I saw today is something special. Riding with superior training is important. But riding with superior intelligence—that's something that no amount of coaching can teach."

"*Grazie.*"

"Ah, but listen, *amico*, I'd like to talk with you about your next steps. Have you given any thought to what you're going to do?"

"Well, no, not actually. I suppose I'll go back to the States." As Cal said it, images of returning to his position as a barista flashed in his mind. He felt his shoulders slump.

Parisi jumped in and continued. "I'd like to talk to you about joining my team, Banca d'Italia. We're in a transition year. Several of our veterans, Colombo, Schmidt, and Puliti are retiring. A couple of our younger riders are getting attractive offers and will be switching to other teams. We need some good young riders. I've got spots on my team for two riders and I was hoping that you'd join us for the next season."

Cal's mind started to spin. Suddenly, he was back in the room with Gerhardt, back on the road with the team, training in rainy, windy Belgium. The fatigue. He felt it now in his legs, as if they each weighed a hundred pounds. It was a reminder of just how brutal professional racing had been. But he wondered, a new start? Was the day's victory on Le Scale just going to be a reprise of his earlier experiences, or was it a new beginning? He tried in vain to organize his thoughts.

"Signor Parisi, I don't know what to say. I'm blown

away."

"Then, it's settled. Just say 'yes' and I'll have the contract sent to you. We don't have a huge budget, but I think you'll find the terms much better than racing for cups of espresso." He turned and smiled at Daniella.

Cal surprised even himself when he replied, "I just don't know."

"You don't know? You're refusing my offer?"

"No. Not refusing. Just that… Well, it's just that I'd decided some time ago that I wanted to leave racing and…"

"And today, you made your rebirth in racing and the results should have convinced you that you have a strong future. With my team, things will be different. You'll see. Ask Gianni."

Gianni set his hand lightly on Signor Parisi's shoulder. "Riccardo and I were teammates for several years. His philosophy on training and racing is very modern. And you couldn't work with a stronger team." Then, he set his other hand on Cal's shoulder. "But the question is this, *ragazzo*. Is it in you? Do you have the hunger to train and to compete? Because without that, the rest is just pain. One race, today, you're a champion. You can retire after today and no one would be critical. You can go out with the sweet taste of success in your mouth. But you know as well as anyone, that a real champion isn't born in a day and a professional career isn't about the glory, only. It's about the dedication to work, to survive, and, if you're good enough, to win."

All eyes were on Cal at that moment. He shifted his gaze to catch the expectant face of Daniella. He searched her eyes for guidance, hoping that the answer would be there. But it wasn't. With a flip of her head and palms raised outward, she indicated that the answer to this question was his, and his alone.

"Signor Parisi, I'm so honored that you would make this offer to me." His head felt light, and he struggled to find a diplomatic way of saying what he felt. "I didn't enter Le Scale to earn a professional contract. I entered it because it seemed like an opportunity to purge some bad memories that I had of racing, something that I loved, and something that I didn't want to remember in only the bad ways. I love this sport. I can't deny it. Your interest is very flattering, but I can't say yes."

The other SD riders who had gathered around were shocked to hear this exchange. Lucca, in particular, moved forward and said, "Cal, *tu sei pazzo*! You're crazy."

"Are you saying no?" inquired Parisi incredulously.

"No. I'm not saying no, either. Just asking if I can have some time to think about it. Can I sleep on the decision and let you know tomorrow?"

"Sure. Take the time. It's a big decision. But unless things have changed a lot since my days racing, you won't be sleeping too much tonight. Tonight is a night to celebrate your victory. So go ahead. Take the night and tell me tomorrow. But keep in mind that time doesn't run forever. If you don't reach a decision by tomorrow, I'll be extending the offer to some other very good riders I saw today."

Cal took a deep breath and turned to his gathered teammates. "Okay. Now, about that celebration. When does that start?"

Lucca popped the cork off of a bottle of champagne and sprayed the gathered team and supporters. "It just did. Drink deeply everyone. Today, we won Le Scale." The team gathered around, each taking a deep pull from the bottle before passing it on to the next.

Cal turned his head and looked around. "Where's

Rocco?"

"I don't know. I saw him throw his bike into his mother's car and head down the hill," replied Lucca. "He left right after the awards ceremony."

CHAPTER 33

The victory celebration was a signature event for the Villa Palma. The hotel had never had the honor of hosting a Le Scale champion. All the SD team members were there with family and girlfriends in tow, and they feasted on a lavish array of fresh bruschetta, prosciutto and bresaolo, plates of *Ziti Fra Diavolo* (in honor of the team's name) and a main course of Beef Florentine. There was a river of champagne and red wine to float the celebration, and the guests toasted their way through the dinner.

At the end of the dinner, Paul rose and lifted his glass of wine. It sparkled like a beacon in the bright lights of the chandelier. "I want to propose a toast to the champ. To my son." He turned to Cal, who saw what was coming and began an intent study of the tablecloth. "I think I'm going to need a larger shirt after today just to contain the size of my heart. They say a father's love has no boundaries. And at no time is that more true than today. Seeing you carrying this crazy flight of fancy through to the end made me so proud. You had so many opportunities to give in, to call it quits, or even just to finish and say 'job well done.' But that isn't you. You not only finished, but you did it in the only way you know how to finish — giving it your all, and coming out today with a total commitment.

The assembled crowd burst into a raucous chant, "Speech, speech!" Reluctantly, and with no small amount of emotional and physical discomfort, Cal rose to his feet.

He looked down at Daniella who was sitting next to him. He gestured for her to give him an idea of what to say, but she motioned for him to get on with it. "Come on, *campione*. This is your turn to address your fans. You need to speak for yourself here." She gave his hand a quick squeeze.

"Damn! I don't know what to say, really. I'm here, I'm here on a vacation, one day. And the next, I'm training, and then I'm racing, and now… I won the fucking Le Scale."

A roar soared up from around the tables.

"But I'm not here alone. As you all know by now, this isn't my first spin around the racing circuit. Since Gianni's generous offer to train with you guys, I've had a chance to think a lot about what happened with me the first time around. You guys have reminded me of what love for the bike can mean. I've been on both sides of the finish line when races have been won, and I can tell you for sure that winning makes the suffering a lot easier to bear than losing. And when we celebrate a victory, we all know that one rider may wear the champion's jersey, but a whole team helps him to put it on."

The cheering got even louder.

Lucca called out, "If you get tired of wearing the medal, I'll wear it for you!"

Cal laughed and shook his head. "It'd be too heavy for you. I'll wear it for now." He continued, "But there are a couple of people I'm especially grateful to." He turned to his father and raised his glass.

"Dad, you believed in me even when I didn't believe in myself. There were times when I hated you for that.

I asked myself why you wouldn't just let me be. Now, I guess I know. And now, I'm going to ask you to leave me alone again." He let the comment hang for a second, until a layer of confusion clouded the joy in Paul's eyes. "Nah, just kidding, Dad. You can bug me all you want." Paul's face cleared, and he laughed.

"And in my short time here in Italy," Cal said, "I've had the opportunity to have a second father. Gianni, you're a champion in the truest sense of the word. As a kid, growing up, I worshipped the great riders of Europe. If I had had the privilege of knowing you back then, I don't think I would have ever dreamt to be a professional racer, because you're so awesome and you embody so much of what is elegant and grand about cycling. I would have been intimidated to dream of being in the same world as you.

"Today, I won a championship. A race. Next year, there will be another champion and he'll feel like I do today, so cool. And after him, another and another, and so on. Victory is special, but it's a process, not an end. And it's a moment in time; it comes and then it goes. Something to savor, for sure, but, in the past weeks, I've appreciated something much more permanent than a trophy or a medal. I've learned about the power of the human heart. And the person that taught me that is here tonight."

Cal leaned over to Daniella, gave her a kiss on the cheek, and pulled her up from her seat. He put his arm around her and drew her close. She hung onto her glass of wine, happily pressing into his side, as if they had been a pair in the world for their whole lives.

"I love cycling. Always have. Even when I was hating it, I loved it. But that was one kind of love. But the love that comes from the people in your corner is something different." Turning to face Daniella, he looked at her. "You taught me so much. You taught me, for example, never to underestimate the power of Italian women, especially when it comes to descending mountain roads." The assembled guests laughed. "No, seriously. You showed me so much. I felt that I knew this race before I even pedaled a single stroke because of your knowledge. More than the roads, though, you taught me that there are opportunities to correct the mistakes that you make and not to be afraid to do that."

As he paused, a shout went up from the audience. "And she can still kick your ass on a mountain bike!"

"And yes, she can still kick my ass on a mountain bike. Which is the reason that I am announcing tonight my retirement from anything that even faintly resembles mountain bike racing."

CHAPTER 34

After the party had come to a finish and the last guest had left for home, Cal and Daniella sat in the bar, enjoying the quiet hotel and a final glass of red. Cal was exhausted from the race. He could tell that something was on Daniella's mind; when she was troubled, he was learning, she couldn't hold eye contact with him in their conversations and her fire crept out of her humor and into her attitude.

"You're thinking something," Cal said finally. "I can tell the wheels are turning in your head. What is it?"

"Today, after the race... Parisi, Banca d'Italia? You want to get back to racing? Yes? What are you thinking? You tell him you have to think about it? What does that mean? What's there to think about?"

"It's so attractive. And the offer to race with him and his team is almost too good to pass up."

"So? You have doubts about it? Banca d'Italia is a premier team. I've known Parisi since I was a baby. He was a teammate of my father. His reputation in the world of cycling is... There just is no one better you could be with. You couldn't ask for a better opportunity."

"Well, I couldn't just say yes, not without talking with you first."

Daniella came up short. "Talking with me? Why? This is your offer, not mine."

"Because I want you as part of my team. I don't want to make a decision that means that this, what has developed between us, is only a vacation fling."

"And you think that taking a contract with Banca would make this a vacation fling? You're pretty smart sometimes, but sometimes you can be as stupid as a cow..."

"Whatever I decide, I'd like you to come with me. If I do take them up on their offer, it means moving to Como for their training camp. It means being on the road for a lot of the time. All over Europe, maybe the world. I'll need a place to come home to, a real home, and I want it to be with you. And I can't make a decision right now, without knowing that it includes you."

Her eyes lifted to his, and the fire danced in them. "You're damned right you can't. Because you need me, and for more than being the best bike mechanic you've ever known."

"Yeah, that, too. And a good lover, too."

"Good lover? Great lover!"

"My mistake. You *are* a great lover."

"But listen to me." She took both of his hands in hers. "Listen carefully. I wanted you to win so bad that I could feel it in my bones. Not just because I wanted my lover to be a champion, but because I felt you needed something like this. That you deserved a win to put you back on your path. I hoped it would complete your dream to land a contract and pick up where you fell off. I even imagined us having this conversation. Maybe with a little less *vino* in us, but talking about a future together."

"And?"

"Who knows what it will be? Between us, I mean. I want to see with my own eyes where it goes. I do know that you're a winner. I also know that we, together, are a team that has magic at its disposal. I'm not afraid to try. I'm not afraid to join in a team with you."

"But?"

"No, but. I just want you to know that I'm happy, thrilled even, to make a life with you. And I have dreams, too…"

"I know you do. I know that you aren't done with your career."

"I can't agree to be a *donna di casa*, a housewife, waiting for you. Seeing you only between races, when you show up to do your laundry, feed you, and then send you on your way to the next race. I watched my mother do that for my father, and it isn't the life for me."

"So…?"

"It means that I'm ready to make a commitment to be with you, if you're ready to make a commitment to me, and my life. And understand that I have every intention of pursuing my own racing career, on the mountain bike."

"Whew! Is that all that's bugging you? That you want to race and being with me might get in the way?

"Well…"

Cal sat up and pretended to transcribe his words on a bar napkin. "I hereby commit to be the support team for your racing season, just like you were the support for mine. And in the meantime, you can teach me some of the tricks of the trade for tuning bikes."

"This I can't promise. Some skills you are born with and some you just can't learn."

"So it's settled, then. Tomorrow I'll tell Parisi. I'll settle the details. And then, we can figure out the logistics of where we go next."

Daniella smiled warmly and stood up, next to Cal's chair, and leaned into his arms. "There is just one more thing I need to do."

"What's that?"

"I need to call my grandmother and let her know. I'm Italian, after all, and no momentous decision is made without *la Nonna's* approval. Can I call her?"

"Of course, but isn't it a little too late?"

Daniella let out a loud laugh. "You really don't understand Italian culture at all. In Italy, there are three types of situations where clock time has no meaning at all: marriage, childbirth, and death. In these times, there's no hour of the day or night. You make the call."

"Wait, wait," said Cal. "Marriage? Is that what we were..."

"No, silly. And I'm not ready either. But here in Italy, if I'm going to move with you, it is, in the eyes of my grandmother's generation, a marriage. And I need to have her blessing before I make any commitments."

Daniella pulled her phone out of her pocket and called her grandmother. While Cal swirled the wine in his glass, he listened closely, trying to make sense out of the rapid fire Italian conversation. Although he couldn't make out the particulars of the conversation, he could tell from the squeals of delight and the fevered pitch of the exchange that it was going well. After a few minutes and with a hearty, "*Grazie, grazie,*" Daniella ended the call. She turned to Cal with an ear-to-ear smile.

"There. That's done."

"Great. What did she say?"

"She told me it was a good thing that I was leaving with you."

"Good thing? Why? I'd think that she'd have been sad to see you leave."

"Well, she told me that with legs like yours if I didn't snatch you up, somebody else would and that the Di Salvo gene pool could use a little input from American stock."

"Sounds more like a breeder than a grandmother."

"In her case, there isn't a lot of difference."

Cal wrapped her in his arms and whispered, "You've taken care of your details. Now, I have a detail of my own to take care of. You come with me."

"What? You have to call your grandmother, too?"

"No. Just a detail that I have to take care of before I go and talk with Parisi tomorrow morning. Let's get your car."

They made their way through the dark of night and climbed into Daniella's Fiat. Daniella piloted the car out of the parking lot. Although she didn't know the purpose of the late-night mission, it didn't take her long to figure out where they were headed. Bassano was a small town and once they had passed the town center, their destination was only a few minutes up the road.

CHAPTER 35

Daniella's surprise lit her face, even in the dark car. "Rocco's house? Cal, the race is over. You won. You don't need to rub it in. You don't need to get even. I've let it go. So should you.."

"No, this is something I've been thinking about all day long. Something I need to do," said Cal, as Daniella pulled the Fiat up to a run-down cottage. Just seeing the condition of the home told Cal something that he immediately understood about Rocco. Nobody ever made it easy for him.

After Daniella eased the car to the side of the road, they got out and strode up the path, their feet crunching on the gravel walkway. Cal led the way with a reluctant and hesitant Daniella in tow. Once on the threshold, Cal rapped on the door, and waited as the door opened just a crack. Through the split, Cal could make out the shape of a weathered old Italian woman, Rocco's mother. She peered through the opening and only after staring for a moment and seeing Daniella behind Cal, opened the door a few more inches. She eyed Cal suspiciously and shifted her gaze from him to Daniella, whom she studied from her toes to the top of her head.

"*Dimmi. Cosa vuole?*"

"Hello, Signora. My name is Cal. I'm a teammate of Rocco's on the SD squad. Is he home? I'd like to talk with him."

Rocco's mother looked at him without speaking. Cal was about to repeat his request when Daniella jumped in.

"*Per favore. Siamo qui per parlare con Rocco.*"

Silently, she turned to leave the door and fetch Rocco, but not before slamming her door shut to her late-night guests.

"Friendly?" Cal chuckled to Daniella.

"And you? What do you expect? I'm sure she has heard all about you, and I doubt you're the person she wants to see at this late hour standing in her doorway."

"Yeah, I suppose."

"And for what?" She was embarrassed. He could see her wanting to leave, fighting to keep her feet at his side and not drag him back to the car.

"You already beat his ass on the road. What do you want to do now? Rub it in? Ask him if he wants to go for a moonlight training ride?" The interrogation was cut short when the door opened, revealing a sleepy, shirtless, and disheveled Rocco, squinting in the light of the hallway.

"You? What do you want with me? I thought you would be off celebrating."

"The celebration is over. I wish you had come. You're a member of the team and it's rude to desert you teammates like that."

"Is that what you came here to tell me? You wake me up and tell me that I should have come to the hotel for *your* damned celebration? Well, great. Sorry to disappoint you, but I needed my sleep." Rocco grasped the door and went to close it. Before he could do so, Cal placed his hand on the door and prevented it from closing.

"That's not it at all. I came to talk with you. There's something I want to ask you."

"You want to ask me something? What?"

"Well, it isn't really just something to ask. I want to tell you something, too."

Rocco motioned with his open hands for Cal to continue. He couldn't avoid noticing Daniella's hand enclosed in Cal's, and his eyes moved to the yard and walkway to avoid the sight.

"For the past two weeks, I've been damned impressed with your riding. There were times when I felt I had to turn myself inside out just to hang with you."

"Thanks." He scrubbed his fingers against his scalp and leaned against the edge of the door. His chest was bluish in the moonlight, and he seemed smaller. "Is that why you came here in the middle of the night?"

"Just listen to me for a moment Today, I was fortunate to get the win. And a team that worked for me. And lucky enough to have a strong group to train with. And you…"

Rocco made a sleepy grunt, betraying what he thought of himself today.

"Well, there's no denying that you weren't much help today on the road. And I don't even want to bring up what you did to my bike. That was pretty low."

His face wakened and guarded itself again. "So?"

"Well, I can't deny that you're one of the strongest racers I've ever had the misfortune to ride against. There were times when you pushed me so hard that I saw stars. But you pissed me off so much, there was no way I'd have given up. Today, I don't know if I'd have won if you hadn't punished me so fucking hard in our training. And I damned sure know that my anger at you was part of the fuel I used to get up that ridiculous mountain."

There was an awkward silence between the two. Rocco waited for Cal to continue. In the darkness, they could barely make out the look on each other's face. The silence between the two was punctuated by the sound of crickets in the night and the heavy hush of a rural valley at night. Daniella took in a deep breath. She prepared herself to step between the two rivals in case either got physical.

"So I still don't get it. Why are you here?" asked Rocco. "You come to my house, you get me and my mother out of our beds, all to hash through…"

"Because today, after the race, I was offered a position on Banca d'Italia for next season."

Rocco's head slumped at the sound of Cal's announcement. In the light emanating from the room behind Rocco, his face seemed to crumple for a moment, and he made one step back into the house. As he did so, he looked up and drilled Cal with his eyes. "I heard that. Well, good for you. And thank you for coming all the way out here to brag to me about it. And to you, Daniella, for helping him rub it in. Good night."

"Rocco." Cal planted his hand on the door. "I have some things to think about before just saying yes to the offer." Cal looked over and caught Daniella's eye. She was still uncertain, and she had crossed her arms tightly over her body and would not look at either man. She looked cold, but the air was mild. Cal fixed his eyes on Rocco. "Before you close the door. Today, Parisi came to me and mentioned he was looking for a couple of riders for next year. Two riders. I want to recommend you to him. He needs two, and together, I think we can make each other better."

The look on both Rocco's and Daniella's faces mirrored their shock at this sudden turn in the road.

"You want to recommend me to Parisi? You want me on the same team as you? You just got through telling me that I was an asshole. And you want me on the same team as you?"

Cal looked down at his shoes. "Yeah, I'm not sure that I get it, either. It's just that talent like yours is too big to stay in this town. Maybe I want you on my team because I don't want to have to chase you, or have you chasing me, on another team."

Rocco stood with his mouth open, speechless.

Cal extended his hand as a peace offering. Rocco, hesitant at first, grabbed his hand hungrily and began to pump it vigorously. A huge grin spread across his face. "I don't know what to say. Banca d'Italia? No shit! You will tell Parisi?"

"Tomorrow morning. Now, in the meantime, I suggest you get some sleep tonight. Because tomorrow, I intend to go on a recovery ride and you're coming with me. And I intend to ride you into the ground."

"You can try, but I doubt you'll be able to drop me," replied Rocco, with a grin.

They shook hands one more time, hardily, almost like friends, before Rocco closed the door.

Daniella hooked her arm through Cal's and led him back toward her Fiat, her feet navigating the old path and the valley shadows from years of memory. She guided him back to the road. "Well, that comes as a surprise," she said.

"Yeah. Surprised me, too. There were times in the past couple of weeks when I hoped that I never saw his face again."

"Me, too."

"But the guy deserves a second chance, don't you think?"

"Everyone deserves a second chance. You're proof of that."

A sound punctuated the silence of the night. Daniella craned her neck back toward the house. She frowned, and touched one graceful finger to her lips. "Shhh, do you hear...?"

In the background, coming from inside the house, Rocco was shouting, "Mama, Mama, Banca d'Italia! Banca d'Italia! *Ho vinto! Ho vinto!* I won!"

THE END

Made in the USA
Lexington, KY
06 December 2011